KT-134-234

Roger Taylor was born in Heywood, Lancashire, and qualified as a civil and structural engineer. He lives with his wife and daughters in Wirral, Merseyside, and is a pistol shooter and student of traditional aikido. He is the author of the four Chronicles of Hawklan, *The Call of the Sword*, *The Fall of Fyorlund*, *The Waking of Orthlund* and *Into Narsindal*, as well as the epic fantasy *Dream Finder*.

Also by Roger Taylor

The Chronicles of Hawklan
The Call of the Sword
The Fall of Fyorlund
The Waking of Orthlund
Into Narsindal

Dream Finder

Farnor

Roger Taylor

Copyright © 1992 Roger Taylor

The right of Roger Taylor to be identified as the Author of
the Work has been asserted by him in accordance with the
Copyright, Designs and Patents Act 1988.

First published in 1992
by HEADLINE BOOK PUBLISHING PLC

First published in paperback in 1993
by HEADLINE BOOK PUBLISHING PLC

A HEADLINE FEATURE paperback

10 9 8 7 6 5 4 3 2 1

All rights reserved. No part of this publication may be
reproduced, stored in a retrieval system, or transmitted,
in any form or by any means without the prior written
permission of the publisher, nor be otherwise circulated
in any form of binding or cover other than that in which
it is published and without a similar condition being
imposed on the subsequent purchaser.

All characters in this publication are fictitious
and any resemblance to real persons, living or dead,
is purely coincidental

ISBN 0 7472 3999 1

Printed and bound in Great Britain by
HarperCollins Manufacturing, Glasgow

HEADLINE BOOK PUBLISHING PLC
Headline House
79 Great Titchfield Street
London W1P 7FN

To my wife and daughters

Chapter 1

Darkness fell cold across Farnor's face, extinguishing the myriad lights that had been flickering behind his closed eyelids and replacing them with shifting, blue-in-black shadows.

He opened his eyes with a start, momentarily fearful that some stranger or menacing creature had silently crept upon him as he lay, half dozing, under the gently swaying trees. It was not so, however. The darkness was only a cloud passing in front of the sun.

He made to smile away his reaction as foolishness, but, oddly, the unease persisted and with a frown he gazed around the sunlit woodland, searching for a sign of anything untoward that might have provoked this response. But there was nothing; just the rustling whisper of the wind-stirred trees and the innumerable splashes of bright sunlight flitting and dancing at their nodding behest.

Guilty conscience, he thought wryly as he struggled to his feet, brushing twigs and grass from his trousers and shirt. Loafing around in the woods when you're supposed to be checking the sheep.

Thoughts of justification jostled for position as he walked to the edge of the wood and out into the brilliant spring sunshine. He hadn't actually gone to sleep – well, hardly, anyway, and not for long – and besides, he'd get the job done – and there wasn't anything special to do on the farm today . . .

He cut them short. They were a remnant from the times when his father would regularly interrogate him about his daily doings – or misdoings. Now, however, he was being treated increasingly as a trusted partner in the running of the farm; as a man, even though he would still be considered a boy in the eyes of the villagers for almost a year yet. It was quite amazing how much his father had learned over the past few years, he reflected.

Pausing, he looked down the valley towards the farm. It was hidden from view by the rolling terrain, but, as ever, he could feel its presence, solid and dependable; always there, always welcoming, a haven from all ills.

And yet, as he turned and began to walk up the valley again, he could still feel the shadow of the unease to which he had wakened. He had a faint memory of strange voices talking all around him . . . talking *about* him. The sound of the trees intruding into his half dreams, he presumed, but . . .

Almost angrily, he drove the end of his staff into the soft turf in an attempt to dispel once and for all the darkness that seemed reluctant to leave him. It hadn't been the wisest of things to do, he supposed, going to sleep up here. Especially not with something worrying the sheep.

'Someone's dog gone wild,' had been the usual opinion of the villagers to such happenings on the few occasions that Farnor had known them in the past; an opinion that was invariably proved correct after some judicious night-watching and trap-laying. The brighter sparks in the village would even take wagers on whose dog it was liable to be.

But it was different this time, for though only a few sheep had been worried, the damage to them had been massive and the traditional conclusion had been spoken hesitantly and in subdued and anxious tones. Then, like a mysterious creak in an empty house, Farnor caught a whisper of the word 'bear'. Somewhat awkwardly, he put it to his father, only to receive a confident shake of the head and a lip-curling dismissal of the author of the suggestion.

2

'Ale-topers' talk. Berries, grubs, the odd fish, that's all bears eat unless they're desperate. They've little taste for meat and generally sense enough to keep well away from people.'

'They say you can get rogue bears,' Farnor offered. 'Bears that have . . .'

His father cut across the tale with his final verdict: 'The only rogues around here are those who should be working in the fields instead of swilling ale during the day and filling people's heads with nonsense.' Though he added, reassuringly, 'It's just a big dog gone wild, that's all, Farnor. Probably from over the hill somewhere.'

From over the hill. The anonymous beyond. Where lived outsiders; people who weren't 'our' people and who must necessarily be odd and thus quite capable of allowing large dogs to run wild and escape.

Nevertheless, and with a deliberate casualness, his father had from that time insisted that his son take a particularly stout staff with him whenever, as today, he was to go any distance up the valley.

As he moved further from the trees the last vestiges of Farnor's unease fluttered away. Unconsciously he patted his knife in its rough sheath, then, impulsively, he swung his staff around in a whistling arc.

He began to daydream. His mind ran ahead along his journey. He would come to his favourite spot near the head of the valley and there sit down to eat the food his mother had prepared for him. Then, just as he was about to eat, he would notice bloodstains trailing across the ground. He would follow them and soon come to their source: the mangled body of a sheep. Almost before he would be able to react however, there would be a rustling in the nearby undergrowth and the culprit would emerge, charging towards him at full tilt: a huge hound, wild-eyed and ferocious, with bloodstained foam spraying from its snarling mouth.

3

A great battle would then ensue in which only Farnor's skill with his staff would save him from the lightning, killing reflexes of this monstrous animal until finally, slipping on the bloodstained grass, he would crash to the ground and the creature would be on him, teeth scarce a hand span from his throat.

Farnor drew his knife with a flourish and thrust it upwards into the sunlit air to emulate the final blow that would unexpectedly finish his attacker at the very last moment.

He laughed out loud in his excitement, and allowed his fantasy to peter out with images of his triumphal return to the village and the wide-eyed appreciation of the villagers – and their children in the years to come – who would beg him to tell them, yet again, the tale of his mighty battle against the beast of the valley.

Then, though he knew he was quite alone, he glanced about, slightly embarrassed at this lapse into childish imagining.

Nonetheless, it *was* a good tale. It was the kind of tale that Yonas the Teller would tell with much drama on his rare visits to the village. Farnor began to embellish it and to mouth it to himself after the manner of Yonas. Then he began to imagine himself to be a great Teller, travelling not only to towns and cities about the land, but even to *other lands* far away. Lands ruled by great princes and kings, and full of noble lords and fine ladies. Farnor stretched himself tall; ladies who would smile knowingly at him and . . .

His foot sank into a cow pat.

An ignoble but vigorous oath rose up amid the unique incense released by the deed, and self-reproaches fell back down on him. 'Dreaming again, Farnor?' he heard his father's oft-repeated comment.

A few ungainly, dragging steps relieved him of the bulk of his burden, but the remainder proved persistent

4

and, despite a further brief, foot-twisting ballet, he was finally obliged to resort to sitting down and finishing the task with a clump of grass.

His poetic mood dispelled, Farnor strode on sourly, content for the time being to be earthbound; neither slayer of beasts nor Teller of tales, but a plain, ordinary farmer's son out looking after his father's sheep.

He was still so minded when he eventually came to the end of his journey: the place where, a little earlier, he had chosen to fight the ravening sheep-worrier.

'That will be far enough,' his father had said. It was his usual admonition; unelaborated, but laden with meaning. Farnor leaned on his staff and stared up the valley.

This was the last rolling hummock before the mountains began to assert their presence on the terrain, closing in darkly and rising steep and rugged out of the lush greenery. But it was more than that: it was, to Farnor, the boundary of the known land. Just as beyond the valley and the village lay a strange and alien world best kept at bay, so beyond this point lay a forbidden world, a world of unspoken dangers and strange menace.

As ever when he was here, Farnor imagined how easy it would be to walk down the grassy slope in front of him and begin the climb up towards the head of the valley. The thought gave him a not-unpleasant shiver of fear, but he could no more take that first step than he could fly.

Such a journey would take him first to the old castle. The King's castle stood stark and desolate, keeping a blank-eyed watch over the valley and, though long abandoned, it was still spoken of only with lowered voices by the villagers. Then beyond that were the caves. Caves that were said to wind down through steep, intricate tunnels into the bowels of the mountains to dark and secret vaults where lay unheard-of terrors; terrors from the ancient times that slept as the world had become civilized but which might be awakened again by the blundering of the unwary. And beyond that yet, never spoken of save by the children in their world of whispering and wonder, was the eerie, silent tree-filled gorge that led to the land of the Great Forest to the north. The land where even the people were different, and where who knew what other creatures dwelt?

For a moment Farnor suddenly felt himself to be constrained, bound by unseen ties. He sensed a part of him struggling, crying out inarticulately.

He drew in a sharp breath, as if someone had dashed cold water in his face, so unexpected and vivid was this sensation. Briefly the mountains became mountains and the castle a castle, then, once again, they were *the* mountains, *the* castle, and the images he saw were those of his upbringing.

Yet . . . not quite so. Something was different. Something seemed to have changed.

He shook his head. You're hungry, he thought.

Swinging his pack off his shoulder he turned towards his favourite seat: a small rocky outcrop which hid him from the ominous region to the north and on which he could sit and lean back and look down the valley.

He settled down with some relish and fumbled with the straps on his pack without looking at them. Ahead of him green fields, white-dotted with sheep and outcropping rocks, lay vivid in the spring sunshine. The shadows of the few small clouds passing overhead marched slowly but resolutely across all obstacles, and the air was filled with the susurrant whispering of distant rustling trees, tumbling streams and the soft shifting of countless wind-stirred grasses and shrubs. Occasionally an isolated sound rose above this harmony: a sheep, a hoarse croak from one of the great

6

black birds that circled high above, the buzz of some passing insect.

Don't go to sleep again, Farnor cautioned himself, as he felt the valley's peace seeping into him.

He sat up and began to concentrate on his food.

After a mere mouthful, however, another matter forced itself upon him, setting aside both appetite and any chance of slipping into sleep. Only a few paces ahead of him the grass was streaked with blood.

What had a little earlier been an exciting daydream was a more sober, not to say frightening, reality. With almost incongruous care he laid the piece of bread he had been eating back in his pack, stood up and walked hesitantly over to the stained grass.

As he neared it he saw more blood. And the grass was crushed. Something had been dragged across it recently. A faint sense of excitement began to return, but it was mingled unevenly with alarm. Then duty and his native common sense took command. He had been sent out to check on the sheep. It was one of the responsibilities that his father had entrusted to him. This was probably no more than a rabbit killed by a fox, but he must have a look around just to be sure, and then he could return to his father and tell him what he had seen and what he had done about it.

He found himself walking along quite a distinctive trail.

It was a lot of blood for a rabbit . . .

He bent down and pulled something that had snagged on a gorse bush.

And that wasn't rabbit's fur . . .

His face wrinkled in distress. He was going to find a sheep. One that might perhaps have injured itself. But that was his head talking; his stomach was beginning to tell him something else.

And it was correct. He was at the end of his search:

the remains of a sheep, its body rent open and its exposed entrails scattered recklessly about. In obscene contrast to the stark stillness of the animal, the gaping wound was crawlingly alive with flies, a shifting shroud glittering iridescent blue-black in the bright sunlight.

As Farnor approached, the writhing mass disintegrated and rose up in front of him in a noisy black cloud. He flailed his arms angrily and pointlessly.

Then, as if released by the departure of the flies, the smell struck him and he took an involuntary step backwards. He swore at his reaction. He'd seen enough dead animals and encountered enough smells in his days . . .

Except this was peculiarly awful.

And the damage to the sheep . . .

It was – had been – a good-sized animal, certainly no weak and ailing stray. And there was a lot of it missing. He had seen worried sheep before, although he had been much younger, but this seemed to be different. Whatever had killed it must indeed have been large and powerful.

Farnor looked around to see if there was any other sign the creature had left that would help his father and the villagers in the hunt they must surely now mount.

But there was nothing. Not even an indication as to which way the creature had gone, no footprints on the short grass, no damage to the nearby shrubbery, nothing.

Farnor was not unduly disappointed. His earlier, dramatic flight of fancy about the animal was now far from his mind. Dreamer he might be from time to time, but the hard-headed farm helper within him knew enough about the reality of wild animals not to wish to meet such a one as this alone, and so far from help. He must get back and tell his father what he had seen.

A sudden sound made him start. He turned round quickly, his heart racing.

The sound came again.

Something was coming through the shrubbery towards him. Something large.

Chapter 2

Wide-eyed and fearful, Farnor stepped back and swung his staff up to point at the rustling shrubbery.

The noise came nearer. Farnor stepped back a little further to give himself more space in which to manoeuvre. Whatever might be coming towards him, he knew that to attempt to flee from a predator would be to draw it after him inexorably.

The shrubbery parted.

'Rannick!' Farnor exclaimed in a mixture of anger and relief as he lowered his staff. 'You frightened me to death.'

The newcomer's lip curled peevishly. It was his characteristic expression. He ignored Farnor's outburst.

'What're you doing up here, young Yarrance?' he said, twisting Farnor's family name into a sneer.

Despite his relief at encountering a person instead of some blood-crazed animal, Farnor took no delight in Rannick's arrival. Few in the community liked the man, but for reasons he could not identify Farnor felt a particular, and deep, antipathy to him. It was not without some irony, however, that while on the whole Rannick reciprocated the community's opinion of him he seemed to have a special regard for Farnor – in so far as he had regard for anyone. For although life had not presented Rannick with any special disadvantages, his general demeanour exuded the bitterness and envy of a man unjustly dispossessed of some great fortune. When he spoke, it was as if to praise or admire something would be to risk choking himself to death. And when he undertook a task it was as if to create something willingly, or for its own sake, might wither his hands.

'Don't let him near the cows,' Farnor's mother would say if she saw him wandering near the farm. 'That face of his will sour the milk for a week.'

He had wilfully neglected the quite adequate portion of land that his father had left him and now he earned his keep by casual labouring on the valley farms and, it was generally agreed, by some judicious thieving and poaching, though he had never been caught at such.

Worse, it was rumoured that on his periodic disappearances from the valley he was thick with travellers and the like from over the hill.

Apart from his invariably unpleasant manner however, perhaps his most damning feature was his intelligence; his considerable intelligence. In others such a gift would have been a boon, an affirmation, but in Rannick it was what truly set him apart. It gleamed with mocking scorn in his permanently narrowed eyes when they were not full of anger or malice, and it could lend a keen and vicious edge to his tongue, too subtle to provoke an immediate angry rebuke but cruel and long-lasting in its wounding nonetheless.

And, perhaps, there were other things.

Farnor remembered a soft, incomplete conversation between his mother and father overheard one night when he had crept down the stairs to eavesdrop on that mysterious world of adult life that awoke only as the children went to sleep.

'Rannick has his grandfather in him, I'd swear. He knows and sees more than the rest of us.' His father's voice, muffled.

Ear close to the door, Farnor had sensed his mother nodding in agreement. 'It's to be hoped not,' she said. 'Not with that dark nature of his. It'll do neither him nor anyone else any good.'

12

And that had been all. But unspoken meanings had permeated the words, and something deep in Farnor's unease about Rannick had resonated to them.

'I'm tending the sheep,' he replied to Rannick's question.

'Not doing such a good job, are you?' Rannick retorted, nudging the dead sheep with his foot and making the flies swarm upwards again. This time they did not travel far, but settled back to their noisome business almost immediately.

Farnor grimaced but said nothing. He looked at Rannick's angular, unshaven face, his unkempt black hair and his generally soiled appearance. He was like someone that Yonas might have described as a bandit or some other kind of a villain in one of his tales.

And yet, even as he watched Rannick examining the sheep, he felt that the man was not without a quality of some kind: a strange, inner strength . . . or purposefulness. And, too, he noted almost reluctantly, with a little cleaning up he might even be quite handsome; that he could perhaps serve as much as a hero as a villain in such a tale.

Abruptly the flies flew up again, surrounding Rannick. He swore profanely and Farnor's new vision of him disappeared. Then Rannick snapped his fingers. Or at least that was what Farnor thought he did, though the movement he made was very swift and the sound was . . . odd . . . strangely loud, and yet distant. Almost as if it were in a different place.

For an instant Farnor felt disorientated: as though he had been suddenly jolted awake as sometimes happened to him when he was hovering halfway between sleep and waking. As he recovered he found Rannick gazing at him, his eyes searching him intently.

'What's the matter?' Farnor heard him say.

13

'Nothing,' Farnor replied as casually as he could, waving a hand vaguely. 'I . . . don't like the flies.'

Rannick sneered dismissively and, muttering something to himself, turned back to the sheep. Farnor noticed, however, that the flies were gone from both the corpse and Rannick. They were hovering in a dark shifting cloud some way away, almost as if they were being constrained there or were too fearful to venture closer. And he sensed that Rannick was observing him in some way, even though he seemed to be totally occupied by his examination of the sheep. Briefly, his disorientation returned.

'What are you looking for?' he ventured after a moment in an attempt to recover himself. Rannick did not reply, but bent forward and retrieved something from the sheep's fleece. He looked at it closely and then he lifted it to his nose and sniffed at it. It was a peculiarly repellent action. Farnor grimaced.

'I . . . I'll have to get back,' he stammered, stepping back as he felt his stomach beginning to heave. Only the fear of Rannick's mockery prevented him from vomiting there and then.

Again, Rannick did not reply. Instead he stood up and moved his head from side to side like an animal searching for a scent. Farnor felt the unseen observation pass from him.

'I'll have to get back,' he said again, continuing to retreat. 'Tell my father what's happened. He'll need to know. And the others . . . they'll want to hunt this thing . . .'

Still Rannick said nothing. He was looking to the north, still, so it seemed, scenting the wind.

Farnor turned and began to run. Not so fast as to appear to be frightened, he hoped, but sufficient to emphasize the urgency of his message. He needed the movement and the wind in his face to quieten

14

his churning stomach. He did not look back until he knew he would no longer be able to see Rannick on the skyline.

The farmhouse of Garren and Katrin Yarrance was little different from any other in the valley, though its stone walls were somewhat thicker than most and its thatched roof a little steeper, in deference to the fact that it was the highest farm up the valley and tended to receive more of the winter snows than those lower down.

The Yarrance family land was not particularly good but it was quite extensive, having grown through the generations as less able, or less fortunate, families had gradually given up the struggle to eke a living from those farms that were then even higher up the valley.

Land ownership, however, was not a matter of great sensitivity to the valley dwellers. Not much was fenced, and cattle, sheep and people roamed fairly freely. The valley was big enough to feed everyone who lived in it and that was all that really mattered.

In any event, technically, the land belonged to the King, being let on lease and liable to the payment of an annual tithe. This was calculated from an ancient and very arcane formula, which approximated (very roughly) to one seventeenth of the dairy produce, a nineteenth of all grains and harvestable grasses, and a sixteenth of all meat produce on alternate years except in the year of a coronation or in the event of invasion or eclipse. (There were also exemptions for some produce and special levies for others during those years in which the King and his family, to first cousin, were blessed with children or diminished by death.) Root crops were exempt, as were strawberries and apples (except where grown for purposes of barter), but not raspberries or pears. All individual tithings were doubled in respect of any produce used in the making

15

of spirituous liquors (of any character, save those used medicinally).

After that, matters became complicated.

How this fiscal wisdom had been so succinctly distilled was beyond anyone's current knowledge, and, indeed, there were only a few left in the valley who could even attempt to calculate the due tithe. And they rarely agreed on the final answer.

Not that any of this was of great concern, for just as Garren Yarrance's farm was at the extremity of the valley so the valley itself was at the extremity of the kingdom, and not only did little or no news of kingly affairs ever reach them, neither did the tithe gatherers. Or at least they had not done so for many years.

Views were divided on this benison.

'The tithe should be collected,' said some. 'It *is* the King's due and *if* the gatherers come and there's nothing prepared, then the penalty could be harsh.'

This could not be denied and was a cause of much furrowing of brows amongst those advocating this cause. Others, less cautious, thought differently.

'The King's got no need for our small offering, else the gatherers would have been around fast enough,' they declared. 'And in any case, we haven't had a tithe master in living memory. How are we supposed to know what's due? We can't prepare for collection what we don't know about, can we?'

This was a telling point and invariably provoked much sage nodding, even amongst their opponents.

'Nevertheless . . .' came the final rebuttal, uttered with great significance but never completed. It needed no completion. The penalties for non-payment of the tithe were indeed severe, and not something to be risked lightly, especially as the tithe, calculated by whatever method, was not particularly onerous.

The debate had reached the status now of being an

16

annual ritual, and so too had the conclusion. On the due date, Dalmas Eve, the estimated tithe would be ceremoniously prepared in the tithe barn for collection by the King's gatherers and the barn officially sealed by the senior village elder.

Although many matters relating to the tithe were contended amongst the villagers, all, both ignorant and knowledgeable, knew *for certain* that the gatherers having failed to appear on Dalmas Day or Dalmas Morrow meant that the King had munificently returned the tithe to his loyal subjects.

Thus, three days into Dalmastide, no gatherers having appeared, the seals would be solemnly broken and the barn opened.

With continued solemnity, a short speech of gratitude would be made to the generosity of the absent monarch and then a portion of the tithe would be distributed to those whose crops had fared least well and those who could not properly fend for themselves from whatever cause. That done, the solemnity faded rapidly and the barn would become a market place filled with loud haggling and bartering over the remaining produce. This would be followed by a large and usually raucous banquet.

During the fourth day of Dalmastide the village – indeed the whole valley – was invariably unusually quiet.

It was the approach of Dalmas, rather than any concern about sheep worrying, that had prompted Garren Yarrance to send his son out to check on the sheep, and he was leaning on a gate pondering the extent of his contribution to the tithe this year when Farnor came into sight over the top of a nearby hill.

Garren clicked his tongue reproachfully as he watched his son running and jumping down the steep hillside.

How many times had he told the lad not to run? 'You

stumble and fall, break a leg, then where are we, your mother and me? Tending you *and* doing your work, that's where. Or getting into debt paying someone else to do it.' He would pause. 'That's always minding we find you, or that old Gryss can put you together again if we do.'

It was a litany that he himself had learned from his own father, as doubtless he in his turn had from his. And Farnor ignored it similarly.

Garren changed the emphasis somewhat as Farnor reached him, sweating and breathless. 'Very good, son,' he said. 'You save ten minutes by risking life and limb to bring me an urgent tale, then I have to wait for ten minutes before you can speak.'

But the reproach faded from his voice even while he was speaking as Farnor's agitation became apparent. 'What's the matter?' he asked, as much man to man as father to son.

Farnor told his tale.

Garren scowled. He had hoped that, the last attack having been some months ago, the dog responsible would have moved on, but now there would have to be a hunt. There was always the risk that there might be more than one dog and that raised the spectre of their breeding and thus turning a problem into a nightmare.

'What was Rannick doing out there?' he asked absently as his mind went over what was to be done next.

'I don't know,' Farnor replied. 'I didn't ask.' He shied away from describing Rannick's behaviour. 'I don't like him. He's strange.'

Garren wrinkled his nose. 'He's not the most pleasant of men, that's true,' he said. 'But some people are like that. Never content with what they have. Always wanting something else, then still miserable when they've got it. He's probably quite a sad soul at heart.'

Farnor curled his lip in dismissal of this verdict. 'Well he can be sad on his own, then,' he said. 'It wouldn't disturb me if he went on his wanderings and never came back. He makes my skin crawl sometimes.'

Garren looked at his son again, considering some reproach for his harsh tone, but the simple openness of Farnor's response forbade it and instead he reached out and patted him sympathetically on the arm.

'Not a nice sight, is it, a mangled sheep,' he said. 'Go inside and make yourself presentable then we'll go into the village and see old Gryss.'

Old Gryss was the senior elder of the village: the one who got things done. He mended broken limbs and cracked heads, cured sick animals, extracted teeth, settled quarrels and generally organized the villagers whenever organization was needed. He was also one of the few villagers who, when younger, had travelled beyond the valley; been over the hill, seen towns and even, it was said, cities.

'Noisy, smelly, and too crowded,' was all that he would say about such places however, whenever he was asked directly. Though, in his cups, he would sometimes regale his audience with tales of his adventures, albeit somewhat incoherently.

The sun had fallen behind the mountains when Garren and Farnor reached Gryss's cottage, and the few clouds drifting overhead were slowly turning pink. The cottage was not unlike its occupant, having a thick but rather scruffy thatch lowering over two sparklingly bright, polished windows and a hunched and slightly skewed appearance due to its original builder having been both wall-eyed and too fond of his ale.

An iron ring hung from a chain by the door. It was attached to a small bell. Garren took hold of it but did not pull it immediately.

'He brought this back from his travels, you know,' he said. 'Heaven knows how many people have tugged on it through the years, but it's not shown a scrap of wear. I'd give something for a plough made of the same.'

Farnor, familiar with this oft-repeated parental wish, gave the ring a casual glance for politeness' sake. Gryss had many relics of his wandering days and, over the years, Farnor had been made tediously familiar with all of them.

Then, on an impulse, he took the ring from his father and looked at it more closely. As if for the first time, he saw the finely etched rows of tiny figures that decorated it. They were warriors, some on horseback with lances and some on foot carrying long spears. They were amazingly detailed and lifelike and, as Farnor moved the ring to examine it further, it seemed to him that they were alive with movement. For a moment he felt he was inside the scene. It was a lull in a terrible battle. A waiting for a final, brutal onslaught from an enemy who . . .

'It's a lucky charm.' Gryss's familiar, authoritative voice made Farnor jump. The old man had opened the door silently and was standing watching Farnor's scrutiny of the ring. Startled, Farnor let it fall. The chain rattled as the ring bounced then swung to and fro, and the bell rang slightly. Thus summoned, an old, sleepy-eyed dog emerged from behind Gryss's legs, gave a desultory bark into the evening and then turned back into the cottage.

Garren laughed at his son's discomfiture.

'You'd think he'd never seen it before,' he said.

'Where did you get it from?' Farnor asked, almost rudely. His father raised his eyebrows and was about to intervene when Gryss answered the question.

'From over the hill, young Farnor,' he said. 'Off a trader from a land far, far away. Could hardly understand a word he said, though he managed to wring a rare price from me for it. Said it would protect me . . . I think.' He chuckled at his youthful folly, then he lifted up the ring and gazed at it. 'Worth it, though. It took my fancy and it's a fine piece of work.'

'And a fine piece of iron,' Garren added reverting to practicalities. 'Those lines are as sharp as they ever were.'

Gryss nodded. 'Indeed they are,' he said, his voice suddenly distant.

A brief awkward silence hung over the group, then Gryss said, 'Anyway, what brings you to my humble cottage, with the prospect of a dark journey home ahead of you? No broken limbs by the look of you. And you're not a man for picking quarrels with your neighbours.' He hunched forward and stared at Farnor, 'Toothache, perhaps?' he said.

Farnor edged behind his father a little.

Before Garren could reply, however, Gryss stepped back and beckoned them inside. As they followed him through a small hallway and into a room at the back of the cottage, the old dog trundled forward again, sniffed at each of them and gave another dutiful bark before retiring, apparently for the evening by its demeanour, to a basket in the corner.

Gryss waved his visitors towards a bench by a long, well-scrubbed table. He sat down opposite them and looked at them expectantly.

'Farnor was checking the sheep for the tithe when he found another one worried,' Garren said, without preamble. 'I think we'll have to get a hunt together.'

Gryss frowned. 'Tell me exactly what you found,' he said to Farnor.

Farnor told his tale for the second time.

Gryss's frown darkened. 'It sounds like the others and it sounds bad,' he said. 'It's something big all right,

21

and it looks as if it intends to stay. I'll have a word with Rannick when he appears, see if he saw anything that Farnor might have missed, then we'll have to organize a hunt as you say.'

As they left Gryss's cottage Farnor let his hand run over the iron ring again. Though he could not see them clearly in the dying daylight, he could feel the etched lines, fine and hard; the strange touch of the world over the hill. Heroic deeds captured in fine craftsmanship. Perhaps not everything out there was darkness and suspicion, he thought, unexpectedly.

Gryss's parting words to his father interrupted his reverie. 'Don't send him out alone again, Garren,' he was saying. 'And don't go out alone yourself.'

Deep in the cold darkness, a black-in-black shadow stirred uneasily.

Mingling with the scents that had returned with it was one it had known before. Long before . . . if it had ever known what time was.

With it came the desires that it had known before. Desires that it had long forgotten . . . if it had ever known what memory was. Ancient, black desires that fulfilled its heart and made it whole . . . it understood desires.

The scent came.

And went.

Elusive. Tormenting.

Deep in the darkness came a low, menacing growl that had not been heard for countless generations.

Chapter 3

The prospect of a hunt might have been a source of some irritation to the adults of the valley, but to the young men and the boys it offered the prospect of considerable excitement although the former affected a haughty indifference to it.

And even the men were making little effort to keep their faces stern as they gathered a few mornings later at Garren's farm with their various dogs and a motley assortment of weapons. There were pitchforks, spades, hatchets, billhooks, even a rusty old sword or two and, of course, the inevitable bows. There were also more than a few ale jugs in evidence.

Gryss looked at them dubiously and then laid down the law sternly.

'No bows,' he declared.

There were injured protests.

Gryss gave his reasons without any concession to the finer feelings of his audience.

'There's not one of you could hit a cottage end from ten paces, sober. The last time bows went out on a hunt we lost the dog we were after and brought down two beaters and three ewes.'

It was somewhat of an exaggeration but not entirely unfair. With all their needs being well met from their farming, hunting skills were generally not required by the valley people.

Denials rose among the continuing protests.

Gryss met them full on. 'Half of you don't know which hand to let go of,' he expanded heatedly.

Hackles rose even further and rebellion seemed

imminent. Gryss's eyes narrowed and his shoulders rose as if he were about to push a large weight. Then he seemed to concede and, swinging his pack off his shoulder, he began rooting around in it.

'Very well,' he said. 'I'm not going to argue with you, but . . .' He pulled a long-bladed and lethal-looking knife from his pack and squinted knowledgeably along its edge. Then he breathed on it and slowly and deliberately whetted it on his sleeve. 'If I'm going to be *gouging* arrows out of people . . .' He made a laboured, scooping gesture with the knife as he laid emphasis on the word 'gouging'. 'Then I'll be needing this. And . . .' He turned to Garren. 'Lend me one of your boring irons and some good dry kindling would you, Garren? Or, better still, a few sunstones if you can spare them so that we can get some *real* heat. It's always best to seal those big wounds in the field. Better a little discomfort than bleeding to death on the way home.'

Interest in archery waned abruptly, as did the protests, and soon the bows and quivers were leaning against the wall of Garren's farmhouse.

Gryss allowed himself no victory celebration, but turned immediately to the next skirmish. 'And you needn't think you're coming, Marna,' he said, pointing a curved arm over the heads of the group. 'I can see you there, trying to be inconspicuous.'

The small crowd parted to reveal a black-haired figure with what could have been a handsome face had it not been for its defiant glowering and a mouth wavering between a grim line and a pout. There was expectant amusement among the crowd and even the dogs fell silent.

Gryss threw up his hands in despair. 'Look at you in those clothes!' he said. 'You look like a boy, for heaven's sake. You should be home cleaning your father's house, mending, cooking . . .'

24

The girl interrupted him with an angry gesture. 'The house is clean, nothing needs mending and my father's downland cutting reeds,' she said, her voice as defiant as her appearance.

'He wants to cut a thick one and lay it across your backside,' Gryss muttered, though very softly. 'Yes. And I've got to look him in the face when he gets back,' he went on, louder. 'I don't want to be telling him his daughter's been savaged by some wild animal.'

'What's going to savage anyone with all you around?' Marna retorted, her tone witheringly dismissive. 'It's only some stupid dog we'll be chasing.'

Gryss cringed inwardly. Having had no mother that she could recall, and a gentle, slightly lost father who was as compliant as the canes he wove into baskets and stools, Marna was wild, outspoken and prodigiously self-willed. That she was also large-hearted and generous in her nature served only to make her more difficult to deal with when she chose to stand her ground.

'You're not coming,' Gryss declaimed, with as much an air of finality as he could muster, though, as ever with Marna, he could feel the argument slipping from him. 'It's too dangerous.'

'It's only a *dog*, for pity's sake, Gryss,' Marna reiterated. Her look darkened further. 'You don't want me along because I'll probably find it while you're all swilling ale. The only chance of me getting hurt is through one of you falling on top of me.'

All eyes turned back to Gryss. He clutched at a straw. 'It might be a bear,' he said.

The eyes returned to Marna. Her hands came to her hips and she shook her head in mock weariness at having to deal with such blatant foolishness.

'Bear, my behind!' she snorted.

Laughter erupted around her, coupled with shouts of

25

encouragement. Marna's cheeks coloured. One swain reached out as if to tug at her trousers, but retreated rapidly to avoid a ferocious blow. The dogs began barking again.

Gryss smiled, but did not join in the laughter. He shook his head. 'You can come, Marna,' he said, unable to take advantage of his inadvertent victory over her. 'But stay by me and Garren.'

The party thus set out in a mood of some merriment, wending its way through the morning sunshine and leaving a dark trail through the dew-sodden grass.

It was a while before they reached the place where Farnor had found the dead sheep and, as a result of stopping once or twice to enable the slower members to 'catch their wind', some of the party were already unsteady.

The remains of the sheep, however, sobered them. The corpse was a little smaller than it had been when Farnor had first found it, but it was alive with crawling activity and the extent of the damage caused by the predator was vividly displayed. The increasingly warm sun did nothing to improve the scene.

The dogs, restrained some distance away, whined. Looking again at the destruction wrought on the animal, Farnor was glad that his father had decided not to bring their own dogs on the hunt, and Gryss unthinkingly laid a protective arm on Marna's shoulder. She made no protest.

'It was big,' someone said eventually, voicing everyone's concern. Then hesitantly, 'It couldn't *be* a bear, I suppose?'

Another voice sniggered, 'Bear my behind,' nervously, but the buzzing air sustained no humour.

'No,' Gryss said at last. 'We'd have seen more sign by now if it was a bear. No . . . It'll be some big dog wandered in from . . . somewhere.' He waved vaguely towards the mountains. 'But this is worse than the others we've lost. It could be two dogs. We must find it . . . or them . . . and we mustn't take any chances.' He became more businesslike. 'We'll work in groups of four. Whatever you do, don't split up. And if you happen to stumble on anything, don't be a hero. Whistle us all in first.'

No one seemed inclined to dispute this advice and, after some further discussion, the party split into its various groups.

Gryss remained by the dead sheep with Garren, Farnor and Marna.

'Did Rannick have anything to say?' Garren asked.

'I haven't seen him since you told me about this,' Gryss replied, offhandedly. 'I've no idea where he is. Probably gone wandering off again. You know the way he is.'

Garren nodded. 'God knows why he was out here in the first place,' he said, his face puzzled. 'But you'd imagine even he had enough sense of responsibility to help us find whatever did this. He's got quite a nose for tracking.'

Gryss frowned. 'Rannick's Rannick,' he said, as if reluctant to pursue the matter. 'He'd be out here for no good, you can rest assured on that. The man's not just irresponsible, he's bad.'

Garren looked sharply at the elder and then, briefly, at Farnor and Marna. Farnor knew that it was his and Marna's presence that prevented his father from reproaching Gryss for this total and uncharacteristic condemnation. For a moment he considered taxing the old man himself, but the thought faded even as it formed. Marna might be able to handle Gryss up to a point, but for all her outspoken ways she was a girl – or a woman, as she would protest – and thus allowed far more latitude than he would be. Besides, Gryss's words

27

were flaring up like a beacon, casting the shadow that Rannick threw across his mind into even darker relief. He realized that he agreed with Gryss's verdict. Agreed with it totally.

Gryss cut across Farnor's thoughts. 'Rannick?' he asked, flicking his hand towards some damage in the nearby shrubbery.

Farnor nodded. Gryss looked around. By now, almost all of the villagers had disappeared from view in the rolling terrain, though an occasional shout could be heard.

'We'll go this way,' he said.

Farnor's stomach tightened. Gryss was pointing to the north. He glanced at his father, but Garren showed no surprise at this decision. In fact, he was agreeing. Farnor made an effort to keep the surprise and excitement from his face in case Marna saw it.

Gryss instructed as they walked down from the top of the rise. The remarks were ostensibly addressed to Farnor, but they were for everyone's benefit. 'The ground's mostly too hard for tracks, but there'll be the odd muddy patch which might be helpful, so watch where you're walking. And keep your eyes open for any broken branches or bits of snagged fur.'

Farnor tightened his grip on his staff and his mind began to wander. He would be like one of the figures etched on the iron ring, grim-faced and unyielding as he waited for the enemy's final assault. Once again he would vanquish the monstrous sheep-slayer – several sheep-slayers – in a great battle. Or perhaps he might die heroically saving Marna from its cruel jaws . . .

He coloured at this unexpected thought and brought himself sharply back to the present. Surreptitiously he glanced at his companions in case he might have given some outward sign of this strange notion: especially to Marna. But there were no knowing looks being directed at him and he congratulated himself on a fortunate escape. Concentrate, hero, he thought.

The temperature rose as they dropped further down the hillside and moved out of the mild breeze that was drifting over the top. Their pace slowed.

Looking about him diligently, Farnor could see nothing untoward: occasional sheep tracks looking deceptively like man-made pathways, rocky outcrops, gorse, ferns, white and purple spring flowers, birds and insects flitting hither and thither. In fact this new terrain they were exploring was little different from the rest of the valley.

At the bottom of the slope a small stream dribbled by and the ground became softer.

'Look around carefully,' Gryss said. 'See if you can find any unusual tracks.'

They spread out and moved through the squelching turf.

Farnor could see nothing other than the footprints of sheep in the muddier areas, except for the occasional skittering trail of some small animal and the busy, narrow scratches left by worm-hunting birds.

'Here.'

It was Garren.

The other three converged on him. He was pointing his staff at a row of footprints.

'You didn't come down here, did you, Farnor?' Gryss asked.

Farnor shook his head. 'No, never,' he said.

'It's Rannick then,' Gryss said, none too pleasantly. 'Damn his eyes.'

This time the presence of Farnor and Marna did not restrain Garren. Farnor respected his father's sense of justice.

'I know you don't like the man, Gryss,' he said. 'But you seem more than usually set against him today.'

29

Gryss grunted by way of an answer, then he waved the party forward again. Farnor looked ahead and then instinctively back for some landmark to guide him should he become lost and have to return alone.

They followed Rannick's footprints as far as they could and then continued in the direction they had been leading when they finally disappeared.

After a while Garren spoke. His voice was soft but Farnor could hear the concern in it. 'This way will take us . . .' He did not finish his sentence, but looked significantly at Gryss.

Gryss nodded, but again did not reply, and the party went on for some time in silence.

'It's not just today,' he said abruptly. 'It's been growing for some time. Years, perhaps. He's getting worse.'

'Who?' Garren asked, puzzled.

'Rannick, of course,' Gryss replied, almost irritably. 'And what you call my dislike for him.'

Garren shook his head as if to recollect his own question. 'What do you mean?' he asked.

Gryss hunched up his shoulders and his bright eyes became almost menacing. 'He's getting worse,' he repeated. 'More unpleasant, more argumentative, more unhelpful.'

'I've never had much problem with him,' Garren said, still feeling the need to plead for the absent Rannick. 'Though I'll grant he's got an unfortunate manner.'

Gryss blew out a noisy breath. 'You'd see good in a raiding fox, Garren Yarrance,' he said, though not unkindly, laying a hand on Garren's shoulder. 'But I've watched Rannick from a lad in the hope that he'd improve as he grew up, and all I've seen is him going from bad to worse. And it seems he's going faster and faster.'

Garren made to speak, but Gryss stopped him.

30

'No, Garren,' he said. 'Don't say anything. I've always given him the benefit of the doubt. You know that, in spite of the fact that I didn't like him. But I know his family farther back than you, or, for that matter, than almost anybody in the valley these days, and there's an evil trait in it which is writ large in Rannick.'

Farnor and Marna glanced at one another as the word 'evil' floated into the sunny air. Farnor shivered suddenly.

Garren was more forthright. The word disturbed him also. 'Evil!' he exclaimed. 'No, I can't accept that. Good grief, his grandfather was a respected elder! A good man.'

'Maybe,' Gryss conceded. 'But he wasn't typical of the family by any means, and even he was a strange one until he married and seemed to quieten down.' He stood still for a moment. 'I think that's perhaps what I've been expecting Rannick to do. Find a nice girl, settle down, become more . . . easy with his life.'

He set off again.

'But Rannick's grandfather was a healer,' Garren said, falling in beside him. 'And they say he had the power to understand the needs of animals almost as if he could talk to them.'

Gryss's face darkened. 'Yes, he could. And you've heard it said that if provoked he could knock a man down without seeming to touch him.'

Garren shrugged. 'Alehouse tales,' he said uncertainly.

Gryss shook his head. 'I've seen him do it,' he said. 'Only once, when he was a young man and I was a lad. But I saw it. And I can see it now, as clear as if I was still there.' He paused. 'I don't know how it came about, but there was some angry shouting, then there was a wave of his hand and this fellow went crashing across the room as if a cart had hit him. I remember the air tingling suddenly, as if a bad storm was due.

31

And I remember the men around him going quiet and then start drifting away. And his face. I can't forget that. Savage and cruel. Only ever saw it like that the once, but I've seen the same expression on Rannick's many a time.' He glanced down at his hands. 'He had some skill . . . some power . . . that was beyond most people's understanding. And his grandfather before him was said to be a wild man.' He shook his head. 'My father used to say the family line was tainted as far back as anyone could recall. I've thought as you do in the past: gossip, old wives' tales, but all these old memories have been coming back lately.' His voice faded away.

Farnor's mouth went dry. Gryss's tale, his patent concerns and doubts and, indeed, the whole conversation between the two men, freely uttered within his hearing, seemed to have surrounded him with a fearful stillness into which the warm sun and the valley scents and sounds could not penetrate. It was as if, after passing over the boundary that had marked the limit of his wanderings all his life, he was now being taken across other, more subtle, boundaries by his father and the village elder. Boundaries to worlds that were at once here and yet far away. An urge rose within him to reach out and thank them both, to reassure them, to . . . comfort them?

Gryss raised his hand hesitantly as if something had lightly brushed against him. He smiled. 'What – ?'

The presence of the valley returned to Farnor so suddenly that he missed his step and staggered forward. He steadied himself with his staff.

'Careful,' his father said sternly, 'I've no desire to be carrying you back home with a broken ankle.'

Before Farnor could reply however, a faint whistling reached them.

'Someone's found something,' Gryss said, cocking his head on one side to see which direction the whistling was

32

coming from. But the sound was rebounding from too many rock faces.

Gryss frowned and swore softly.

'Let's go on towards the castle,' Garren suggested, pointing up a nearby slope. 'We'll be able to see and hear better from up there, and it's not too far.'

Gryss nodded. Farnor's excitement returned, though it was laced with trepidation.

The castle! The *King's* castle! This was proving to be a remarkable day.

Standing almost at the head of the valley, the castle was large and impressive by the villagers' standards, but although it commanded a view of much of the valley it did not dominate. No man-made structure could dominate the peaks that towered over it.

To the children of the valley however, it was a haunted, frightening and forbidden place: both the door to, and the protection from, the world that lay to the north. The world that was even more alien than the one over the hill. The world that lurked on the fringes of their darker dreams.

At play around the village, safe in their secret huddled conclaves, they would touch the darkness and run, whispering, 'The caves . . .' and, 'The forest . . .' And shivering breaths would be drawn.

To the adults of the valley on the other hand, the castle seemed to mean little, although they were not above saying 'The King's men will come for you' to quieten their more awkward offspring. At most it was perhaps a reminder of the existence of the world over the hill, with its needs and, by implication, its powers. And, to that extent, people would tend to glance up at it more frequently towards Dalmas. Normally, however, it was just another unseen and ignored part of the landscape.

Yet even in the sober adults childhood shadows

lingered, and most were content both to laugh at and to perpetuate them as 'harmless tales', while being happy that the castle was comfortably far away from the normal avenues of their lives. Few ever found it necessary to discuss the regions beyond, though the unkinder parents would occasionally extend the menace of their threats by declaring, 'The *Forest People* will come for you!'

The four hunters moved off in the direction indicated by Garren.

'Go ahead, if you want,' he said to Farnor and Marna. 'You'll see the castle when you reach that ridge, but wait for us there. We don't want to go trailing all the way unless we have to.'

Farnor wanted to ask his father how it was that he was so familiar with the terrain, but Garren was motioning him to follow Marna who had already set off.

'Do you think we'll catch it?' he said, as he caught up with her.

The girl shook her head and made a disparaging noise. 'Your father and Gryss might, and some of the other upland farmers, but the rest are only out here for the ale. Most of them need both hands to find their backsides.'

Farnor grinned at Marna's manner, but made a hasty gesture for silence and glanced quickly behind in case Gryss or his father were near enough to hear this cavalier disrespect. The two men were well out of earshot, though, trudging along at their own steady pace. He noticed however, that they were deep in conversation.

Not all boundaries were to be swept aside today, he sensed.

The thought brought a shadow back to him.

'And Rannick,' he said to Marna, not knowing why. 'Could he catch it?'

He felt her stiffen. 'Oh yes,' she said flatly. 'He could catch it.'

Farnor pressed on. 'What do you think Gryss was talking about back there?'

'Nothing I didn't already know,' Marna replied. 'Rannick's a mad dog. Bad and dangerous. The valley would be a quieter place without him.' She shuddered.

Farnor could not keep the surprise from his face. Marna could be blunt to the point of considerable rudeness at times, but it was usually to someone's face. And he had never heard her speak so brutally of anyone before. He found himself instinctively trying to take his father's part as defender of the man against this condemnation, but he remained silent. Just as Gryss's words had illuminated his own feelings about Rannick, so too had Marna's.

But feelings were feelings. There must surely be reasons for such vehemence.

'What's the matter with him?' he half stammered. 'I don't like him much myself but—'

'He wants things, Farnor,' Marna replied before he could finish.

'We all want things,' Farnor retorted.

Marna shook her head. 'No, not like that,' she said. 'He wants to be what he's not. Wants to . . . push people about . . . make them run when he tells them . . . jump when he tells them. Wants to be in charge of everything.'

'An elder?' Farnor said though sensing immediately that this was a naive response.

'No, of course not,' Marna said impatiently. 'Nothing like an elder. He wants to be like . . .' She waved her arms about, in search of a word. 'Like a . . . great lord of some kind . . . a king, even.'

Farnor looked at her intently. 'You mean it, don't you?' he said. Then, without waiting for a reply, 'That's stupid. Why on earth would he want to be something he couldn't possibly be? No one in the whole valley would

35

let him.' A thought came to him. 'And how would you know something like that, anyway?' he added, suspiciously.

Marna glowered at him. 'Because he's a man, and men think stupid thoughts like that, that's why, you donkey. And I know because it's written in his face, in his eyes. Just look at them one day.'

Farnor felt that he had inadvertently wandered into a thorn bush, and he retreated in haste. He sensed that Marna was blustering to hide some other concern, but he wasn't going to ask about it.

They continued in an uneasy silence.

As they walked over the rounded top of the rise, the castle came into view ahead of them. It was still some considerable distance away, but neither Farnor nor Marna had been so close to it before. They stopped and gazed at it in awe.

Its high, grey stone walls crawled purposefully over the uneven ground, between great buttressing towers. These for the most part were circular, but wherever the wall changed direction they were six-sided. From some of them more slender towers rose up haughtily as if disdaining the earthbound solidity that actually supported them. Other towers, too, could be seen, rising from behind the walls, as could the roofs of lesser buildings. The walls themselves were made strangely watchful by lines of narrow vertical slits and, at intervals, small turrets jutted out from the battlements to hang confidently over the drop below. A tall, narrow gate wedged between two particularly massive towers fronted the whole.

'It's so big,' Marna said softly. 'It really is like something out of one of Yonas's tales.'

But this is *real*, Farnor wanted to say, but he just nodded dumbly. He felt the hairs on his arms rising in response to the sight. Questions burst in upon him.

36

What must it have been like here once, when it was first built back in the unknown past, or when the King's soldiers occupied it? He saw lines of riders clattering up to the open gate, surcoats and shields emblazoned with strange devices shining bright amid the glittering armour. Servants and grooms ran out to greet the arrivals; dogs barked, orders were shouted, voices were raised in welcome, trumpets sounded . . .

'Come on!' Marna was tugging at his sleeve, the child in her showing through her stern adult mask. 'Let's go!'

Farnor hesitated. The castle was at once inviting and forbidding.

'Wait there!' A faint voice reached them from below to spare Farnor the need for a decision. He turned to see his father gesticulating. The command was repeated and he waved back in acknowledgement. Marna's mouth tightened as she bit back some comment, and with a soft snort she sat down on the grass. Farnor felt awkward.

Eventually, Garren and Gryss reached them. Gryss was puffing heavily.

'It's been too long since I went sheep-herding,' he said, smiling ruefully as Garren motioned him to a flat rock on which he could sit.

'I walked too quickly for you,' Garren said. 'I'm sorry.'

Gryss brushed the apology aside and looked up at the castle.

'It doesn't seem to change, does it?' he said.

Garren shook his head. 'There's craftsmanship there that we can't begin to equal,' he said.

Farnor could remain silent no longer. 'You've been here before?' he said, almost rhetorically. 'Why? You never told me. You've always said it was a place where we shouldn't go.'

37

'And so it is,' Garren replied, his manner authoritative. 'I've been here from time to time, just to look for sheep, that's all. But it's a . . .' He paused and his authority seemed to fade. 'It's a place you should avoid,' he concluded lamely.

Unexpectedly, Farnor felt affronted. An indignant protest began to form, but Gryss intercepted it.

'All things in their time, Farnor,' he said. 'There's nothing here for any of the valley folk. The ground's too poor for cultivation, and not even very good for grazing sheep.'

He looked at Farnor, who could not keep his dissatisfaction at this answer from his face. He seemed to reach a conclusion.

'It's a limit, Farnor,' he said. 'A boundary. You'll meet them all your life. Things that can't be done . . . for many reasons. Things you can't have.' He pointed beyond the castle, to the north. 'The land over the hill is a strange enough place, with not much to commend it. But over there . . .' He shook his head slowly. 'Over there, there's a world stranger still. It's best let be. Kept away from.'

'How do you know?' Marna asked. Farnor started at her tone, part true enquiry, part challenging taunt.

Gryss scowled and turned to speak to her, but the whistling that had brought them to the top of the rise reached them again.

'Over there,' Garren said, pointing. He clambered up on to a small outcrop. 'I can see them. They've found something.'

Chapter 4

Rannick looked down at the tiny figures below. He took a long grass stem from his mouth and threw it away, spitting after it.

Ants, he thought, with scornful elation. Ants. Scurrying about in the valley all their lives and not even realizing they were trapped there just as generations before them had been trapped. The idea drew his eyes upwards toward the enclosing mountains, and his lip curled. It would not be so for him. Not for him, that blind captivity. He saw and knew the bars of his cage and knew too that he would break free of them.

Undimmed for as long as he could remember was the knowledge that he was destined for greater things than could conceivably be offered or attained here. At some time he would know a life beyond the valley and its people, with their suffocating ways; a life that would be full of power over such lesser creatures.

This certainty sustained him daily, yet, too, though he had not the perception to realize it, it burdened him; for the expectation it bred twisted and turned within him endlessly, and constantly drew his heart away from matters of the moment. Rannick lived ever in his own future, his joys marred, his miseries heightened.

Abruptly his elation vanished and his mood lurched into darkness. He clenched his fists in familiar frustration as the reality of his circumstances impinged on him with its usual relentless inevitability.

Where was this greatness to come from? And, above all, when?

Soon it would be Dalmas again. Like the other annual

festivals celebrated in the valley, Dalmas had meant little to him for most of his life, except as an excuse to do even less work than he normally did and an opportunity to eat and drink not only more than usual, but at the expense of others. Over the last few years, however, it had also begun to serve as a reminder that he was yet another year older. Its imminence invariably served to sour his manner even further.

A year older and still bound to this place, his life remaining resolutely unchanged while his ambition burgeoned with time. Indeed the reality of his life was probably becoming worse, so increasingly at odds with the people of the valley was he growing.

He looked back down the valley again. This place where his family had always been mistrusted – feared, even; as near outcast as could be without actually being so. Only his grandfather had escaped this treatment.

He gazed at his hands. Part of him wanted to be like his grandfather – a healer – a person thought highly of; someone at whom people smiled whenever they met him strolling through the village. With Rannick they would turn surreptitiously away rather than risk catching his eye and be obliged to acknowledge him.

It was a small and diminishing part, though. What the greater part of him wanted was to increase the power that had come down to him from the darker reaches of his ancestry. But here his grandfather's presence intruded more forcefully. The old man's words, spoken to him long ago when he was very young, had burned into him like fire and were as fresh now as they had been then.

Eyes had looked deep into him, dominating him, pinioning him. He had never known such total helplessness before, even when his father had beaten him, seemingly endlessly, with his thick leather belt. Yet, and to his bewilderment, the eyes were also full of affection and concern.

'You have it, Rannick. You have our family's taint.' He remembered something inside him struggling, as if it wanted to avoid discovery, but it seemed that nothing could escape the searching eyes. The words went on: 'It is no blessing, Rannick, and never think it so. However it shows itself, set it aside, ignore it, bury it, let it wither and die. It is master, not servant. It will deceive. And it will enslave you utterly.'

But even as his grandfather had spoken Rannick had sensed another presence within, far beyond his grandfather's searching. A presence shining clear and bright like a single silver star in a golden evening sky. And with it came a voice; distant, too, but still sharp and certain. A voice that gave his grandfather's words the lie; that showed Rannick the fear in the old man's voice.

'*I am the light,*' it said. '*The one true light. Follow me.*'

And still it shone, guiding him forward. A lodestone lure drawing him inexorably into the dark knowledge beyond knowing that his grandfather had declared tainted.

Rannick turned away from the mountains and the valley and slid down to the ground, his back solid against the rock he had been peering over. With the thought of his power came the desire to use it; to test himself again.

He extended his left hand.

Birds and insects nearby fell silent, though Rannick was oblivious to the change. The air around him began to stir and, slowly, small pebbles some way in front of him began to tumble over as if caught in a sudden breeze. Then larger stones began to move. And larger ones still. Rannick smiled and his narrow eyes widened. His mouth worked noiselessly.

41

He withdrew his hand. It would not be needed now. He felt the power rising from wherever it lay within him and moving through him to do his will.

'It is no blessing, Rannick, and never think it so.' His grandfather's words returned to him as they always did at this point.

'*I am the one true light,*' said his deeper guide.

I hear you. I see you. I will follow you. Rannick paid silent homage to his chosen mentor.

'Set it aside, ignore it, bury it, let it wither and die. It is master, not servant. It will deceive. And it will enslave you utterly.'

'No,' Rannick whispered in defiance of the shade of his father's father. 'No. I smell your desperation now, old man. You feared me. Feared my power. As will others. This gift is mine. Given to me to use. And I will use it. I *will* use it!'

He felt himself amid the tumbling, rolling rocks. Touching each one, from the least grain to the largest boulder, effortlessly guiding, directing. They were his, utterly. His to lead to whatever destiny he chose.

He laughed breathlessly as he felt exhilaration rising within him. Then his rumbling charges began to move faster and faster, round and round, and he fell silent.

His face became ecstatic.

Abruptly, the circling movement ended and the captive stones and boulders hurtled straight into a nearby rock face. They struck with such force that several of them shattered. Rannick drove his fingernails into his palms.

Slowly, stillness returned to his eyrie and the breeze caught the dust rising from the commotion he had made and carried it gently away. It was like a soft healing hand, but it passed unnoticed. Rannick slumped forward. Sweat was forming on his forehead and he was weak and drained. It was ever thus. If only he could use the power without this awful weakness, then . . .

Vistas of a glorious future opened in front of him, but he ignored them. They were all too familiar and they had nothing to offer him other than to distract him and drag him down. He must follow his chosen discipline. He must look for what he had gained from this day's work.

His skill was growing, he knew, as was the range and strength of the power he could exert. And, he confirmed to himself with growing satisfaction, although he felt battered and empty, his weakness was less than it would have been but a few months ago.

Something was happening. Something was in the air. Something new.

And even as the thought occurred to him, a strangeness touched his still-raw awareness.

Instantly, he became motionless and silent, like a hunter who has just seen his prey. Then, tentatively, he reached out and touched the strangeness again.

It was alive!

Hastily he withdrew the power. Had some oaf blundered up this way as part of the hunt and seen his display with the rocks? He struggled to his feet and gazed around fearfully. But there was no one in sight save the distant figures below.

No, he reassured himself after a moment. They might perhaps wander as far as the castle, but none of them would dare go beyond it, no matter how many sheep had been worried.

What was it he had touched then?

He reached out again; gently, carefully. This time the power felt different, as if that slight touch of a living thing and his response to it had transmuted it – or him – in some way. His exhaustion slipped from him, and he probed more confidently.

43

It was still there.

He sensed a vision through tangled, swaying branches. Felt an unconscious shifting of balance in the gently buffeting breeze.

It was a bird, he realized. Then, in confirmation, he felt alarm calls strangled in his throat. Felt the wings that would not move. Felt the fevered tremor of a tiny heart.

It was terrified.

Yet it did not fly away. *Could* not fly away. It sensed his touch, but it could not fly away!

It was in his thrall! Bound to and by him as totally as any of the lifeless rocks he had just sent hurtling to their destruction.

Come to me, he willed, drawing the bird towards him.

There was some kind of resistance that he could not identify, then he felt it yield. Wings fluttered and the balance shifted again. Come to me; he set forth his power more urgently.

Then, abruptly, there was nothing.

He held his breath. What had happened?

His eyes narrowed as he realized that the frantic tattoo of the tiny heart had stopped. Startled, he let his control slip.

The faint sound of something falling through the leaves in the trees nearby reached him, but Rannick would not have heard the roar of an avalanche, so loud was the exultation ringing in his head.

Throughout his life, following the voice beyond his grandfather's, Rannick had applied himself to the development of his gift with an assiduity that would have made him a master of *any* craft had he studied it with the same intensity. Hitherto his progress had been marked by the movement of increasingly large objects at increasingly greater distances. Exhaustion had been the price paid for each use of the power, but even had this not begun to diminish with practice he would have tolerated it for the exhilaration that the use of the power gave him.

But now his progress had taken an entirely unexpected leap forward. He had touched a living creature. Touched it from within. Controlled it. *Killed it!*

For a long time, Rannick sat leaning against the rock, breathing heavily, his mind incoherent with the welter of feelings and ideas and schemes that were cascading through it. The rational part of him knew that he must retreat and rest; think. Above all he must think. The destiny that but minutes before had been quite certain, yet infinitely beyond him, was flittering tantalizingly amid this chaos. He had but to grasp it.

The turmoil, however, showed little inclination to diminish. With an effort he forced himself to stand up and to walk. It was no easy task; he was trembling from head to foot.

He shook his head in an attempt to clear it, but to no avail. The excitement burning through him seemed to be drawing its energy from some unquenchable source.

He must try again. Try immediately. Try to reach some other living creature. Learn. Learn now, while the power was so alive in him. He must not let this slip away.

He lurched forward in the direction of the nearby trees. Pebbles and stones jumped and bounced out of his path as he neared them, branches rustled away from him as if he were the heart of a great wind.

Though aware of this turmoil, Rannick ignored it, letting his power flit to and fro indiscriminately. He felt a myriad tiny scrabblings and burrowings, panic-stricken, terrified. Insects, worms, ants, all the inconsequential creatures of the woodland, he divined. But nothing larger. And yet there must be birds about, perhaps squirrels, even a fox . . .

He stopped and forced himself to become calmer.

The uproar in his mind silenced, the sounds around him began to impinge again. He leaned forward, listening carefully. Beneath the ceaseless rustle of the trees he began to detect other noises, though they were diminishing rapidly. There were cries and squeals, and the crackling of undergrowth being hastily swept aside and trodden underfoot.

They were fleeing! All those creatures that could do so were fleeing from him. Running from him as if he were a summer fire.

He smacked the edge of his clenched fist against a tree in both frustration and elation. The rough bark grazed his hand but he did not notice. They knew what he could do. The simple creatures of the forest *knew*. They needed no painstaking reasoning and explanation. No demonstrations. They did not have to struggle with disbelief. They had confirmed his new-found skill with their flight as effectively as if they had remained there to be hurled to and fro like the rocks themselves.

It was good.

Then his hand throbbed. He looked at it. The skin had been broken and peeled back slightly. Absently, he raised his hand to his mouth, bit off the torn skin and sucked the small, bleeding wound clean.

It was good, he thought again as he spat out the dead skin.

Good . . .

The sensation resonated in his mind as if it had echoed and re-echoed from some towering cliff face, and his mouth suddenly became alive with the taste of blood; bitter . . . warm . . .

Good . . .

For a moment terror flooded through him. As surely as he knew his own power when it reached out and

46

touched things, so he knew now that that same power was reaching out and touching *him*.

The realization transformed his terror on the instant. No! His whole being cried out in rage. Grasses and bushes bowed flat before him and the branches of the trees around him swayed frantically. Somewhere, stones rattled. This could not be. This would not be. This was *his* gift, *his* power. He would share it with no one and he would destroy anyone who sought to use it against him . . . He would destroy anyone who even possessed it.

The strange touch, however, was gone. Seemingly vanished at the instant of his furious inner cry.

Watchful, Rannick waited.

Slowly he sensed a faint shadow of the presence returning hesitantly. It was almost as if it were reluctant to depart.

Rannick gathered himself for some berserker onslaught to expunge this lingering remnant. The touch slithered away from his rage again. But it did not flee utterly. Rannick hesitated, curious now. He closed his eyes and covered his ears to shut out the sights and sounds around him so that he could the better feel this strange presence that was both within and without him.

He sank to the ground, unwittingly increasing his isolation from his surroundings by crouching low and drawing his arms up over his head.

Cautiously he reached out. The presence moved away, wary, nervous. Yet Rannick sensed great strength in it; and its power was both the same and different from his own. It was more whole, more balanced, more assured. But it was also more feral, savage, unfettered.

It was an animal, he realized. A powerful, predatory, animal. Rannick's curiosity grew. What kind of an animal could it be, and how could it have his power?

47

And why did it stay with him like this? What did it want?

Then amid the nervousness he began to sense something else. It was familiar, but it eluded him for a moment. Only gradually did he recognize it as subservience.

And need!

The presence lingered because it needed him in some way!

No sooner had he reached this conclusion than the character of the presence seemed to change. A profound, black sense of loneliness, eternal loneliness, passed over him. But for all that, it evoked no sympathy, for it was riddled through with a dreadful malice, a malice that Rannick found drawing a like response from somewhere deep within himself.

Whatever this creature was, it was a kindred spirit.

And it needed him.

A small part of him whispered tentatively, *Why?* but the question died almost before it could be formed. Deeper forces within Rannick were guiding him now. Forces that knew that this creature could serve their needs.

Yet Rannick knew that it was a fearful thing. Could it not in its turn become the master instead of the servant?

It was the last lingering doubt.

No. He had never encountered an animal that he could not master if need arose, with whip or with will. And this one had already accepted him as its superior. Powerful and savage this creature might be, but it would be his to command.

A malevolent glee swept over him as the presence began to fawn on him.

Farnor and Marna were the first to join the growing group of hunters converging on the edge of a small

48

lake. Garren and Gryss had again fallen behind despite the downhill slope.

The group had formed into a circle at the centre of which lay another brutally slaughtered sheep.

From the peaks above came a sound like distant thunder. Farnor's flesh tingled.

'Rock slide,' someone said casually, and attention reverted to the dead animal.

Garren and Gryss arrived, the elder quietly pushing his way to the front of the circle. He bent over the remains of the sheep. 'This hasn't been dead as long as the other one,' he pronounced after a brief inspection. 'It's getting hungrier.'

'Or it's just acquiring the taste,' Garren said. Gryss nodded. It was irrelevant which. Both knew that the attacks on the sheep would now become more frequent.

'It's making itself at home,' someone said, by way of confirmation.

Gryss looked up at the sun. 'We've quite a lot of the day left. We must try and find it or we'll be having to round up the flocks and set a night watch.'

This observation sobered even the merriest members of the group. A hunt was a hunt, but night watches were a different matter altogether. Dismal affairs at best. Small groups chosen by lot to mount guard on a few huddled sheep. Waiting silent through the cold, dark night, with no fire, no light, not even any talking to set aside the brooding presence of the unseen mountains. And certainly no ale. Fall asleep out there full of ale and glowing and, blanket or no, you could expect to wake up dead.

'Where do we start?' a young man asked. 'There aren't any tracks to follow.'

Gryss glowered at the speaker. 'It's a *big* dog, or more than one,' he said, pointing at the corpse. 'There'll be signs somewhere if we bother to look properly. If not footprints, then fur snagged on the gorse or a bush. Or bits of this poor beast dropped somewhere. Just spread out carefully and keep your eyes open.'

Subdued, the hunters did as they were bidden.

'What can we do?' Farnor asked his father.

'The same,' Garren replied. 'But keep us in sight.'

As Farnor made to walk away, Garren laid a hand on his shoulder. 'I mean that,' he said sternly but softly so that Marna would not hear. 'I don't want you, by the way, drifting off into some thicket with milady there.'

Farnor coloured and opened his mouth to deny the implicit accusation, but too many protestations formed at once and culminated only in an incoherent stutter which Garren waved to silence. He repeated Gryss's comments. 'We *have* to find whatever's killing these sheep as quickly as possible now, but it's marked this place out as its territory and it's liable to attack anyone who stumbles on it carelessly. So be alert. No foolishness of any kind. Do you understand?'

'What's the matter?' Marna asked as Farnor joined her.

Farnor, still a little indignant, fought down a petulant 'Nothing!', and substituted, 'He was just telling me to be careful.'

Marna looked at him and then back at the two men. They were laughing about something. Her eyes narrowed, but she said nothing.

Inexorably, Marna and Farnor's search carried them back in the direction of the castle, though, in conscience, they were diligent in their duties, scanning the ground for signs of the passage of the predator. It was, however, with mixed feelings that Farnor noticed some flattened ferns at the edge of an overgrown area bounding the grassy slope up which he and Marna were walking.

He bent down to examine the damaged fronds. They were bloodstained

'I'll call the others,' Marna said and, putting two fingers in her mouth, she gave a piercing whistle.

'Don't touch it,' she said. 'The dogs might be able to pick up a scent.'

They did. But instead of a chorus of excited barking rising to greet this find, an oppressive silence fell on the group as each dog in its turn sniffed the ferns and then started back, ears flattened and tail curled deep between its legs. Some whimpered.

'Leash them,' Gryss said softly. 'It looks like we'll have to finish this without them.'

The dogs' unease, though, had spread to the hunters and such enthusiasm as they still had waned markedly as they did Gryss's bidding.

'So it's big,' Garren said, speaking the silent concern. 'We knew that. We've got staves and axes enough for any dog, haven't we, for pity's sake? Do you really want to come back up here on night watches? Come on. Let's find the damn thing and kill it.' And without waiting for any debate, he plunged off through the ferns. Rather shamefacedly the others followed, some of them raising their spirits by roundly swearing at their dogs.

After his initial rush Garren soon slowed down for, large though it might have been, the animal had left little in the way of clear signs to follow: a broken stem here, long grass trampled there.

Then some fur snagged on a bush.

Garren untangled it and rubbed it pensively between his fingers. It was a mixture of black and dark brown and unusually coarse. He offered it to one of the dogs, but again the ears went back and the tail drooped, and the dog looked reproachfully at its master.

Garren pulled a rueful face as he staightened up and threw the fur away. 'Well, at least with this colour it should be easy enough to spot,' he said.

Farnor bent and picked up the fur as the group set off again. It had a peculiarly unpleasant feel to it, and he felt his skin crawling again just as it had when he had heard the rumble of the rock slide earlier.

He rubbed his right arm to still the sensation but his touch felt odd, as if both hand and arm were someone else's, someone in a different place, at once near and far away. He glanced down, momentarily fearful. His arm and his hand looked as they felt, near yet distant; his, yet not his. Only the dark fur of the strange, slaughtering animal held in the familiar, alien fingers seemed to be truly real and present. Indeed, it was vividly present, as if it alone belonged here.

Something somewhere began to form the idea that he was light-headed with the sun and the walking and the excitement of events that day, but it faded into the background as, abruptly, a dreadful malevolence seemed to possess him.

That it was the spirit of the creature they were hunting he knew as surely as he knew his father and Gryss and the others about him, pressing forward through the ferns in their own distant world.

He heard the breath being drawn from him at the horror of the sensation, while at the same time he felt two responses rise within him like ill-matched horses drawing a wagon. Sword-swinging rage to destroy this abomination and all its ilk for ever. And pity for this creation, into which so much wilful evil had been nurtured.

Part of him reached out . . .

* * *

52

Following a path of his own, Rannick faltered as the presence about him momentarily vanished, then returned, heightened tenfold and full of bloodlust and desire. Desire for vengeance.

With a gasp, Farnor fell headlong forward.

Chapter 5

Many sounds filled the swimming darkness that was another place. Sounds and sensations. Clamouring, pushing. Unfocused and incoherent.

Confusion, bewilderment, concern. And, too, anger; human anger. And a different anger: a demented anger; an unfettered animal anger. The two were mingled in an unholy union.

Then they were gone, snatched away brutally. In their wake was a strange void that gradually filled with a myriad voices whispering and calling softly. There was a sense of a vast . . . family? filled with surprise and enquiry; and some disbelieving alarm. How could it have come here?

But that too drifted away . . . softer . . . and softer . . .

And then he was many people, staring, talking, anxious for the downed young man.

Mostly anxious.

And finally there was only confusion. Eddying to and fro, slipping tantalizingly into coherence then slipping away before it could be grasped. Until, slowly, a rhythm made its way through the swirling din and demanded attention. Drawing all to it like mountain streams to a valley lake.

'Farnor. Farnor.'

Light entered the darkness, painfully bright.

And blue.

'Farnor. Son.'

And he was back: the focus of a ring of worried faces centred by Gryss, head cocked on one side, and his father and Marna gazing down at him. The heavy scent of crushed ferns filling his nostrils.

He held up his hand and stared at it curiously. It was there, and solid, and, beyond debate, his. He felt unexpectedly relieved at the revelation.

'Are you all right?' His father's voice impinged on his reverie.

Farnor looked up at him and smiled. 'Yes,' he said. 'What happened?'

'You tell *me* what happened,' Gryss replied, almost indignantly. 'You fell over. You've been unconscious for a good few minutes.'

Farnor made to sit up but Gryss restrained him. 'Give yourself a moment,' he said. 'It's probably the heat. When did you eat last?'

Farnor scowled. A surge of rebellion stirred in him. He wouldn't be treated like some sticky child out on his first round-up. The humiliation!

But a quieter part of him set the indignation aside.

He looked again at the watching faces. People he had known all his life. Down-to-earth people. Some he liked, some he respected, some made him laugh, some were just friends.

He wanted to tell them that in some way he had touched the creature that they were hunting. Touched it and other things also. He wanted to tell them that the creature was profoundly evil and that if it were caught – and that would be no light task – then it would wreak appalling destruction on its captors.

There was no doubt about his new-gained knowledge of the creature, though how it had come to him he could not begin to fathom. But they would not understand. Not even his own father. Gryss, perhaps. But still . . .

'I'm fine,' he said. 'Truly. I must have snagged my foot and tumbled. Winded myself. Or banged my head on the ground.'

Garren looked at him closely and then stood up, relieved normality closing about him. He made a small pantomime of searching for damage to the ground as he gave his son's shoulder a squeeze. 'I can't see a dent,' he said. There was some laughter from the spectators at this antic, and several hands helped Farnor to his feet. As he stood he caught Gryss's eye; the eye of old Gryss, the healer, from whom little could be kept.

Farnor shrugged.

'Watch where you're putting your feet then, young Farnor,' Gryss said significantly. 'I doubt anyone here's anxious to be carrying you back home.'

And the hunt set off again.

Farnor was relieved to have avoided further interrogation by Gryss, but sensed that this was only a postponement.

'Are you all right? What happened?' The questions this time came softly from Marna.

'I told you, I tripped,' Farnor replied irritably, though equally softly.

'You didn't,' Marna hissed. 'You were looking at the fur, then you went down like a log. I saw you.'

'I don't want to talk about it,' Farnor said, recognizing the mistake even as he made it.

Marna seized it. 'Talk about what?' she demanded.

'Nothing!' Farnor snapped as loudly as he dared. Marna took his arm and shook it. 'I'll tell you later,' he surrendered, and Marna released him grudgingly.

The group continued in silence for some time until the ferns petered out, and with them even such small signs as the creature had left. And there were other problems.

The path they had been following had taken them away from the castle, but they were almost level with it. Ahead the valley floor rose gradually, and the tree cover became thicker.

57

Without any command they stopped. To continue would be to go beyond the castle. They had reached the boundary of their territory, and though no obstacle opposed them only some grim necessity would make them go further.

Gryss swore under his breath. He knew that for every reason he could put forward for continuing, two would be raised for turning back and trying some other method of catching the creature. Even night watches. As leader he would have to follow.

'This is far enough,' he said, voicing the silent consensus. 'It seems as if it's hiding in the woods up there. It could be anywhere. We'll have to wait for it to come to us, after all.'

Farnor looked around, registering only faintly the unspoken unwillingness to travel beyond this unmarked boundary. Having been drawn past his own limits, he saw nothing in this place to restrain him. On either side of the valley the high peaks were closing in, but they were not yet oppressive. Ahead lay rising undulations of easy mountain turf no different from those parts of the valley that he knew. And the trees too were no different. Swaying and whispering gently. Almost as if they were calling out to him.

To the left, some way away and much higher than the motionless group, was the castle, oddly dominant now in spite of the mountains behind it.

'We might see something from up there,' Farnor offered, pointing towards it.

Gryss looked at him thoughtfully. 'Maybe,' he said. He cast a glance at the others, watching him uneasily after Farnor's suggestion. 'But it'll be too late to be going much further even if we do.' He spoke to the watchers. 'You head back. Start making arrangements for a round-up, and schooling yourselves to the idea of night watches. I'll go to the castle with Garren and these two' – He nodded at Farnor and Marna – 'Perhaps we can see something from there.'

There was no dispute and the group divided.

As he trudged slowly up the long slope to the castle, Farnor found himself next to Gryss while Garren and Marna walked ahead.

'What happened?' Gryss asked bluntly.

'What do you mean?' Farnor tried.

'What happened when you passed out?'

Farnor shrugged his shoulders and repeated his earlier explanation.

'You were neither winded nor stunned, young Farnor,' Gryss declared. 'And even if I didn't have the wits to see that, I've known you since before you were born and I certainly know when you're lying. Now what happened?'

'I don't know,' Farnor said, after hesitating as long as he dared and taking refuge in a version of the truth. 'I just remember feeling light-headed. As if I was far away but here at the same time. And then I was waking up with you all round me.'

Gryss looked at him narrowly but did not press his interrogation. Instead, he admitted his ignorance.

'Well,' he said, 'you're not cursed with the falling sickness, nor are any of your family. And you're too strong to be overcome by the sun and a little walking.' He rubbed his chin. 'And I'd swear you were dreaming. It was almost as if you were awake and just had your eyes closed.'

'I wasn't pretending!' Farnor exclaimed, heatedly.

Gryss was taken aback at this response. 'I know,' he said both reassuringly and apologetically. 'But I've never seen anything like it before. Can't you remember anything?'

Farnor suddenly wanted to spill out the strange contact he had had with the creature they were hunting,

59

but even as the thoughts formed he set them aside. Besides, as time had passed the incident had become less vivid in his mind. Perhaps indeed he had only been dreaming.

'No,' he replied.

Gryss nodded resignedly and seemed to accept this answer as final, though Farnor sensed that in due course the incident would be returned to again. He knew Gryss's persistence and patience of old. For the nonce, however, they walked on in companionable silence until they reached the top of the slope. Garren was sitting on a rocky outcrop waiting for them while Marna was wandering over towards the castle.

'Go on,' Gryss said to Farnor with a nod in her direction. 'Have a look while you're here. It's an interesting place and I doubt you'll get much call to come up here in the normal course of events. Your father and I will see if we can spot our predator on its prowl.'

Farnor needed no urging and strode after Marna. Watching him, Gryss turned to Garren and spoke quietly.

'Keep an eye on him,' he said. 'I'm not quite sure what happened when he fell over, and he seems to be deliberately keeping something from me.'

Concern then irritation crossed Garren's face and he made as if to call after his son, but Gryss took his arm and directed his gaze back to the valley. 'No, Garren,' he said. 'Leave him. He's no child any more. He can't be forced to do anything he doesn't want to do, at least not without hurting both of you. If he's choosing not to tell us something, then we'll have to trust his judgement. But you just watch him. If he looks like wanting to talk, you look as if you want to listen. Man to man. A friend rather than a father.'

Garren looked unconvinced. 'He's child enough still,' he said stiffly. 'If he's keeping something from you I can get it out of him.'

'No,' Gryss said. 'Trust me in this, even if you can't trust him. You're too close to him to see what he's become. He's a good son, but you'll find you're dealing with someone near your equal if you try to lord it over him too much now. Besides, it may not be that important.'

Garren grimaced. 'Well, what's all the fuss about then?' he said testily. 'You suddenly telling me how to bring up my own boy.' Then, almost immediately repenting his manner, he raised an apologetic hand. 'I'm sorry, that was rude of me,' he said. 'I think seeing him go down like that must have upset me more than I thought.' The look of concern returned. 'He's not ill, is he?'

Gryss sat down on the rock next to the farmer. 'No,' he said, wilfully using his healer's authority. 'I'm sure he isn't . . .'

There was an implied 'but' in his voice as it faded away. Garren waited, then voiced it himself.

'But?'

Doubt came into the old man's eyes. 'There's a strangeness in the air, Garren,' he said. 'I've sensed it ever since Farnor brought the news back about the sheep. And it seems to have been growing worse as the day's passed.'

Garren frowned, unsettled by this down-to-earth elder talking almost like Yonas the Teller. 'What do you mean?' he asked.

Gryss gesticulated vaguely. 'There's the extent of the damage that's been done to the sheep for one thing,' he said. 'I've never seen anything quite so bad before. And the dogs. They've scented something they really don't want to meet.'

'They're not stupid,' Garren said. 'They can probably tell better than we can that it's more than one dog and that they're wild to boot. A chase and a kill is one thing. Risking getting hurt is another.'

Gryss shook his head. 'That would make them nervous, cautious. But you've been watching them. They grew quieter and quieter as we moved on, and when they smelled that fur . . .' He turned to Garren, his eyes piercing underneath his scruffy hair. 'They were really frightened. Half a chance and they'd have been back down the valley at the run.'

Under the old man's gaze, Garren could not disagree.

'And it's not a pack, it's one animal,' Gryss added definitively as he turned back to look out over the valley.

Garren stared at him in surprise. 'You're very certain all of a sudden,' he said.

'I'm very certain after some reflection,' Gryss corrected. 'I've been thinking about the size of the wounds in that sheep, and the way some of the big bones had been broken. It's one animal, and it's big.'

Still there was a hint of some unspoken concern in his voice that disturbed Garren.

'And?' he ventured, almost in spite of himself.

Gryss frowned, as if wrinkling his forehead would squeeze an answer out of his troublesome thoughts.

'And there's Rannick,' he went on. 'What was he doing so far up the valley the other day? And why did he go beyond? And where is he now?'

Garren shrugged. 'You said yourself he's irresponsible,' he offered. 'Besides he knew Farnor would tell us.'

'I said he was bad,' Gryss corrected again. 'And Farnor or not, it's still out of character for him not to tell us. For one thing, he enjoys bringing bad news and for another hunting is one of the few things he does with anything approaching enthusiasm.'

'He's no great loss,' Garren said dismissively.

'Maybe,' Gryss replied, half to himself. He fell silent and the sounds of the valley filled the warm air around the two men. Then he held out his hands and, looking at them, he seemed to reach a decision.

'But it's just one more . . . strangeness,' he said.

The word unsettled Garren once more.

Gryss went on, purposeful now. 'Farnor was holding that piece of fur when he fell over, and when I took it from him it gave me the shudders. For an instant I felt something bad . . . evil, almost.'

He appeared almost relieved, having spoken the words.

'I felt nothing,' Garren said, after an awkward silence.

'It was only a brief impression, but it was very strong,' Gryss said, adding, as if to a nervous patient, 'I get similar flashes of certainty sometimes when I'm healing. I've always found it worthwhile to pay heed to them.'

The descent into explanation seemed to ease the tension that Garren had felt building within him, and, almost incongruously, he smiled. 'What are you trying to say?' he asked.

'I'm not sure,' Gryss said. 'I just have a feeling that there's a lot more to this sheep-worrier than meets the eye and that we'll have to be both craftier and more careful if we're going to catch it. Much more careful.'

The words that Gryss had spoken a few days ago, when Farnor had first brought the news, returned to Garren. 'Don't send him out alone again, and don't go out alone yourself.' For a moment he touched on the depths of Gryss's unease.

Wordless and indefinable though it might have been, it chilled him.

* * *

Marna patted the stone wall and, holding herself close to it, looked up at the ramparts above. Suddenly she gave a little cry and jumped back, lifting her hand protectively.

Farnor, standing some way away, laughed.

'What are you doing?' he asked.

Marna ignored the condescending taunt in his voice and beckoned him. 'Come here, come here,' she ordered. Then, seizing his arm, she dragged him forward and pushed him face first against the wall of the castle.

'Look up, look up!' she insisted.

A strong arm kept him pressed against the wall, but he managed to turn his head round to give her a look full of suspicion.

'Up! Up!' Marna said excitedly, pointing. Uneasily, Farnor did as he was bidden, gazing up the foreshortened perspective of the lichen-stained wall.

After a moment a cloud, brilliant white against the blue sky, passed overhead and began to disappear past the top of the wall. In direct imitation of Marna, Farnor let out a startled cry and jumped backwards as the wall seemed slowly but inexorably to lean forward towards him.

For some time they tested this phenomenon with a relish that was more befitting young people considerably their junior.

'It's so high,' she said in some awe when the game had begun to pall a little. 'It must be three or four times the height of the inn.'

'Even more than that,' Farnor said, shading his eyes and squinting up at the battlements. The noise of battle rose around him. Overlain with the ringing tones of Yonas, men surged up unsteady ladders propped giddily against the walls only to be felled or overturned by the castle's valiant defenders. Swaying wooden siege towers were laboured forward under lethal cascades of arrows . . .

'Let's look at the gate,' Marna said, cutting the thread of Farnor's burgeoning saga.

As they walked towards it, Farnor felt other impressions making their way through the dramatic clutter of the siege. The stones from which the walls had been built were old and weathered but they were also finely worked and very tightly jointed. He had heard a tale once of a general who had become separated from his army in the heat of battle to find himself trapped inside a walled city by a hastily closed gate. His men, on the outside, had been so enraged and distraught that they had driven spears into the joints of the wall and mounted these impromptu ladders to fall upon the enemy from above and rescue their leader.

Farnor ran his fingers along one of the fine masonry joints and peered again at the towering height above. The idea of such a feat made him shiver.

They moved to the gate. Over it was an arch held solid by an enormous keystone on which was carved an ancient coat of arms. Practicalities began to intrude into his imaginings.

How could they have lifted that? he wondered. Memories came back to him of the stone door lintels that he and his father and no small number of helpers had struggled to lift into position on a simple storehouse for a neighbour. There had been sweat, effort and bad language enough in that to last for some time. Not to mention a narrow escape for someone's finger on at least one occasion and a crashing collapse on another. At times it had been for him a frightening and desperate affair with the lumbering weight of the stone seeming to have a relentless will of its own.

And as for the towers now soaring above them: they were so high. How could they have been built?

His attention turned to the huge double-leaved gate itself and he ran his hand over the long-seasoned wood. He imagined them crashing open to release a charging column of riders grimly intent on breaking a siege, but at the same time he marvelled at the size of the timbers and the skill with which they had been joined together. Where could trees be found that could provide such timbers? And where the men to hew and shape them? He thought of the rough beams that formed the ceilings and roofs of most of the village houses.

He came to a wicket door. What must this place be like on the inside?

'Impressive, isn't it?'

His father's voice intruded on his thoughts, though not harshly. Farnor turned and smiled. 'I'd no idea it was so big,' he said. 'Whoever built this could have built all our houses and barns, even the inn, in an afternoon.'

Garren laughed. 'A little longer than that, I suspect. This place probably took many years in the building, maybe several lifetimes, and doubtless it cost more than a few lives.' He gazed at the battlements and the towers rising beyond them. 'How are you feeling?' he asked.

Farnor affected to be looking at the wicket door. 'I'm fine,' he replied casually. 'Does this open?' He pushed at a brass cover plate behind which was presumably a keyhole.

A hand reached out and restrained him. It was Gryss. 'Quite possibly,' he said. 'But the keyholder, whoever he was, is long gone and entering this place without permission would be treated as an offence against the King's person. Best leave be.'

'Why is it so big?' Marna asked.

'Time was when it held a garrison of several hundred men, so my grandfather used to say,' Gryss replied.

Marna wrinkled her nose in dissatisfaction at this reply. 'But why so many? In a place like this. At the end of a valley at the end of the Kingdom?'

Gryss waved a schoolmasterly hand. 'Enough questions. Who am I to question the ways of kings? I shouldn't imagine for one moment that things have always been as quiet and peaceful as they are now. Certainly Yonas is never short of warlike tales to tell.' The notion seemed to disturb him and he became almost brusque. 'Anyway, from what I've seen of soldiers and their ilk, consider yourself more than fortunate that the castle *is* empty and locked.' He glanced at the sun. 'Come on. Time we were heading back.'

Marna seemed to be considering pursuing her questions, but Gryss's manner forbade it.

For a while they followed the old castle road back to the village, but it was overgrown with brambles in places and uniformly hard and uneven underfoot. Further, being intended for carts and wagons, it wound too leisurely a way round the contours of the route for the pleasure of the quartet, and very soon they cut off it and began walking across the steep grassland directly towards the village. They spoke little, each pondering the events that had occurred to make the present so radically different from what they might have expected at the outset of the day.

Rannick moved cautiously forward. Following the lure of the creature, he had gradually dropped down from his high vantage and now found himself passing through increasingly dense woodland.

The eerie, tenuous contact he had made had been maintained constantly, a mutual anxiety keeping it whole. What part of it was guiding his feet he could not have said, but he knew that he was moving steadily towards his goal.

Occasionally flutterings of doubt arose, urging caution. What was this creature he was so blithely breaking new ground to find? Judging from the sheep it had taken it was large and powerful, and hadn't he himself lured many animals into his traps with suitably tempting bait? And, should some ill fate befall him, then even assuming that the villagers would notice he was missing and be concerned enough to send out search parties, they would not even think to look for him out here.

But he dismissed such thoughts out of hand. The need of the creature for him was beyond doubt, as was his certainty that he could master it when finally they met. And, too, he conceded that there was a desperate recklessness in his behaviour. This creature knew and used the power that he possessed; something he had never known before. True, he had sensed occasional, flickering sparks of contact at times, even when he had been in the village, but these were rare and fleetingly elusive, and could have been nothing more than imagination. But this was not. This was as real and solid as the mountains themselves. This, he knew, was the key to his future greatness and it was better to die contending for that than to shrivel and die like an autumn leaf within the stultifying confines of the valley.

He glanced around. There was little to be seen; the trees obscured almost everything save the sky. But he knew that he was well beyond the castle, and he felt a brief frisson of alarm as childhood memories rose to the surface. He had long grown used to wandering in parts of the valley that were not commonly used by the villagers, such as the far downland where he had met travellers from over the hill, or upland, around the castle, where most of the villagers were almost too afraid to tread.

But here was beyond where even he had trodden

before. Here was the region where the caves were said to lie, with their deep, winding tunnels and, so the tales had it, the chambers where lay ancient, evil creatures. Creatures from a time long dead. Creatures that were sleeping until . . . until when?

Now?

He ignored the question, but he paused for a moment and looked around again. He was hot, tired and thirsty, but he could not rest. He had an inner momentum that was carrying him forward inexorably. Nothing would stop him now until he had reached . . . whatever it was that was calling him.

He shrugged off the discomfort and strode on. There would probably be a stream across his path where he could pause to cool himself and take a drink.

Soon, however, he found that he was moving upwards again. The terrain became steeper and rockier and the trees less dense, then, quite suddenly, he was at the edge of the trees and clambering awkwardly along a scree slope, a sheer rock face looming above him to his right and a view over an unfamiliar tree canopy to his left. Looking back, he could make out the taller towers of the castle rising above a ridge on the far side of the valley. He had come much further than he had thought.

The presence of the creature was almost palpable now, filling him completely with its desire; a desire to which his whole being resonated in response. He turned away from the castle and continued his journey.

There was little of it left, however. Scrambling over a tumbled mass of rocks that had fallen on top of the scree, he found himself on the edge of a great cwm. But it was not the majestic, arcing sweep of the weathered rock face that drew his gaze: it was the dark mouth of a cave only a short way above and beyond him.

He began running towards it, almost falling over in

his haste as he leapt across the rocks. Small stones and boulders, dislodged by his passage, went clattering down towards the trees below.

Reaching the entrance to the cave, he stopped and gazed into the forbidding darkness. A damp coldness rolled out to greet him, carrying with it a scent of musty rottenness. Once again, childhood terrors rose up to test him, but he swept them aside. The cry of need that was now ringing through him was so all-pervading that he no longer knew whether it was his or the creature's.

Here everything came into focus. Here lay his destiny: drawn mysteriously from an unknown, inaccessible future to the solid present.

Rannick stepped into the cave and disappeared from the light.

Chapter 6

In bed that night, Farnor lay awake. Normally such a day's exertions would have sent him straight to sleep the instant his head touched the pillow, but the events of this particular day had unleashed a host of thoughts and imaginings which conspired noisily to keep sleep at bay.

Gryss and his father had taken him over the boundary that had marked the whole of his childhood existence. And he had seen and touched the castle and found it to be a wondrous place, though for reasons quite different from those he would have imagined even as recently as that morning.

The great, finely jointed stones piled relentlessly one upon the other high into the spring sky sat in his mind with the same feeling of massive solidity that the castle itself exuded. So also did the huge gate timbers with their echoes of the trees that had yielded them. The who and the how of its building tantalized him. As too did Marna's questions: why was it so big? And why was it there?

And, it occurred to him, there were no large quarries nearby, nor trees of that size. What must the valley have been like when convoys of wagons were wending to and fro, bringing in all those stones and timbers and all the other paraphernalia that would have been used in the building of such an edifice? And what would the castle itself have looked like with its great walls and towers half completed and with masons and joiners and all manner of other artisans crawling about it like so many ants?

At the thought of joiners he found himself perched

giddily high on one of the castle's towers, struggling perhaps to secure some heavy roof rafter. The swaying perspective that he and Marna had viewed from the base of the walls he imagined downwards from those half-built eaves. Even in the dark safety of his bedroom, Farnor felt his hands start to shake at this vision and, toes curling, he had to clench his fists and close his eyes tightly to dismiss it.

Then, feet on the ground again, he pondered the valley when the castle was garrisoned.

Soldiers?

He had no conception of what they were, really. On the one hand were Yonas's tales of mighty armies fighting great battles against hordes of cruel invaders, and valiant knights searching always for heroism and glory. On the other was Gryss's revealing and sour response, 'From what I've seen of soldiers and their ilk, consider yourself more than fortunate that the castle *is* empty and locked.'

The iron ring outside Gryss's house came back to him, with its vivid representation of the lines of sombre, waiting soldiers; these seemed to be different again from either Yonas's or Gryss's view: ordinary men made extraordinary by evil circumstances. A lucky charm, Gryss had called it. Lucky? Farnor smiled to himself in the darkness and wondered for a moment if the old man had ever really looked at it properly.

Probably he had, he decided after a moment's reflection on this silent act of disrespect for the village elder.

But there must have been soldiers in the village once. Or was the village even there when the castle had been first built and manned? Perhaps in fact it grew into being afterwards because of the need to grow food for the garrison.

Farnor had never had such thoughts in his entire life before.

And then there was still the why of it.

Had there once been enemies to the north? Had the lush green valley once rung to the cries of battle?

Round and round his mind went. Then, as he drifted towards sleep, the real concern of the day emerged like nemesis. What had happened to him when he had picked up that piece of animal fur? The sensation had been so intense. He had touched something. Something desperately wicked. And it had been as if he had touched it in another world; a world that had been real and solid, while the valley and his father and the others had become but distant dreams at the edge of his awareness.

He turned over and plunged his face into a cool part of his pillow. Could it have been the sun, and the general strangeness of the day?

Please let it be that.

But it could not be. He had laboured long and hard in the fields many times under hotter suns than today's. He might sweat and stink and have a mouth like a cowshed floor, but he didn't become light-headed, nor did he drift into vivid waking dreams. And still less did he faint.

So it *had* happened. Somehow he had gone into another place and touched the creature that was killing the sheep.

The conclusion came slowly and fearfully and not without much anxious denial and backsliding. But come it did, despite his resistance. And it stayed, showing the same immovable solidity as the castle itself.

Farnor suddenly felt very alone. And he had lied to Gryss and to his father; a further act of isolation. He had told them he remembered nothing.

But how could he have done otherwise? How could he have said, 'I've been into the heart of the creature and known its evil,' when he had been all the time lying unconscious at their feet?

His father would have supported him gently, his

73

manner a mixture of concern and impatience at such unmanly nonsense. Gryss would have recommended this, that or the other physic, and the rest would have pulled knowing faces at one another.

Then cold, black panic surged up inside him. What did it really mean? Was he some kind of oddity, a freak? He recalled Rannick standing over the slaughtered sheep. He saw again the black cloud of flies swarming up around him to be despatched to hover at a watchful distance like a waiting army by a snap of the fingers. And he knew that Rannick had touched them in some way. He remembered, too, his own momentary disorientation.

Was he like Rannick? Did he have in him those traits – evil traits – that would bring Gryss's condemnation down on him? Some power beyond most people's understanding? 'Going from bad to worse . . . faster and faster.'

He found himself trembling and, for the first time in many years, he felt his throat tighten with the need to weep. He swallowed hard and forced the urge down though the effort involved left him drained and unhappy. The haven of his familiar room could not protect him from the desolation he began to feel.

For a long time he lay motionless, painfully wide awake and his heart and mind blacker than the surrounding darkness.

Then the memory of the creature's evil came back to him. He would have to tell someone about it, somehow. Men would be sent out on night watches soon and they would be slaughtered as easily as the sheep if they came across it unprepared.

But how could he do that?

No answer came, but the comforting practicality of the problem took his mind away from his darker, less tangible anxieties and as he pondered it his young body, wiser than he, eased him gently into sleep.

He had no solution to his problem when he woke the following day, and it remained at the forefront of his mind as he pursued his early morning routine of jobs about the farm.

'You look tired,' his mother said when he eventually came into the kitchen.

'I am,' Farnor yawned ungraciously as he hung up his leather cape dripping from the fine drizzle that was misting the landscape outside.

'Yesterday was a long one by all tellings,' his mother said. 'Sit down. Eat your breakfast. Your father's gone to Gryss's to get something sorted out about the night watches.'

Untypically, food had not been dominating Farnor's mind since he had awakened, and such appetite as he had shrank further at this news.

He was careful to keep his reluctance from his mother, however, and he watched her surreptitiously as she moved busily about the kitchen. Her greying hair was pulled back into a loose bun, setting off a round face that even he could see was still attractive. And small agile hands pursued long-familiar tasks with practised ease, pausing only now and then to smooth down her white apron.

It came to him that he had never really looked at her. Never seen her for what she was. He had looked at his father, particularly of late, and seen him slowly, almost imperceptibly, change. Change from being just a father to being also a friend; a respected, older and sometimes stern friend admittedly, but a friend nonetheless. Vaguely he could understand how such a thing could come about. His mother, though, was his mother. It was beyond him to imagine her as anything else. She couldn't ever be just a friend. It wasn't possible.

Perhaps it was a father and son thing. Perhaps mothers and daughters too became friends while fathers and daughters stayed always fathers and daughters.

The thought brought Marna, unbidden, to his mind and as he watched his mother he felt guilty about the richness of his own good fortune. Marna had only her gentle, easy-going father, perhaps neither friend nor support to her. Was that why she was so strong, so belligerently independent? And one day he would have this farm, but what would she have? As far as he knew she had little, if any, of her father's skill at the weaving, and it would be a rare one indeed that would take her on as a wife.

And yet she was a very whole, solid person, and she loved her father, and he her. You only had to see them together to realize that.

'You're not eating.' His mother's voice ended the voyage he had set forth on before he wandered into territories beyond charting. 'Are you all right?'

'I'm fine,' he heard himself saying. 'Sorry. I was daydreaming.'

Better a confession to a lesser crime than to try to explain that he did not want to eat, could hardly eat, while his secret knowledge of the creature lay so heavy inside him.

Better, too, to force the food down with affected enthusiasm than to risk further enquiry.

'I'm going down to Gryss's,' he said, rising to his feet the instant he had finished his first plate. 'They might want some help with the arrangements.'

His mother looked at him enigmatically, but said nothing.

As he fastened his cape about him he returned her gaze. Suddenly he wanted to reach out and embrace her and say, 'Thank you, mother. Thank you for everything. Thank you for my whole life and for being what you

76

are.' But instead he shrugged awkwardly and gave her his usual clumsy kiss on the forehead as he left.

Unusually she came to the kitchen door and watched him as he strode across the farmyard and clambered over the gate in preference to opening it. She watched him until he had disappeared from view.

Once out of sight of the farm, Farnor slowed. He was glad that his father had inadvertently given him this opportunity to be alone and to think. He was glad also to escape his mother's perceptive eye; he would not have been able to keep his preoccupation from her for very long.

The cool, grey dampness of the day soothed him. It made everything wonderfully quiet and still.

Within minutes the fine drizzle had soaked his black hair and pressed it flat against his skull, and his face was shiny with rainwater. His leather cape had been well oiled and would protect most of him from a soaking, but it would be damp with condensation on the inside by the time he reached Gryss's cottage and the rain would have leaked coldly down his neck.

He was unconcerned about such discomforts, however, sensing that this journey to Gryss's would perhaps be the last opportunity he would have to decide what he should do about the danger that he knew the creature offered to the night watchers. And know he did, he reaffirmed to himself. Despite his night's sleep, the memory of the creature was as vivid as ever.

Carefully he rehearsed a number of explanations for Gryss and his father as to why the watchers should go out in larger groups than usual and why they should be better armed. It wasn't going to be easy but he would have to say something. He'd just have to watch and listen until an opportunity presented itself for him to speak.

Arriving at Gryss's cottage he was greeted first by his father, who opened the door and looked pleasantly surprised to see him, and then by a belated and indifferent bark from Gryss's old dog.

'It's Farnor,' Garren said, as he entered the back room with his son. Gryss, seated in a large wicker chair, smiled and raised a hand in greeting.

'You'll forgive me if I don't stand, Farnor,' he said. 'I'm afraid I did rather too much yesterday and my legs aren't what they were.' He motioned the new arrival to a chair facing him across the empty fireplace. Garren sat down at the long wooden table on which were some papers and an open box containing various writing materials. He picked up a long pen and carefully wiped the nib on a cloth. Then, to complete the ensemble, the old dog entered and lumbered over towards Gryss. It bumped heavily into Farnor on the way and then slumped to the floor noisily at Gryss's feet. After settling itself wheezily, it let out a great sigh as if to declare that the meeting could now continue following this unwarranted interruption.

Gryss rooted down by the side of his chair busily, and retrieved a towel from somewhere. He threw it at Farnor. 'Here, dry your hands and face. You look like a drowned rat.'

Gratefully, Farnor rubbed his damp hair into an untidy mass, then wiped his face. The smell of the towel was the smell of Gryss's room. Welcome familiarity closed protectively around Farnor's concerns.

'Did your mother send you?' Garren asked as Farnor completed his brisk toilet and handed the towel back to Gryss.

'No,' Farnor replied. 'I just thought I'd come and help with the arrangements for the night watches if I could.'

He was pleased when he saw his father successfully fighting back an urge to ask his once-usual, 'Have you finished all your jobs, my lad?'

He glanced around. 'Is no one else here?' he asked.

Gryss chuckled. 'Only the people who matter,' he replied. Garren smiled and nodded knowingly.

Alarm lit Farnor's face. 'We're not doing night watches *on our own*, are we?' he asked.

Gryss's chuckle became a soft laugh. 'How many people do you think would like to go out on night watch?' he asked.

'Not many,' Farnor replied.

Gryss shook his head. 'None,' he declared, firmly. 'But we'll all have to do it, and if I get the whole crowd in here they'll spend half the day concocting excuses as to why such and such a night will be inconvenient and why such and such a place will be awkward, and why we should do this and why we shouldn't do that. Then they'll spend the other half saying it all over again. And in the end they'll decide they need to go to the inn because their throats are dry with all the talking.'

Farnor thought that this judgement was a little harsh, but he could see some truth in it. Gryss went on.

'So what your father and I will do is decide on the watch places, prepare the lists of watchers and just tell them.'

Farnor looked at the old man uncertainly. 'Won't they mind?' he asked, after a moment.

'Probably,' Gryss said, laughing again. 'But they'll get it out of their systems by haggling with one another about who should do what when, not why they shouldn't be doing it at all.'

Rather to his surprise, Farnor felt mildly indignant at Gryss's high handed treatment of the villagers. 'Surely no one would try to avoid helping to catch this thing?' he said.

Gryss's eyes widened at this response, then he put his head back and stared up at the ceiling. Farnor's insides curled up in anticipation of a rebuke or, worse, some

79

acid rejoinder. It wasn't his place to reproach a village elder, for any reason.

But no axe fell. Instead, Gryss threw an acknowledging salute to Garren who accepted it with an unusually proud smile.

'You shame me in your innocence, young Farnor,' he said, his tone half serious, half mocking. 'You put me in my place. You're quite right,' he conceded. 'Probably none of them would try to avoid helping if asked outright. It's just that I'm so used to people turning to me to sort out the most unbelievably foolish quarrels and disputes that I tend to forget they're quite capable of thinking for themselves at times.' He chuckled again. 'However, it's still the only way to organize these night watches if we're to get it done this side of the summer solstice.'

Farnor was not disposed to try his good fortune too far and took the opportunity to pursue practicalities. 'How much have you done?' he ventured.

Garren picked up one of the sheets in front of him and pushed it along the table to his son. On it were various lists. One was of times, another of places. The longest was a straightforward list of names, and a final one seemed to be of equipment, food and general advice.

Farnor looked at it for a moment, uncertain what was expected of him, and then handed it back to his father. One of his prepared speeches clattered awkwardly round his head and he cleared his throat as casually as he could.

'How many men will there be in each group?' he asked.

'We usually work in pairs,' Gryss replied 'Six or seven scattered around where we think the dog is prowling. Setting aside the grumbling, night watches *are* a nuisance. They interfere with everybody's work and we try to keep the disturbance to a minimum.'

Two people. Alone and isolated in the dark night. The memory of the creature's savagery returned to Farnor. He had to say something.

'This creature's big and vicious,' he said hurriedly. 'I think it would attack two people alone. I think you should send them out in groups of at least four.'

His suggestion was made with considerably less subtlety than he had hoped, but immediately he felt easier in himself.

Gryss and Garren exchanged a glance. 'Why do you say that?' Gryss asked quietly. 'No dog's going to attack a man when it can have a sheep. You know that. If we send out men in larger groups there'll be fewer groups and the chances of catching it will be that much the less.'

Farnor cringed inwardly. He could not deny Gryss's answer without explaining in some way his knowledge of the creature. And yet he could not sit silent when men might be sent out to face it, oblivious of its malevolence.

'It's just that it's so big,' he said uncomfortably. 'Didn't you notice the size of the wounds on that second sheep?' He held up his hands, his fingers curling clawlike. Reluctantly he edged away from his intention to warn. 'Perhaps it won't actually attack, but if it were cornered or caught with its prey I don't think it would run away.'

Neither Gryss nor Garren spoke.

A memory came to Farnor's rescue. 'You yourself said we shouldn't go out alone when we came to tell you about the sheep the other day,' he said to Gryss.

Gryss nodded. Even as he had spoken it he had thought it a strange remark, and now it returned to confront him. Like Farnor, he had had a troubled night, with dark, ill-formed thoughts keeping sleep at bay and refusing resolutely to come clearly into focus. Dominant

81

amongst them was the sensation he had felt when he had touched the creature's fur. The merest whiff of something admittedly, but he was wise enough to take heed of such happenings, however transient, and it had been bad, without a doubt.

And then Farnor, down-to-earth, strong, young Farnor, a steadfast son following a long, steadfast line of sons if ever there had been one. But he had fallen into some kind of trance at that same touch.

Discreetly, Gryss looked at the young man. He was patently troubled in some way, and, it seemed, turning from a boy into a man almost as he watched.

What was moving here?

He wanted to question Farnor, persuade him to speak out and bring his concerns into the open, but he had to be patient. Farnor was teetering on some unknowable edge, and an injudicious enquiry might send him the wrong way, plunging him into deeper silence.

Besides, he knew that the urge to bring Farnor's secrets into the light was merely a reflection of his desire to have his own confusion clarified. Whatever was amiss would have to wait events. For now he could simply use his authority to advocate the caution that he too felt was necessary.

'I agree with you, actually, Farnor,' he said, levering himself out of his chair with some effort and moving to the table to sit next to Garren. 'And I commend you for noticing the size of the wounds to the sheep. It *is* a big dog, as I mentioned to your father yesterday. A very big one.' He took the cork from a bottle of ink and stood it carefully on end. 'And I'm far from certain what it might do if it comes across anyone in what it now probably thinks as its territory. Four men per group it is. And well armed at that.'

Farnor breathed a discreet sigh of relief. Garren

looked mildly surprised. 'That'll cause problems,' he said.

Gryss pushed a clean sheet of paper in front of his scribe. 'That's what we're here for,' he said.

For most of the rest of the morning they worked through those problems, deciding who should go with whom, and where and when. Farnor contributed little, but sat in some awe as he listened to Gryss's detailed knowledge of the everyday affairs of the villagers and farmers being used to arrange a system of watch nights that they would be likely to accept. He was impressed, too, by his father. He had never seen him doing anything like this before, but at the same time he realized that his methodical and orderly approach actually pervaded the whole of his daily, weekly, even seasonal routines at the farm. At intervals the two men came to an agreement, and Garren diligently wrote down the details, his tongue protruding between his lips slightly as his weathered hands pursued this untypical task.

'I think that's all we can do,' Gryss said finally. 'We'll discuss it at the tithe meeting tomorrow night. Everyone will be there. A time of great healing.'

The two men chuckled conspiratorially. Knowing that arrangements for night watches were being prepared, more than a few of the interested villagers could be expected to find tasks out in the fields for the next day or so. But absence from a tithe meeting was potentially disastrous, as those attending would determine the tithing to be paid by those absent. Many a bed-bound invalid had been miraculously cured by the announcement of a tithe meeting.

'I'll put these away,' Garren said, gathering up the writing materials and the unused papers.

Gryss nodded his thanks then, as Garren left the room, he took a risk. He leaned towards Farnor and spoke softly and urgently.

'In your own time, Farnor, talk to me about this creature and what happened yesterday. I'm troubled by something I felt. Something bad.'

To his alarm, he saw panic filling the young man's eyes. He raised his hand reassuringly but Farnor was speaking even as he did so.

'Am I related to Rannick?' he asked hoarsely.

Garren's footsteps sounded along the hallway.

'This is a small community, Farnor,' Gryss said hastily. 'We're all related in some way.' The panic grew. 'But no. You're no more related to Rannick's line than I am.' He waved a hand for silence as Garren returned.

'We'll leave you to rest,' Garren said. 'I must admit it's been a day or two since I walked so far and my own legs are letting me know it. Is there anything I can fetch for you before we go?'

Gryss declined the offer and rose to see his guests out. The air was pleasantly fresh as they stepped outside. The drizzling rain had stopped and a warm sun was yellowing the thinning grey sky.

Farnor rested his hand on the iron ring as he passed it, causing the bell to tinkle slightly. A faint bark wandered down the hallway.

Gryss laid his hand on Farnor's shoulder. 'I'm glad you came, Farnor,' he said. 'You helped me get some things clear in my mind about this business.' Farnor smiled awkwardly by way of acknowledgement. Not only for the words, but for the pressure on his shoulder that said again, 'In your own time, speak to me about this creature.'

Chapter 7

When they had gone Gryss returned to his wicker chair. He had been right to risk speaking to Farnor. The boy – he corrected himself – the young man, was indeed troubled in some way. But the question he had asked, Am I related to Rannick? was puzzling.

Why in the name of sanity should Farnor suddenly imagine he was related to Rannick? And be so terrified at the prospect? Distaste Gryss could understand, but fear?

What had happened the other day when Farnor had met Rannick? And what had Rannick been doing so far up the valley?

He frowned. Alone now, he felt a much greater sense of urgency about these recent happenings than he had hitherto. He really must seek out an opportunity to be alone with Farnor with a view to tackling these questions head on. Then he swore at himself for a dull-witted old fool and, slapping his hands hard on the arms of his chair, he heaved himself up and almost ran to the front door. The chair creaked unhappily at this treatment, and the dog, caught in this sudden maelstrom of activity, scuttled indignantly out of his way and, grumbling darkly, went to lie down in a corner.

Farnor and Garren had not walked very far, and both turned at the sound of Gryss's penetrating whistle. The old man beckoned them back.

'I'm sorry, Garren,' he said as they reached him. 'There *is* a little job that Farnor can do for me if it's not too much trouble. Can you spare him for a while?'

'Of course,' Garren said. 'Any time. Just ask. You know that.'

As he closed the door, Gryss motioned Farnor to the back room.

'Sit down,' he said, indicating the chair that Farnor had been sitting in previously. Then he dropped back into his own chair opposite and, without preamble, said simply, 'Now. Tell me everything.'

Farnor looked at him for a moment, then, clearing his throat, said, 'Did you really sense something about the . . . sheep-worrier . . . yesterday?'

Although he had already admitted this to Farnor only minutes before, Gryss found that the prospect of giving a more detailed explanation was more daunting than he had anticipated. He made his face stern, fearing that he was going to look as sheepish as the young man in front of him.

'Yes,' he managed to say, authoritatively. 'Just a flash of something when I held that piece of fur. But my guess is that you felt much more. That's why you passed out. Please tell me what happened to you. I think it's important.'

Farnor grimaced and turned away from the old man's gaze.

Impatience crept into Gryss's voice. 'Farnor, you're not remotely interested in organizing the night watches, are you?' he said. 'Least of all if it means walking here through the pouring rain.' He paused to let the words take effect. 'You came to warn us about something. And you called that animal out there a creature. Not a dog, a creature. And why have you suddenly got the idea that you're related to—?'

Farnor lifted a hand before he could finish the question. 'Rannick touches things . . . animals . . . insects,' he blurted out. 'Controls them.'

Then, scarcely pausing for breath, he spilled out the

86

details of his meeting with Rannick and the strange behaviour of the flies.

'And, yesterday, I touched the . . . thing . . . that's out there.' He waved his hands vaguely. 'When I held that fur I seemed to go into . . . some other place. And I touched it. And it's more than just savage, it's bad . . . evil. It'll kill people without a doubt. It might even prefer people to sheep.'

He stopped and looked intently at his interrogator.

Gryss had received Farnor's outburst like a man trying to catch several things falling simultaneously from a shelf; only with an effort did he prevent his mouth from dropping open. He wanted to dismiss this young man's nonsense out of hand, but he could not deny what he himself had felt. And there was the strange trance that Farnor had fallen into.

He met Farnor's gaze. The lad was imaginative. He knew that, having watched him many times sitting spellbound as Yonas the Teller had spun his sonorous tales of wonder. Yet, too, he was solid and practical, with his feet well on the ground. His father had seen to that. Farnor would be a fitting heir to the Yarrance land when the time came.

Despite their clamour, he set the how and the why of it all firmly to one side.

'I believe you,' he said quietly. 'Though what it all means and how it's all come about, I can't say.' He went on, anticipating Farnor's next question, 'And we have to accept that we can't tell this tale to the others as you've told it to me.' He smiled weakly. 'They'll think we've both gone down with brain fever.' Then he made his face become thoughtful lest Farnor misconstrue his levity, and when he spoke again his manner was bluntly practical. 'What we must concern ourselves with is the danger that this creature offers. Nothing else. Perhaps what you and I felt was . . .' He shrugged. 'Something

87

like the tension we feel when a thunderstorm is about to break, or that quality in the air that tells us winter is coming . . . who can say?'

'But why now?' Farnor's question burst through. 'I've never had anything like that happen before, have you?'

'No, not really,' Gryss admitted. 'But we've never known a sheep-worrier like this before, and we mustn't fret about it. Not yet, anyway. We must stick to practical matters. We must protect ourselves when we go hunting and, above all, we must protect our herds – our winter food and our future. If we catch this thing, or kill it or drive it away, then perhaps we can give some thought to what's happened and why, but for the moment it's not important.'

Although Farnor would have preferred answers from the elder, he found that the acceptance of his tale had lifted a burden from him that he had scarcely realized he had been carrying. And the practicality of Gryss's response heartened him.

Gryss reached out and took from the table the sheet of paper on which Garren had written the arrangements for the night watches. He nodded slowly as he studied it. 'I think we can do it without causing too much stir,' he said. 'I'll attend to it when you've gone.'

Yet something lingered between the two men. Lingered like foul air over a stagnant pond.

'Rannick,' Gryss said, like a cold, dispelling breeze.

Farnor looked at him but did not speak.

'It's just occurred to me that you heard me talking about the taint of Rannick's family yesterday, didn't you?' Gryss said.

Farnor nodded.

Gryss paused for a moment. Farnor's concern had become clearer. He voiced it.

'Looking back, you think that when Rannick snapped

his fingers he moved that cloud of flies away, controlled them in some way, don't you? Then, within days, you found yourself mysteriously drawn out beyond the place you were in and touching a strange animal presence. It occurs to you, therefore, that you might be like Rannick. And Rannick is tainted, you heard me say.'

Farnor nodded again, his face pained.

Gryss held a brief debate with himself. Better the truth, he decided. Or at least such truth as he knew, and an honest admission of his uncertainties.

He held out his hands. 'When people come to me with their ailments and their aches, I use what knowledge I've gathered over the years to try to help them. Some of it I was taught by another healer when I was younger, some I've learned from books, most I've probably learned by experience. But sometimes . . .' He smiled ruefully. 'Only sometimes, sadly, and far from often, these hands seem to heal things on their own. They sense things. They go straight to a hurt and put it right almost as if I wasn't there.' He gave a disclaiming shrug. 'I get the credit for it, but I don't begin to know how it happens. It's just some attribute that I seem to have been born with.' He looked at Farnor squarely. 'For all I know, now you've made me think about it, such a trait could be some remnant of the strangeness that runs in Rannick's family. The strangeness that yesterday I referred to as a taint. So also might be the brief awareness of . . . the creature . . . that I sensed yesterday.'

Farnor shook his head. 'I don't understand what you mean,' he said. 'Are you saying that you're related to Rannick in some way, and because of what happened yesterday you think I might be too?' Fear came back into his eyes, mixed with anger. 'I don't want to be related to Rannick,' he said. 'I don't want anything to do with him. I can't stand him.'

'It's not something you've got any choice about,'

Gryss replied starkly. 'This is a small community and very few here have either the inclination or the opportunity to marry outsiders. It's always been that way and if you go back a few generations and think what it means, you'll soon realize that by now everyone's related to everyone else. We're all cousins at some degree and at one remove or other. The blood of Rannick's family is in all of us, just as all of ours is in his.'

Farnor knew enough about the breeding of animals to understand this, though it did nothing to make him feel any easier.

'But it's diluted, Farnor,' Gryss went on reassuringly. 'Spread thin. And mixed with the blood of many other good solid folk before it came to you from your mother and father.'

'I've heard of traits coming out in sheep after five generations and more,' Farnor said in rebuttal.

'And what traits do you have in common with Rannick, Farnor?' Gryss said. 'His surly, self-destructive disposition? His sour idleness? You've certainly none of his looks.' He did not wait for a reply. 'Just consider what's happened. You *think* you've seen him exert some mysterious control over animals, or flies anyway.' He allowed a hint of scorn to colour this last remark. 'Then you *think* that you've . . . touched . . . one particular animal. How can you draw any profound conclusions from such vagueness? It might all be no more than coincidence.' He jabbed an emphatic finger at the young man. 'And in any case, Farnor, while you're half your mother and half your father, you're *wholly* yourself. Whatever traits you were born with, bad or good, and whoever they might have derived from, they're yours now and how you use them is up to *you*! Whether they become masters or servants is your choice.'

Farnor grimaced. 'I suppose so,' he conceded reluctantly, though the thought of being related to Rannick, however distantly, made him feel as though he were wearing a shirt full of hay chaff. He fidgeted uncomfortably in the wicker chair.

'Don't suppose so, *know* so,' Gryss insisted. 'It truly doesn't bother me if part of my healing skill is something inherited from Rannick's line.' His face darkened as the memory of tragic failures he had known rose to overshadow his many successes. 'I only wish I had more of it,' he added softly. 'And you yourself. How has this ability shown itself?' He leaned forward, his voice compelling. 'It warned you about something, Farnor. And you warned us. Perhaps because of it some of our friends and neighbours will be alive next week instead of being dead. It was your choice, Farnor, and you made it correctly. How can that be bad? Be grateful to whatever fate gave you such an opportunity to help others.'

Farnor's remaining resistance crumbled in the face of this assault. 'Yes, you're right,' he said, his face lighting up. 'Thank you.'

Gryss warmed to this simple, unconditional gratitude. It was like seeing a fever patient pass through a crisis. He was both relieved and more than a little pleased with himself that in helping Farnor he had also been able to shine some light into the darkness of his own recent concerns. He looked at Farnor. Young people could be monumentally tedious at times, he mused. But at others they were quite splendid. And they certainly kept you on your toes.

He raised a cautionary finger. 'But,' he said, 'this is still *our* secret until we know more. I can quietly arrange for our hunters to be better protected, but you must tell me if anything like this contact happens again. However slight, however odd.'

'Of course,' Farnor said, almost off-handedly. Most of his anxiety having been taken from him he wanted to be away; to be outside; to breathe cool, fresh air and feel space about him.

Gryss released him with a flick of his hand. 'And if you see Rannick, ask him if he could drop in and see me urgently,' he concluded as Farnor rose to leave.

By dint of his knowledge of the villagers and farmers, coupled with some shrewd talking and some straight-forward alarmism based on the results of 'a further detailed examination' of the damage to the two corpses, Gryss persuaded the hunters to go out in groups of six and armed with, amongst other things, sharpened staves, axes, sickles and the inevitable rusty swords.

The sheep were rounded up and brought lower down the valley, except for a few that were left to act as bait for the marauder. With varying degrees of patience the hunters kept their nightly vigils, but apart from an occasional alarm prompted by a curious fox, or some night bird, nothing happened, and after a few nights spent thus any enthusiasm there had been for night watches disappeared completely.

'It's left. We've frightened it away,' was the consensus among the yawning and by now bad-tempered watchers. Gryss could scarcely disagree. In the past, offending animals had invariably been caught by the third night at the latest. And, too, Dalmas was imminent and there would be a great deal of work involved in agreeing the final value and distribution of the tithe and then collecting and preparing it.

The night watches were thus abandoned without further debate, and village and valley life reverted to normal, enlivened by a rash of new tales being told, retold and exaggerated about the many small incidents that had coloured the tedious nightly outings.

Superficially Gryss was satisfied with this outcome, though something inside him could not accept that it was yet finished. And two more specific matters lingered uncomfortably in his thoughts. One was that Rannick had still not appeared.

The other, though vaguer, Gryss found more disturbing.

When the sheep had been rounded up, one of the farmers thought that some of his were missing. He made no great issue of it as the round-up was necessarily not a particularly thorough one, and Gryss gave the remark little heed. In due course, however, independently and equally casually, some four or five other farmers made the same observation and Gryss realized that the possible total number of sheep missing was disturbingly large.

But, with Dalmas pending, and general disenchantment at the fruitless night watches dominating village affairs, Gryss held his peace. It felt like an act of cowardice however; something that he might come to regret in due course.

Farnor, not privy to these concerns and to some extent still glowing from Gryss's secret approval of his actions, happily let the whole affair slip into the past. And as Dalmas approached, like everyone else, he became increasingly occupied with the business of gathering the tithe.

To Farnor there was something comforting about the particular reliability of Dalmastide, with its long-winded and almost ritualistic haggling over who had to pay what and why, and the subsequent communal effort involved in the gathering.

Daily routines were changed, carts and wagons were borrowed, as were casks and kegs and barrels and all manner of other containers. Special breads and cakes were baked and meats prepared. The village had a smell of spring awakening and of cooking that was uniquely Dalmastide. People were not where they usually were and, bumping into friends and acquaintances they had 'not seen for ages', invariably stopped too long to gossip and chatter – usually in the inn.

Overall, a sense of excitement, expectation and, not infrequently, dire emergency filled the air.

Farnor was less taken by the details of the preparation, affecting to regard it as women's work, though it was not a comment he would have said out loud in the vicinity of his mother or any of the other women. And, notwithstanding this affectation, he always found the careful arrangements of the stored produce decorated with elaborate patterns of spring flowers and leaves a happy, even moving, sight.

On the evening of Dalmas Eve there were the usual last-minute alarms but, as ever, the preparation was eventually declared adequate and the tithe barn was ceremoniously closed and sealed at sunset.

Gryss stepped back from the door of the barn and performed the final task of the ceremony, the striking of a sunstone which was to be mounted on the ridge of the barn. In earlier days this had involved a hair-raising climb up a long and invariably shaking ladder, but following a series of unfortunate happenings to one particular elder an ingenious rope-and-pulley system had been devised so that the matter could be attended to with dignity from the safety of ground level.

Farnor watched the shining sunstone as it rose to the top of the barn in its open metal bowl. It swung hypnotically from side to side until with a click it came to a halt. The barn being on raised ground, the sunstone would be visible from many parts of the valley and at night would look like a bright new star set low in the sky. It seemed like a good omen, a celebration of the end of the strangeness that had begun with his finding of the dead sheep and to some extent still lingered with him, albeit greatly lessened by Gryss's lancing.

* * *

Dalmas Day passed quietly, as always, it being regarded as a rest day following the flurry and bustle of the tithe gathering. Dalmas Morrow, too, was quiet, though, as usual, it had a livelier air about it as final preparations were made for the cooking of the special meals that were a feature of the following day.

At risk of being drawn into this activity by his mother, Farnor judiciously opted to observe another Dalmastide tradition, namely the sunset watch. This was ostensibly the oldest of the Dalmastide ceremonies though, whatever the truth of this, it had undoubtedly changed in character from its original form.

Once believed to have been a gathering of worthies charged with the task of watching for the arrival of the King's tithe gatherers, it was now an excuse for the young sparks of the village to gather with a view to making merry. Accompanied by knowing looks, unorthodox bottles full of 'my father's best fruit cordial' and 'my mother's liniment' appeared, as did food more properly destined for the morrow. Instruments were brought and played, songs sung, dances danced and other activities pursued as the mood of the moment dictated. There was much talk and laughter and the 'ceremony' always extended well beyond sunset, the time by which the gatherers had to arrive if the tithe was not deemed to be unrequired by the King. Indeed, the ceremony did not normally begin to get properly under way until the light began to fade.

It was still some time to sunset when Farnor arrived at the hillock to the south of the village where the sunset watch was traditionally held, and after greeting those already there, he flopped down on the short springy grass and lay back luxuriously to await events.

It had been a fine warm day and it promised to be a fine warm evening. The atmosphere on the hillock was already lively and happy and Farnor felt a euphoria

95

seeping over him; a feeling of gratitude such as he had felt for his mother the day after the hunt; a feeling of gratitude for his father and Gryss and all his friends, and the good life that was to be found in the valley. Yonas's ringing tales of wars and battle and heroism in distant magic lands, and Gryss's quiet reticence about the world over the hill, swung in easy counter-balance to one another against this contentment. Tonight, whether it be quiet and reflective or noisy and boisterous, would be good, he knew. It always was.

Through half-opened eyes he watched his friends. Some were lying idly on the grass as he was, some were standing and talking, others were just wandering to and fro. The buzz of their conversation and the smell of the grass seemed to flow right through him. His friends appeared to be at once here, around him, and a long way away. He wanted to reach out and thank them for being.

Abruptly a great spasm shook him wide awake as if he had been lifted gently off the ground and then dropped violently. It was a familiar enough experience often happening as he was drifting into sleep.

He smiled ruefully to himself. A lucky escape, he thought. Had he gone to sleep there was no doubt that some atrocity would have been committed on him by his friends that would have served as a topic for merriment for the rest of the year. As he levered himself on to his elbow, he noticed that the hillock was suddenly silent and that many of his companions had raised their hands as if something had touched them or as if to catch a distant sound.

He clapped his hands loudly, making several of them jump and immediately restoring the noisy hubbub to the top of the hillock twofold.

He laughed as he dodged various missiles, then

looked around to decide which of the groups he should favour with his company.

As he did so, however, something caught his eye. For a moment it confused him, then he sought it out again and studied it intently.

Silence once again descended on the gathering.

To the south, winding slowly over the undulating ground, was a long line of riders.

Chapter 8

A clamorous knocking filled the house.

Gryss's eyes opened first in shock and then in disbelief as he eventually identified the noise, and it was a far from genial village elder who struggled out of his chair to answer the door.

His dog was not pleased either, and the two of them wore almost identical expressions of world-weary irritation as they lumbered sleepily down the hallway towards the cause of this unconscionable disturbance.

'It's Dalmas Morrow, you know . . .' Gryss began crossly as he opened the door. He stopped. There was no one there.

'Gatherers, Gryss sir, gatherers! The gatherers are coming!' An anxious and disembodied voice startled Gryss further into wakefulness. Struggling to gather his wits he glanced from side to side, looking for the bearer of this strange message. There was no one in sight. Then a tug on his jacket drew his eyes downwards. They met those of one of the younger village children. The boy was red-faced and breathless, jumping up and down agitatedly, and pointing down the valley.

'Gatherers!' he shouted again. This time it was the import of the message that impinged on Gryss and the residue of his peaceful doze fled completely. Almost immediately however, a suspicion entered his head.

He crouched to bring himself level with the boy. 'Is this some Dalmas jape, young Pieter?' he demanded. 'Disturbing the peace with your racket and waking up folk from their well-earned rest?'

The boy shook his head in wide-eyed earnestness.

'Farnor Yarrance sent me, sir,' he said. 'He said to tell you that the gatherers are coming and he and the others are going to get the rest of the elders. He said to come to the tithe barn.'

'Others?' Gryss frowned, trying to come to grips with what he was hearing.

'From the watch,' the boy replied, almost impatiently. 'The sunset watch.' He tugged at Gryss's jacket again. 'He said to come right away.'

The old dog emerged from behind Gryss's legs having finally decided that it was safe to bark. The boy smiled and bent forward to stroke it. Gryss eyed him narrowly. There was little doubt about his innocence in whatever was brewing here; he was merely the expendable foot soldier sent out as bait for some ambush.

'Right away, eh?' he echoed sternly. The boy nodded.

Gryss looked around. It was a fine evening and a stroll would not go amiss. No harm in playing this through, whatever it is, he thought, though the mention of Farnor's name was a little disturbing. It was some time since he had been involved in any Dalmastide mischief.

He motioned the boy to lead on and, saying, 'stay' to the dog's reproachful gaze, he closed the door and set off after the youngster at a leisurely pace.

As he neared the tithe barn he heard voices carrying through the quiet stillness of the evening air.

Several voices.

And talking loudly at that!

Forehead furrowing, he quickened his pace, and soon he was walking up the slope towards the tithe barn. The sunstone was shining brightly, reinvigorated by the light it had received during the day, but what drew Gryss's attention was not this fine star-bright glow, but the crowd of people gathered

100

in front of the barn. Others were arriving, young and old.

If this was indeed some prank by the youngsters it had all the hallmark of one that was going to go badly wrong, disturbing so many people on Dalmas Morrow. He shook his head, his mind already running through the kind of recriminations that were liable to be heaped upon the perpetrators. Doubtless they would have asked for it, but it always gave him a twinge of regret to see youthful scapes, as much full of enthusiasm as folly, dashed against parental displeasure with its underlying tinges of envy and regret for times gone.

As he approached, Farnor emerged from the group and strode towards him. All notions of youthful pranks disappeared from his thoughts as soon as he saw Farnor's face.

'What's the matter?' he asked before Farnor could speak.

'The gatherers are coming,' Farnor said, pointing south, his voice a mixture of excitement and concern. 'We saw them from the sunset watch hill.'

Gryss's stomach tightened and his breathing became cold and shallow. He did not speak for a moment for fear that his voice would shake.

'Tell me what you saw,' he said eventually.

'Riders,' Farnor replied, simply. 'A long line of them coming along the valley. There must have been about a hundred of them. They'll be here within the hour, I imagine. Shall we open the barn?'

Gryss shook his head though more in the mode of someone who did not wish to be troubled with questions rather than someone making a denial. Indeed that was the case, for Farnor's news seemed to have struck a sudden and cruel blow at the heart of something that was very precious about life in the valley, and Gryss would have preferred to be able to walk away for a

101

little while and think before he faced his friends and neighbours.

In spite of the vigour and heat of the yearly arguments about the tithe, Gryss, like everyone else, had pursued them as if they were no more than a harmless and comforting ritual which duly performed would, like one of Yonas's tales, inevitably lead to a happy ending. Now reality was riding steadily along the valley towards him, and it seemed that whatever the outcome of this day the Dalmastide he had always known could never be again.

Many good things would be lost with it.

Worse, frightening even, the world from over the hill was about to intrude upon them. The world of the King and his needs. The vast world of towns and cities and strange peoples with strange ways and little concern for such as lived in the valley. And, too, the world of other, more distant lands and peoples. He had touched upon such things in his youthful travels and had subsequently valued the valley the greater for his experience.

Please don't let it be war, he thought desperately.

'Are you all right?' Farnor's voice interrupted his fretful reverie.

He forced a smile to his lips. 'Yes,' he said. 'Your news took me by surprise, that's all. I thought young Pieter had been sent on some errand of mischief. Now I'll have to try to remember what it is I'm supposed to do when the gatherers arrive.'

He realized that he was slouching, 'like some old man', and, straightening up, he took Farnor's arm and set off towards the noisy group by the barn.

Immediately he was the focus of attention. He raised his hands to silence the clamouring questions. 'Well, my friends,' he began, his voice as hearty and reassuring as he could make it, 'it looks like our annual market tomorrow has been called off. It's an unfortunate

102

surprise for us, to say the least, and I can't pretend to be pleased about it after all these years.' He shrugged. 'But I tell you, I'm well pleased that we've kept up the tithe gathering as was our duty. I'd hate to be standing here tonight with the barn empty.' Much sagacious nodding greeted this remark. 'What we've got to remind ourselves of now is that these men will be the King's men come for what's *his* due. No matter what we feel like, we'll have to put on welcoming faces and see that they get all the help we can give. Especially as we'll probably find that the tithe's been calculated wrongly.'

'That's not our fault,' someone shouted. 'We've never had a proper tithe master.' A chorus of defensive voices rose in agreement.

Gryss acknowledged the remark. 'We know that,' he said. 'And I'm sure that whoever's in charge of these gatherers will know that too. But this has been a shock and I know most of you will not be relishing parting with some of tomorrow's bargains, so I'll emphasize again that it's important for us to be as pleasant as we can manage, no matter what. Then if there's any problem with the tithe, we'll be more likely to get the benefit of the doubt.'

''Tain't fair!' This surly comment received even more support than the previous one.

Gryss slapped his hands on his chest. 'Don't tell me about it,' he shouted with exaggerated injury. 'There were more than a few things I had my eye on for tomorrow, I can tell you.' He became more serious. 'But if you think you can't keep your mouth shut, then go home now and lock yourself in until it's over. Do you understand?'

His firm manner and common sense stilled the noisier complaints and people began to turn to practicalities.

'What are we supposed to do?' a woman called.

'Nothing,' Gryss decided on the spur of the moment.

'The official procedure, as I recall it, is for the barn to be unsealed in the presence of the chief gatherer, an elder and something like at least ten villagers.' He paused and scratched his head. 'And then for the sunstone to be lowered and used to light up the inside.' He nodded to himself. 'Yes, that's it . . . I think. Anyway I'm sure one of the gatherers will be only too happy to tell us.'

'Where are all these outsiders going to stay?' someone asked. He was a stocky, ill-shaven man with a round, heavy face and black hair that clung closely to his skull.

Gryss threw up his hands. 'Let's deal with one thing at a time, Jeorg,' he said impatiently. 'Most of them will probably be soldiers. I imagine they'll have . . . tents . . . or something.' He levelled a finger at his questioner. 'And don't go calling them outsiders. At least not in their hearing. They're the King's men and don't forget it. Apart from any problems with the tithe, the less stir we make the more likely we are to be forgotten again in the future.'

Jeorg curled his lip derisively, but Gryss's last point was a sound one. The elder turned to Farnor. 'You and the others get back to the hillock and act as look-out for us. We'll come down to the end of the village to meet them when they're a bit nearer.'

Farnor and his friends needed no urging; the arrival of the elders allowing them to let excitement begin to dominate their initial alarm.

Gryss watched them striding down the hill talking noisily to one another. Some of the younger ones were running ahead to see who could be first to reach the top of the hillock. He found himself re-organizing the future Dalmastide activities. A sunset watch like it was once, supposedly? With a prize for the first sighting of the gatherers? Or a race to the hillock for the young ones? A feast to greet the gatherers? He dismissed that one immediately. It was important to make their visit routine and unmemorable.

But truly he felt empty. Shock and grief, he diagnosed, at this unexpected loss.

The thought *please don't let it be war* surfaced again in his inner silence, and he realized it had been repeating itself over and over, underlying all his thoughts since he had arrived like the drone on a sinister bagpipe colouring the lightness of the dance with its ominous monotony.

For something momentous must have happened if the King suddenly needed his tithe from this small and distant valley, and had sent so many gatherers to collect it. Nearly a hundred, did Farnor say? And he could think of nothing other than war. Surely the celebration of a royal wedding or birth, or the mourning of a royal death would not warrant such an action? For a moment it occurred to him to send after the young folk, to call them back and tell them to hide lest the gatherers brought with them such dark news and its inevitable consequence: a calling of the young men of the land to arms.

Memories that he had long buried emerged to heighten his anxiety. Memories of beggars wandering the streets of a town near the capital city of the land. Beggars with limbs missing and faces scarred by long-healed but dreadful wounds. Old soldiers, he had been told. Ignore them.

He felt shame still that he had heeded this advice.

Grimly he crushed the memory and sought to follow his own advice: one thing at a time. Whatever nightmares he might choose to torment himself with here, the reality would be on them soon enough.

The crowd had fallen silent, as if the young people had taken all the noise and energy with them. Gryss was once again the focus of attention. 'We might as well follow them,' he said, turning away and setting off slowly down the hill. The group drifted after him, like an uncertain funeral procession.

The general mood was little changed when they reached the end of the village and began to spread out into a well-worn patch of land much used by the children.

A variety of indignant and defiant noises had reached Gryss's ears from the menfolk as they came to terms with the prospect of losing Dalmas bargains, but he let them pass without comment. Better spat out now and into the ears of friends than when the gatherers were here.

Jeorg was the last defender of this position. Scowling, he planted himself firmly in front of Gryss. 'They'd better be here by sunset,' he said. 'Or the tithe's ours.'

Gryss stared at him. 'You'll be telling them then, will you?' he said. 'All one hundred of them? All one hundred soldiers and officials?'

The women were quieter, infected, Gryss suspected, by the same concerns as himself. It was ironic, he had mused more than once in the past, that of the two sexes the one best suited to cope with change and upheaval was the one that valued security the most. They would be watching, thinking, learning, even if they were not aware that they were doing it. And their very presence would be quietly curbing the more foolish excesses of the menfolk.

When Farnor and the others came back, the crowd spread out on both sides of the road to hear their news.

'They're a funny looking lot,' Farnor said, self-consciously. 'Not like I imagined soldiers to be at all.'

Gryss laid a hand on his arm which he hoped felt reassuring.

Then the first riders appeared around a bend in the road some distance away and Gryss stepped to the front of the crowd. He had no idea what formalities, if any, had to be observed when greeting the King's tithe gatherers, so he decided that simple courtesy would be his best approach when first contact was made. That, and a willingness to apologize and explain any shortcomings in the welcome that was being offered.

He began forcing his mouth into a smile.

Slowly the riders approached, swaying shadows against the darkening landscape. Gryss squinted, trying to bring them more clearly into view, but it was not until they were almost upon him that he began to understand Farnor's comment.

Apart from the beggars, the only soldiers he had ever seen were those performing formal duties, guarding public buildings or marching in ceremonial parades. Those had been dressed in colourful, braided liveries and armed with polished swords and pikes with finely etched blades and intricately carved handles and grips.

The new arrivals, however, were dressed in all manner of attire, and carried about them all manner of arms: swords, maces, axes, bows, spears, pikes and no two of them alike. Indeed, more than a few carried weapons which had obviously been farm implements at one stage. Further, Gryss noted, they were, to a man, scruffy and unkempt. Some were bandaged and others, his healer's eye noted, looked far from well. There was a wildness about them that somehow he had not expected.

And their horses were no better, he noted in passing; ill-groomed and lifeless.

He set aside the questions that their appearance raised. They were after all on active service, as it were, and far from the capital and their homes. And, for all he knew, perhaps some communities had chosen to argue about the need to pay the tithe. It would be foolish indeed to imagine that this valley was the only one that had been remembered after such a long time.

107

It was not a happy thought. Such occurrences could bode ill in any negotiations that might ensue even though the gatherers could soon be assured that they would find neither ill-will nor resistance here.

Gryss passed a hand through his hair in an apparent and highly uncharacteristic attempt to smooth it down. It returned to its normal condition as he stepped forward to greet the lead rider.

The man, however, gave no sign of even having seen him, and his horse continued walking steadily forward. Gryss stepped aside when he saw that the horse was not going to stop, then took a pace back. The rest of the villagers did the same.

Slowly the line of riders walked past. Gryss kept his face locked into a welcoming smile, but it was not easy. The soldiers were not merely an unprepossessing sight; they had a hard, even brutal quality about them that was almost palpable. And it was difficult to say which was the more chilling: the stony indifference to the watching crowd that most of them exhibited, or the cold-eyed curiosity of the remaining few.

The villagers watched this parade with a bewilderment that gradually turned into a foot-shuffling unease, and there was silence for some time after the last rider had passed by.

It was Jeorg who broke it. 'They treated us like so much cowshit!' he declaimed angrily, but his voice faded as Gryss raised a hand for silence. He was at a loss. Of the many things he had envisaged happening since Farnor had told him of the approaching riders, being ignored was not among them. Surely if there was some special greeting ceremony for the gatherers they would have at least stopped and waited for it?

'I don't understand,' he admitted. 'I think we'd probably all better' – He hesitated and shrugged – 'go back to our normal business and . . . await events.'

The silence of the passing troop seemed to have infected the watchers, and such conversations as were struck up were held almost in whispers as the villagers took Gryss's advice and gradually dispersed. At Gryss's signal, Farnor and a few others remained.

'Not much heart for finishing the sunset watch, Farnor?' Gryss asked, largely for want of something to say.

Farnor shook his head. 'Not much need now, is there?' he said, attempting to smile. But he could not keep his true feelings hidden. 'I don't know why I feel so upset . . .' He paused, and Gryss saw his mood suddenly change. 'No, not upset,' he decided. 'Angry. Ignoring us like that. They treated us as if we were *less* than cowshit. At least there's a use for that. We were like . . . nothing . . . smoke in the wind . . . bubbles in a stream.'

'Would you rather they'd rode in at the charge, sabres drawn?' Gryss asked, with gentle mockery, glad to find himself recovering from the stultifying effect of the riders' silent passage.

'No, of course not,' Farnor replied needlessly, though with some heat. 'But they could have . . . stopped, or something. Acknowledged us in some way. Told us what they wanted, what we were supposed to do.'

'I'll confess it wasn't what I expected, to be sure,' Gryss said. 'But in my experience being ignored by strangers, especially strangers who look as they did, is probably better than being noticed.'

Farnor pulled an unhappy face. 'Yes,' he agreed. 'They were . . .' He hesitated, loath to form the words he was thinking for fear of scorn from the others. 'Frightening,' he conceded eventually. He wrapped his arms about himself and hunched his shoulders as if he were suddenly cold.

No scorn greeted the remark, however, for it chimed

with the unspoken thoughts of too many of the others. 'They're only men,' Gryss said flatly, after a long pause.

He turned to the others. 'Still, we can't leave it like this,' he went on in a tone that implied he would very much prefer to. 'We'll have to find out what's happening.' An idea came to him. 'Perhaps they've gone straight to the tithe barn,' he said, snapping his fingers. 'Come on.'

It took the group only a short time to reach the foot of the slope that led to the barn. The sunstone was shining like a guiding star, but even without its light they could see that no riders were waiting for them outside the sealed doors.

Gryss scratched his head violently with both hands, making his grey thatch even more disorderly than normal. 'We'd better go after them,' he said in exasperation. 'They're outsiders, after all. It could be they don't even know where they are. They might think there's another village further up the valley.'

'Let's wait for them to come back, then. It'll be easier on our legs,' Jeorg said.

Gryss seemed half inclined to agree but he shook his head. 'No,' he said. 'That lot were hardly in the sweetest of moods, for whatever reason. They'll be even sourer if they trail up to the castle and find they have to turn back. Besides, we shouldn't respond to their bad manners with bad manners of our own.'

Progress through the village was slowed by large numbers of people coming the other way, people who had not been disturbed by the initial alarm but who had peered out of their windows simply to see, 'Who that could be, riding at this time of the evening.'

By the time he had explained the tale some four times to different enquirers, Gryss's temper was beginning to

110

fray, and he delegated the task to Yakob, one of the other village elders.

It soon became apparent, however, that though the riders might have only been walking their horses they were already beyond catching.

'Well, I'm damned if I'm riding after them,' Gryss said, stopping abruptly in the middle of the street and wiping his shining forehead. 'They can go all the way to the Great Forest for all I care. We'll take your advice and wait for them to come back, Jeorg.'

'In the inn?' Jeorg enquired, inclining his round head significantly towards the nearby establishment.

Gryss nodded solemnly, as one about to prescribe a special medicine. 'Indeed,' he said, lifting the morale of the crowd with a single word as befitted a leader.

Farnor took his arm as he began to lead the assault on the inn. 'I think I'll go home,' he said. He was worried about that line of ill-favoured horsemen going past the farm with his father and mother alone there and unaware.

Gryss caught the uncertainty in his voice. 'Probably the best thing,' he said. 'Tell your father what's happened. I'll borrow a horse from the inn and come along myself later.'

Unhindered by the others, Farnor let his feet take up the pace of his concerns and as he reached the outskirts of the village he broke into a leisurely, long legged trot that he knew he could maintain for mile after mile.

Stars were beginning to appear in the darkening sky, though a moon was rising that would soon wash many of them aside.

Farnor had no eyes for the heavens, though. Away from the apparent security of the village his mind began to wander unrestrained through many dark avenues, fed by his vivid imagination and remnants of tales he had heard from Yonas.

111

All that was truly clear to him was the increasing certainty that, whatever the gatherers were doing, they boded no good and the sooner they were gone the better. He echoed Gryss's relieved proclamation that he was glad the village had always collected the tithe. The prospect of greeting King's men of such an ilk having failed to do so verged on the terrifying.

'They're only men,' Gryss had said. The rational view, stated to dispel the primitive and ancient fear of strangers that is in all people.

But reason is the newcomer and less rooted in its ways, and the juxtaposition in his mind of the grim outsiders and the warm security of his home and parents made Farnor grimace despite himself.

He wanted to be home desperately, both for shelter and support.

Then for a while his thoughts ceased and he simply ran; on and on, relaxed and easy, despite his concerns, until at last he came to the gate that led to his home. It was too dark now for him to see any signs of where the riders had gone, and his anxiety began to return as he ran up the pathway towards the farm.

Rounding the final corner, he saw the house. A sunstone lantern hung by the door, illuminating the yard. The empty yard.

Farnor wanted to shout with relief as half-formed images of the place filled with milling horsemen emerged from the recesses of his mind and vanished.

'You look puffed,' Garren said, as his son banged into the house. 'Some irate father been chasing you from sunset watch for dallying with his daughter?'

He chuckled, until his wife shot him a menacing glance over the top of the book she was reading.

Before either could speak, however, Farnor had launched into his tale. As it unfolded, his mother laid down her book and joined her husband in staring at their son spellbound.

'Riding up the valley, you say?' was all that Garren could say as Farnor finished his tellling.

Farnor nodded. 'I didn't catch them,' he said. 'I suppose they've gone on up towards the castle.'

Katrin looked nervous and Garren puffed out his cheeks and blew a long breath as he struggled to assimilate all that he had just been told.

'Gatherers!' he said eventually. 'After all these years! That's not going to go down well.' Then the questions began to pour out. 'How many were there? What did they look like? Why didn't they go to the tithe barn? Why didn't Gryss speak to them?' And in increasing bewilderment. 'And what in the world are they doing trailing all the way out here?'

In the small spaces between these and other questions, Farnor shook his head, shrugged and managed the occasional 'I don't know', until inspiration prompted him to say, 'Gryss said he'd come along later.'

It stemmed the flow of questions, but not his father's agitation. Garren got up and walked out of the house and across the yard. Farnor followed him, leaving his mother silhouetted in the open doorway. The farm's two dogs emerged from their kennels and loped after them.

At the gate Garren stopped and, placing his hands around his eyes to shield them from the light of the sunstone lantern, he peered intently towards the castle. Farnor did the same but, despite the moonlight, it was too dark for anything to be seen other than the sombre shapes of the mountains themselves.

'Do you think we should go and look for them?' Garren said. 'See if they need any help . . . food . . . water? If they're as weary as you seem to think they are, they could get lost up there.'

113

'They had pack horses with them,' Farnor said. 'They must be used to travelling through strange countryside by now if they've come all the way from the capital.'

'You're right,' Garren said, turning back towards the farmhouse. 'And I doubt they'd take too kindly to a stranger barging in on their camp.'

As they were crossing the yard one of the dogs growled and edged towards the gate. The whinny of a horse floated out of the darkness and slowly a tall shape emerged into the outer fringes of the sunstone lantern's light. It was a rider.

'Sorry if I startled you,' came Gryss's voice as he dismounted to open the gate. His tone was matter-of-fact. 'Did you see any sign of the gatherers on your way back, Farnor?' he asked.

Farnor shook his head.

Gryss reached down to stroke the two dogs, then he looked northwards. 'I imagine they've gone wandering off up there, then,' he said, turning to Garren. 'Farnor's told you everything, I presume?'

'Yes, but I'm none the wiser.'

'Nor I,' Gryss said. 'But I've had a quick word with most of the Council at the inn, and I thought I'd have one with you too before we have a formal meeting tomorrow.'

Garren smiled. It was Gryss's normal way of dealing with such rare matters as had to be dealt with through the village's Council. After making up his own mind, he would then persuade the elders and Council members to his way before the meeting, 'to save time'. Sometimes it worked. Sometimes, spectacularly, it did not.

At the word 'Council' Farnor's interest in the proceedings evaporated. The excitement and the alarm of the arrival of the gatherers could not survive the dead hand of any Council deliberation. As the two men disappeared into the house, Farnor clicked his tongue at the dogs and clambered over the gate. After his dash from the village and his father's interrogation, a quiet moonlight walk would help him clear his thoughts.

The two dogs scrabbled under the gate and ran after him, tails wagging.

As he walked, the dogs came and went, running twenty paces for his every one and generally terrorizing the nocturnal wildlife. At the roadway he debated for a moment and then turned left, northwards.

A short walk would bring him to the top of a rise from which, during the day, more of the castle would be visible. Perhaps he might be able to see some sign of a camp – distant fires burning, perhaps even voices carried through the still night air.

When he was about halfway up the rise the two dogs bounded up to him once again. Abruptly they stopped and, lowering their heads, began to growl.

'What's the matter?' Farnor asked, crouching down between them and following their gaze.

Ahead, the road ended as a black hummock against the moonlit sky where it topped the rise. Trees on either side waited, motionless.

Then, slowly, the black hummock began to change shape.

Chapter 9

Farnor's eyes widened in terror as the silhouetted crest of the rise ahead of him changed into moving, swaying life. Visions of the sheep-worrier, monstrous and malevolent, emerging from some dark and terrible lair for vengeance against its pursuers rushed in upon him before he had time to think more calmly what might be happening.

Though his legs were trembling in readiness for flight, no instruction reached them and as the shadow grew Farnor remained transfixed, his arms around the hackled shoulders of his dogs. He could feel the vibration of their growling, but all he could hear was the sound of his own heartbeat pounding in his ears.

The shadow continued to grow, then:

'Ho, you there!'

The voice cut through the internal din of his terror.

Part of him queried, *me?* Another part advised a hasty retreat. But yet another at last identified the eerie shapes ahead. They were riders, he realized with relief. The gatherers returning, presumably.

'Yes?' Farnor said, in a voice that surprised him by the absence of tremor.

'Come here.'

'What do you want?'

The shadows shifted. 'Come here!' the voice repeated irritably. It sounded unusual and there was an inflection in it that Farnor did not like.

For a moment he again considered fleeing, or, more correctly, slipping away. This was his land and he knew it intimately, by day or by night. He could disappear into it on the instant and make his way back to the farm in secret to draw Gryss and his father into this strange happening.

The thought of this option calmed him.

But then, he reflected, what had happened?

Nothing (he glossed over his initial terrified response), except that he had been addressed by a stranger who was certainly benighted and almost certainly lost. Further, the stranger was a gatherer, a King's man whose goodwill might prove important over the following days. He would get short shrift from either Gryss or his father if he abandoned such a man by running off into the night like a frightened child.

'Stay,' he commanded the dogs. They lay down but Farnor was glad of their snarling presence, for all he had resolved to play ambassador for the valley. A horse whinnied and Farnor heard what he took to be an oath, though the words were unfamiliar.

As he walked forward, he made out someone dismounting and coming to meet him.

A dozen paces further and he found himself in front of a tall, slightly slouching figure. The moonlight threw deep contrasting shadows across the man's face, and Farnor could form no impression of how old he might be or even what he looked like; or anything about him, for that matter.

Except his eyes. He could not see them for they were sunken and dark, but he knew they were narrowed and searching. He tried to stare into them but the effort made him uneasy.

'You live around here, boy?'

The appellation made Farnor stiffen indignantly, but he offered no rejoinder. And again the voice sounded strange. The man pronounced his words in a peculiar manner, and with a hesitation that was at odds with the confidence of his physical presence.

'Yes,' Farnor replied.

'We need a healer,' said the man. 'Some of my men are sick. Where can I find one?'

Farnor felt as if the sun had come out. He became almost garrulous.

'You're lucky,' he said. 'The healer's at our house right now. Come with me. I'll take you to him.'

The man tilted his head to one side as if he were listening very carefully.

'How far?' he asked after a moment.

'A few minutes' walk,' Farnor answered, pointing back down the road.

Once more the man seemed to be pondering something, then, with a flick of his hand, he said, 'Lead.'

For some reason he could not have explained, Farnor made a slight bow by way of acknowledgement of this instruction. The man turned back to his still-mounted companions and beckoned them forward. One of them spoke.

Farnor's mouth dropped open. The man was talking gibberish! There was a brief return of his earlier alarm. A long-forgotten childhood tale of night demons which whisked away unwary travellers to become slaves in some terrible world of their own making, passed briefly through his mind. Then it came to him that these men were not merely King's men from the distant capital, but *foreigners*: people from an entirely different land.

What was the word that he had heard Yonas use?

Mercenaries, that was it. It had a splendid sound to it, though, as he recalled, Yonas's mercenaries were sometimes loyal and true, other times treacherous and deceitful. But that was Yonas. This was real life. And the King would surely only have selected the finest men to act as his gatherers.

He put aside his thoughts as the other riders reached

him and, mounting his horse, the first man motioned him on.

Farnor clicked his tongue and the dogs left their vigil and came to his side. They seemed to have lost any relish for their nocturnal rampaging however, and, tails uncertain, ears pricked, they stayed close by Farnor as he walked ahead of the riders.

For the most part the riders were silent, though there was an exchange at one point that was ended by a sharp command from their leader. Both, again, in their own alien language.

Farnor was enthralled as he walked ahead of these strangers like some mysterious shepherd.

Reaching the farm he opened the gate and the men rode past him into the brightly lit yard. There were six of them and it seemed to Farnor that on entering the light they became uneasy. They spread out and glanced around a great deal as if looking for something . . . or, perhaps, someone. Their horses, too, became restive and the night was soon filled with the sound of hooves clattering nervously on the well-packed stone that surfaced the yard. The light from the sunstone lantern took up the agitation and danced great shadows about the yard and over the walls and roofs of the enclosing outbuildings. One of the men spoke anxiously to the leader, who muttered something and swung down from his horse.

'Wait here,' Farnor said to him. 'I'll get my father.'

But the noise of the riders entering the yard had already brought Garren and Gryss to the door in some alarm, with Katrin at their back.

'What's the matter? What's happening?' Garren said to Farnor as he took in the scene.

'Are you the healer?' the leader of the riders asked Garren before Farnor could reply.

Garren stared at him, taken aback by the strange accent.

Gryss stepped around him quickly. 'Foreigners,' he

120

murmured to Garren by way of explanation, then, addressing the question, replied, 'I have some small knowledge of healing. Has anyone been injured?'

The man waved his hand northwards. 'At the castle there. Some of my men are sick,' he said.

Gryss nodded. 'A few of them looked none too well when you rode through the village,' he said, and, briefly the querulous physician, 'You should have spoken then. I've no equipment or medicines with me here.'

'Come anyway,' the man said. Farnor thought he heard a threat in his voice, but decided it was probably the peculiar accent.

Gryss simply nodded and went over to his horse. 'I'll come with you,' Garren said, walking after him, but Gryss shook his head. 'No. You stay here with . . . Katrin and Farnor. If it's not too late I'll call in on my way back.'

The two men looked at one another for a moment.

'Call anyway,' Garren said, in unconscious imitation of the riders' leader.

As the riders left, Garren frowned. 'What's the matter?' Farnor asked. 'I did right to bring them here, didn't I? It'll be good for us to have helped them, won't it?'

Garren's frown darkened. 'I suppose so,' he said thoughtfully. 'But why would they need six men to find a healer?' He glanced at his son and a smile forced its way to his lips. 'Yes, you did right,' he said. 'It was a happy meeting. It could well do us some good if we end up having to negotiate with these people about the tithe.'

With casual firmness, he shepherded his wife and son inside.

As he closed the door, however, he peered out into the darkness beyond the yard. 'Foreigners?' he mouthed silently, his face puzzled and grim.

'A little slower if you don't mind,' Gryss said to his companion, speaking carefully and clearly. 'I'm no rider at the best of times, and this horse isn't mine.'

The man reined his horse back a little.

'My name's Har Grysstson,' Gryss said, smiling and extending his hand. 'But everyone calls me Gryss. Or old Gryss if they're feeling particularly superior.'

'Gryss,' the man said to himself as if testing the word, then he took Gryss's hand. 'Nilsson,' he said. 'Halfvrin Nilsson.' His grip was powerful and his teeth gleamed for a moment in the moonlight in what Gryss took to be a smile.

'You're captain of this company?' Gryss asked.

'I lead them,' Nilsson replied tersely.

Gryss changed tack. 'What's the matter with your men?'

Nilsson shrugged. 'If I knew I wouldn't have sought a healer,' he replied. Gryss frowned slightly at the indifference in the man's voice.

Sensing futility in any further questioning Gryss resigned himself to completing the journey in silence, which indeed proved to be the case.

He had been honest when he had said that he was no rider, and he was more than relieved when they eventually reached the castle. A shout rang out as the great bulk of the gatehouse towers loomed ahead of them. The group halted and Nilsson answered the challenge. In response the wicket door opened, cutting a dark rectangle in the moonlit gate. Nilsson and the others dismounted.

With much noise and little dignity, so too did Gryss. None offered to help him.

'Thank you very much,' he muttered to himself sarcastically.

Then, pulling a rueful face and rubbing his behind

gingerly, he took the reins of his horse and followed Nilsson through the door.

He could not have said what he had expected to see within the castle walls, though what he saw was without doubt an anticlimax. A few men were wandering about carrying pitch torches, and the fitful light of these was sufficient to obliterate the moonlight that flooded into the courtyard while illuminating little.

Nilsson spoke to someone then turned to Gryss. 'This way,' he said, taking the man's torch.

Another rider took Gryss's horse from him and he set off after Nilsson towards a nearby building. As they entered it Gryss noticed that the door was damaged; it had been forced open. He frowned, then realized that probably all the locks were rusted solid by now, and tired soldiers at the end of a long journey would not be looking to spend time delicately greasing and manipulating old door furniture before they could get in and rest, especially if some of them were ill.

Inside, Gryss found himself in a large antechamber with several passages leading from it. Nilsson looked around for a moment, uncertain which way to turn. Gryss pointed to a door under which a light was showing. Nilsson grunted and pushed the door open.

It led into a small hall lit by a dozen or so torches. The smoke from them was acrid and had filled the high ceiling like winter cloud. Around the hall men were lying almost as if they had been dropped like so many sacks of meal.

Nilsson inclined his head towards the men. 'That's them,' he said curtly. 'Get them on their feet if you can. We can't carry passengers.'

Gryss looked at him sharply, shocked by the harshness of his tone. Reproaches came to his mouth but he left them unspoken, knowing that he knew too little about

123

these people to stand in judgement over them. He turned to his charges.

It was not easy examining them by the light of the torches. 'Have you no lanterns?' he asked at one stage. There was no reply, but Nilsson brought his torch closer.

Crouching, Gryss moved from one man to the next, looking into eyes and mouths, feeling brows and taking pulses, testing limbs and generally prodding and poking. The replies he received to his few softly spoken questions were answered haltingly with the same accent as their captain's.

When he had finished, he straightened up with a grunt of discomfort and turned to Nilsson. 'As far as I can tell after such a short examination, whatever else might be wrong with them, these men are suffering from severe exhaustion. Make sure they get a good night's rest and I'll come back and look at them more thoroughly tomorrow.'

Nilsson glowered at him and then at the men. His lips pulled back in a snarl to reveal tightly clenched teeth. Gryss wondered if that was what he had assumed to be a smile as they had ridden together through the darkness.

'You mean they're malingering because they're tired?' Nilsson said. His jawline was tense and the snarl still lingered nearby. For the first time since they had met, Gryss looked properly at the man. He was taller than average and heavily built, with a slight thrusting slouch to his shoulders that gave him a menacing appearance. A full face, that would in time probably become jowled, was marked by deep-set lines and his eyes added to the sense of menace he exuded by their searching coldness.

And the brief snarl had made him look peculiarly savage.

Gryss felt afraid.

He sought safety in reason. The man's a soldier, he told himself quickly. And a captain at that. A man with responsibilities and one used to imposing his will on others in order to fulfil them. And, too, one capable of using extreme violence when need arose. What else should I expect to find in him except a fearsome, perhaps cruel determination?

And he's a foreigner, came the afterthought. A species of stranger necessarily much more . . . unusual . . . than even those fellow countrymen from over the hill.

Some unease in his presence was inevitable. The conclusion gave him a little comfort.

'No,' he replied. 'They're not just tired, they're physically *exhausted*. Their bodies are ceasing to work properly. You might get them on their feet by using brute force, but it'll only be a matter of time before they fall over again and then they'll be unable to move no matter what you do.' He did not add that given such encouragement his men might also be galvanized sufficiently to cut their captain's throat. Exhausted or not, and his patients or not, Gryss still found them as unsavoury looking a crowd as they had been when they rode through the village.

Nilsson seemed inclined to disagree, but Gryss pressed on. 'You don't look too good yourself, Captain,' he said starkly. 'How long have you been riding?'

'Too long,' Nilsson replied without hesitation, taken unawares by the question.

Gryss sensed a pain underneath the flat tone of this response and, despite the man's demeanour, reached out to take his arm.

'Your diligence does you credit, Captain,' he said. 'But I'm sure the King wouldn't want you and your men driven into the ground just for the gathering of his tithe.'

125

Nilsson's expression became puzzled. Gryss began to speak more carefully again, presuming that the Captain had not understood properly. 'He wouldn't want you to work so hard for him that you fell ill. Especially as I imagine our small tithe won't make much difference to his revenue.' He became avuncular. 'Good grief! No one can even remember when the tithe was last collected from here. Your taking a day or so to rest and recover your strength isn't going to make any difference after all these years, is it?'

The possible answer to this rose frighteningly in his mind once again. 'There *is* no great need, is there? A war or something?' he added anxiously.

As Gryss had spoken, Nilsson's look of bewilderment had been replaced by one of shrewd-eyed calculation, and this in turn had given way to one of studied blankness. He was silent for a moment after Gryss had finished.

'No, no,' he said suddenly with a shake of his head, as if he had just recalled the question. 'No . . . war. Just . . .' He finished with a casual shrug.

Gryss reflected the movement in a shrug of his own. 'Well, then,' he said, 'you must stay here and rest until your men are fit again. It won't be too long, I'm sure. Only a few days.' He gazed around at the smoky hall with distaste. 'I'm afraid I've no idea what rooms there are in the castle, but there must be plenty better than this. I wouldn't bother disturbing your men now, let them sleep. But perhaps tomorrow you can find something . . . more comfortable.'

Nilsson's eyes were fixed on Gryss. 'We don't have enough food to allow us to stay here,' he said.

'I'm sure we can come to some arrangement about any food that the King's tithe gatherers might need.' Gryss made his reply airy, though he was pleased that he had remembered to keep a note of impending barter in his offer.

Nilsson nodded and moved towards the door. Gryss took this to be both an acceptance of his suggestion and an end of his visit.

'I'll come back tomorrow,' he said.

As he was about to open the door it swung towards him and two men entered. He stepped aside to let them pass then made to leave. As he moved, one of the men shot a questioning glance at Nilsson and Gryss felt a powerful grip close about his arm. He gave it a tug, but knew immediately that no effort he could muster would free him. Alarmed, he turned to Nilsson.

The Captain was engaged in an urgent conversation with Gryss's captor that ended abruptly in a stern, almost vicious command from Nilsson, which, though Gryss did not understand their language, obviously meant, 'Let him go!' with a strongly implied 'or else'. It was obeyed only after the second utterance, and the release was as rough as the seizure. Independent of this, however, Gryss deemed it advisable to remain where he was until Nilsson spoke to him directly.

Motioning the new arrivals to one side, Nilsson opened his arms apologetically and smiled at Gryss. It was a real smile this time.

'I'm sorry,' he said. 'We've been too long in the saddle, as you say, and tempers are not what they should be.' He became confidential. 'To be honest,' he went on, lowering his voice, 'we weren't quite sure where we were. There aren't many . . .' He snapped his fingers in search of the word. 'Maps . . . of this part of the country, and we've had considerable difficulty finding our way here.'

Gryss smiled back relieved, but still did not move until Nilsson guided him through the door and out into the courtyard. It was almost deserted now, and

Gryss's horse had been tethered to a post by the door.

Nilsson opened the wicket door for him. 'Would you like an escort back to your farm . . . Har Grysstson?' he asked.

'No, thank you, Captain,' Gryss replied. 'It's a clear night and, unlike yourself, I'm lucky enough to know where I am.'

With an effort he mounted and, nodding a farewell to the Captain, urged his horse forward. As he heard the door close behind him he felt as if a great burden had been lifted from him. He had not realized how oppressive the atmosphere in the castle had been.

Looking down the valley, he saw the sunstone shining on top of the tithe barn. He halted his horse and gazed at it for some time. Then he half turned and looked back at the castle. Once familiar yet mysterious, it seemed now to have been totally transformed. The familiar had become alien. The mysterious, haunted and fearful.

He closed his eyes and released a long, slow breath. He was tense. Too much had happened today. Far too much.

When he opened his eyes, the tithe barn sunstone again filled his vision. He looked at the bright, hopeful light of the Dalmastide symbol. The light that had meant so much to him and, indeed, the whole valley for so long.

Now he found himself wishing only for darkness to cover and protect the valley and his people.

Chapter 10

'What the devil do you think you're playing at, Halfvrin? First bringing him here and then letting him go like that!'

The complaint came from the man who minutes previously had seized Gryss's arm to prevent him leaving: Arven Dessane. He was shorter than Nilsson and of a similar, heavy build, though where there was a stillness about Nilsson there was a restless nervousness about Dessane.

Nilsson stared at him coldly. 'More to the point, Dessane, what the devil were you doing grabbing hold of him like that?' His voice was low and full of menace, and Dessane edged back. He managed to maintain some of his defiance, however. 'I was trying to stop him leaving,' he replied bluntly. 'The last thing we want is news getting out about us being here.'

Nilsson's teeth glinted an unhealthy yellow in the dying torchlight. He let out an audible breath in which weariness just overcame anger, and pushed past Dessane to head back towards the building housing his exhausted men. 'How you've survived this long defies me,' he said. He stopped and turned to face him. 'Didn't you learn anything from our late unlamented leader? Didn't you learn to watch and listen and wait? To smile and keep your knife up your sleeve?'

'Much good his plotting and scheming did him in the end,' came Dessane's unhesitant reply. His tone became scornful. 'And don't you go pretending you're like him, or have you suddenly found the secret of his *special* kind of protection?' He made a disparaging noise. 'You'll get us all killed, wandering off like that and bringing strangers back to spy on us. We should keep things simple. Strong arms and sharp steel. That's all we've got, that's all we need and that's all we should bother ourselves with.'

Nilsson clenched his fists and seemed to be giving serious consideration to striking his companion. Instead he leaned towards him, like a huge swaying tree. 'Really?' he said caustically. 'An elegant and perceptive analysis. I hadn't appreciated that you had such a subtle grasp of our position. How fortunate I took the others with me for a little pleasant company when I went out looking for a healer. There'd probably have been enough of us to deal with anything untoward that we ran in to, or don't you think so?' Dessane held his ground, but only with difficulty in the face of this viciously soft onslaught. 'But, fortunately, it wasn't necessary, was it?' Nilsson went on. 'We found no ambushes, no spies, no . . .' He paused significantly. '. . . pursuers. Just a lad out with his dogs and a healer visiting a friend.' He paused. 'But perhaps I made a mistake, thinking, planning, like our erstwhile leader did.' He pointed to the wicket door. 'You go after the old man. Cut his throat before he gets back to that farm.' Then his rage came through. 'And see where that gets us. The whole valley up in arms and us stuck up the wrong end of it while they'll be raising the entire countryside.'

'We can seal the valley and deal with a few villagers easily enough,' Dessane replied defensively.

'With what, you donkey?' Nilsson hissed. He jerked his thumb over his shoulder. 'It may have escaped your attention, but we've virtually no food left and damn near a third of our men are too sick and exhausted almost to mount, let alone fight. That's why we stopped at this place when we found it, if you can remember that far back, and why I went looking for a healer. And *you'd*

130

kill him. In one stroke make sure the men would get no proper treatment *and* start a war they couldn't fight. Brilliant.'

His tone was withering, and Dessane made no response for some time, though, momentarily, his eyes blazed. The fire faded however, and when he spoke his manner was defeated and sulky. 'Even so, I don't like the idea of that old man knowing we're here and that we're so weak,' he said. 'He could be sending messengers right now.'

Satisfied that his companion was subdued, Nilsson became conciliatory. 'Look, you're nearly as tired as that lot in there. You're not thinking. Where would he send his messengers to? We haven't seen another village in days, let alone a town with a garrison. This place is the back of beyond. I'll wager no one's been out of this valley in years, nor anyone visited it except the odd tinker. And why should he send for help? What have we done? Nothing. Rode quietly through the village, that's all.'

Dessane was still unsettled. 'We broke into this place,' he said. 'And it's been a major garrison fort at some time, judging by the size of it.'

'Once. Maybe,' Nilsson agreed. 'But you saw the state of that road.' He waved an arm around the courtyard. The last torch had guttered out, and the cold moonlight gave the ancient walls a sepulchral look. 'And every lock we've come across in this place is rusted solid. I wouldn't be surprised to find most of the roofs rotted through when we see them in daylight. This place hasn't been used in decades.' He came close to Dessane and lowered his voice to a conspiratorial whisper. 'If need had arisen, I was going to tell him that we'd had to break in because of our sick men.' He tapped his head and bared his teeth again. 'But if you'd watch and listen, like I said, instead of reaching for your knife every time you see a stranger, you'd learn.' He paused. 'He didn't even seem surprised about us being here. He even suggested that we stay on for a few days. Said they could come to an arrangement about some food for us. That's all we need. Food and rest and we'll be on our feet again. If we make no trouble here then we can slip away quietly along the valley on to pastures new and it'll be years before anyone finds out about where we've gone.'

'You seem very sure about the old man,' Dessane said, a faltering rearguard.

Nilsson smiled. 'Oh yes,' he said. 'As far as I could understand him, he seemed to think we were some kind of king's men.' He searched for Gryss's words. 'Gatherers, that's it. Tithe gatherers he called us. You speak the language better than I do. What are they, do you think?'

Dessane thought for a moment, brow furrowed, then he chuckled, relieved to be standing with his captain instead of against him. 'They're tax collectors, by the sound of it,' he said. His chuckle became a low laugh. 'Yes, I'm sure of it. They think we're tax collectors.'

Nilsson snapped his fingers. 'That's why that crowd was waiting in the village.'

'And looking so miserable.' Dessane laughed maliciously.

Nilsson clapped his lieutenant on the back, the tension between them gone. The two men's laughter floated up into the bright sky, twisting around the thin columns of smoke rising from the dead torches.

Gryss called at the farm as Garren had asked. He had little to say. 'They don't look any better by torchlight than they did by daylight,' he said. 'But those I saw were in a poor way. In need of rest and good food, I'd judge.'

132

'Shouldn't they have had enough supplies to come this far?' Garren asked.

Gryss shrugged. 'One would think so, but perhaps they've had problems. The Captain did say they'd got themselves lost. Understandable, I suppose, after all this time. There'll certainly be no one alive who could remember the way since the last time the tithe was gathered. Although, to be honest, I think he's a harsh one. I certainly wouldn't like to try knocks with him. He's probably been driving them too hard.'

'You did say they were foreigners,' Garren said. Necessarily, that comprehensively explained many evils.

Farnor surreptitiously hugged himself as these revelations and speculations fed off one another, though he would have preferred to have been without the chilly note that filled Gryss's voice when he spoke of the Captain.

'Where do you think they come from?' he ventured. 'And why would the King use foreigners as gatherers?'

Once again Gryss shrugged. 'Anywhere, and he alone knows, are the best answers I can give you, Farnor. We might find out in time, I suppose, but my main concern now is to have the tithe agreed and get them out of here.' He sighed. 'Though they'll have to stay for a few days at least. They've got some very tired men there.'

Katrin entered the room, her fingers threaded through the handles of four cups. Gingerly the men unhooked them. A savoury smell filled the room. Gryss sipped his noisily and then patted his stomach.

'Splendid, Katrin,' he said. 'It's a clear night out there and chillier than you'd think. And the company so far's not been too warming.' He became businesslike. 'I think it'd be a good idea to take some food to them as soon as possible. Be friendly, but not too friendly. Just enough to get them on their feet and to get us a good deal, but not so much that they'll remember us next year.'

He laughed. 'Better not give them any of this, though, Katrin,' he said, holding his cup up like a formal toast, 'Or they'll never leave.'

Katrin gave him a knowing look and raised a finger to rebuke him for such foolishness.

'Pity about Dalmas,' Farnor slipped into the easy silence.

The others nodded. 'I think I'm about used to the idea now,' Gryss said sadly. 'When this is over, we'll have to see if there's anything else we can do. It'd be a shame to lose the whole celebration.'

There was a short debate about what could be done, and how, but the day had been long and, filled with his mother's warm drink, Farnor found himself falling asleep. He jerked himself awake a couple of times, then finally had to concede defeat and retire to bed after being awakened by Gryss and his parents laughing when he almost fell out of his chair.

In bed, he lay, half awake, half dozing, for some time, basking in the steady rumble of the voices percolating through his bedroom floor. I must remember to ask what they were talking about in the morning, he thought, as he turned over, relishing his growing adult privileges from the childish security of his familiar bed.

Gradually he sank deeper and deeper into a luxurious drowsiness; his thoughts pursuing their own strange, incoherent ways and he happening upon them from time to time and thinking he understood where they were going. From nowhere, his mother and father and Gryss flowed into this meandering stream and he felt their thoughts and hopes and fears with extraordinary vividness. Instinctively, he reached out to cherish the love and to soothe the pains.

Then, as on the hillock, he jerked violently. The impact left him winded and shaking and wide awake.

He swore, and twitched his right leg once or twice, deeming it to be that limb which had offended, then he turned on to his back, and flopped down into the pillow again.

As the small noises of this upheaval faded, he realized that no sound was coming from down below. The room, in fact the whole house, was silent. For a moment, ominous shadows began to form at the edge of his awareness, but, almost immediately, they were scattered as his mother's laugh suddenly rose up to reassure him. It was closely followed by echoing laughter from Gryss and his father. The sounds merged and peaked a few times and then drifted back into their steady drone.

Farnor turned over and went to sleep immediately.

'Dalmas stayabed, young man,' was Gryss's greeting as Farnor entered the kitchen the next morning. 'Your father's gone to collect some of my medicines and food for our guests. Would you like to come with me to the castle when he gets back?'

'Jobs and then breakfast first, Dalmas or no,' Katrin intervened. 'Then he can go if he wants.' She wielded a large spoon like a judicial sceptre.

Both men bowed to this higher authority.

A little later, Farnor and Gryss were sitting on one of Garren's carts and being drawn steadily along the remains of the castle road by Garren's old mare. Much of the vegetation that had overgrown the road had been trampled by the riders the previous night, but twice Farnor had to jump down and lead the animal as the unevenness of the neglected surface caused her problems.

He complained after the second time but Gryss shut him up. 'Don't mention anything about the state of this road,' he said. 'For all I know it might be our job to look after it.'

135

'Why? We don't need it,' Farnor protested. 'If they want it, they should—'

'Never mind,' Gryss interrupted firmly. 'Just do as I say. Paying tithes and the like is bad enough, but there's all sorts of queer things can happen when you start getting involved in the affairs of folks from over the hill, and I'd prefer you didn't go giving them any ideas. You just look and listen when we get to the castle and keep a guard on your tongue. There'll be bargains to be struck soon, and the more we know, the better.'

Though quietly spoken, there was an authority in this instruction that was not to be argued with. Farnor nodded and urged the mare on.

The rest of the journey was uneventful. The soft clop of the horse's hooves, the creaking of harness, the muffled rumble of the wheels and the swaying rhythm of the cart conspired with the warm sunshine and the scents of the valley to lull both passenger and driver into as deep a state of relaxation as is possible short of actually falling asleep.

Farnor scarcely noticed when they passed beyond the point where, but days earlier, he would have considered his world as ending.

As they neared the castle two riders came out to meet them. Farnor had had in mind, albeit vaguely, that once in their proper home the soldiers would be wearing some kind of formal uniform, and he was disappointed to note that they looked as unprepossessing as they had the previous evening.

In fact, everything about them had a patched and worn look: clothes, weapons, tackle. They could not have been further from any of the notions Farnor had held about what a soldier should look like. And they were none too fragrant, he discovered, as one of them moved upwind to peer into the cart. *That* was something

Yonas had never seen fit to mention even in his most down-to-earth yarns.

More disconcerting however were their suspicious, fast-moving eyes and their hands which were never far from the knives in their belts.

'Would you tell Captain Nilsson that I've come to look at your sick again? And we've brought you some food,' Gryss said. 'Can you get the gate open?'

Gryss's news succeeded in making the two soldiers a little less surly, although his question caused some frowning.

They held a brief debate in their own language, then one of them rode back to the castle while the other motioned Gryss to follow.

It transpired that the answer to Gryss's question was that they couldn't get the gate open, and Gryss and Farnor found themselves waiting in front of it listening to a great deal of hammering and banging intermingled with much swearing and some unkind laughter.

'For pity's sake, we've not brought them that much,' Farnor said, softly, with a world-weariness that made Gryss smile. 'They could've carried it through the door in half this time. There's enough of them.'

Eventually, amid raucous and ironic cheering, the gates creaked ponderously open. Despite his growing disenchantment with the soldiers, Farnor felt a surge of excitement at the sight. The two great timber leaves were even thicker than their outside appearance had indicated and he could scarcely believe the size of the iron bolts and hinges. He tried to imagine the village blacksmith drawing them from his furnace and beating them out on the anvil, but the image eluded him. How in the world were such things made?

A nudge in the ribs from Gryss brought him out of his wonderment. He clicked the horse forward. As the cart passed underneath the gate arch he almost fell out of his seat as he stared up at the huge keystone above him.

'Steady,' Gryss said, catching his arm. 'Your father and mother won't be too pleased with me if I fetch you home with a wheel track across your ribs.'

'Sorry,' Farnor exclaimed. 'I was—'

'I know what you were doing,' Gryss said, a serious edge to his voice. 'And I understand. But I don't want you daydreaming here, Farnor. I want you to watch and listen as I told you.'

As the cart trundled across the courtyard, more men began to appear from various doorways. Again, Farnor felt a twinge of excitement as he saw himself the centre of this martial attention, but it faded quickly enough when he saw that they all seemed to have the same demeanour as the first two they had met. He also found the sound of the gates closing behind him disconcerting.

Then Nilsson emerged from a nearby building and walked across to the cart. He had long, easy strides and the small crowd opened up before him like a flock of sheep before a dog.

'Har Grysstson,' he said, smiling and holding out his hand to help the old man down. 'And our guide, if I'm not mistaken.' He nodded curtly at Farnor who, uncertain what to do, gave a hesitant nod in reply.

Nilsson peered into the cart. 'Ah, food!' he exclaimed. 'That's most welcome. What do we owe you for this?'

Gryss waved his hands vaguely. 'This, I think . . .' He hesitated as if deliberating. 'Is a . . . a Dalmas gift from the village. Some consolation for your bad journey.'

Farnor recognized the opening ploy of a long barter and wondered if Nilsson had noted the same. He doubted it somehow as the Captain, having thanked Gryss, began to shout orders to his men to unload the cart. He'd find out in due course, Farnor thought, when bargaining about the tithe began.

138

In the meantime the alacrity with which the cart was being unloaded gave Farnor the impression that if he was not careful wheels, horse and even himself would be spirited away to some mysterious storeroom before Gryss would even notice that he was missing. He jumped down and moved the horse's head to steady it as men clambered noisily on and off the cart.

'Would you like me to look at your sick again?' Gryss was saying.

'I would, yes,' Nilsson replied. 'They seem better just for the night's rest and your food should have them up and about again very soon. But I'm no healer.'

'Shall I stay here?' Farnor asked, stroking the horse's cheek.

'You might as well,' Gryss said. 'I shouldn't be too long.'

As Gryss and Nilsson walked off, Farnor led the horse round so it was facing the gate. Muscled with ironwork, the gate looked even more formidable than it had from the outside. Under other circumstances Farnor could see that that would be a source of reassurance for the people sheltering within, but at the moment he would have preferred to see it standing open.

He gazed around.

He was *inside* the castle! Only now did the thought really impinge on him. It was only a week or so since he had come close to the castle for the first time, and now he was inside! He looked up at the enclosing walls and the various buildings that fringed the courtyard. Without exception, they were all larger than anything he had ever seen before, and his mind filled again with the wonder of how they could have been built, and, to a lesser extent, why.

He left the horse and began to walk towards the gate. Glancing down he saw that the stone slabs which formed the courtyard were as finely jointed as those of

139

the buildings and that hardly anywhere could he see weeds or grasses forcing their way through.

'Where are you going?'

The questioner was Dessane. Farnor started.

'I was only going to look at the gates,' he stammered.

'Why?'

'I've never seen anything like them before,' Farnor replied simply.

Dessane's mouth curled uncertainly. 'Don't wander about. Stay by your cart where I can see you,' he said harshly.

A rebellious retort formed in Farnor's mind, but he managed not to speak it. He was helped in this by the menace in the man's solid presence.

Then Dessane seemed to recant. 'It's dangerous round here,' he said. 'It's not been manned for years. We don't know how safe some of these buildings are.'

Farnor nodded slowly and turned studiously away from him to examine the horse's harness.

'What's to the north of here?'

Farnor jumped. He had not heard Dessane come up behind him. He gaped.

'What's to the north?' Dessane repeated, indicating the direction with his eyes.

'I don't know,' Farnor answered after a moment. 'Just forest, I think.'

Dessane's thin veneer of friendliness buckled. 'What do you mean, you don't know?' he asked, his jawline working as he fought to be pleasant. 'You live here, don't you?'

'I live there,' Farnor pointed down the valley. 'We don't come up here. There's no call to. The best grazing's down there, and what would anyone want to trail all the way up here for, let alone go further? All I've ever been told is that there's forest to the north.

140

As far as the eye can see. A whole country full of trees. The Great Forest.'

Dessane gave him a penetrating look. 'How old are you, boy?' he asked.

Farnor told him.

'And you've never been up the valley in your whole life?' Dessane made no effort to conceal his disbelief.

Whirls of fear and anger twisted inside Farnor. 'No,' he said, firmly, the anger predominating. 'I've never even been this far until we came here hunting a sheep-worrier the other week.'

Dessane pursed his lips. 'A sheep-worrier, eh? That must have been exciting. Did you catch it?'

'No.'

Dessane's expression announced that he wasn't in the least surprised, but when he spoke he said, 'And I suppose you've never been *down* the valley either, have you?'

'No, I haven't,' Farnor replied with increasing heat at this belittling assault on his integrity and, he suspected, his whole world. 'Not all the way, anyway. Why should I? Why should any of us? There's no need.'

Dessane did not seem disposed to debate the point.

'Hardly anyone ever bothers to go out of the valley,' Farnor added, fearing a further rejoinder.

'Or come into it?'

Farnor shook his head. 'Yonas the Teller, sometimes. And the odd pedlar now and then.'

'And . . . gatherers?'

Farnor looked straight at him. 'You're the first gatherers to come here within living memory,' he said. 'We presumed the King had sufficient and didn't want our small tithe.'

Dessane seemed to relax. 'We must have frightened you turning up like we did.'

'Not frightened,' Farnor lied. 'It *is* Dalmas. No one

141

was really expecting you to come for the tithe after all these years, so everyone was a bit put out. But not frightened. Why should we be frightened?'

'Why indeed?' Dessane said after a long pause. Someone called his name.

'Go and have a look at the gate if you want,' he said, almost friendly now. 'But stay round here. Don't wander off.'

And he was gone.

Farnor frowned. He knew that he had told this stranger a great deal about something important, but he did not know what. He cast his mind back through the conversation and resolved to repeat it to Gryss as fully as possible.

A short time later Gryss reappeared, and after exchanging a few courtesies with Nilsson, he and Farnor were again on the cart, watching the great gates being hauled open.

As they drove out of the castle, two riders passed them, turning northwards as Farnor steered the cart towards the old road. He stared after them curiously.

He was not the only one watching. High on a tree-lined slope opposite, Rannick, thinner than he had been, watched them also, his narrowed eyes ablaze with some strange inner light.

Chapter 11

The room was empty of furniture save for a large wooden table and a few chairs. A cursory attempt had been made to clean it though this had consisted largely of brushing the dust into the air and allowing it to redistribute itself as it settled. As a result, swooping tangles of cobwebs that had been invisible for years across the high, curved ceiling were now weighted and thickened and all too visible, making the room look dingier than ever.

Dying daylight did little to improve the scene as it filtered in through two narrow windows and rendered pallid the light of two lamps, one on the stone mantelshelf which beetled over a cavernous and empty fireplace and one on the table.

This latter illuminated half of Nilsson's face as he sat sideways on to the table, his shoulders hunched, and stared at his lieutenant.

'Tell me again,' he said.

Dessane made no effort to disguise his irritation at this request. 'They rode north for half the day and found nothing but forest,' he said wearily. 'Yeorson eventually climbed a tree but, he says, there was nothing to be seen except more trees. Trees filling the entire valley floor and disappearing north into the distance.'

'And they came back because the trees felt . . . bad,' Nilsson said, his voice heavy with anger and sarcasm.

Dessane gave a disclaiming shrug. 'That's what Storran said, and Yeorson didn't disagree. Don't ask me what they meant. I'm just passing on the message.' Then, remembering that it was he who had chosen them for the task, he rallied. 'But they're good scouts, you know that,' he said, tapping the side of his nose with his forefinger. 'With noses that have got us out of trouble more than once before now.'

Nilsson, however, did not seem to be disposed to reminisce. 'Get them in here,' he snapped impatiently. He rested his elbow on the table and the lamp flame wavered. After a brief hesitation, Dessane gave another shrug then went to the door and shouted.

Eventually the two men appeared. Yeorson was tall and thin while Storran, by contrast, was short and stocky. An injudicious person might have been inclined to smile at the sight of them side by side, but as with all those who followed Halfvrin Nilsson it would have been a mistake to be seen doing it. Their characters had marked their faces: Yeorson wore a permanently peevish and supercilious expression, while Storran might have had a jovial look about him had it not been for a large, voluptuous mouth and small, mean eyes.

Nilsson gestured them towards two chairs set beside him. As Yeorson moved forward a long hanging cobweb brushed his face, leaving a dusty scar. He flicked it away silently as he swept the chair away from the table and sat down. Storran ignored the chair and hoisted himself on to the table. They waited, eyes fixed on their leader.

Nilsson straightened. 'What's this Dessane tells me about the trees frightening you?' he asked, but with enough humour in his voice to temper the bluntness.

'The truth.' Yeorson's equally blunt reply made Nilsson start, though he disguised the movement. He had expected some reproach to be levelled at his lieutenant for misrepresentation. Now it was he who waited.

'There's a bad feeling about the place, Captain,' Storran added. 'And the further north we went the worse it seemed to get.'

Nilsson allowed some exasperation to show. 'The places we've been, things we've seen, things we've done . . . I can't believe I'm sitting here listening to you two, of all people, telling me you were too frightened to go into the woods.'

Yeorson and Storran were an odd, cold-blooded pair, he knew, but again he was surprised that such a taunt produced so little response. Yeorson tilted his chair back and Storran began swinging his legs, but both continued looking at him.

'That's how it was, Captain,' Yeorson said. 'Nothing particular you could see or hear, but it was bad. As if we were being watched all the time.' He paused and looked thoughtful. 'Or perhaps more as if something knew we were there. I've no other words for it; there was just a feeling about the place.' He glanced at his partner and his next words came as if reluctantly. 'Something . . . I . . . we haven't felt since . . .'

He stopped. In the silence, an errant draught caught some of the ancient cobwebs and motes of dust drifted down to join those already afloat, moving and hovering, dancing to the whims of a music beyond hearing.

'Since?' Nilsson prompted, uneasy at this hesitation.

'Since we . . . started our travels,' Yeorson finished as awkwardly as he had begun.

Nilsson frowned and turned away. This he had not expected. Dark memories seemed to flood into the room and for a moment Nilsson found his thoughts paralysed.

Somehow he freed himself; the needs of the present were too pressing to allow inaction, and, though it had been brought here by his own questioning, Nilsson had no desire to pursue this unwanted revelation.

'We *have* to find out what lies to the north,' he said, as if the previous question had never been asked and answered, and as if, by ignoring it, he erased it. 'We

145

need to leave this land as soon as we can and north is effectively our only way out. I'm not doubting what you felt,' he continued, skirting as close to the topic as he dared, 'but I think perhaps I was too hasty sending just the two of you out, scarcely rested.' He pushed his chair back noisily. 'Pick twenty men and try again . . .' He thought for a moment, businesslike. 'The day after tomorrow, I think.' He smiled. 'Thanks to the generosity of our . . . new neighbours . . . we can spare ourselves a day or so to recuperate from our journeying, and to plan our next move.'

He signalled the end of the exchange and Dessane left with the two men. After they had gone, Nilsson looked round the room sourly. The memories were still there, stirred up and hovering like the dust. Making visible what had lain unseen for a long time.

The following day Gryss arrived bringing more food, though not as much as on the first journey.

He saw none of the sick, however. 'They're all fine now,' Nilsson assured him as he signalled his men to begin unloading the cart. 'It was as you said: fatigue, hunger. It's been a bad journey. The rest and your food has put everyone back on their feet. And we've managed to find better quarters for everyone. The place is in remarkably good order.'

Gryss pressed. 'Are you sure? It's no hardship to look at them now I'm here.'

Nilsson waved his concerns aside. 'These are soldiers, Gryss. They learned long ago that if they didn't recover quickly they died. Illness, exhaustion, what you will, is a luxury they can't afford.'

Gryss found himself torn. He had no great desire to keep visiting these people, as, indeed, not only were none of them truly sick but almost without exception they seemed to exude a quality which made it difficult for him to raise any feeling of the true goodwill towards them that was essential if he was to heal. It distressed him. *They* distressed him.

On the other hand, he did not wholly believe Nilsson. Despite the Captain's flashes of pleasant, even charming, behaviour, there was a cold menace about him that cut through the old healer. And more than a few of the men he had examined bore signs of physical brutality about their persons.

Still, he thought resignedly, there was nothing he could do if he wasn't asked. Like Nilsson, he must look to his own, and their ends would best be served by getting rid of these unwanted newcomers as soon as possible.

'Whatever you say, Captain,' he replied. 'If you need any further help, you can always send for me.' He looked towards his now empty cart and then back at Nilsson. 'Incidentally, while I'm here can you tell me what we need to do about the tithe-gathering ceremony? It's been so long since there's been one that no one knows anything about it.'

'The tithe ceremony,' Nilsson echoed, nodding his head slowly and purposefully while he tried to think what to say. Inspiration came. Taking on as sage an expression as he could, he said, 'In a garrisoned . . . region . . . like this, albeit abandoned for the time being, the practice . . . indeed, the requirement . . . is that the tithe be brought to the garrison headquarters for . . . checking, prior to being taken to the capital.'

Gryss frowned. 'That's a deal of trouble – bringing everything all the way up here when you have to go back past where it's being stored on your way home.'

Nilsson shrugged. He was warming to his idea. 'It's not something I have any authority over, I'm afraid,' he said. 'I'm sure you've realized by now that many things have changed of late, and I would be answerable to my superiors if one of the King's . . . examiners . . . were suddenly to appear and find me blatantly ignoring the procedures that the King himself has authorized.'

Gryss pulled a wry face. He was about to say that hardly anyone ever came to the valley, but the very fact that Nilsson and his men were there destroyed that as an effective argument. He could offer to have people sent downland to act as look-outs, but he was far from certain as to how Nilsson might react to such a suggestion with its hint of collusion. Besides, there was a lot of produce to be loaded, and who was to say that one of these . . . examiners . . . might not suddenly arrive at full gallop? More than a few certainties had disappeared with the arrival of these gatherers.

'Very well,' he conceded with a sigh. 'If that's the way it has to be then I suppose that's the way it has to be. But it does seem to be remarkably foolish in this instance.'

Nilsson agreed. 'I'll mention it when I get back,' he said, extemporizing. 'Perhaps they'll allow some other arrangement next year.'

Gryss gave a resigned nod of acknowledgement and turned to matters practical. 'When shall we start bringing the produce up, then?' he asked. 'Do you want to be present when the barn is opened?'

Nilsson faltered. He did not want to leave this place with its strong walls and gate, other than to move northwards and away from this country for ever. But having stumbled upon this unexpected supply of free food it would be madness to jeopardize it for what must be, in reality, a small risk.

'Oh yes,' he said firmly. 'That's most important.' He paused as if considering many tasks ahead. 'I'll be along tomorrow. Three hours after daybreak.'

'Should there be anyone special from the village?' Gryss persisted.

Nilsson shrugged. 'Anyone,' he said simply. 'Providing

148

one of them has the key.' He smiled, but he was becoming increasingly anxious to end this business before he said something that might expose him. He changed the direction of the conversation abruptly. 'Tell me, Gryss, what lies to the north of here?'

'As far as I know, the Great Forest,' Gryss said.

'As far as you know?' Nilsson queried.

'I haven't actually visited the place myself,' Gryss replied. 'In fact, no one's ever been further up the valley than the castle. There's no cause to, is there?'

'Then how can you know what's up there?' Nilsson asked, an exasperated edge creeping into his voice.

Gryss laughed. 'I can't, I suppose, if you put it like that,' he said. 'But the existence of the Great Forest has been accepted by countless generations of families here, and I've no special reason to doubt it. Don't forget that most people here haven't seen the capital, or for that matter even any of the nearer towns and villages, but that doesn't mean they don't believe in them.'

Nilsson seemed to be disconcerted by this powerful innocence. To help him, Gryss pointed. 'Certainly if you go to that crag over there, you'll see the valley's solid with trees further along.'

Nilsson still looked bemused by Gryss's unashamed ignorance. 'We'll have to look for ourselves, then,' he said after a moment, unable to keep the irritation from his voice.

Gryss watched him. Farnor had told him of the similar conversation he had had with Dessane the previous day. Why should tithe gatherers be so interested in the land to the north? Once again the most troubled of the thoughts that had been stirred up in the wake of the new arrivals swirled into his mind. He could do no other than blurt it out.

'Is there . . . trouble . . . to the north?' he asked softly, as if his voice might ring out from the castle and inform the whole valley. 'Something we need to know about? A foreign enemy gathering for an invasion?'

The question further discomposed Nilsson. This old man was a peculiar mixture of country oaf and sharp-minded politician. He was almost impossible to read and thus unpredictable and dangerous. Who knew what information he might be picking up from the most seemingly casual conversation? Nilsson reminded himself that whatever else Gryss might be, he was the head man of this village and doubtless not without skill in manipulating people. It would be unwise to take him for granted. He resolved to keep him at arm's length for the remainder of his stay.

Starting now.

'No,' he said, with great sincerity, 'there's nothing to concern you. I told you before, many things have changed lately and we've simply been given the task of reporting on the state of the borders as well as . . . gathering . . . the tithe as we move around the country.' He laid a hand on Gryss's shoulder and gently turned him back towards his cart.

Gryss followed the lead and contrived to look relieved at the news. He was not wholly convinced by Nilsson's manner, but he sensed that further enquiry might well yield only a rebuff. 'I understand,' he lied. 'But if you're going up there I think you should know that the place has an evil reputation.'

Nilsson stopped walking and raised his eyebrows. 'Explain,' he demanded.

Gryss coughed awkwardly. The remark had slipped out for want of something to say, as much as anything. Now he felt embarrassed at having to amplify it.

'They say . . . The tale goes, that is, that there are caves along the valley where . . .' He wished he had not started this. Nilsson's expression urged him on. 'Where there are . . . creatures . . . from times long gone . . .

150

sleeping. Just waiting to be wakened.' He gabbled the last part despite his best endeavours. 'It's only legend, of course,' he added hastily in an attempt to forestall Nilsson's scorn. 'But legends often have roots in the truth somewhere in their history and, as I said before, for whatever reason any of us here might give, no one from the valley has ever been further north than this castle – within my memory, certainly. There may well be something unpleasant up there, even if it's not . . .' He coughed again. 'Legendary monsters.'

Somewhat to his surprise, however, Nilsson's manner became serious and attentive rather than scornful. 'That's interesting,' he said when Gryss had finished. 'As you say, such old tales often contain a vestige of truth. We're not here to take risks. I'll see that due precautions are taken when I send the men out.'

They parted without speaking again, save for their cursory farewells.

As Gryss drove through the gates and out into the sunlight, Nilsson stared after him. Monsters, he thought. But he could not bring the derision to the idea that he would have liked. The tale that Storran and Yeorson had returned with still lingered unpleasantly in his mind. And *they* were not foolish old men who were too afraid to move beyond their hearths. When they spoke it was foolish not to listen. He would have to do as he had told Gryss: make sure that whoever went out next to explore the way through the valley was prepared for trouble.

Gryss, too, was uneasy as he drove away from the castle. Try as he might, he could find little to like about Nilsson or his men and he hoped fervently that he was keeping his dislike well hidden, if only for the sake of the negotiations that would probably ensue during the collection of the tithe.

As the cart bounced over a particularly uneven part

of the road and rocked him violently from side to side, he swore roundly at the folly of the King and his advisers sitting idle in some distant palace and devising fatuous schemes that involved honest folk trooping all over the countryside carrying his precious tithe. Had he *no* idea what such a thing was going to involve?

But that was not his predominant concern. That still lay with the persistent interest of these strangers in the land to the north. And, he reflected, he was quite surprised by Nilsson's response to his account of the caves and the creatures therein. An outright laugh would have been understandable, if not excusable, but there had not been even a flicker of amusement in either his face or his manner. Gryss reached a similar conclusion about Nilsson as Nilsson had about him but minutes before. The Captain was a strange mixture of genial host and brutal leader. And too difficult to read. It would behove him, as senior elder of the village, to keep his distance and to watch his words carefully tomorrow when the barn was opened and the tithe assessed.

Yet the concern about the north returned to him. Were there enemies there that the Captain knew of but for various reasons could not speak about? The prospects were coldly awful. Was the castle to be manned again? He found himself cringing more at the idea of the valley being invaded by the likes of Nilsson's men than at the possibility of some enemy army descending upon them.

He had no time to ponder this paradox, however, as a figure suddenly emerged from the trees on his right.

It was Rannick.

Gryss started but took in Rannick's appearance in a single glance. He was thinner, his angular features now almost gaunt. He's not eaten in days, Gryss diagnosed instantly. And yet there was some more subtle change; he looked at once wilder and more composed . . .

Gryss frowned.

'A poor greeting,' Rannick said.

'You startled me,' Gryss responded.

Rannick nodded and walked forward. The horse whinnied and tried to move sideways causing the cart to creak in protest. Gryss shouted at it, but to no avail. He yanked on the reins but the horse ignored him.

Slowly Rannick turned to the horse and stared at it. 'Whoa,' he said, very softly. The horse stopped moving immediately, but it turned its head to one side slightly, and Gryss saw its eye, white with fear.

'You always had a way with animals, Rannick,' Gryss said, by way of thanks. Rannick smiled, though in a manner which indicated that it was because of some inner pleasantry of his own rather than any compliment that Gryss had paid him.

'Where have you been, Rannick?' Gryss asked. 'I was concerned about you. And you look half starved.'

'I thank you for your concern, Gryss,' Rannick said, without a hint of irony. 'But it was unnecessary. I'm used to fending for myself and I've been away on . . .' He smiled his strange inner smile again. This time Gryss felt chilled by it. 'On a voyage of exploration.'

'Where?' Gryss asked. 'What's to be explored around here?'

'Many things,' Rannick replied enigmatically, then: 'Who are the men in the castle?'

The bluntness of the question took Gryss unawares. 'Tithe gatherers,' he answered.

Rannick looked straight at him. The change in him rang through Gryss. His eyes, normally narrowed and full of bitterness or scorn, were wide and penetrating. Gryss met them with difficulty.

Where had Rannick been? What had happened to him? Was he feverish, delirious through exposure and lack of food?

No, whatever other impression he gave, Rannick had a vigour about him that Gryss had never seen before.

'Rather spoiled our Dalmas celebrations,' Gryss went on in an attempt to come back to normality. But Rannick had turned away and lifted his head, like an animal scenting the wind. 'Gatherers,' he said softly to himself. Then he shook his head as if in denial.

'Do you want a lift down to the village?' Gryss asked, finding himself increasingly unnerved by Rannick's presence. Rannick cocked his head on one side as if he had heard the question from some great distance.

'No,' he said eventually, still scenting the air. 'Tell me about these . . . gatherers.'

'What's to tell?' Gryss shrugged.

'Everything,' Rannick said, turning his attention back to Gryss and staring at him intently. The horse shifted, restlessly, making the cart shake. The noise sounded faint and distant in Gryss's ears and he realized that he was surrounded by a peculiar silence. It was as if the very air about him was pressing in on him. He could see the trees swaying in the light breeze and he knew that the many other sounds of the valley were all about him, but they, too, were now distant. And he could hear no birds singing. Rannick moved his hand slightly and the horse became still again.

'Tell me.' Rannick's voice demanded total attention through the silence.

Gryss found himself talking about the unexpected arrival of the gatherers, of meeting their leader and tending their sick and giving them food. 'Foreigners they are, too.' And of the broken locks in the castle and the unsettling menace they seemed to carry with them. And, too, their curiosity about what lay to the north. '"It's the Great Forest," I told them. "Nothing there but trees. And there's caves up the valley before you get there. Bad place." But I think they'll be sending someone before long. In fact, they seem more interested in that than in the tithe. I hope there's no trouble brewing.'

He was aware of Rannick watching, listening; his eyes, his new vigour filling his whole attention.

And then he was free. The birds were singing again, the ubiquitous sounds of the valley folded about him.

And Rannick was gone. Gryss looked around, but there was no sign of him.

He could not remember seeing him go. Had he been dreaming? Or momentarily ill? He was certainly breathless. Then, without command, the horse began to move again and jerked Gryss sharply back to the practical.

It was trotting.

Gryss tugged on the reins to slow the animal, but it did not respond until he applied some considerable force. It occurred to him that the horse was anxious to be away. And indeed, he decided, so was he. The strange meeting with Rannick had served only to add more confusion and turmoil to the many thoughts and speculations that were already tumbling through his mind.

Where the devil had he come from so suddenly? And where had he disappeared to? And, for that matter, where had he been these past days, and what had happened to so change him? He had no answers, though he could not set aside the impression that such answers would be important.

As they moved further away from the place where Rannick had appeared, so the horse began to pull less and, after a while, Gryss gave it its head, and devoted himself to searching for some order out of his whirling thoughts.

By the time he had reached Garren's farm he had given up. One thing at a time, he had decided. The tithe was his business, and getting the gatherers out of here. Then getting the village back on a straight furrow

155

after the upheaval. The tithe day had been a bizarre experience, with the traditional celebratory meals being eaten in atmospheres ranging from forced jocularity to downright ill-humour. It was as if the guests at a wedding had suddenly discovered it was a funeral.

And whatever the interest of these foreigners in the north and the Great Forest, their actions were beyond both his control and his persuasion and he would have to await events.

As for Rannick, maybe the man had finally gone melancholy mad and would end his years a demented recluse dwelling in a cave up the side of the valley somewhere. It had happened before and, frankly, at the moment he couldn't care less.

Rannick, however, was far from melancholy mad. He was exhilarated. Old Gryss had been like so much malleable clay in his hands. And these soldiers . . . these so-called gatherers. They were his kind of people, he knew; the air was full of their presence. They must be brought to his service.

Silently he moved on past the castle and up into the woods beyond, treading the golden road that had been opened for him and which he had only to follow to achieve the greatness that was his true destiny.

Chapter 12

The next day was bright and sunny again, but a strong wind was buffeting noisily through the valley. Trees and bushes, grasses and flowers, all followed its urging and leaned with it as if striving to hear the insistent command that was drawing the armies of clouds so purposefully overhead and sending their shadows scuttling over fields, fences and rooftops in frantic pursuit. People, on the other hand, followed their own urgings and when the whim took them set their faces resolutely against the wind and leaned against it in direct and wilful opposition, not hesitating to curse it when it unbalanced them in mid-step or threw dust in their faces.

Gryss was standing dutifully by the tithe barn door with Garren and the full village Council when Nilsson and his party eventually arrived. The rest of the area in front of the barn and the sides of the road leading to it were filled with almost the entire population of the village.

Nilsson was over an hour late and Gryss had repeatedly had to reassure his companions that this was probably just a bargaining ploy, as their mood had shown signs of souring during the delay. Fortunately, and to Gryss's considerable relief, little discontent was outwardly apparent as Nilsson arrived, and the Councillors, although somewhat dishevelled by the wind, still made quite a dignified group: well scrubbed, and decked in their best holiday clothes, this having been Gryss's instruction to them in the absence of any more specific knowledge about what was required on such an occasion.

Nilsson dismounted and led forward a sharp-featured individual with a florid face and restless eyes. He smiled broadly at Gryss, but offered no apology for the delay. 'May I introduce you to Saddre?' he said. 'He's the . . .' He searched for a word. 'The clerk of the tithe.'

'Tithe master?' Gryss suggested.

Nilsson shrugged. 'You must forgive me if I have difficulty with your language from time to time,' he said. He turned to Saddre. 'I don't think you're a . . . tithe master . . . are you?' he asked. Saddre's eyes fixed on him momentarily then he smiled regretfully and shook his head.

Nilsson turned back to Gryss. 'He's just army, like the rest of us,' he said, by way of explanation. 'Co-opted to this duty and trained in what's needed for routine work.' Then, concerned that he might have laid a trap for himself, he added significantly, 'He has full authority here, though. In tithe matters his word is law, and whatever he decides I have to enforce. Serious disputes have to be sorted out later by . . . palace officers. If necessary.'

Gryss nodded. 'I'm sure we'll have no difficulties,' he said, amiably. 'Shall I open the barn?'

Nilsson motioned him to proceed.

Somewhat self-consciously, Gryss lowered the sun-stone and carefully capped it, then he handed it to Garren who passed it to someone else. It disappeared quickly into the crowd. That was a damn good stone and nothing to do with the tithe, and it wasn't going to be allowed near any bargaining!

Gryss beckoned Saddre forward. 'You can see how we've sealed the barn,' he said, pointing to a decorated and waxed rope that was elaborately wound round two plain wooden handles. 'And this' – He rooted awkwardly inside his jacket and eventually produced a small sheaf of papers – 'is an account of everything we've collected, and the basis on which we've calculated it.'

The papers flapped noisily in the wind as Saddre took them and carefully thumbed through them. He maintained a sage expression throughout and, after a moment, he pursed his lips and nodded. 'Seems reasonable,' he said. 'But show me what you've done as we examine the tithe in detail.' His voice had a rasp to it that seemed to fit his sharp features.

'As you wish,' Gryss said. He gestured to Garren, who stepped forward and deftly untied the decorated rope. Then, producing a large key, he unlocked the barn door.

Such dignified formality as there was in these proceedings ended with this act, as several hands were needed to control the large doors in the wind as soon as Gryss began to open them. After a brief but noisy struggle they were fastened back against the wall and, urged on by the wind, Gryss, flanked by Nilsson and Saddre, scurried into the barn. The villagers moved forward to fill the doorway but, following Gryss's prior instruction, they remained outside.

Decorative ribbons and floral displays fluttered and danced as if in welcome as the wind ignored protocol and surged inquisitively around the inside of the barn, performing its own audit of the contents. The high-timbered roof creaked ominously.

Standing next to his father in the doorway, Farnor looked at the carefully piled barrels and sacks of produce, the elaborate displays of fruits and vegetables, the rows of kegs and bottles. For the first time the enormity of what was about to happen struck him. All that, going to outsiders. And foreigners at that! His outward expression of this outrage, however, was mild.

'What a shame,' he said quietly.

'It is indeed,' Garren agreed. 'Just try and think of it as a hail storm flattening the corn, or a wind like this costing us most of our fruit. One of those things, and quite beyond our control.'

'I'll try,' Farnor said. 'But it's not really the same.'

'True,' his father replied. 'But it's the best I can offer to stop it hurting so much.' There was an unexpected humour in his voice that caught Farnor's attention. 'It's not without its funny side,' he seemed to be saying. 'Gathering this ostensibly for the King but really for ourselves, and finding that the King wants it after all.'

The unexpected lightness shifted Farnor's perception of the event. There'd be other years. It wasn't that bad.

'It's bad enough—' Farnor started as a surly voice behind him muttered this contradiction of his unspoken thought '—them taking all our stuff. But manhandling it up to the castle is the sodding limit. And in our own carts at that!' Farnor glanced over his shoulder to confirm the speaker. It was Jeorg.

'The *King's* stuff,' Garren corrected with an uncharacteristically malevolent chuckle at Jeorg's discomfiture. He offered him the same consolation he had offered his son. 'Just imagine that the barn's been struck by lightning.'

Jeorg almost growled. 'I can just about cope with losing the tithe, Garren, but your good humour is too much.'

To Gryss's surprise, Saddre made no comment on the way in which the tithe had been calculated. To each of Gryss's, 'We've never been quite sure about this, so . . .' he nodded indulgently and waved a dismissive hand, concluding finally that, in the absence of a tithe master, the villagers had made a remarkably accurate assessment. 'It's an excellent piece of work. Your diligence is to be commended.' He went on to say that there might be one or two minor adjustments after he had had an opportunity to examine the calculations and inventory at his leisure, and he was about to say more when he caught Nilsson's eye and, instead, closed the ceremony quite abruptly.

The rest of the blustering day was spent in transporting the produce to the castle. Despite Gryss's best urgings to look cheerful, it was done for the most part with a very ill grace, although this was confined to sullen attitudes and nothing overtly unpleasant was said within earshot of the gatherers.

And then the barn was empty. Bits of paper and torn sacks and the remains of floral displays scurried hither and thither about the dusty floor as the wind continued its own relentless search. Farnor gazed round at the echoing emptiness. It looked as it always looked after tithe day, but now it seemed sad and empty whereas previously he realized now, it had always seemed happy in some way . . . contented at a task well done, perhaps. He watched the whirling, wind-inspired dance of dust and litter for a while then half-heartedly reached for a brush.

'Leave it, Farnor,' Gryss said. 'It'll be there tomorrow.'

A logic that could not be disputed, Farnor thought, though he had never been able to make his mother see it on similar occasions. Deferring to the elder's wisdom, he conscientiously put the brush down.

There was another short but alarming struggle to wrest the doors from the wind until they were finally shut and locked, then the few remaining villagers wandered off down the road. There was little conversation.

At the castle, however, there was a great deal of conversation, and even more mirth as the entire complement gathered in a dining hall and proceeded to 'assess' the tithe by eating and drinking it – mainly drinking it.

'Here's to you, tithe master,' Nilsson said, raising a tankard to Saddre.

'Clerk of the tithe, Captain,' Saddre corrected, raising his own tankard in return. 'I'm army, you know, not civilian. Co-opted and specially trained.'

'Trained to pick pockets and cut throats,' Dessane intervened raucously. This shaft, sharpened by the ale, made the trio relapse into uncontrollable laughter.

'This is rich,' Nilsson said, wiping his eyes and still laughing. 'All this!' He pointed to the piles of produce occupying one end of the hall. 'We've raided bigger villages and come away with less on more than a few occasions. And delivered to us as well.'

'They didn't enjoy it, judging by their faces,' Dessane said.

'They'd have enjoyed it a damn sight less if we'd collected it the usual way,' Nilsson said.

'Maybe I should tell them that not enjoying paying their taxes is an offence against the dignity of the King, and fine them for it,' Saddre declared. 'In my capacity as—'

'Clerk of the tithe,' Nilsson and Dessane said simultaneously.

Again the laughter that greeted this was disproportionate to the humour of the remark, but it went unnoticed in the general uproar that was filling the hall.

None of the three, though, was truly drunk. The presence of the other revellers forbade that. To lead such meant that to be without control around them was to risk death.

Saddre pursued his thought. 'Perhaps I could fine them a few women,' he said, leering lasciviously. 'For the entertainment of the King's officers in the field. I saw some tasty ones in that crowd.'

Nilsson chuckled but his eyes were cold as he looked at his lieutenant. 'No,' he said categorically.

Saddre, abruptly possessed by his idea, protested. 'Just a few,' he pleaded. 'For crying out, we can't—'

'You can and you will.' Nilsson's voice was icy, and all trace of humour had gone from his face. Recognizing the change, both Dessane and Saddre sobered. Dessane eased his chair back, ready to move quickly, and Saddre held out his hands. 'Just my joke, Nils,' he said, smiling desperately. 'Just my joke. No harm meant. You know I wouldn't—'

The crash of a table falling over and a sudden shouting rose above the din to cut across Saddre's plea. Nilsson turned away from him and scanned the hall. He focused on the source almost immediately. Like a whirlpool suddenly appearing in a turbulent river, a circle of hastily moving bodies was forming around two struggling figures. Its power drew other bodies to it and soon it would occupy the whole hall.

Nilsson swore and stood up clumsily. His chair clattered over behind him. Without pausing, he strode into the melee. Saddre and Dessane looked at one another with expressions of open relief and Saddre drew the back of his hand across his mouth nervously. He let out a trembling breath.

The object of his alarm was gone however, ploughing violently through the crowd, at times lifting men bodily off their feet and throwing them effortlessly to one side.

When he reached the centre Nilsson's face was a mask of fury. The inner circle widened to reveal two men rolling about the floor amid a mess of food, ale and broken dishes. They were pummelling one another mindlessly. With a snarl, Nilsson reached down and seized them both by the hair. Then he hoisted them upright and brought their heads together with a resounding thud. Some of the spectators winced at the impact while others, the majority, laughed, always glad to see other than themselves being hurt. Nilsson released the two men who slumped unconscious to the floor.

163

'You'd no call to . . .' a drunken voice began behind Nilsson's back. Before it could finish however, Nilsson had spun round and, using the momentum of his turn, delivered a punishing blow to the protester's face. The man crashed backwards, taking several others with him as he fell. Blood was streaming from his nose and mouth.

As those felled with him crawled hastily away, the man struggled into a sitting position, his face livid with rage. He reached inside his jacket. A bystander's foot kicked him over and planted itself on his chest. Nilsson stepped forward and looked down at the bleeding man. Gently he motioned the owner of the foot to one side, then he held out his hands, to the fallen man, palms upwards. His eyes were wide with a mixture of rage and exhilaration.

'I'd every call, Avak,' he said. 'That was summary field punishment. You know the rules. No fighting amongst ourselves. Pain of death if weapons are drawn. And my word is law until you elect yourselves another leader.' He leaned forward. 'Are you thinking of running for office?'

Avak's mouth worked, but no sound came.

The man who had kicked him spoke up tentatively. 'I think he was reaching for something to wipe his face with, Captain,' he said. 'And I'm sure he's just wondering how to apologize for disturbing you when you were administering discipline. I'm afraid this good ale you've won for us today has addled the remains of his wits.'

Nilsson kept his eyes fixed on his victim throughout this respectful intervention, and acknowledged it only with a slight inclination of his head. He raised his eyebrows questioningly.

Avak, rage now gone from his face and replaced with sheer terror, nodded frantically. His lips were trembling, but from somewhere he found his voice. 'That's so, Captain,' he said. 'An ill-considered remark . . . the ale . . .' His tongue seemed to stick to the top of his mouth.

Nilsson placed his own foot on Avak's chest and tapped it thoughtfully.

The hall became very silent.

Then, settling his weight on to his foot, Nilsson turned and stared at the spectators.

There was nothing but fear all around him.

He turned back to the pinioned Avak then, with a final tap of his foot, abruptly released him. Avak scuttled away frantically. No one moved to help him.

'The celebration's over, gentlemen,' Nilsson said. 'These villagers with their ale have nearly cost us as many men as if we'd raided them.'

He began walking back to the table where Saddre and Dessane were standing waiting. The crowd parted before him.

'Listen carefully, all of you,' he said as he walked. 'We've fallen lucky with this place and I'll personally disembowel anyone who makes any trouble for us here, because of ale, women, anything.' He stopped and looked intently at his audience. 'As far as these villagers are concerned we're soldiers, tax collectors of some kind. As a result of that, they've voluntarily given us enough supplies to last us for months. I needn't tell any of you what a gift that is. You've all had to risk getting killed for a damn sight less in your time. Tomorrow Yeorson and Storran are going north with a patrol to find a way through the valley and to see what lies beyond. When they come back, we'll load up our supplies and slip away. If this is done *quietly*, it'll be months before . . .' He paused and his jawline stiffened. 'Before anyone . . . finds out where we've gone. In fact, it's a possibility they'll never find out; this place is so far

165

from anywhere.' His shoulders hunched, and his voice became menacing. 'I'm an easy-going man, you know that. I don't interfere with your pleasures normally. But this time it's too important. If these villagers begin to suspect we're not who they think we are, we'll have the whole countryside down on us. So this is the way it's going to be. None of you are to go near the village. None of you are to have contact with any of the villagers. Any of them come to the gate on business, send for me.' He raised his voice. 'Do any of you need to hear that again?'

There was a general muttering of, 'No.'

'Do any of you disagree with this strategy?' He lifted his hand before anyone could speak. 'I give you fair warning that once you've agreed to these orders, it'll be death for any man who disobeys them. I'll kill him instantly . . . Or worse.' There was a long silence before he spoke again. 'Now, does anyone disagree?'

This time the voices were louder. Nilsson looked slowly over his audience once more, then, with a wave of his hand, dismissed them.

As they dispersed, Nilsson returned to his table. 'That includes you two as well,' he said to Dessane and Saddre. 'Whatever chance has thrown this our way, we're never going to get another and I'll allow no one – no one – to jeopardize it. Do you understand?'

Both men nodded, well sober by now.

'How long do you think we've got here?' Saddre asked, anxious to redirect his leader's menacing mood.

'Quite some time, I'd think,' Nilsson replied. He indicated Dessane. 'According to the tales we've both heard, hardly anyone ever comes to this valley and no one ever leaves. They seem to have everything they want here.' He paused and became pensive for a moment as if the remark had stirred something within him.

166

'And what if the real tithe gatherers arrive?' Dessane asked.

'It'll be the first time in living memory, according to that old healer,' Nilsson replied dismissively.

'But . . . ?' Dessane let the doubt hang in the air.

As each of them knew, Dessane's remark about the tithe gatherers was in reality a reflection of another, rarely spoken of concern.

Nilsson screwed up his face as if in pain. As he himself had acknowledged, the chance that had brought them to this valley and to this reception verged on the miraculous, and the benefits should not be lightly risked; indeed they should not be risked at all. 'I suppose we could mount lookouts down the valley,' he said, almost reluctantly. 'It's just that I'd rather keep all the men here, where we can see them. Once they're out there they'll do something stupid for certain.'

'Small groups. Three or four. Good men,' Dessane suggested. 'We've enough for that.'

'Perhaps,' Nilsson said, then motioned the two men away.

After they had left, Nilsson sat for a long time in the deserted hall. Around him lay the debris of the celebration like the aftermath of a small riot. The ale he had drunk lay heavy on his stomach and he knew that it fogged his perceptions to some extent. It did not worry him too much; he had many years ago learned to drink heavily and still maintain his lethal fighting capacity. Indeed, as a protection against former 'companions' he had trained himself to become more savage and unrestrained in drink than he was when sober. And as he had tempered this with heightened cunning, a fearful reputation had grown up about him.

What he had not trained himself to cope with was the dark melancholy that would sometimes seep into his thoughts when, as now, he was alone after such revelries.

167

A melancholy that would turn everything about him into so much dross, and whose bitter taste would rule him utterly until such time as it chose to pass. Only the lethargy that it brought to his limbs prevented him from purging himself of this clinging inner miasma by some act of monstrous violence; a fact of great benefit to his companions, had they known it, for Nilsson was not of a suicidal or even a self-reproaching disposition.

Now darkness reigned inside his motionless form. Darkness full of anger and bitterness at the one he had followed and who had betrayed him; at the chain of violence and mayhem that he had forged and that had led him here; at those pursuing him. From this jaundiced perspective, even the chance turning that had brought him so fortuitously to this valley, with his men on the verge of mutiny, was seen as being little more than his rightful deserts, an ordained reward as acknowledgement of simply the rightness of his being.

His dead eyes drifted over the scene around him, sullying it even further: scattered tables, overturned chairs, smoking lamps, the whole strewn with uneaten food and splattered with spilled ale and vomit.

Not even the stacks of produce so easily taken from the village brought a respite to his soured vision. Rather they tarnished it further with their silent implication of effort and toil; assiduous, willing, patiently applied toil to gain a desired and beneficial end.

He put his head in his hands. The patient, if wary, good nature of Gryss and Garren and the others he had met, the well-tended fields and animals, the well-built and cared-for houses and cottages rose like gorge in his throat.

All this should be his. Yet he did not want it; knew he could not have it. For though it could be destroyed on a whim it was not such as could be given; it was something derived from within and through years of quiet endeavour.

He did not want it.

He could not have it.

The thoughts circled maliciously, taunting him, seeing themselves and knowing themselves to be both true and false.

Many sounds drifted through the echoing corridors of the castle that night. Shuffling, restless, creaking, muttering. Men talking, crying, laughing in their stupefied sleep. Men groaning with surfeit. Men disgorging surfeit.

No one heard the solitary cry that came from the dining hall as Nilsson saw briefly into his own soul.

Chapter 13

Life in the valley began to settle back to normal after the tithe had been transported to the castle. Although the valley dwellers were quite capable of sustaining petty quarrels for months, if not years, this was largely a superficial trait used, as much as anything, both to vary and to confirm the soundness of the texture of their everyday existence.

Patient, farming people living lives that were founded deeply and wisely in the ways of nature and which knew and danced to the slow rhythm of the seasons, they showed a true measure of reality when need arose. From the moment the gatherers had been identified for what they were, the villagers had begun to relinquish their emotional ties to the goods gathered in the tithe barn. After all, the justice of the matter lay squarely with the gatherers and, looked at squarely, it concerned only a few odds and ends that would be grown again next year.

Thus, although the initial grief at the loss of their Dalmastide bargains was sharp and the keening voluble, there was little true pain and the noise faded quickly. Indeed, the dominant feeling soon became one of relief that they had in fact dutifully gathered the tithe and not been caught unprepared by the arrival of the King's men.

And, too, it could not be denied, there was frothing on the surface of their lives a certain . . . excitement . . . at these new arrivals; new topics to be raised around the table, at the fireside and, of course, in the inn.

* * *

No such return to normality faced one group of Nilsson's men the day following the collection of the tithe however, when Storran and Yeorson moved through the castle some time before dawn and roused them with the news that they had been chosen for the patrol that was to explore the northern section of the valley.

Nilsson gathered the men about him in the courtyard. 'I know the state some of you are in,' he said. 'This village ale will take some getting used to. But check your weapons and make sure you keep your wits about you. Storran and Yeorson think there's something odd up there. That's why they came back, and that's why you're going out in force now. I can't see it being bandits or the like, as the villagers would have known, but work on the assumption that if you nod off in the saddle or on watch you mightn't wake up.'

This advice was greeted with a surly silence.

Nilsson was in no mood for the niceties of morale-raising. He bared his teeth and pointed northwards. 'That's our best way out of here,' he said, starkly. 'Just go and see what there is and get back as quickly as you can. Routine reconnaissance, that's all. Anything gets in your way, ride over it. Then we can be on the move again. At least we don't have to fight for our food this time.'

Yeorson and Storran led the patrol away from the castle as the rising sun was beginning to throw long shadows on the mountain turf, and late morning saw them travelling at less than foot pace as they threaded their way between the trees. Some had chosen to dismount, preferring to lead their horses rather than contend with the frequent low-hanging branches. At intervals they would hack gashes into the trunks of the trees to mark their route through this deceptively treacherous terrain. Sap oozed from the cuts.

In places the trees grew close together, and the canopy

172

overhead became so dense that it shut out much of the sunlight. The riders fell silent as they passed through these dark and gloomy canyons, and there was always a marked air of relief when they emerged into the light again.

Eventually, reaching a small clearing, Yeorson called a halt and cast about for a suitable tree to climb. Finally selecting one, he stretched up like some grotesque, unfolding creeper and, seizing a branch, disappeared into the foliage with an easy heave. Storran stared up after him for a while, but he was soon lost from sight and his progress could only then be measured by the sound of the disturbed branches. Then there was a brief period of silence until the sound of his descent began.

'Anything?' Storran asked as the long figure emerged from the lower branches.

'Not much,' Yeorson said. 'Same as last time. Trees north and south for as far as I can see.' He pointed. 'But there's a cliff obscuring the view further along. It looks as though the valley turns east. If we can reach the edge of the trees we might be able to get part way up it and get a better view from there.' A few grumbling minutes later the patrol was under way again, leaving behind it its extending trail of hacked and weeping markers.

It proved impossible to reach the edge of the trees on horseback as they rose steeply up the valley sides in most places. However, by moving some way up from the valley floor, the patrol was able to follow a line quite near to the edge and which gave them occasional views across or along the valley. At each of these panoramas Yeorson's lip curled in dissatisfaction, enhancing his naturally supercilious expression.

'I don't like this place,' he said quietly to Storran. 'It still feels bad.'

Storran nodded. He, too, was uneasy about the seemingly deserted woodland they were travelling through, though he had no words to define his unease clearly.

'We'll just have to carry on,' he said. 'It's probably because it's so still.'

Yeorson curled his lip again, but offered no reply.

Towards evening, they reached the rock face that had obscured Yeorson's view. It came on them like an ambush, appearing suddenly and towering above them, massive and rugged against the darkening sky as they entered a clearing full of fallen trees and tangled undergrowth.

Studiously unimpressed, Storran concentrated on their immediate surroundings. 'Rock fall,' he said, simply.

Looking at the eminence above gave the patrol no comfort. The trees rose up it some considerable way and it would be no easy task struggling through them to reach the rock face proper. Certainly there would be no question of taking the horses. Then there was no way of assessing how negotiable the cliff would be when they got there.

Storran shook his head. 'Tomorrow,' he said.

No one demurred. Most of the men had shaken off the effects of the previous night's revelries, but none of them seemed to be able to muster any enthusiasm for the task in hand.

As the light faded the horses were tethered, undergrowth was cleared to make a camp, wood was collected, a fire was lit and food cooked – all efficiently enough, but with an untypical and wary silence. Even the customary insults about the cooking were either left unsaid, or larded with unusual viciousness.

In an attempt to break this strange and growing tension, Yeorson repeated Nilsson's remarks as they sat around the fire. 'The sooner we find a way through

174

here, the sooner we get out of this place,' he said. 'And the quicker and quieter we leave, the longer it will be before anyone finds out.'

A burning log collapsed noisily, sending a great cascade of sparks dancing and weaving high into the darkness. Yeorson's words went with them, unheeded and futile.

'This place gives me the creeps,' someone said as the small disturbance faded.

His words hung ominously in the air and the ill mood of the group seemed to congeal about them. Yeorson and Storran glanced at one another, puzzled, and uncertain as to what was about to happen. Dangerous though the men were, to a man they had a loyalty to each other borne of mutual need that bound them far tighter than even their own sworn oaths. And there had been no particular signs of discontent on the journey so far. But . . . ?

Yeorson and Storran were excellent trackers because they listened to and trusted their instincts. Needing no reason other than this inner prompting, both of them simultaneously and surreptitiously moved their hands towards their knives.

Even as they did so however, they felt the mood about them suddenly change, then they saw that most of the men were staring at something.

Yeorson followed the gaze.

Only a few paces from them, and well within the circle of the firelight, stood a solitary, motionless figure.

Yeorson swore softly to himself. How had this intruder come so close without being heard?

Before he had time to issue any orders several of the men were on their feet, knives and swords drawn. They made no attempt to advance on the figure, though, and it remained still and silent for a long, oddly timeless interval. There was an eerie unreality about the whole

175

scene as if the figure were in some other place. Then, it extended its arms slowly and spoke. 'I apologize if I startled you, gentlemen,' it said.

'Who the hell are you?' Yeorson demanded, his voice harsh, and disregarding the easy manner of the apology. 'And what are you doing creeping about out here?'

'My name's Rannick,' the figure replied calmly. 'I've been hunting. I was concerned when I saw the flames through the trees. I thought I was going to get caught in a forest fire.'

Yeorson looked at him narrowly. 'You move quietly, Rannick,' he said. 'Sneaking up on an armed camp like that could get you killed.'

Rannick remained where he was and extended his arms again, this time accompanying the gesture with a leisurely shrug. 'I've said I was sorry for disturbing you. I'll leave.'

He turned.

'Stay where you are!' Yeorson shouted.

Rannick stopped, his head bowed and half-turned towards the fire.

With a series of short, sharp gestures, Yeorson dispatched several of the men into the darkness.

'Are you alone?' he asked.

'Yes.'

'Come here,' Yeorson said curtly. 'And keep your hands in sight. I warn you, if this is some trick to ambush us you should know you're not dealing with village clods this time. And you'll be the first to die.'

Rannick walked towards the fire, seemingly unperturbed by Yeorson's threatening manner.

'You must be the gatherers,' he said as he stopped a few paces away from Yeorson. His tone and his smile were mildly ironic.

'This amuses you?' Yeorson asked menacingly. The men casually surrounded the new arrival.

'A little,' Rannick admitted.

A knife appeared at his throat. 'How would another smile across your face amuse you, farm boy?' its holder asked viciously.

Rannick looked at his assailant calmly. 'Put the knife away,' he said, very quietly. 'I'm no danger to you.'

The man did not move but, to Yeorson, it seemed for a moment that he was immobilized by Rannick's gaze rather than by any determination to stand his ground.

There was a long silence.

Yeorson's voice broke it. 'Let him be, Meirach,' he snapped, pushing the man away none too gently. There was a flicker of relief on Meirach's face as Yeorson's blow tore him away from Rannick, and he gave only a cursory indication that he wanted to return to the fray.

As Yeorson watched Meirach the men he had sent out began to reappear from the darkness. They shook their heads as Yeorson looked at them. The man *was* alone, then.

He studied Rannick carefully. Under normal circumstances, a lone traveller encountering a group under his charge would have little likelihood of surviving, but the prospect of Nilsson's bloody retribution rose before him if such a deed were to cause problems with the villagers. And, almost certainly, someone, somewhere, would be keeping a discreet eye on this oaf, for all the protestations that no one ever came up here. They would surely know where he was and when he would be back. He decided; there would be no sport from this one tonight.

'Sit down and join us . . . Rannick,' he said, gesturing to the others to do the same. 'I'm sorry for the welcome, but it's the way we are. You're lucky you weren't killed on sight.'

Rannick came forward, but made no response to this remark. As he sat he looked from Yeorson to

177

the other men around the fire. After a moment, he
nodded.

'I understand,' he said, eyes wide. 'You're soldiers.
Your life must be full of adventure and excitement. I
suppose you're always ready for danger.'

There was awe and sincerity in his voice and manner
that no one in the village would have recognized. The
mood around the fire relaxed almost palpably. Just
another village simpleton was the unspoken consensus.
There was some laughter, though in anticipation of the
torments that would most likely befall their visitor before
long rather than at his seeming naivety. Yeorson made
no effort to hide his disdain from Rannick. 'We'd been
told that no one ever comes here,' he said.

'Nor do they,' Rannick said. 'I only come here because
the rabbits and the birds aren't as shy as they are in the
valley.'

'Where's your catch?' Yeorson asked.

Rannick shrugged self-deprecatingly. 'I've not done
too well so far, but I'll give it another day or two.'

He looked expectantly at the food that was lying about
the fire.

'Do you know these woods well, Rannick?' The
speaker was Storran. He picked up a piece of meat
and offered it to him.

Rannick's eyes widened as he took the meat but as
he raised it to his nose and sniffed at it, he closed
them.

'Yes,' he said. 'I know them very well.' He bit into
the meat. It had only been lightly cooked, and a trickle
of blood ran slowly down his chin. At the same time,
Yeorson applied his foot vigorously to the fire. It flared
up brightly and for an instant in its ancient light Rannick,
with his hand clawed around the meat, his bloodstained
teeth bared and his eyes turned into black shadowed
orbs, looked like the spirit of some terrible predator

from an age long dead, had any there had the wit to note it.

'Very well,' he repeated, as the flames died down.

Yeorson nodded approvingly at Storran; a little local knowledge could save them a great deal of time and effort.

'How far do these woods go north?' Storran asked.

Rannick stopped chewing. 'Up to the Great Forest,' he said in some surprise. 'Anyone could have told you that.'

Storran's mouth forced itself into a smile. 'They did,' he said. 'But they never come here, do they? So how can they know? They could be wrong. We've had it before. People not knowing what's on the other side of their own mountain. But you're here. You know this place.'

'Oh, yes. I'm very familiar with this place,' Rannick said, his voice enigmatic as he looked around the makeshift camp.

'You've actually been through the valley? Seen this . . . Great Forest?' Storran persisted.

'Why do you want to know?' Rannick asked.

Yeorson started slightly at this sudden reversal in roles. 'We need to know,' he said brusquely. Then, tempering his reply, he added, 'It's the King's orders. We have to find out what lies beyond the borders of his land.' His invention began to amuse him. 'And if you can help us, then we'll tell him how you helped. There might even be a . . . reward . . . for it. A medal, perhaps.'

With the hand away from Rannick's gaze, he beat down the rising sniggers of his companions.

Rannick's eyes widened innocently. 'A reward?' he said, then his shoulders slumped.

'What's the matter?' Yeorson asked in genuine surprise.

'You can't go through to the Great Forest,' Rannick replied.

'What do you mean?' Yeorson demanded. 'We can't go through. Are there bandits or something? Or a river or a gorge we can't cross?'

Rannick shook his head. 'No,' he said. 'You just can't go. It's too dangerous.' He lowered his voice and looked around as if someone in the surrounding shadows might be listening. 'It's cursed. It's an evil place. Guarded by demons.'

In sharp contrast to Rannick's almost whispered concern, the listening men, ignoring Yeorson's restraining hand, broke into raucous laughter.

'Stretch him over the fire,' someone said amid the din. 'Show him what we do to demons.'

'Or anyone else,' another added.

The idea gathered momentum and Rannick looked at Yeorson fearfully.

'Shut up,' Yeorson roared. '*Captain Nilsson* won't appreciate us treating him badly. Him having friends in the village and all.'

Nilsson's instructions of the previous evening had been quite unequivocal and, as all present knew, his response to disobedience would be equally so. The mention of Nilsson's name and the reference to the village thus had the desired effect, and the laughter faded into a mixture of scornful sneers and surliness. Yeorson looked round the group angrily, to ensure that all had understood the full import of his remarks.

Rannick turned to the man who had called for the roasting. It was Meirach, still smarting from his earlier rebuke. 'You shouldn't say things like that,' he said, almost plaintively. 'Even as a joke. You're liable to bring them down on yourself.'

Meirach, half lying by the fire, glared at him, but a gesture from Yeorson stifled any reply. Irritably he extended his foot and kicked some smouldering branches back into the fire.

There was an awkward silence.

Rannick turned back to the fire, his eyes squinting as if disturbed by its brightness. Then he looked up into the darkness.

The unseen tree tops around them began to rustle as if a breeze had caught them. Rannick returned his gaze to Meirach. Their eyes met.

Suddenly part of the fire collapsed and a large burning log tumbled out of it and fell across Meirach's legs. He pulled them back immediately with an oath, but a branch on the log tangled in his long jacket and as he jerked his legs the log bounced into his lap almost as if it were alive.

Seeing his plight, his companions started to laugh, though a couple of them kicked out at the log in an attempt either to dislodge it or perhaps to harass him further. Frantically Meirach struggled to his feet, but the log remained entangled in his jacket and the flames, in continuing to rise upwards, began to play over his chest and face. Some of the laughter increased in intensity, but cries of alarm also began to make themselves heard.

As Meirach started to flail his arms about in an attempt to free himself from the burning log, a gust of wind blew through the camp. The fire roared and flared violently, and flames, sparks and glowing embers blew in every direction. The men sitting and lying around the fire scattered in confusion, leaving only the fire itself and the thrashing figure of Meirach at the centre.

Then someone ran forward, hurled the struggling man to the ground and beat out the flames with a jacket. It was Storran.

The wind fell as quickly as it had arisen and the fire became quiet again.

Although the flames had been extinguished however, Meirach was still rolling about on the ground, beating

181

desperately at smouldering portions of his clothes. The laughter returned.

At last Meirach realized that he was free of his blazing burden and he scrambled to his feet. His beard and eyebrows were singed and there were black smudges and red weals on his face that would doubtless become painful in due course, but apart from this he was remarkably undamaged. His appearance, however, made his indignation appear incongruous, and the laughter redoubled.

He spun round, glowering at his companions, then he fixed on Rannick. He levelled a hand at him and, his face contorted with rage, spoke rapidly and loudly in his own language.

The laughter faded.

'What's he saying?' Rannick asked, nervously.

'He's saying that you did that,' Yeorson answered after a moment.

'Did what?'

'Set fire to him,' Yeorson replied irritably. His irritation, however, was at Meirach, not Rannick. 'Shut up, Meirach,' he shouted above the man's complaints. 'It's your own damn fault for sitting too near the fire. You're lucky Storran bothered to put you out. I'd have left you there. It would've saved us collecting more firewood.'

Meirach swore at him. Without pause or comment Yeorson strode forward and, lifting his clenched fist high as if to strike a blow, swung his leg up and caught Meirach squarely in the stomach. The man doubled over and staggered back, but managed not to fall. Even through his pain he knew that to fall was to risk being kicked to death by this long, sneering individual who had been given charge over him.

Yeorson indeed seemed set to pursue just this course when he remembered the presence of Rannick. With a conspicuous effort he stepped back and returned to his position by the fire. 'Go and clean yourself up, Meirach,' he said. 'And get the cook to put some grease on those burns. Nilsson's going to be less than pleased if you go sick on us now.'

Several hands grabbed Meirach and dragged him away before he could compound his initial folly in abusing Yeorson. 'Discipline has to be stern,' Yeorson said to Rannick as he watched the departing figure. 'That kind of carelessness and wild behaviour could get us all killed.'

'How could I have moved that log?' Rannick said, affecting still to be shocked at such a bizarre and impossible accusation. 'I was nowhere near it. The fire collapsed. You saw it . . .'

Yeorson gazed skywards. A part of him wished dearly that Nilsson's instructions no longer constrained him and that he could have pursued Meirach's suggestion and roasted this dolt. A larger part, however, accepted both Nilsson's reasoning and his cruel authority. And, too, a half-burned Meirach had been quite an amusing diversion.

'Don't worry about it,' he said. 'He was just looking for someone to blame for his own carelessness.' Then, anxious to set the incident aside, he reverted to his original questioning. 'Tell me again why we can't head on to this . . . Great Forest in the north.'

Again, Rannick looked around nervously. 'I told you before,' he replied. 'It's dangerous. There are—'

Yeorson waved a hand to silence him. 'I don't want to hear about demons,' he said. 'We've all of us here seen some rare things in our time, things that'd chill your blood, but in the end they've all been in the shape of men, not fairy-tale monsters. Explain what you mean properly. We *have* to go ahead. Those are our orders. And I need to know what kind of dangers we're likely to run into. Do you understand?'

'I can't explain like you want me to,' Rannick said. 'It's not something you can see. It's just dangerous. You can feel it in the air.' Abruptly, he placed his hand on Yeorson's arm affectionately. 'Stay here,' he said, his voice both pleading and full of enthusiasm. 'Stay in the castle. There's plenty of food in the valley for everyone and an easy life for you if you want.'

Yeorson was taken aback by this unexpected and oddly powerful appeal. He found himself staring open-mouthed at Rannick.

'We can't—' he began.

Rannick's grip tightened on his arm. 'Yes,' he said. 'Yes, you can. The valley's very secluded. A good place for you.' He pointed north. 'There lies only danger and death. You mustn't go.'

Yeorson yanked his arm free. Despite himself, he found that Rannick's words had released images into his mind of a life of ease and comfort being tended by the villagers. He dashed it away. Too many vengeful shadows lay in the past for that to be a possibility, at least in this land. He became suddenly angry with this village oaf and his simplicity, his tales of demons and dangers and the Great Forest beyond. And fawning over him like some faithful dog, oblivious of the fact that he was alive only because of the word of a man he had never met and who wouldn't scruple to snuff him out like a candle if the whim so took him.

Yet, he realized, there was something familiar about him. Something in his manner, his speech, his attitude? Something disturbing; sinister, even.

Rannick stood up. 'I'll go now,' he said. 'Thank you for the meat. Don't go any further along the valley.'

There was menace in his voice. Clear and unmistakable menace.

Once again, Yeorson found his mouth dropping open, but before he could speak Rannick was gone. Swift but unhurried strides had carried him beyond the range of the firelight and into the forest darkness.

Yeorson jumped to his feet and swore. 'Bring him back!' he shouted. 'Bring him back!'

As several of the men ran off in the direction that Rannick had taken, Storran joined Yeorson. 'Weird, some of these village people,' he said. Then, his voluptuous mouth twisted in puzzlement. 'He reminds me of someone, though.'

Yeorson nodded slowly in agreement. Someone.

But who?

The men had no success in finding Rannick. The forest was impenetrably black beyond the light of the fire, making the tangled undergrowth and low branches singularly dangerous.

'Tomorrow,' Yeorson said.

Later that night, when the men were asleep and the fire had fallen to a dull red mound, Yeorson remembered who it was that Rannick reminded him of.

He sat up suddenly, his heart racing and sweat starting from his brow.

Chapter 14

Yeorson roused the camp early the following day. He was in a foul mood, his night having been racked by grim and fearful dreams, and he had no hesitation in venting his ill humour indiscriminately amongst his men.

Noting his mood, most of the men knew from experience that it was best to bear his conduct in silence. Meirach, however, opening his eyes to see his immediate neighbour being kicked awake, purposefully drew his knife from under his rough blanket and pointed it at his leader.

The two men held each other's gaze. Meirach's demeanour radiated his clear intention, regardless of consequences, to skewer Yeorson if he chose to bring his bruising feet any closer. After a long moment, Yeorson snarled, 'Shift yourself, Meirach, we've got work to do,' and turned away.

Despite the blue sky overhead, indicative of another fine day ahead, the clearing was cold and damp, being sheltered from the sun by the lowering cliff face.

Firewood was gathered and the fire rekindled. Its smoke, undisturbed by any breeze, slowly filled the clearing as a subdued, grumbling breakfast was cooked and eaten.

Gradually, as the routines of the morning carried him further from his troubled memories and dreams, Yeorson's mood became less vicious and by the time they were ready to move, he had mellowed into his usual, supercilious self.

He stared up at the cliff. 'I'll have to go with them myself,' he said to Storran. 'No point sending any of these up there on their own. They'll only come back with half a tale. Will you take the rest and see if you can find that yokel? He's sure to have left tracks.'

'What do you want us to do with him?' Storran asked, drawing a finger across his throat enquiringly.

Yeorson shook his head and smiled unpleasantly. 'Just *invite* him back here, then we'll decide on the details,' he said. 'It was a mistake to let him get away last night. There's something about him that we need to get to the bottom of whether he likes it or not.'

'I agree. But Nilsson? And the villagers?' Storran said.

Yeorson shrugged. 'If we're careful, we'll be able to take his remains back sorrowfully and say we found him . . .' He hesitated.

'At the foot of a cliff?' Storran offered.

Yeorson nodded shrewdly. It was one of several alternatives that would suit their ends without bringing Nilsson's wrath down on them.

Thus, Rannick's fate agreed, the two parties set off, leaving the horses tethered and in the charge of Meirach, who was too sore to do much walking.

Yeorson's group headed up the hill towards the cliff. It was an untidy and awkward journey, there being little in the way of a clear route and a great deal of dense undergrowth and treacherously loose ground.

As they toiled upwards, however, Yeorson's mood became almost cheerful. He buried rather than set aside his foolish night thoughts, and began to look forward to the return to camp and the sport that would be had with Rannick when Storran brought him back.

The prospect was still cheering him when they eventually rose above the tree line and found themselves scrambling over the mounds of rocks that footed the cliff face proper. Wiping the sweat from his forehead, he turned to look across the valley. It was as it had been when he had climbed the tree the previous day: trees in every direction, a sea of rich and varied greens, motionless in the windless morning and with faint wisps of mist rising here and there. It was a scene of great beauty and peace. Yeorson, however, curled his lip in irritation.

He had been right about the valley turning, though.

'Move on,' he said, pointing north along the cliff face. 'Let's get to that headland. We should be able to see quite a way from the other side.'

Storran's group had easier going of it. Rannick had indeed left tracks, tracks that needed no great skill to follow: footprints, crushed grass, broken twigs. Storran pouted with delight when he encountered them. There should be no difficulty in finding him. He could not have travelled far at night, and he had probably never thought that anyone would bother to follow him.

He chuckled and motioned his group forward. 'Quietly, lads,' he said. 'We don't want to disturb him, do we? And show some diplomacy when we catch up with him, please. I'd much rather we persuaded him to come back with us of his own accord.' He chuckled again. 'Save us the trouble of carrying him.'

As the two groups moved further apart, Meirach wandered aimlessly about the camp. From time to time he took his water bag and splashed his hands and face. His burns were sore as the devil and he could not wholly dispel the feeling that it had been Rannick who had caused the log to fall on to him. He did not dwell on the fact that Rannick had been sitting on the far side of the fire and well away from it.

He splashed his face again and winced. What wouldn't he do to that village idiot when Storran brought him back!

And yet . . . ?

There had been something unpleasantly familiar about Rannick. Something that at least part of him was not entirely sure it wanted to meet again.

His reverie was broken by an urgent whinnying from one of the horses. The noise spread rapidly to the others and they began to mill around, tugging at the tether line.

Swearing, Meirach strode towards them. Stupid animals, it was probably a fox nearby.

'Meirach,' came a voice.

It had an edge to it that made his skin crawl. He spun round, searching for the speaker.

A figure came into focus emerging from the trees. Meirach felt a frisson of both elation and alarm. It was Rannick.

But even at this distance Meirach could see that he had changed. His gait alone was confident and assured.

He must have seen the others leave, Meirach thought. Perhaps come back to steal from the camp.

Still, he had met and dealt with cocksure individuals often enough before today, and they all went the same way; there was a world of difference between looking confident and being capable.

The horses became more and more disturbed as Rannick drew nearer. Meirach roared at them furiously, but that served only to increase their distress. He picked up a stick with the intention of beating them into submission, but as he reached the tether line one of them swung sideways in panic and caught him full on, sending him sprawling backwards to the ground.

A powerful hand yanked him to his feet.

'Tell me about yourselves,' Rannick said, without preamble.

Meirach tore himself free and stared at him in disbelief. 'Go to hell,' he shouted.

Rannick turned to the frantic horses irritably. He

closed his eyes slightly and the horses became suddenly still.

He turned his attention back to Meirach. 'Tell me about yourselves,' he said again.

Meirach's already livid face coloured further in a combination of fear, bewilderment and rage as he struggled to find some way of coping with this bizarre development. Faced with such uncertainty, his old fighting instincts prevailed. He'd master the situation better when he'd mastered its creator.

Without a vestige of warning he swung his clenched fist straight up to strike Rannick's chin. Coming from such an angle, it was a blow that would not be seen by the victim until it struck, and it was invariably effective.

But some animal reflex seemed to take command of Rannick and he jerked back and flailed his left arm in front of himself, effectively spoiling the attack. A seasoned fighter, Meirach allowed himself no dismay at this unexpected setback, and without pause, he drove his other hand forward.

There was a brief flicker of surprise in Rannick's eyes, then they became cold and without pity. Almost casually he stepped to one side to avoid the oncoming attack.

Increasingly angry at this peculiarly elusive victim, Meirach spun round, preparing to follow up his second failed attack. As he did so however, he caught Rannick's gaze.

And he could not breathe.

All thoughts vanished from his mind except the single one of mortal terror at the leaden weight that had suddenly filled his chest. Convulsively his mouth began to work in an attempt to take in more air. But nothing happened.

'The air is mine to command, Meirach,' Rannick said, off-handedly, still staring at him. 'An ancient gift. You

191

will breathe no more until I allow it.' He shrugged. 'And if I feel so inclined then you'll die.'

Meirach lurched forward, his eyes bulging and his hands clawing the air as if he could seize it and force it into his burning chest or perhaps seize and destroy his tormentor. But his body's resources were focused totally on its need for air, and his legs failed to respond, buckling underneath him. Rannick watched him like a disinterested spectator.

Then Meirach was free. Crouched on all fours and gasping desperately.

Slowly, his breathing settled into some semblance of rhythm.

Then he heard Rannick speaking again.

'Do you wish to continue attacking me?'

Meirach clenched his teeth and glowered at his assailant.

'I understand,' Rannick said, sympathetically. 'But you won't, will you?'

'Who in Murral's name are you?' Meirach gasped.

Rannick smiled slightly. It gave his gaunt face an even more menacing appearance.

'Tell me about you and your companions,' he said.

Meirach grimaced. His impulsive attack, a hitherto infallible stand-by, had failed. His companions were too far away to be of any immediate help, and this . . . creature . . . had some frightening tricks in his repertoire. It was contrary to his nature, but he must try a more subtle approach. He had learned one or two things from Nilsson in his time.

'A minute,' he said, twisting himself round to sit on the ground. He beat his fist gently against his chest. 'How did you do that?' he asked.

Rannick smiled again, but did not answer.

'Bad joke of mine, that, last night,' Meirach said, still breathing heavily but attempting to return the smile.

'Saying throw you on the fire. We're not used to your ways. We've got a harsh humour. It was only a joke, you know.'

'No, it wasn't,' Rannick said. 'You'd have done it if Yeorson hadn't stopped you. I'm interested to know why he did. In fact, I'm interested in everything about you.'

A commotion interrupted him. Some of the horses were becoming restless again. Meirach looked at them. Though tethered, they seemed to be struggling desperately against other, unseen, restraints. Fear and curiosity vied within him.

'What's happened to them?' he asked, getting unsteadily to his feet.

But Rannick was not listening. He was peering past him into the trees at the edge of the clearing and shaking his head as if in denial. Meirach followed his gaze. For an instant he thought he caught a glimpse of something moving there, a large shadow. But it was gone even as he saw it, vanishing into the deeper shadows of the forest beyond.

The horses became quiet again.

Rannick turned back to Meirach. 'Now you've recovered your breath, stop wasting my time and tell me about yourself and your companions. These so-called gatherers.'

Mindful of Nilsson's instructions, and despite his own terrors, Meirach equivocated. 'We *are* gatherers,' he said indignantly. 'We're King's—'

He felt the air being drawn out of his lungs. Rannick stared at him with an expression of weary resignation. Unable to speak, Meirach desperately waved his hands. Rannick released him.

Meirach gaped at his tormentor, fear now dominating all other emotions. He spoke in his own language, his voice low and full of awe. Rannick frowned. Meirach waved his hands again in frantic apology to forestall any further retribution for this mistake. His voice was thick with his foreign accent when he spoke. 'Is it you, Lord? Come again?'

Rannick put his head on one side, his brow furrowed in puzzlement. 'What do you—?' he began, then he stopped and straightened and his face hardened. He spoke slowly and very deliberately, his forefinger emphasizing his words. There was a finality in his voice that was unmistakable.

'Tell me about yourself and your companions, Meirach,' he said. 'Now!'

He opened his mouth wide with this last word and it seemed to Meirach that Rannick was not a man, but the heart of a terrible storm. A blast of air struck him, scouring his burned face. He covered it with his hands, but to no avail. The wind seemed to seep around his fingers, tearing at his burns with relish.

He sank to his knees.

'For pity's sake, no more,' he said hoarsely. 'What do you want to know?'

'I told you before,' Rannick replied, almost gently. 'Everything.'

Moving carefully along the rock face above the tree line, Yeorson and his men gradually made their way around the headland until, at last, they found themselves able to look along the valley for some distance.

The valley wound and twisted away from them, and throughout the length that could be seen, the majestic peaks and ridges rose out of a dense, continuous forest. A strong breeze was blowing around the vantage that the climbers had reached, cooling damp foreheads and tacking chilly shirts and tunics to damp backs, but the forest below seemed unaffected by it, lying serene in the spring sunshine.

Its serenity, however, did not encompass the watchers. Yeorson swore and wiped his arm across his brow. He looked up at the cliff looming over him, and thence at the neighbouring peaks. It was beyond him or any of his men to scale it, and, as far as he could judge the ridges, he doubted that they could be traversed easily by anyone capable of reaching them.

One of his men spoke. 'That Rannick said the valley led to the Great Forest. Just getting through this lot is going to be a major expedition, and if there's only more forest at the end of it . . .'

He left the observation unfinished.

Yeorson offered him no rebuke; the words chimed too closely with his own thoughts and the speaker was Haral, as bloody-handed a follower of Nilsson as any and by no definition either a grumbler or a faint heart.

He nodded but entered no debate. 'We've seen what we came to see,' he said. 'Let's get back down, then we'll decide what's to be—'

'Hush!' someone said, holding up his hand urgently for silence.

The group froze into alert immobility and the speaker craned forward in concentration.

A faint high-pitched sound drifted up to them. It continued for a few seconds then it was gone, submerged under the wind soughing around them.

There was a brief silence. Though scarcely perceptible, there had been an unsettling, even frightening, edge to the sound. 'Never heard an animal make a noise like that,' Haral said, voicing everyone's thoughts. He frowned, uncharacteristically uncertain. 'What if that Rannick was right about this place being bad, dangerous?' he said.

Yeorson looked at the forest stretching ahead, then at the treacherously easy-looking journey sloping away from them back towards the camp. He saw both for what they were and his face became contemptuous. '*We're* dangerous, Haral,' he said. 'And certainly more dangerous than anything that lives down there.' The sneer curled into a dark smile. 'Anyway, when we get back to camp we might be able to encourage friend Rannick to explain himself in more detail.'

It was an encouraging prospect.

When they arrived back at the camp, however, it was to the news that Rannick had not been found, and that Meirach was gone.

'What do you mean, gone?' Yeorson demanded.

'What I said,' Storran protested. 'He's taken a horse and left.'

'Didn't he leave a message?'

'No.'

There was some debate about why Meirach had left but Yeorson was in no mood for reason. Something about this place was unnerving him. He lashed out.

'And where's Rannick, for crying out loud?' he shouted angrily. 'How could you not find him? He was only on foot.'

Storran's round face coloured and his mouth tightened warningly. 'And what did *you* find, after your climb?' he asked with menacing softness.

Yeorson told him.

'Marvellous,' Storran exclaimed witheringly. 'Nothing but forest ahead of us. Meirach wandering off when he's supposed to be guarding the horses. And that bumpkin, Rannick, running us round in circles.' He swore violently and, suddenly drawing his sword, aimed a savage blow at the trunk of a nearby tree. It was an uncharacteristic outburst and the men moved away from him warily. Nevertheless, it served to bring the two leaders back to their senses.

'What happened?' Yeorson asked as Storran sheathed his sword.

Storran clenched and unclenched his fists as the residual irritation expended itself. 'He left tracks a blind man could follow,' he said. 'Here, there, everywhere. Wandering aimlessly, by the look of it.' He waved his hands vaguely. 'We couldn't see any traps he might have been visiting. Then we came to a rocky outcrop and the tracks just disappeared.'

'Disappeared?' Yeorson queried.

Storran nodded. 'We looked all around it and couldn't find any sign of a camp or of him leaving,' he replied. 'My nose tells me he knew we'd follow him and that he was leading us on. It was a mistake to let him go last night.'

'Well, we did,' Yeorson said philosophically. 'But right now we've got other things to worry about, namely Meirach and where we go next: forward through this damn forest or back to the castle.'

There was no serious alternative. They would have to search for Meirach.

'He's a troublesome son of a whore, but he's too handy in a fight to lose,' was Yeorson's conclusion. 'We can decide whether to go on or back when we find what kind of a state he's in.'

They would all go, it was agreed, leaving a note for Meirach should he return to find the camp deserted, and marking their route well. Not knowing what they were going to find, there was no point in splitting the patrol again.

An examination of the ground around the tether line showed them the direction in which Meirach had left. It was to the north.

'And he's leading his horse,' Storran said, crouching down to study the tracks more closely.

Both pieces of information were puzzling. What

could have possessed him to head further away from the castle?

After some congestion around the edge of the clearing, the trees became more widely separated and the undergrowth less dense. The patrol was obliged to move slowly and carefully as they followed Meirach's tracks, and their progress took on the appearance of being nothing more than a group of friends enjoying a leisurely afternoon ride across a stately parkland as they moved through the leaf-shadowed shafts of sunlight.

They travelled thus for some time.

Then Haral touched Yeorson's arm and pointed. Yeorson squinted into the distance and in turn reached out and touched Storran.

Ahead of them lay a mound. It was not possible to make out what it was from a distance because of the shadows being thrown across it by the surrounding trees, but when they reached it, such quietness of spirit each might have been secretly relishing in the silent search, vanished abruptly. The mound was a horse. Its belly and throat had been ripped open and its entrails strewn about the forest floor. Flies were beginning to gather.

For a while the men simply stared at the carnage. They had seen worse in their time, but this had a peculiar horror by virtue of the sunlit calm about them and the implications for their companion.

'What kind of an animal could've done that?' someone said eventually, his voice hoarse with shock.

Storran ignored the question and moved to stem any outburst of conjectures. 'Stay mounted,' he said sternly, swinging down from his horse. 'And keep still. We don't want to disturb any tracks.'

His voluptuous mouth twisted in distaste, he approached the carcase. Yeorson joined him.

'Good question,' Yeorson said softly as they both crouched by the body. 'What *could've* done this?'

'And what did it do to Meirach?' Storran added.

'We heard some kind of a scream when we were up the mountain,' Yeorson said. 'Did you hear anything?'

'Faintly,' Storran replied. 'We were a long way from here.'

'Well, I'll wager that tells us when this happened,' Yeorson said, standing up. 'How do you think we should go about finding out *what*?'

Storran was prodding the body thoughtfully. 'I'm not sure I want to,' he said.

'We've got to find Meirach,' Yeorson said, uncertain about Storran's intentions.

Storran glanced up at him. 'Look at the size of this bite.' He poked the jagged edge of a wound in the horse's side. 'Whatever did this won't have left much of Meirach.'

'We've still got to find him. Or whatever's left of him,' Yeorson said. 'Morale's bad enough, and on the whole I'd rather face whatever did this than have to tell Nilsson we lost someone and didn't look for him.'

Storran looked at the waiting men then heaved himself upright. 'I know,' he said, blowing out a resigned breath. 'Let's get on with it.' He turned to the men. 'Those of you who've got them, string your bows,' he said. 'And if you see anything big, shoot it and ask after.'

'Even if it's Meirach?' someone shouted.

'Especially if it's Meirach, the trouble he's caused us,' Storran said.

The raucous laughter floated up to the sunlit canopy overhead, where sat two figures.

'Your friends don't seem to be taking your loss too much to heart, Meirach,' Rannick said softly.

Meirach's face had a deathly pallor which made his burns peculiarly livid. He stared at Rannick wide-eyed, but made no answer.

Chapter 15

'What do you mean, you couldn't find him?' Nilsson thundered, bringing his two fists violently down on to the table.

Yeorson and Storran held their ground before his onslaught, but barely.

'Just that, Captain,' Yeorson said. He summarized his account again. 'There were the tracks of a horse and someone walking it up to where we found its body, then . . .' He shrugged in exaggerated helplessness. 'Nothing. Literally nothing. No sign of anyone or anything moving away from the body. We circled out to over a hundred paces, and there was still nothing. We went back to the camp site to see if we'd missed anything else, but we hadn't. We'd followed the only track out other than those we'd made ourselves. There was nothing we could do but return.' He leaned forward. 'That place is bad, Captain,' he said. 'Me and Storran felt it the first time we went. This fellow, Rannick, said the same, and he was a weird one. We've got problems to the north, Captain. My guts tell me it'll cost us dear if we go that way and if there's only this . . . Great Forest . . . at the other end . . .'

Nilsson met his gaze ominously. 'I don't want to hear this, Yeorson,' he said, eventually.

'I didn't want to have to tell you, Captain,' Yeorson replied, doggedly.

Nilsson's eyes narrowed, but Dessane, sitting next to him, whispered, 'Steady, Nils. Listen to him. You didn't see the men when they came back; they were badly shaken up. We're going to have a serious morale problem on our hands if we're not careful. Something's frightened Yeorson to make him talk like that. He's a good man, you know that. So is Storran. Better with us than against us.'

Nilsson remained motionless for a moment then he nodded and relaxed.

'Sit down,' he said to the two men. Hesitantly they did as they were bidden, judiciously placing themselves at the opposite side of the table.

Silence filled the room as Nilsson pondered the news he had received. When he spoke, his heavy face had a grim set about it. 'I suppose everyone knows about Meirach and the horse by now, but have you told anyone about *your* feelings about the forest?' he asked.

'No, Captain,' Yeorson and Storran replied simultaneously.

'Good. See it stays that way. And anything we discuss here, now, stays between us also. Is that clear?' Nilsson twisted his chair sideways and, leaning backwards on it, swung his leg on to the table. 'This is a cosy niche,' he said, looking round at the stone walls whose bareness seemed to lend no small irony to his words. 'And we've reached it without making any great stir. Without . . . anyone . . . knowing where we are. We've been lucky.' He rocked his chair to and fro gently. 'In fact, very lucky indeed to stumble across such a place with its plentiful food and its quiet people.' He paused for a moment, then drew in a noisy breath through his bared teeth. 'However, we can't stay here for ever, and if we go south we'll be going towards trouble. Back towards the consequences of our past activities. It's not something we can even consider unless all other avenues are closed to us.' He tapped out an uneasy tattoo on the table top with his fingertips. 'Completely closed to us,' he emphasized.

He looked at each of his listeners in turn as he

continued. 'Gentlemen, we have mountains to the east and the west, shades to the south and doubts to the north. The first impassable, the second undesirable, the third . . . ?' He shrugged. 'We have no choice. We go north unless it proves absolutely impossible.'

He drummed his fingers on the table again, then brought his palm down on it with a sharp slap to mark the end of his reverie.

'North, gentlemen,' he said briskly. 'No choice. But I trust your judgement in this matter. I always have, you know that. You've spared us problems enough in the past with your ability to judge the whims and fancies of . . .' His voice faltered. 'Of our previous leader.'

The atmosphere in the room grew suddenly chilly and for a moment Nilsson appeared reluctant, or unable, to continue. It was as if the memories that this inadvertent reference invoked were so powerful that they forbade the very existence of the present. With an effort, he recovered his composure and continued.

'So I accept there's a problem in the north of this valley that we must contend with.' He became increasingly businesslike. 'And to contend with it, we need to know what it is. This is what I sent you out for,' he waved his hand to forestall any protests. 'But I accept that what happened left you no alternative but to come back.'

Both Yeorson and Storran breathed out silently.

'But what did happen?' he mused. It was a rhetorical question and not an invitation to repeat the telling. 'Meirach first got himself burned, then got himself lost. 'Storran couldn't find this . . .' He snapped his fingers for the name.

'Rannick,' Yeorson supplied dutifully.

'Rannick,' Nilsson echoed. 'And finally you find a mauled horse. A badly mauled horse. This is so?'

'Yes, Captain,' Yeorson confirmed, cautiously.

Nilsson nodded. 'Overlying all of which is your and

Storran's general . . . unease about the place,' he went on. 'Though this has not really manifested itself in any tangible way so far. This, too, is so?'

'Everything was unusual, Captain,' Yeorson said, almost unwillingly, a tic beginning to flicker beneath his left eye. 'Meirach's burning and then his disappearance, Rannick's manner, the damage done to the horse . . .'

'True,' Nilsson said. 'But, equally, a camp fire burning is a camp fire burning. Hardly an unusual occurrence. Meirach could have gone down with a fever in the night. From what you tell me he was lucky not to have been burned far worse, and he was obviously in a rare state to draw a knife on you when you woke him, wasn't he?' He did not wait for an answer. 'Then a local man, meeting strangers – King's men, as he thinks – and reasonably expecting hospitality, is threatened with a roasting no less. Very wisely he runs away at the first possible opportunity and subsequently makes damn sure you can't follow him by laying a false trail.' He smiled. 'And, good trackers though you might be, he *was* a hunter and on his own territory.'

He stretched his extended leg and eased his chair back a little further. 'And finally we have a mauled horse.' His brow furrowed slightly. 'I seem to remember that healer-cum-headman . . . Gryss . . . mentioning something about sheep being worried. I'll lay odds it's nothing more than a big hunting dog gone rogue, or maybe even a pack of dogs. You know how vicious they can be. And if Meirach was with the horse, and feverish, when it or they attacked, he was probably up a tree and away like a frightened squirrel. Hence no tracks.' He turned to Yeorson and Storran again. 'This *could* be so?' he said, a hint of menace seeping back into his voice.

'Yes,' Yeorson conceded. 'But we found no animal tracks. Certainly no evidence of a pack—'

'No buts,' Nilsson commanded. 'That's the way it was as far as the men are concerned. Is that clear?'

Yeorson was still uncertain.

'I'm not dismissing your concerns,' Nilsson said, swinging his leg down. 'Perhaps there is a savage dog wandering about out there but we can contend with that, for pity's sake. What we have to concern ourselves with now is the fact that the men will be nervous and unhappy about what's happened, not least because we've apparently had to abandon one of our own, and you know how they feel – how we all feel – about that. But I don't want their alarm aggravated by tales of mysterious forces at work in the woods. Some of them have never recovered from seeing what . . .' Again he faltered and a great unease seemed to fill the room. 'From what they've seen in the past,' he managed eventually. 'And it's not in our interests to feed such memories.'

He paused as if waiting for comments, though his eyes forbade any.

'So we must confine ourselves to simple practicalities,' he went on. 'You two will take another patrol north tomorrow. Same men as before and as many again.'

Dismay filled Yeorson's face and Storran's eyes became smaller than ever at this news, but Nilsson ignored their silent protest.

'You'll tell the men you're going out again to do two, maybe three, things,' he continued. 'You're going to find Meirach who's probably sick. You're perhaps going to hunt the animal that killed the horse and, above all, you're going to get through the valley and see what lies to the north.' He stood up and, resting on the table, he loomed over the two men as ominously as the great rock face had done earlier that same day. 'And get through you will, if you've got to cut down every tree that stands in your way.'

'What about this Rannick?' Yeorson asked.

'If you come across him deal with him as the fancy takes you,' Nilsson replied. 'But don't leave any evidence that could cause problems back here; the silence of these villagers is important. It's as good as having a regiment guarding our rear.' He levelled an emphatic finger at the two men. 'And don't waste any time searching for him. You've more pressing matters to attend to than chasing some village oaf who's probably safely back in his hovel by now.'

Nilsson's tone precluded any further debate and the two men rose to leave just as Saddre entered the room.

'They look less than pleased,' he said, as the door closed behind them.

'How are the men?' Nilsson asked, disregarding the comment.

Saddre scratched his cheek. 'Not good,' he said. 'No one's happy about Meirach being left, especially with this horse-killing animal on the loose.'

Nilsson nodded. 'And?' he prompted, detecting reluctance in Saddre's voice.

'And this Rannick seems to have . . . unsettled them,' Saddre said, eventually.

'In what way?' Nilsson asked.

Saddre's eyes moved about the room almost frantically. 'Some of them say he reminds them of—' He stopped and his eyes finally came to rest on Nilsson's in mute appeal. Nilsson did not press him.

Very quietly, but with that menacing purpose that had made him the leader of these men, he reached out to calm this seething unease and to crush any rebellion before it found shape.

'I will attend to Rannick myself,' he said.

Garren Yarrance looked up in surprise as the sound of

206

the dogs in the yard reached him. The insistence of their barking told him that someone was coming.

Farnor, however, was first to the door, throwing it open and stepping out into the yard almost before Garren could hoist himself from his comfortable chair.

He ordered the dogs to silence as the shape of a horseman appeared at the gate. The barking fell to a rumbling growling.

'It's the Captain,' Farnor said to his father, who was standing in the lighted doorway.

The rider was leaning forward and struggling with the latch on the gate. 'I'll do it for you,' Garren called, striding forward. 'It's a little awkward until you get the knack of it, and that's a big horse you're on.'

'It's all right,' Nilsson shouted back, abandoning his task. 'I was only calling on you to find out where Gryss lives.'

'I'll show you,' Farnor said, before his father could speak. 'I'll come with you if you want. It'll be difficult for you at night.'

Nilsson hesitated for a moment then looked enquiringly at Garren.

'It *will* be easier in the dark if he goes with you,' Garren said. Then: 'Have you someone sick again?'

Nilsson, taken aback by this unexpected concern, frowned before almost stammering out, 'No . . . I need to talk to him about . . . a tithe matter.'

'So late?' Garren remarked, with undisguised surprise.

Nilsson managed a smile. 'I'm used to city hours,' he said.

Garren chuckled. 'Gryss isn't,' he said.

Nilsson gave an apologetic shrug. 'We've a lot to do, I'm afraid.'

Farnor clambered over the gate.

207

'Get on behind me, boy,' Nilsson said, anxious to avoid further conversation.

Farnor did as he was bidden, rather self-consciously putting his arms around the big man for support. Seeing his son's discomfiture Garren chuckled again, but Nilsson allowed him no time to give his amusement voice; with a wave of acknowledgement he pulled his horse's head around and urged it forward into the darkness.

The journey to Gryss's cottage passed in silence except for Farnor's occasional instructions. Not that that distressed Farnor in any way. Being seated astride this horse, which like all the gatherers' horses was larger than any that had ever been seen in the valley, and hanging on to a King's man, more than compensated for the slight of being referred to as 'boy'.

For a while he imagined himself galloping over the rolling valley fields on the great horse in search of bold adventures. But rather to his annoyance it soon palled, causing him to muse ruefully that his imaginings of late seemed to have less power, to hold less interest for him, since . . .

Since when?

Since little more than two or three weeks ago, he realized quite suddenly. Not since his encounter with Rannick had he found the old excitement in his daydreams.

He felt the patient, powerful movement of the horse beneath him carrying him relentlessly on.

I must be growing up, he thought. The notion caught him unawares and, surreptitiously, he glanced from side to side into the darkness as if concerned that some unseen eavesdropper might have mysteriously caught wind of this embarrassing admission.

'What's the matter?' Nilsson asked.

Farnor started. How could this man have noticed such a slight movement?

'Nothing,' he said. 'We're nearly there.' He leaned to one side and pointed to a light shining through the trees. 'That's it, over there.'

The light came from a small lantern that, like most of the valley dwellers, Gryss lit every night. The origins of the practice had long passed from memory. Certainly the lights were rarely of any value as anyone who was likely to be about at night tended to carry his own small sunstone lantern. Farnor, in fact, found the practice annoying. Living away from the village, he was used to walking about in the darkness, and the presence of bright lights destroyed his night vision. As far as he was concerned, they obscured more than they illuminated.

As Nilsson drew his horse to a halt, Farnor slithered down and walked to the door of the cottage. Nilsson dismounted and followed him. At the door Farnor tugged on the iron ring. The small bell tinkled cheerfully.

Then the ring was taken from his hand. He released it without any resistance but turned, curious. Nilsson was examining the ring intently. But his face was a mask; its heavy lines etched so deeply by the light of the lantern that it seemed as though the night itself had carved them.

A surprised and slightly indignant bark from the other side of the door forestalled any questions that Farnor might have been considering and, almost immediately, the door was opened.

'Where did you get this ring from, old man?'

Nilsson's question was asked abruptly, and none too pleasantly. Farnor looked at him sharply, shocked by this unexpected rudeness.

'Good evening, Captain, Farnor,' Gryss said, wilfully courteous. 'What brings you here so late? One of your

209

men sick? Someone injured?' He leaned forward. 'You look a little pale yourself, actually.'

Nilsson seemed to recollect himself. He made no apology for his sudden question but he gently lowered the ring so that the bell did not sound. The dog barked again however.

'No,' Nilsson said, a little awkwardly. 'I . . .'

'Do come in, Captain,' Gryss said, cutting across the hesitation. Nilsson stooped unnecessarily as he stepped into the cottage. Uncertain what was expected of him, Farnor followed and quietly closed the door.

'I bought the ring many years ago from a trader when I was away over the hill,' Gryss said with forced amiability as he shuffled down the hallway. 'Have you seen something like it before? I'd be interested to know where it came from.'

'No, no,' Nilsson said hastily, as he narrowly avoided tripping over the dog which was lumbering along in front of him. 'It just . . . caught my eye.'

Gryss nodded and grunted but did not pursue the matter.

He led Nilsson into the back room and offered him the wicker chair opposite his own. Nilsson, however, sat down on the bench by the long table and leaned forward on to his folded arms. Farnor hovered in the doorway, seemingly forgotten by both men.

Gryss settled himself into his chair then looked at Nilsson purposefully.

'How can I help you, Captain?' he asked.

Nilsson was direct. 'Do you know a man called Rannick?'

Farnor's attention sharpened.

'Yes,' Gryss replied.

'Tell me about him,' Nilsson said, straightening up and looking at the old man directly.

'Is he in trouble?' Gryss asked.

'He might be.'

'What's he done?'

'Just tell me about him,' Nilsson persisted.

Gryss shrugged. 'There's nothing much to tell,' he said. 'He's a general . . . labourer, I suppose you'd call him. Has a cottage just outside the village and a small piece of land, which he assiduously neglects. He earns his keep by doing odds and ends about the place. He's capable enough when the mood takes him. Very intelligent, I suspect. But he's got a surly, not to say downright unpleasant disposition. Seems to think that someone owes him a living. He's not one of the most popular people in the valley.' He paused briefly then repeated his question: 'What's he done?'

Nilsson again did not answer. 'Can you show me where he lives?' he asked, instead.

'Certainly,' Gryss replied. 'But he's not there at the moment, nor has been for the last few weeks.'

A flicker of annoyance passed over Nilsson's face. 'Where can I find him then?' he asked.

Gryss leaned back in his chair. 'I've no idea,' he said. 'Rannick often disappears for days, sometimes weeks, on end. No one knows where he goes, no one asks.'

'And no one cares, I gather,' Nilsson added.

Gryss nodded. 'If you'll tell me why you're interested in him I might be able to help in some way,' he said.

Nilsson thought for a moment. 'Some of my men met him when they were exploring the valley beyond the castle,' he said. 'They were concerned about him.'

Gryss could not keep the surprise from his voice. 'They met him to the *north* of the *castle*?' he said, his eyes wide with surprise, yet oddly piercing.

'Some considerable way to the north,' Nilsson replied, watching Gryss carefully.

The old man shook his head. 'I can't think what he was doing up there,' he said. 'As far as I know, no one from the valley has been beyond the castle within living memory.' He gave Nilsson a stern look. 'But it's no crime to wander the countryside as far as I'm aware. Why should he be in trouble?'

Nilsson seemed to be taken unawares by this question. His answer was hesitant. 'There's some kind of vicious animal out there,' he said awkwardly. 'A large dog gone wild, I imagine. Or perhaps a pack. We lost one of our horses to it.'

Standing behind him, half in the room and half in the hallway, Farnor felt his insides go cold. The memory of his contact with the creature that had been worrying the sheep had faded since the abandoning of the night watch and he had deliberately turned his thoughts away from it, though it lay in the background of his life like a storm cloud on a far horizon. Now, however, in the wake of Nilsson's words it returned in all its horror and the storm clouds were dark and ominous overhead. For a moment he felt nauseous and dizzy. He steadied himself against the door jamb.

'A horse?' Gryss gasped, lurching upright in his chair. 'You had a *horse* killed?' He was almost shouting. 'Whatever killed our sheep was big, but . . . a horse!' He stared at Nilsson, genuinely alarmed. 'And you think Rannick's up there, in the same area as this . . . creature?'

Nilsson waved the question aside almost irritably.

'Is there something strange about Rannick?' he asked abruptly, blurting out the question.

Farnor stood very still.

'Strange?' Gryss queried, momentarily taken aback.

Nilsson shifted uneasily on the bench. 'Has he any . . . unusual . . . skills? Ways with . . . animals, people? Anything . . . ?' He left the word hanging.

Gryss's eyes narrowed. 'Not that I've ever seen,' he replied straightforwardly. 'But I don't really know what you mean. Rannick's an awkward and unpopular character. The kind of man who lives in bitterness and who dies miserable and alone or on the end of someone's sword through a quarrel he's provoked. That's all I can tell you.'

Nilsson looked as if he had further questions to ask, but he remained silent.

Gryss watched him closely. 'I did caution you that the valley to the north has an evil reputation,' he said. 'Maybe old women's tales, maybe not. But has anything happened up there that might bring problems to the rest of us here in the valley?'

Farnor, his unease persisting grimly, tightened his grip on the door jamb, as Nilsson stood up suddenly. His bulk dominated the room and ended any further debate.

'No,' he said bluntly. 'Nothing's happened that concerns you, but I do need to find this Rannick. Will you show me where he lives?'

Farnor shrank back into the hallway. What had begun as a small excitement, escorting this king's man through the night, had abruptly begun to turn into a nightmare, and his dominant wish now was to return home in the hope that the resurgent memories would once again fade away.

'He won't be there,' Gryss said.

'Nevertheless,' Nilsson insisted.

'Whatever you wish,' Gryss said, standing up with a disclaiming wave of his hands. 'I'll show you with pleasure.'

As the trio emerged from the cottage, Gryss issued his customary command, 'stay', to his sleeping dog, and gave Farnor's arm a sustaining squeeze. Catching his eye, he flicked a glance towards Nilsson's back and raised his forefinger to his lips. Farnor nodded an acknowledgement. He had had no intention of

213

saying anything anyway, but Gryss's silent injunction was comforting.

'It's not far,' Gryss said, as Nilsson made to untether his horse. 'We can walk.'

Rannick's cottage was a countryman's 'not far' however, and it took them some time to reach the narrow, twisting lane that led to it. The lane was bounded by overgrown hedges. Long brambles snaked out of the undergrowth to catch on clothes, and branches hung low brushing the heads of the passers-by. Gryss's lantern threw a tunnel of light through the darkness, that was brought alive by the moths and night insects dancing in it. The odd small animal scuttled away in a flurry and, beyond the light, tiny bright green or red eyes occasionally shone briefly and then blinked out.

Nilsson swore softly as a large bramble tangled in his long coat.

'Rannick's neglect, I'm afraid,' Gryss said. He looked regretful. 'He could have done very nicely out of this little plot if he'd wanted, but . . .' He let out a small sigh and left the sentence unfinished.

Eventually they reached a gate at the end of the path. Like the path, it bore signs of long neglect and as Gryss tried to open it it slipped from his hand and fell over with a weary groan. He shook his head as he stepped over it. The small garden it led into was as overgrown as the path.

'Mind where you put your feet,' he said. 'I wouldn't like to hazard what might be lying about under this lot.'

He held up his lantern and the light from it illuminated the cottage. The thatched roof was battered and dishevelled, the walls were stained where rainwater had seeped through the thatch and run down them. One window was crudely boarded up while the others, and the door, were unpainted and obviously rotten.

Nilsson picked up a stick and began beating aside the straggling plants that were growing across the remains of a decorative path that led to the door. Reaching it, he struck it violently with the edge of his clenched fist.

The sound fell flat in the dense foliage of the garden.

There was no reply.

'He's not there,' Gryss said with some impatience.

Nilsson tried the latch. The door swung open. He stepped back hastily as if suspecting an ambush. 'It's not locked,' he whispered to Gryss.

'Why should it be?' Gryss asked, moving past him and going into the cottage. Nilsson followed.

'Rannick,' Gryss shouted. 'It's Gryss. There's someone wants to see you.'

Again there was no reply. 'I told you,' Gryss said. 'He's not here.'

Nilsson began wandering around the cottage, casually inspecting the many odds and ends that were littered about. Farnor, who had discreetly followed the two men inside, felt an unexpected sense of outrage at this intrusion, though at the same time he felt reassured by the substantial presence of this soldier amid the unpleasant aura that pervaded Rannick's home.

And there *was* something unpleasant about it, he decided. Something other than the dirt and squalor. Something . . . Gryss's word for Rannick's family came back to him. Something tainted.

He stayed near the door.

Abruptly Nilsson wrapped his arms about himself and shivered. He muttered something in his own language and then, without further comment, strode out of the cottage and across the garden. Gryss and Farnor followed hastily.

Nilsson did not speak as they walked back to Gryss's

215

cottage, other than to issue a terse command to the effect that if Rannick was seen he was to be detained.

'Detained!' Gryss exclaimed. 'I can't do that, I haven't—' He flapped his arms '—the authority.'

'You've mine now,' Nilsson said starkly. 'See it's done. And send me word at once.'

Gryss did not argue, but his posture as they walked on showed that he was deeply disturbed.

'I've some work needs doing tomorrow, Farnor,' he said as Farnor clambered up on to Nilsson's horse, 'if your father can spare you first thing.'

There was a subtle urgency in his manner which Nilsson did not note.

'I'll ask him,' Farnor said. 'I'm sure it'll be all right.'

Where the journey from the farm to Gryss's cottage had been tinged with excitement, the return was leaden with a brooding darkness. Though whether this was Nilsson's manner or whether it was a result of his own revived memories of the creature and the strangeness he had felt in Rannick's cottage, Farnor could not have said. Nevertheless, he was more than a little relieved to slide down from the horse at the end of the path that led to his home.

'No point you coming further,' he said, as cheerfully as he could. 'It'll only disturb the dogs again.'

Nilsson may have grunted a reply, but Farnor did not care. All he wanted was to be away from the man and to be surrounded by the security of his home.

As Farnor disappeared into the darkness Nilsson urged his horse forward then let the reins hang loose, allowing the animal its head.

Faithfully it carried him, rapt in thought, through the starlit darkness along the castle road.

And then it stopped suddenly.

Nilsson started out of his reverie. He frowned. They

216

were still some way from the castle. He spurred the horse on.

It would not move.

Nilsson's teeth showed faintly in the darkness as again he used his spurs on the animal, then:

'Captain Nilsson.'

A voice came out of the darkness.

Instinctively he reached for his knife. A plot by some of the men disgruntled by his decision that they should go north, or at his orders for them to leave the village unmolested?

Yet he knew that was not so. Such plots invariably cast their shadows forward to anyone with eyes sharp enough to see them, and he had been nothing if not sharp-eyed for many months now. And there was a quality about this voice that resonated through and through him. Memory after memory rose like spectres out of the dust of his long and wilful forgetfulness.

He drove his spurs savagely into the horse's flanks. The animal quivered in distress, but still did not move.

A shadow, dark in the darkness, came towards him.

'Captain Nilsson,' the voice said again.

Nilsson drew his knife.

'My name is Rannick, Captain Nilsson,' the shadow said. 'You and I have matters to discuss.'

Chapter 16

'Who are you, Rannick?' Nilsson said flatly.

The shadow nodded approvingly. 'You call my name and yet you ask who I am. I commend your perceptiveness, Captain. No false blustering about your bewildered men, or Meirach, or your slaughtered horse. Just a simple, direct question. You seek to know my true self. And yet in asking that question you affirm that you know who I am.' His voice was leisurely and calm, as if they were old friends relaxing over a quiet noonday drink in some peaceful inn, but it seemed to Nilsson that it came in some way from another place, and the slow trickle of old memories that it had invoked at first grew and grew until it threatened to become a flood.

Rannick's voice cut through the mounting tumult. 'Do you feel it is meet that *I* should stoop to tell you what you have told me you already know?'

There was a long silence.

'You have no answer, I see. At least you do not compound your folly by remonstrating with me.' The shadow nodded again and the voice became conciliatory. 'And there is about you the quality of a once true and stalwart servant, so I shall answer your question. I shall tell you what you know. I am a wielder of the power.'

Nilsson's eyes narrowed. This Rannick had a skill of some kind, beyond a doubt, but the *power*? That was a nonsense. Then he realized that his hand holding the knife was beginning to sweat.

The survivor in him tested his grip in case it should slip at some crucial moment, then his other hand moved casually over it lest the faint starlight betray its presence.

He cursed himself for a fool and sternly took control of his voice before he spoke.

'The power!' he said contemptuously. 'Spare me your riddles and foolishness, Rannick. I'm no village peasant who thinks these mountains bound the entire world. I've seen countless shamans conjure up grandiose fantasies of deceit from alehouse tittle-tattle and snatches of camp-fire chatter that they've picked up. Seen them build themselves great castles of seeming power for the deception of others from what was no more than gossamer.' He was almost spitting out his words. 'In short, I've seen too many diviners, priests, necromancers, thaumaturgists and all the other mountebanks of your weary ilk to be other than irritated by you. Or, worse, angered.'

Rannick inclined his head but otherwise gave no response.

Nilsson continued, his anger mounting. 'Your true prey are the foolish and the gullible. And while you may have deceived some of my men with your trickery, and halted my horse with' – He shrugged – 'some noxious nightweed laid across its path, don't think I don't see you for what you are. And don't imagine you'll live to boast of the deed if you don't take your leave of me, *now!*, and look to leave the valley while you can. My men would relish hunting you.'

Despite his anger Nilsson felt his mouth go dry, but old reflexes tightened his grip about his knife.

Rannick came closer and rested his hand on the horse's nose. The horse trembled violently, but did not otherwise move. When Rannick spoke his voice was soft, but a terrible menace permeated it.

'Your lack of faith disturbs me, Captain. Do not ask me for proof of what you already know. You will find my patience even less than your own.' He paused. 'I am your past, Captain. And your future. I am your destiny, just as you are mine.'

The hand patted the horse's nose and, unexpectedly, Nilsson felt a dark, assured amusement leavening Rannick's manner. It was more chilling than any threat could have been. 'I feel your old desires returning, Captain. So many desires whose fulfilment you'd thought had slipped away for ever.' He paused again, as if listening to something.

'So many.' There was a hint of surprise and even admiration, albeit edged with mockery, in his voice. He breathed in audibly. 'They are like sweet air to me, Captain.'

Nilsson's reply was harsh. 'Stand aside, Rannick,' he said. 'I told you I've seen too many such charlatans to be gulled like my men.' He bent low towards the shadowy figure by his horse's head and his voice fell, as if what he had to say would bring a retribution upon him if it were spoken too loudly. 'And, for your guidance, know that though the one I followed is long dead, and his followers scattered far and wide, it would behove you to keep even the *thought* of him from your mind lest his shade alone stir and shrivel your stunted soul into dust.'

'Sweet air, Captain,' came the soft response, indifferent to this advice.

Enough, Nilsson decided, and, without warning, he struck. With a speed learned from years of cruel necessity he leaned further forward and thrust his knife at Rannick's throat.

Rannick did not seem to move, but suddenly Nilsson found himself swept from his saddle and hurled high into the air.

He landed some way from his horse with a winding thud. But worse than the impact of the landing was the fear that swept through him. Fear such as he had not known in many years. Rannick had laid no hand on him, and yet he had been lifted from his saddle effortlessly.

He looked up.

Rannick's form loomed over him, a deep blackness cut into the dark, starlit sky.

'Is it you, Lord?' He heard himself asking, his voice tremulous.

'No, Captain. Your erstwhile master is truly gone, but his mantle has fallen on me. I am his heir. I shall raise again the banner that he let fall, and you will be at my side leading my army.'

Despite his fear, denial rang through Nilsson.

'No,' he said, struggling painfully to his feet. 'This is madness. Whatever skills chance of birth has given you, or you've gleaned in this forsaken valley, you're not he, nor could you ever be. His knowledge was ancient and his power was beyond even your imagining.'

Rannick's form shifted in the darkness, as if some strange wind were tugging at it.

'And he failed,' Nilsson concluded, almost desperately. 'There were others greater who came unheralded and unexpected and slew him. And slew his companions also. And those others live yet, and will slay you if you seek to emulate him.'

'No,' Rannick said coldly. 'My power is guided by an ancient knowledge that even he was not privy to. A knowledge far beyond your understanding. He came but to prepare a path for me. Choose now, Captain. Lead my army and, in the glory of my passing, rekindle and fulfil those ambitions which were promised and which were so cruelly and unjustly torn from you.'

Yes, part of Nilsson cried out. Yes! There was too much truth in the words for his denial to be born.

Yet when he spoke it was the haggler, the survivor, the soldier who gave him the words.

'Or?' he asked, faintly.

Rannick seemed amused again. He opened his arms wide as if to encompass the night. 'If you would turn from the one true light, then you must face the darkness.'

In the silence that followed, Nilsson felt another presence sharing their discourse. A presence full of hard-sinewed power and cruel will that paced silently at some unseen distance. A presence ancient in malevolence and cunning and bloodlust but young in the strength of its rending teeth. A presence waiting with infinite patience for a command.

It was the final confirmation.

Yes, the whole of Nilsson cried out this time. Too long he had been hunted and harried for his past service to his lord. It must be no more. Some power had led him to this lonely valley with the shelter offered by its long-sealed castle and the sustenance offered by its foolish people. To deny its will would not merely be futile, it would be . . . the word teetered at the edge of his mind . . . it would be blasphemous.

'Forgive me, my Lord,' he said, lowering himself on to one knee in obeisance. 'I will serve you again if you feel me worthy.'

Rannick's voice was that of a man who had known no doubt about this conclusion. 'Continue on your way, Captain. I shall come again to you tomorrow.'

In the lonely darkness, Rannick communed. 'This one, above all, must be ours. This one, above all, *will* be ours.'

He laughed.

'So easy, my friend. So easy.'

Gryss was standing at the door of his cottage when Farnor arrived the following morning. It was a fine sunny day, but clouds were beginning to move slowly

223

overhead and there was a slight edge in the air that betokened rain later. Gryss was staring at the yellow spring flowers growing in profusion on an embankment nearby.

'Have you ever looked at those?' he asked as Farnor approached.

Farnor gave the flowers a cursory glance. 'Sun's eyes,' he said, off-handedly.

'Indeed,' Gryss acknowledged. 'But have you ever looked at them?'

'Of course,' Farnor replied, puzzled. 'Many times. You can't miss them at this time of year, can you?'

Gryss smiled. 'How many petals do the flowers have, Farnor? What shape are the leaves? Is there one stem or many, divided? Why do they grow there and not there?' He pointed to a bare area. 'What kind of insects visit them? And why some and not others?'

Farnor waved his arms and spluttered vaguely in the face of this gentle barrage, but offered no coherent reply apart from reaffirming a few times that they were sun's eyes, weren't they?

'Not looked at them as much as you'd thought, have you?' Gryss said, grinning now. 'Try it one day. You won't regret it, I promise you.'

Farnor shuffled his feet. 'You said you had some jobs for me,' he said, in an attempt to forestall any further embarrassing interrogation.

Gryss's face became serious. 'I told you to come here because we need to talk about Rannick and this . . . Captain Nilsson and his slaughtered horse, don't we?'

Farnor turned away from Gryss's scrutiny. 'I suppose so,' he muttered, almost sulkily.

'You know so,' Gryss said, sternly. 'From now on, let's you and me see and say things the way they are, eh? Then we'll know where we are.'

'Where are we, then?' Farnor asked abruptly, somewhat to his own surprise.

'I don't know,' Gryss replied, ignoring the sharpness of the question. 'But wherever it is I'm involved because, for my sins, I'm the senior elder and you're involved because you're involved. All I know for sure at the moment is that we both need someone to talk to freely, directly; someone to trust, to speak foolishness with and not be afraid.'

Farnor looked at him uncertainly. This was a Gryss he had never seen before. A man. An ordinary man. For an instant he felt the young man, no different from himself, bound and hedged about by the old man's body.

'I'll trust your young judgement in this,' Gryss continued. 'Will you trust mine?'

Part of Farnor wanted to turn and run. To fly across the fields and into the woods, and lie on the soft grass there watching the sun flickering through the leaves overhead while he wove his familiar tales of heroism and glory.

But even as the thoughts formed, they palled. A different light had been shone upon them from somewhere. Their colours had faded, their ringing resonance had become thin and weak. He found himself regretting the passing of something, but he was uncertain what.

'Yes,' he said after a moment.

'Good,' Gryss said. 'Let's walk to Rannick's cottage and talk as we go.'

'Why?' Farnor asked.

Gryss gave him a reproachful glance. 'You'd break our agreement so soon?' he said.

'Sorry,' Farnor replied. He tried to make amends. 'Rannick's at the heart of this, isn't he?'

Gryss laid a hand on his shoulder, and they set off towards Rannick's cottage. 'At the heart, or near it,' he said. 'There's been some kind of encounter between

Rannick and Nilsson's men, and it's badly disconcerted our Captain Gatherer in some way, if I'm any judge.'

Gryss's surmise seemed reasonable, but Farnor did not know what to say, except, 'If we don't know what's happened, what can we do? And should we bother? He did say nothing had happened that would affect us down here.'

An unsettling thought formed. 'You don't think that . . .' He hesitated. Gryss inclined his head but did not speak.

They turned off the wide road that went through the village and began walking down the narrower one that led to Rannick's cottage.

'You don't think that the tales about the caves are true,' Farnor managed to say at last, though he could feel his face burning. 'That there are ancient . . . monsters . . . asleep up there . . . just waiting?'

Gryss's brow furrowed and he did not reply for some time. He returned a friendly greeting from a passer-by. 'Reject nothing,' he said, eventually. 'Examine everything.'

Farnor looked at him. It still felt very strange, talking to the old man like this. Almost like an equal.

'Then you think . . .' he began.

'I don't think anything,' Gryss said firmly, turning to him. 'At the moment, I'm just looking. How many petals, what shape leaves, how many stems? You understand?'

'I think so,' Farnor answered, adding after a moment, 'If I'm allowed to think, that is.'

Gryss laughed loudly and aimed an affectionate blow at Farnor's head.

Then they were once again walking along the narrow, overgrown pathway to Rannick's cottage. It seemed wider than it had the night before, constrained as it had been then by the light from Gryss's lantern. But the overgrown hedgerows on either side were more alive, full of mysterious movements and rustlings, and the brambles appeared to have taken on a new life in the sunlight.

Stepping over the fallen gate, they halted.

Gryss shook his head. The darkness had hidden much of the condition of the cottage. He looked at the torn and ragged thatch, and at the stained walls. All seemed worse than the night before, as did the boarded window and the rotten windows and door. 'Such neglect,' he said. 'I'd no idea he'd let it get into this state, or I'd have had a word with him.'

'He wouldn't have listened,' Farnor said.

'Maybe,' Gryss said. 'But I'd have felt better about it, and perhaps a little less guilty now.'

'Guilty! You?' Farnor exclaimed in surprise. 'What for? Rannick does what he wants. Always has, as long as I've known him, anyway. How could you have done anything about this?'

Gryss stopped him. 'I feel what I feel, Farnor,' he said. 'Perhaps a word here, a word there, who knows?'

Farnor made a disparaging noise.

'That's a young man's privilege,' Gryss said. 'Unfortunately, as you get older you realize that a small change at the beginning can have a profound effect on the conclusion.'

'The empire was lost for want of a nail?' Farnor said, recalling one of Yonas's tales and seeing it now in a new light.

'Exactly,' Gryss said. 'Let's go inside.'

The inside of the cottage, like its outside, looked very different than on the previous night. The daylight coming through the windows heightened the gloomy corners and exposed more vividly the stained walls and floor. Though Farnor felt a wave of disgust at the general squalor of the place, he also felt unexpectedly sad at the sight of the faded furniture and the dusty ornaments with their lingering hints of homeliness and caring. He righted a small vase that had fallen over. It left its fallen image, dust free, on the shelf like a reproachful shadow.

Gryss watched him and nodded.

'What do you feel?' he asked.

Farnor shrugged. 'Nothing much,' he replied. 'It's very different from last night. For one thing it doesn't have that captain hulking around in it. Perhaps it was him made the place feel strange. Him and the darkness.'

Gryss chuckled. 'Let's have a look round,' he said.

'Suppose he comes back?' Farnor said, suddenly conscious of what they were doing. Doors were invariably open in the valley, but deliberately nosing around someone's house was another matter.

'I'll have plenty to ask him, don't worry,' Gryss replied tartly, as he headed for the kitchen.

Farnor followed him about, growing progressively more uneasy.

'There is something . . . unpleasant . . . about the place,' he decided eventually as he retreated from the bedroom. 'Apart from the general mess and decay. There's a—'

The front door of the cottage opened.

Chapter 17

Nilsson had little or no recollection of the remainder of his journey back to the castle. It was a swirling maelstrom of fears and doubts, of re-awakened and burning ambition, of elation and black despair, the whole interwoven with long-dead memories risen anew and richly lit by the fire of the promise that had been kindled in him.

'What did you find out, Nils?'

The question reached to draw him from his deep preoccupation. He looked at the speaker vacantly for a moment. It was Dessane.

'What did you find out?' The question came again, Dessane concerned at his leader's abstractedness. 'About Rannick?' he prompted. He stepped back a pace. The light of his torch illuminated both rider and horse. 'Ye gods!' he exclaimed. 'What have you been doing to your horse? It's in a lather, and it's petrified.'

Nilsson ignored the questions but swung slowly down from the horse. His face was still intensely preoccupied and he held up his hand for silence.

Despite this unspoken injunction, however, Dessane confronted him urgently.

'Nils,' he hissed. 'What's happened? Did you run into trouble in the village?'

Nilsson's eyes focused on him eventually. 'What's happened, Arven?' he echoed. 'A great deal's happened. Things that were ended are begun again. From tonight we go in a different direction.'

Dessane scowled in bewilderment at this enigmatic reply. He was half inclined to ask his captain if he had been drinking, but apart from the intrinsic risk in such a question it was patently obvious that he had not. Nilsson when drunk was either dangerously jovial or savagely, coldly, cruel.

Nilsson ended his quandary for him.

'Tomorrow, Arven,' he said. 'Tomorrow. He'll be here tomorrow, then your questions will be answered.'

'Who? Who'll be here?' Dessane asked in frustration. 'And what questions?'

'Tomorrow,' Nilsson repeated. 'Leave me now. I need to think, to sleep. I'll need a clear head when he arrives.'

Dessane opened his mouth to ask 'Who?' again, then gave up. Whatever had affected Nilsson thus, there was no indication of any immediate danger to the group in his behaviour, and it could prove as dangerous to press him in this strange mood as when he *was* drunk.

'As you wish, Nils,' he said, taking the reins from the Captain's hands and stroking the frightened horse. 'As you wish. I'll tend your horse for you.'

But Nilsson made no answer, he was striding purposefully away into the darkness.

The morning did not bring Nilsson the clarity he would have preferred, however. He had spent the remainder of the night tossing and turning fitfully, unable to control the uproar in his mind and, indeed, for much of the time unable to tell whether he was awake and imagining or asleep and dreaming.

Nevertheless he was quieter and his thoughts were to some extent more ordered when daylight struck through the narrow window and finally lured him from his bed. The leader in him rose to the fore as he dashed cold water in his face and began to repair some of the ravages to his appearance the fretful night had wrought.

Had it been a dream?

No. Beyond a doubt, no. Cautiously he flexed his

back and felt the stiffness and bruising of his fall, an all-too-tangible confirmation of the night's event.

Had it been some trickery by Rannick? Nilsson had told the truth when he said that he had seen many wondrous things apparently miraculously conjured into existence which transpired to be no more than base trickery by equally base fraudsters.

Unlikely, a quiet – not to say awed – part of him declared. Apart from some subtle, familiar quality in the man's very presence, there was the vivid memory of being lifted from his horse and hurled effortlessly through the night at the very moment when his knife should have been ending Rannick's life.

That had been the power. He had known and felt it before. And Rannick it had been who had wielded it as he stood there motionless in the darkness.

And, too, there was that other, sinister, presence that had touched him briefly. Nilsson shivered. *That* he had not known before, and whatever it had been he had no desire to know it again.

Yet, though his convictions were more solid in the morning light, his doubts and questions too, were stronger. Where and how could this man have acquired his skills if, as Gryss had said, he had lived in the valley all his life? And how truly adept was he? Nilsson could not begin to answer the first question, and found it impossible to conceive that *anyone* could have the same awesome ability as his erstwhile lord, but . . . ?

The schemer and tactician in him began to take control. He would have to watch and measure Rannick's power; watch and measure his skill in dealing with men; discover and direct to his own ends whatever plans this mysterious valley dweller had. Because, unless he learned more about him, that was all Rannick could be: another valley dweller, presumably simple and

231

unlettered. Almost certainly he would be, in some ways, as gullible as the rest of the people here.

Nilsson ran his wet hands through his hair and drew himself up straight, pleased with his conclusion. Whatever happened today, *he* must be seen to be in authority either as Rannick's indisputable second in command or as his executioner. He checked his various knives and, taking out his favourite, tested its edge. He replaced it with a nod of satisfaction. Whatever hint I gave you last night I'll not give again, he determined. If a thrust is necessary it'll be after a smile of support, in your back and *fast*.

There was always the possibility, of course, that Rannick would not appear. That presented problems. He could easily fabricate some yarn to explain the previous night's conduct to Dessane, but future plans would be thrown into confusion.

He pondered various alternatives. He could postpone Yeorson and Storran's second exploration of the valley, but that would cause awkward questions as everyone knew that, sooner or later, they would have to leave here. Or he could send it out as he had intended. But what danger was there in that? Why had Rannick chosen to intercept the first group? It occurred to him suddenly, that it might have been solely for the purpose of kidnapping Meirach, or someone – anyone. And the implications of this? Rannick now knew everything about Nilsson and his men; or at least as much as Meirach knew, and that was enough. Adept or crafty faker, it would give him no small advantage in their future dealings.

Too many alternatives and too little information for detailed planning, he decided. He must deal with each thing as it happened, as in battle. The strategy, after all, would be no different: first his personal survival, second his best personal interests.

The morning passed for him in a disjointed, spasmodic manner, punctuated as it was by intervals of unreality as he drifted occasionally into deep reveries, plans and schemes forming and re-forming in his mind while the castle pursued its morning routine.

Not that there was a great deal of routine to be pursued. As usual, those who had risen too late for the communal breakfast made their own or did without. The rest did nothing apart from those detailed to guard the walls and the gate, and those who were preparing to leave with Yeorson and Storran.

These latter were acting with commendable efficiency. Generally callous in their dealings with other than their own, and typically brutal with one another, Nilsson's men had an almost incongruously chivalrous horror of abandoning each other and there had been no shortage of volunteers to join the patrol in its search for Meirach.

Feelings were mixed however, as the tale brought back by the first patrol was told and retold, wilfully exaggerated and embellished, inevitably misunderstood and generally allowed to assume a significance far greater than its original reality. Nilsson, assisted by his aides, poured icy scorn on such of these excesses as reached their ears, but it was obvious that a serious morale problem was developing and would continue to develop unless positive action was taken to stop it.

Looking down from the castle walls, Nilsson watched the comings and goings of his men. Like eddies in a stream, they had a rhythm and a pattern seemingly full of purpose but with no discernible cause or conclusion. Yet the movement was too fast, too erratic. To his experienced eye, there were ripples present that betokened the onset of a sudden and dangerous flood.

And, like a flood, a timely intervention would be needed to divert its energies if harm was to be avoided.

He turned to Dessane. 'Call a congress,' he said.

Dessane stared at him in surprise. 'Now?' he asked, eyebrows raised. 'The patrol will be ready to leave shortly.'

'Now,' Nilsson confirmed.

Dessane did as he was bidden. The procedure was simple and devoid of formal ritual. He walked to the stairs that led down to the courtyard and shouted, 'Congress!' at the top of his voice.

The hubbub in the courtyard faltered momentarily before returning with renewed vigour and a quite different character. The cry 'Congress!' was taken up by whoever heard it and was soon echoing around the smaller yards of the castle, along corridors and into every inhabited room and hall.

Within minutes, almost the entire company was gathered in the courtyard gazing expectantly at their leader.

Nilsson walked slowly down the stairs and stopped on the first landing next to Dessane. Saddre emerged from the crowd and came up the stairs to join him.

The gathering gradually fell silent.

'I'll keep this simple, men,' Nilsson shouted.

There was a murmur of surprise and almost alarm from the crowd as his voice boomed round the court-yard, magnified many times by some feature in the shape of the walls or quality in the stonework.

'You can keep it quieter too,' someone shouted, to general laughter.

Nilsson smiled and acknowledged the jest with a wave of his hand. That was useful: the laughter alone would remove much of the tension that had built up.

He lowered his voice and found that it carried adequately over the entire courtyard.

'I'll keep this simple,' he said again. 'I've been hearing some rare tales this morning.' He exaggerated, mockingly. 'Tales of fire-breathing warlocks invading our campfire. Tales of monsters wakened from their ancient sleep to snatch away our men and devour our horses.' He shook his head and laughed. 'For months we've lived hand to mouth, scratching the meagrest living from this country. Now we find this cosy billet, with shelter made for us and food thrust upon us, and what happens? You've so little to do you begin to rave.'

He did not wait for a response but shouted, 'Now!' and clapped his hands together loudly. It had the effect he had desired, as the noise boomed back off the walls, startling all present.

He continued without pause, his voice normal again. 'We can tolerate such children's tales for a little while, but no longer. What we have is an injured, perhaps feverish man who's wandered off into the forest and a horse killed probably by a small pack of wild dogs. Just that. Nothing more. No irate locals marching out on the hue and cry, no groups of mercenaries, no so-called bandits looking to ambush us. One lost man and a wild dog or two.'

Delivered with a carefully judged measure of scorn and fatherly amusement, the brief speech brought the gathering to foot shuffling hesitation almost immediately.

'What about Rannick?' someone ventured, though not too loudly.

What about him indeed? Nilsson thought. Time to prepare the ground for his coming . . . or his not coming as the case should prove.

'A local character,' he replied with a dismissive shrug. 'That's all.' He paused, then continued, 'Though from what I've heard there may be more to him than meets the eye. On the whole, I think we'll benefit more from his friendship and local knowledge than from his enmity. He's to be treated well if those of you going out on patrol come across him. Give him every courtesy and my best wishes and tell him he's welcome to visit the castle and sup with us whenever he wants to.'

Yeorson and Storran were standing a little way up the first flight of stairs. Nilsson nodded to them significantly to confirm this change from his earlier orders. Then he put his hands on his hips and moved towards the edge of the landing. His presence filled the courtyard.

'I'll tell you this, men,' he said. 'No idle chance brought us here. My guts tell me that we're at the start of something new; something big. Something that'll mean an end to our looking over our shoulders all the time.' He paused to let this unfamiliar optimism seep into his listeners. 'Whatever it proves to be, I want us to be ready for it. Opportunities don't come to people who aren't ready to seize them. We're banded together by common consent, but we're still soldiers so let's behave like it. Those of you who're going out on patrol, put your best face to it. No moaning, no malingering. Those of you who're staying here, get yourselves and this place cleaned up. Check your weapons, check your kit, check your horses. Check everything that needs to be checked for us to begin a new beginning.'

Some of the men were actually open-mouthed at this declamation but the balance of the gathering was beginning to show marked signs of enthusiasm for Nilsson's new vision. Before any of them could mar it with injudicious questions however, he raised his hand.

'No questions, men,' he said with a knowing look to indicate that he knew more than he could say at the moment. 'Not yet. Our first job is to find Meirach, and look to his needs, our second is to find out what lies to the north and our third is to get this place operational. Let's have all efforts directed to those ends.'

He stepped back and dismissed the congress. One

236

or two camp-fire lawyers amongst the men muttered that a congress was only supposed to be held when an important decision was to be made, and that such a decision should be made by acclamation after a free discussion. But the mood of the meeting was too buoyant for their grumblings to be listened to, and they held their peace.

Nilsson smiled to himself as the meeting dispersed. He motioned to Yeorson and Storran and they joined him on the landing.

'I can't tell you everything yet,' he said, quietly, 'but I don't want any misunderstanding. If you come across Rannick, then do as I ask. Give him every courtesy and tell him he's welcome here, as I said. Do you understand?'

Both men nodded, though with some reserve. 'Some of the men won't be happy,' Yeorson said. 'They think he was responsible for Meirach getting burned.'

The anger in Nilsson's voice was barely concealed. 'I appreciate it's a change of direction,' he said. 'But it *is* necessary. I don't even want him put on the wrong end of anyone's tongue, let alone their knife. Explain it to the men in whatever fashion you feel's most effective, but warn them that if they seek to deal with him in their own way in the hope that they can leave him dumped in the undergrowth somewhere, *I'll* know about it and the consequences for them will be singularly unpleasant.'

There being nothing else to be discussed after this lucid exposition, the two men left. As they walked down the stone steps Dessane moved closer to Nilsson, drawing Saddre with him. 'Do you mind telling *us* what's going on?' he said. 'All this talk about a new beginning. And what the devil happened to you last night? When you came back you looked like—'

A loud banging on the castle gate interrupted him.

* * *

237

'What are you doing here?'

'What are *you* doing here, is more to the point, Farnor. You've gone as white as a sheet.'

'You frightened the daylights out of me, bursting in like that,' Farnor protested vehemently, his face colouring red as quickly as it had blanched.

'And you frightened the daylights out of me, jumping like that, you ninny,' Marna countered fiercely.

'Ninny?' Farnor's jaw jutted.

Gryss interposed himself between the two antagonists. 'We were looking for Rannick, Marna,' he said. 'We haven't seen him for quite a time and were getting worried. What have *you* come here for?'

Marna's truculence faded. 'The same,' she said.

'Since when have you been interested in Rannick?' Farnor taunted.

Marna rounded on him. 'For mercy's sake, Farnor, don't be so . . .' She flailed about for a word. 'Dense,' she decided, after considering several less charitable alternatives. 'I've no great liking for the man, but he doesn't normally disappear for this length of time, does he? He could be lying injured somewhere, for all we know. Ye gods, we'd be more bothered about a missing sheep! I came here because I thought I should . . .' She shrugged her shoulders and her anger fizzled out. 'Do something.'

Gryss gave Farnor a look of amused reproach, but Farnor could only manage one of injured indignation.

'You put us both to shame, Marna,' Gryss said, putting a hand on her arm. 'But I think I can set your mind at rest, or at least partly so. Apparently some of the gatherers met Rannick when they were exploring the upper part of the valley.'

Marna's eyes widened. 'The upper part of the valley!' she exclaimed, in some alarm. 'Past the castle? What was he doing up there?'

Gryss shook his head. 'I don't know,' he replied. 'But I think perhaps you needn't concern yourself about him any more. At least he's not lying hurt somewhere, and if he's survived this long he's not going to starve to death.'

'I suppose so,' Marna said. 'I needn't have bothered then, need I?' she gave an awkward little smile. Gryss was about to commend her again for her concern when she frowned and wrinkled her nose. The state of the room had begun to impinge on her. 'This place is disgusting,' she announced. 'I've seen cleaner stables.'

'Yes, well, I think we'd better leave it as we've found it, don't you?' Gryss said, turning her towards the door. 'We shouldn't really be here at all.'

Marna followed his gentle urging out of the cottage and towards the broken gate. Suddenly she stopped, causing Gryss to stagger.

'What are you two doing here, anyway?' she asked forcefully, returning to her original question.

Not having a clear answer, Gryss, a lifelong bachelor, made a mistake. He ignored the question in the hope that it would go away. 'How's your father, Marna?' he said, looking purposefully towards the gate. 'I haven't seen him for some time, I—'

Marna's eyes narrowed. 'What's going on?' she demanded. 'Rannick wandering about beyond the castle for weeks on end. And running into gatherers. And you two skulking about his cottage . . .'

'We were not skulking,' Gryss protested. But Marna raised scornful eyebrows by way of reply and allowed an embarrassing silence to develop until another thought occurred to her.

'And how did you know that the gatherers had seen him?' she asked.

Gryss capitulated and briefly told her of Nilsson's visit the previous evening, confining himself to the

239

simple facts and omitting any references to the slaughtered horse and Nilsson's concern about Rannick's
'strangeness'.

'What did he want to look at Rannick's cottage for?'
Marna asked, when he had finished.

Gryss took refuge in his ignorance. 'I've no idea,' he
said. 'I don't know what happened when his men met
Rannick, and he didn't say. He just asked me to show
him where Rannick lived, so I did.'

Marna set off for the gate. 'It wasn't very polite, was
it?' she said, incongruously.

Gryss agreed with some relief. 'But he is a soldier
and he does have the King's authority for anything
he does.'

Marna sniffed. 'I shouldn't imagine the King's so
ill-mannered,' she said.

Gryss could not help but laugh at this observation and
its solemn utterance.

'How's your father?' he tried again, as they walked
back down the pathway.

'He's well, thanks,' Marna replied off-handedly.

Then she stopped again abruptly, and her face
clouded. 'I don't like any of this, Gryss,' she said,
her voice uncharacteristically anxious and urgent. 'I
didn't like the look of those gatherers when they rode
in, nor what I saw of them when they came to collect the
tithe. Now there's this business about them wandering
around the top of the valley and finding Rannick there,
of all people. It all feels wrong. No one ever goes up
there, Gryss. Not ever. And why should that wretched
captain be sniffing about Rannick's cottage? And why
you two as well?'

She looked at Gryss squarely. He reached out to put
an arm around her shoulders then thought better of it.

'Just changing times, Marna,' he said gently. 'Changing times.' He pointed towards the mountains. 'We live

a good life here, very sheltered, very secure. But out there, over the hill, there's another much bigger world full of all sorts of strange people and strange things, a lot of them not particularly nice and some downright bad. Believe me, I've been there. It's not for no reason that we've developed our way of living here through the generations. Now a little of the outside world has come into the valley and unsettled everything. If we keep our wits and our manners, these gatherers will probably forget about us completely after they've left and things will soon be back to normal.'

Marna shook her head. 'You can't unbreak a pot,' she said, simply. 'What's gone is gone and can never be the same, and there's no point fretting about it.'

Momentarily, Gryss looked distressed at this stark verdict, not least because he knew it to be accurate. He searched for words to soften its impact, but none came. And, in any event, he realized, Marna needed no comforting about the implications of her own conclusion. But there was need in her manner, without a doubt.

'I feel so . . . vulnerable,' she said, unexpectedly.

Gryss tried again. It was just change . . . The King must need the tithe for something . . . Everything would settle down again . . . more or less . . .

But Marna swept the answers aside.

'No,' she said. 'Something's wrong.' She looked at Gryss squarely, her dark eyes concerned but determined. 'I don't think those men are tithe gatherers at all.'

Chapter 18

'Hold!' Nilsson shouted to the gate guard as he started to run down the stairs that led to the courtyard.

A few swift strides carried him to the gate where he was intercepted by the man who had been on sentry duty on the wall above the arch. He, too, was breathless from his own reckless descent of the stairs.

'He came out of nowhere, Captain,' he protested before anything was asked of him. 'I was listening to you, but still on look-out, honestly. I don't know where he came from. He just—'

'It's all right,' Nilsson said, as he pushed him aside, almost gently. The man turned to others standing around him, with a desperate, pleading expression, as if the need to justify his apparent lapse had to run the course he had plotted for it in his dash down the stairs. It spluttered to a halt only when he registered the fact that his captain intended no summary punishment for him. Puffing out his cheeks he wiped his brow, then quietly slipped back up to his post.

Nilsson had thrown open the wicket door and stepped outside.

Rannick stood there. His gaunt face and unkempt black hair testified to some neglect, and he was dressed like any of the farm labourers in the valley, with his rough shirt and soiled and patched trousers. But his demeanour was quite different. He stood erect and relaxed, exuding an assuredness that was far beyond either mere confidence or brittle arrogance. And his narrow eyes were bright and piercing, as if lit from within by some awesome fire.

Nilsson's own eyes narrowed at the sight of him, as if he were looking at a bright light, or at something that was a long way away. It seemed to him for a moment that although Rannick was motionless, some strange, other-worldly breeze was tugging at him, ruffling his hair. He blinked and the image was gone, but the weight of Rannick's presence remained. He felt it now in the clear daylight just as he had in the starlit darkness of the previous night. He was in the presence of one who could use the power.

Yet at the same time as he confirmed this he recalled that even his erstwhile lord had had need of lieutenants and advisers, indeed there had been a huge hierarchy of lesser men to implement much of his will. And when he had been drawn to rely too greatly on his power, then he had been thwarted by the lesser servants of other lords. And, Nilsson knew now, powerful though he might be Rannick was not remotely the equal of his former lord. He would have an even greater need of others to implement any plans he might have. And plans he would have, as sure as fate.

Once again Nilsson found himself torn between different ambitions. The one: to pursue his present, meandering aimless existence; effectively a fugitive from his past, and dependent on his ability to manipulate his men to his will, through both superior intellect and physical force, and his ability to turn circumstances to his own ends. The other: to take up again his quest for power and wealth by serving in the train of another, far greater.

A vista of endless wandering opened before him, with its inexorable conclusion, the gradual loss of his authority, or the retribution of others, and some weary, lonely death. It was a vision that he had contemplated many times before in his quieter, darker moments, and one that he had resolutely turned his face away from.

Things would change, he knew. Things always did, if you kept your wits about you and your sword sharp.

And they had again! he realized. His journeying so far had been but a preparation for this moment. His vision of the future changed and took him towards the wealth and power he had always coveted. Took him beyond this life of little more than miserable banditry, and far beyond the vengeful reach of his past. And, his thoughts gathering a momentum of their own, perhaps it might even take him to reconquer what had been lost. To expunge the past!

He felt his whole body alive with exhilaration. Yet his soldier's instincts kept his feet solidly on the ground, for drawn along with these whirling thoughts was a small, dark one which whispered, coldly, 'Anyway, if the worst comes to the worst, I *can* kill this one.'

'You've come,' he said prosaically, moving to one side and extending an inviting arm to the open wicket. Rannick stepped through it.

Inside he gazed around the courtyard, first at the towers and other buildings and then at the men, who were staring at him.

Like a breeze unfelt below but rustling through the leaves of the trees above, a whisper hissed around the courtyard, and with it came a slight stirring.

'It's him!'

One or two edged towards him, torn between Nilsson's commands and the vengeful gossip that had returned with the patrol and which demanded immediate action.

The look on Nilsson's face stopped them.

Rannick affected to ignore the threat he had been offered. 'You spoke well,' he said to Nilsson. 'I am indeed better as your friend than your enemy. And my . . . local knowledge, as you call it, is indeed remarkable.'

Nilsson could not keep the surprise from his face. He

glanced up at the high, solid wall surrounding them. 'How did you hear what I said?' he asked bluntly, without thinking.

Rannick made no response. He gazed around the courtyard again, and at the men still held back by Nilsson's will. Then he spoke as if there had been no interruption. 'And while this is a good beginning, it is a small one and it would be a shame to waste the lives of any of your men needlessly.'

Nilsson felt the menace in the words but knew that he must assert himself without delay if he was to achieve the position he desired in his proposed partnership.

'They hear me and they obey me because I advise them well,' he said. 'But they've other loyalties, and not least among these is a battlefield obligation to collect their dead and wounded and to rescue anyone who's been taken prisoner.'

Rannick smiled at the motley collection of men who were watching him. 'And they . . . you . . . need to know the fate of their comrade, Meirach?' he said.

'If it is . . . an honourable one,' he said after a pause, adding in a lowered voice, 'If it isn't, then a lie will be the simplest expedient.'

Rannick nodded slightly, then held up a hand for silence. The quiet that fell across the courtyard was almost tangible, until . . .

'Someone's coming.'

It was the sentry who had been so anxious to exonerate himself for failing to notice the arrival of Rannick.

'That's a good man up there,' Nilsson said to Rannick. 'Why didn't he see you?'

'Local knowledge, Captain,' Rannick replied, smiling darkly. 'Local knowledge.' He chuckled to himself, then nodded towards the gate. 'Let your visitor in,' he said.

Nilsson signalled to the gate guard to open the wicket

again and all eyes were turned towards it, bright in the shade of the gate arch. Then a figure was silhouetted in it briefly, before emerging into the light of the yard.

It was Meirach. And his face and hands were clear of their burns. He grinned broadly and threw out his arms as if he were returning from a great victory.

The silence was shattered as the men, turning their attention from Nilsson and Rannick, began advancing on the new arrival, cheering and shouting.

Yeorson ran with the others, but paused as he passed Rannick and Nilsson. 'What's happened to his hands and face?' he asked. 'The burns?'

Nilsson shrugged and flicked a glance at Rannick. 'Maybe later,' he said. Yeorson nodded hesitantly and went on to push his way through the throng moving to greet Meirach.

Nilsson caught Rannick's eye. 'I'm glad to see him,' he said.

Rannick pursed his lips thoughtfully. 'It was a close thing, Captain. Scarcely a hair's breadth in my thinking when I decided to let him live.'

Nilsson, emboldened by this confidence, risked a venture. 'The horse, Lord . . . ?' he began.

Rannick's slight intimacy vanished like a candle flame snuffed out by a winter wind. 'Is a forbidden matter,' he said. The voice cut through Nilsson, and his chest went tight.

'As you wish . . . Lord,' he said. He was about to apologize for his effrontery, but decided against it when he noted a flicker of a response from Rannick at the word 'lord'. That would be enough concession for the moment.

Nevertheless, if anything else was eaten in the woods he wasn't going to ask about it.

The throng that had gathered round the returned Meirach was spreading and opening up now to enclose

Nilsson and Rannick also. Questions and praise filled the air. Nilsson shouted above the noise.

'Men. This is . . . *Lord* Rannick,' he said. He gave a broad smile of welcome to Rannick and noted with relish, his fleeting discomposure. 'Lord Rannick has come to help and advise us. To set us on the new road that I hinted at only a few minutes ago. He's to be given the courtesy that befits a lord, and' – He became emphatic – 'he's not to be pestered with idle questions. Our ways aren't his. I'm sure you'll find that Meirach'll be only too keen to tell you what he's been up to. He's not known for his ability to stay quiet as a rule.'

This was greeted with raucous jeering, which Meirach accepted as justly his own, then Nilsson spoke again. 'The Lord and I have things to discuss. When you've finished listening to Meirach's yarn, get back to your duties.'

Nilsson led Rannick quickly to the rooms that he had taken as his own private quarters, before the men could think about what he had said and, despite his injunction, begin to level some very searching questions at him.

'It's rather basic,' he said, by way of apology. 'There was little here when we arrived and over the years we've learned that dragging luxuries along can sometimes carry a high price while, conversely, simplicity can be quite life-enhancing.'

'I know,' Rannick said, sitting on a wooden chair and resting his arm on a table.

Nilsson looked at him carefully. 'How much *do* you know?' he asked.

'Everything,' Rannick replied.

Nilsson shook his head. 'No,' he said. 'Only what Meirach could tell you, and that's not everything by any means. He's just a stupid foot soldier.'

'Do the men know the high regard in which you hold them?' Rannick asked.

'We're bound together,' Nilsson said. 'Regard is of no account. They know I'll not betray them, that's enough.' There was a silence between the two. 'What do you want?' Nilsson asked eventually.

'What do *you* want, Captain?' Rannick replied.

Nilsson returned his gaze for a long moment, then slowly shook his head. He must risk all now. 'No,' he said softly. 'You've skill enough in the use of the power to destroy me, I'm sure, and probably many others. But you've not the skill of our former lord.'

Rannick's eyes narrowed dangerously.

'And even he needed the help of ordinary men such as myself,' Nilsson continued. 'Ordinary men who could command ordinary men and fight ordinary men, and do the many ordinary things that have to be done in the ruling of a land.'

Rannick's expression did not change. 'In the ruling of a land,' he echoed. 'Is that what you think I seek?'

'Yes,' Nilsson said, starkly.

'And what place do I see for you and your men in my scheme, Captain?'

'I'd not presume so far,' Nilsson replied cautiously.

'Though loyal service is loyal service,' Rannick suggested. 'And a loyal servant might reasonably look to loyalty and support in return? And advancement?'

Nilsson nodded.

Rannick stood up and walked over to a window. For a long time he stared out over the still busy courtyard. Nilsson watched him closely, but neither spoke nor moved.

Rannick turned but remained at the window, thus throwing himself into silhouette. 'This castle is now mine,' he said. 'You shall command it as you have hitherto but will submit to my authority.'

Nilsson, aware of the light from the window falling on him, willed himself to absolute stillness. He knew that any angry outburst against this assertion would yield him nothing but pain, or worse.

'Just like old times,' a small ironic voice whispered deep inside him.

'What are your plans?' he asked.

'You accept my authority?' Rannick said, with a faint hint of surprise in his voice.

'What are your plans?' Nilsson repeated both wilfully and blandly.

There was another long silence. Nilsson felt his expectations rising. Unlike his former master, this one *he* would be able to use.

Rannick turned back to the window. 'Those horsemen,' he said, pointing. 'Where are they going?'

Nilsson joined him by the window. Feeling your way, aren't you? he thought. As I am. 'That's Yeorson and Storran. They were going to look for Meirach. Now they're going to see what lies to the north.'

Rannick frowned. 'The Great Forest lies to the north,' he said. 'There's nothing for you there. Your future lies down the valley and beyond. Have them stand down.'

'No,' Nilsson said, categorically. Rannick swung round on him, his eyes blazing. Nilsson knew that he could not meet his gaze, and kept his eyes on the men below. 'Down the valley and beyond lies our past, and it pursues us,' he went on. 'The only way forward for us is to the north, away from here. If I order the men to stand down they'll want to know why. And if I've no answers then my authority over them will be fatally undermined.'

Rannick seemed to ponder something for a moment, then, without speaking, he turned and left the room. Both concerned and intrigued, Nilsson went after him.

As he strode along the dark passages of the castle and clattered down its stone staircases, Nilsson wiped his forehead with his hand, then wiped his hand down his jacket. He had not realized how profusely he was sweating after his confrontation. *Just* like old times, he thought again, darkly. A small twist of nausea swirled in his stomach like a caution against such levity.

He composed himself as he reached the courtyard and set a pace that kept him only slightly behind and to one side of Rannick: action that could be interpreted either as sharing a common purpose with him or maintaining a close supervision over him.

Rannick went over to Yeorson and Storran, now mounted at the head of their patrol and preparing to set off. He stopped in front of them and laid a hand on the nose of each horse. The eyes of the two horses bulged with fear, but, apart from shivering, they did not move.

'You must not go to the north,' Rannick said, his voice unexpectedly concerned.

Startled, both men looked at Nilsson.

'Listen,' he said pointedly.

'There's nothing for you there but terrible danger and then the Great Forest,' Rannick said.

'Captain?' Yeorson said with an imploring shrug.

'Lord, you must tell them,' Nilsson said. 'It's our way that all matters of import are determined by debate and acclamation. Debate that sets aside all rank and status,' he added significantly. 'If you call it then you'll be treated as one of them and, not having called it myself, I'll have no say.'

He glanced at the landing on the wall stair that he himself had spoken from. Rannick nodded. 'I understand,' he said.

As they walked towards the stair, Nilsson said, softly, 'It *is* our way, and even I have only such authority in the congress as I can muster by craft and cunning. You must bear with whatever decision is reached unless you're prepared to control everyone here by force.'

'*Must*, Captain?' Rannick said, menacingly.

251

'Must,' Nilsson replied unequivocally. 'Or there'll be bloodshed, make no mistake, and I doubt that'll serve anyone's ends.'

Rannick did not reply but walked steadily up the stone steps to the landing. Once there he moved his head from side to side a little, as if scenting the air. Nilsson found the movement peculiarly unnerving.

'Congress.'

The word was at once soft and very penetrating as it echoed round the courtyard. Small whirls of dust rose from the floor and the horses responded with alarm.

The reaction of the men to this call, however, was quite the opposite to that which had been given only a little time previously to Nilsson's call. They turned and stared, and then cautiously began to converge on the solitary figure standing part way up the stair.

There was an uneasy, unfriendly silence as the crowd gathered and finally became still.

'It's not for you to call a congress . . . Lord,' someone said. 'You're not one of us.'

Rannick did not single out the speaker, but addressed the whole group. 'And you are not what you were, now that I have arrived,' he said. 'But, that aside, am I not entitled to receive a hearing for saving your comrade Meirach?'

There was some muttering which, on balance, seemed to concede this claim.

'Men,' Rannick began. 'I drew you to this valley for a purpose, a purpose that will serve both my and your own ends. We have need of each other.'

'We need no one!' someone shouted, to some acclaim. 'We can best anyone who comes against us.'

'Is that why you live like dogs and look over your shoulders all the time?' Rannick said.

There were angry cries in response to this. Rannick swept them into silence with a scornful gesture. 'We go nowhere together if you cannot see the truth of your condition.'

Nilsson, standing part way up the stair, watched him carefully. If this speech should turn into a diatribe against his leadership he would have to kill Rannick here and now, ambitions or no. Then again, he mused, listening to the anger of the men, they might do it for him first.

'Be silent!' Again Rannick's voice carried softly yet powerfully around the courtyard, though this time it was laden with menace. The effect was immediate. 'Do you truly wish to continue as you were?' Rannick went on. 'Where would you have been now if I had not brought you here to this shelter, and to this village which has fed you so willingly, if unwittingly?'

No one ventured a reply.

'Wandering who knows where,' he announced. 'Growing increasingly weaker and more desperate with every step, your future extending no further than your next meal and your past gathering like a storm cloud behind you, growing darker and more ominous by the hour.'

Your own future will be less than you imagine if you continue in this vein, Nilsson thought, though outwardly his face was quietly serious.

'We've been through worse, and survived,' a man called. 'Could you have led us better? Tending Meirach will only give you so much credit. If you want to teach us our affairs you'll have to do better than sneer and talk poetic.'

Nilsson was grateful that the comment had been relatively good-humoured. Others might have told Rannick he had to fight if he wanted to be heard.

And they might yet.

'I'm not teaching you your affairs,' Rannick said. 'I'm telling you what you already know. You're well led, that's why you've come so far. But from here you must join with me and together we go an entirely different way.'

'We go north . . . Lord,' cried another voice. 'North and away from this place. And we have ways of choosing our own leaders.'

'You go north and you die,' Rannick said, starkly.

There was abusive denial from the crowd. 'Whatever kind of land lies up there, we'll get there and we'll cope,' was the consensus.

Rannick shook his head. 'Up there is the Great Forest. No people. Nothing. Just trees and birds and animals. There's nothing for you to live off except whatever your own labours grow or hunt down. And that's not your way, is it? But . . .' He levelled a finger at the crowd before anyone could remonstrate with this comment. 'You'll not even get so far.'

There was more denial, this time indignant.

Rannick pointed north. 'I came to your camp the other night to warn you, but I could see you were in no mood to listen so I had to let matters take their course. But beyond where you were the valley is a bad place. Nothing that does not already live there enters and survives. You saw what happened to the horse,' he added quietly.

There was an uncertain silence. 'Just some animals. Dogs probably,' someone said eventually. 'We've faced *real* dangers in our time.'

Rannick shook his head. 'You've faced men. Creatures like yourselves. But up there . . .' He left the sentence unfinished and another uncertain silence descended on the crowd.

Nilsson watched intently. His men were in an odd mood. The early return of the patrol with its account of the slaughtered horse and Meirach's disappearance, followed by the arrival of this strange person who seemingly had the protection of their leader and who

254

had brought back Meirach, cured of his burns, all conspired to unsettle them. Ironically, he thought it made them more amenable to listening.

But not *that* amenable!

'We don't have to put up with this,' came a disparaging voice. 'You want to lead us, then state your case and take your chance. We don't want to hear children's tales. You said yourself you needed us, Rannick. Well, as far as I can see, we don't need you. You're not even a good teller of tales. We've given you credit for helping Meirach but unless you've anything worthwhile to say, stand down and let us get on with our business. We need to see what's to the north for ourselves then *we'll* decide what we're going to do.'

Shouts of agreement greeted this.

Rannick did not reply for a moment, but stood with his head bowed slightly.

Then he spoke. His voice was low and menacing and it once again filled the courtyard, hissing around it like a biting winter wind. 'In deference to your captain, I have indulged you enough,' he said. 'Know this: I come in the wake of the one who once led you. I come with his power to take up his mantle and to lead you back to what was unjustly torn from you by his weakness. I do not vie for leadership with the likes of you any more than does the eagle with the sparrow. If you wish to go to the north and test the truth of my words, then go and I'll not hinder you. And if any of you are fortunate enough to return then you may try your fortune further by prostrating yourself before me and begging my forgiveness for your arrogance and folly.'

There was uproar. Still Nilsson watched. Surprisingly, the men were divided. Indeed, it was the disarray among them that prevented them from attacking Rannick. There was every conceivable reaction to his powerful declaration: disbelief, anger, confusion, fear

255

and, strangest of all, adulation. It was a reflection of Nilsson's own inner feelings when he had confronted Rannick earlier. They feel it, too, he thought. The power again.

'I leave you to choose now,' Rannick went on, his voice overtopping the din. 'Those of you who wish to go on to the greatness that was denied you, remain. Those of you who wish to follow your old way, go north and accept the consequences.' Then he turned and walked down the stairs to Nilsson, motioning him back to the castle.

As they left, the crowd, though noisy, parted for them freely.

Back in Nilsson's quarters Rannick sat silent, while Nilsson watched the continuing proceedings from his window. Various figures mounted the stairs to state their piece, some haranguing, some persuading, some reasonable, some emotional. He listened as all the minor jealousies and differences in his troop came to the surface. A wave of anger passed through him. You'll blow some wind now, won't you, you dogs? he thought. Now that you're well fed and housed again. But it was Nilsson this and Nilsson that, look after us, Captain, only a few weeks ago.

The anger passed as quickly as it had come, to be replaced by some satisfaction. He had effectively manoeuvred Rannick into calling the congress, and the outcome could only be an improvement. A rowdy congress was essential from time to time and, being formally absent from it, he could view this one with unusual equanimity.

And, too, it had revealed interesting details about this new saviour. He was particularly amused to hear Rannick lying about luring them into the valley: a politician's device if ever he heard one. Whatever chance had brought them here, it had nothing to do with Rannick, he was certain. Even his former lord would not have claimed such skill; indeed, he had feared chance happenings.

Then there was the sweat that Rannick had surreptitiously wiped from his brow as they had stepped out of the courtyard and into the shade of the castle interior. Good human traits, he thought. They confirmed his earlier conclusion that though Rannick could indisputably use the power, he was still just another scheming, grasping mortal; at heart, his own kind.

Definitely now he would bind himself to this man.

There was a roar from the courtyard.

Chapter 19

'I don't think those men are tithe gatherers at all.'

Standing in Rannick's dishevelled garden, Gryss felt his insides go cold. Marna's words were perhaps only the petulant grumblings of an over-sensitive young woman disturbed by recent events, but their effect was like that of a gentle leaf-stirring breeze which tilts an aging tree that final fraction too far and sends it crashing down, seemingly without apparent reason.

'What makes you say that?' he asked, struggling to keep his voice from reflecting the turmoil within him that had abruptly been released.

Marna pulled a wry face. 'I don't know,' she said. 'Their appearance. Their behaviour. Everything. They're a shifty-looking lot, not to say nasty-looking. Why would the King hire a motley crew of foreigners like that to collect the tithe? And that . . . Saddre . . . didn't really seem to know what he was doing when he was going round the barn with you. Did you see the way he kept looking at that captain for instructions?' She began to warm to her revelations. 'And why did everything have to be taken to the castle to be checked?'

Gryss gestured to stop this outpouring. 'I don't know,' he conceded. 'But soldiers are soldiers, Marna. They're not chosen for their looks, and I've no idea where the King gets them from or how he decides who does what. All I've ever seen are soldiers on ceremonial parades and on guard outside public buildings, and that was a long time ago. And I didn't speak to any of them; they could all have been foreigners for anything I know, even then.'

Marna looked at him, unconvinced and waiting.

'And they can't go wandering about the country in their fancy city uniforms, can they? They're bound to wear more rough and ready clothes when they're out in the field,' he offered.

'Rough and ready!' Marna echoed with a snort. 'You and me are rough and ready . . .' Farnor glanced down at his clothes indignantly. '*They* look more like beggars than soldiers. They should have some kind of uniform. And what about Saddre? And hauling the tithe all over the valley?'

Gryss scowled. He never could handle this girl, and she was the very devil when she started.

'Saddre's just an army clerk,' he said crossly. 'Nilsson told us that.'

Marna's lip curled.

'And I've no idea why they've had the tithe taken to the castle,' Gryss went on, struggling unsuccessfully to keep the desperation from his voice. 'They said it was the law and that there might be inspectors—'

'Examiners,' Marna corrected.

'Examiners, then,' Gryss growled, 'coming to check up on them.'

Marna's expression indicated that she was confirmed in her suspicions rather than unburdened of them by Gryss's explanation.

'And if they were coming to collect a tithe why didn't they bring any carts, for heaven's sake?' she added, in what was intended to be a final blow, until another occurred to her. 'And why didn't they have produce from any other villages with them?'

Gryss gave a small sigh of defeat. Marna's questions merely served to clarify ill-formed thoughts of his own. He had been too concerned with the forgotten niceties of procedures, and with his hopes that these men would quietly move on, to stand back and look at what was happening – or so he pleaded to himself in mitigation.

Or perhaps he was just getting too old!

'I can't answer any of your questions, Marna,' he said. 'And I don't know who could. I certainly can't ask them of the Captain.'

He stepped over the broken gate and set off down the narrow lane. It was darker than it had been, the hint of rain to come that had hung in the bright morning had become a threat as they had pursued their examination of Rannick's cottage. Now the sky was grey, and a distinct dampness pervaded the air.

As they walked along the lane, the sound of intermittent raindrops striking the surrounding foliage became evident. Marna led the way, followed by Gryss. Farnor watched them both as they wended their way through the weeds and grasses tangled across the path.

A raindrop struck his hand, sharp and clear in its coldness.

He wished his thoughts were as clear. It did not help that Gryss, the senior village elder, was openly uncertain, all too human. And Marna's biting bluntness, as ever, held no comfort. Her questions added their uncontrolled momentum to his thoughts about Rannick and the gatherers, and the creature that had killed the sheep and now, seemingly, a *horse*, and which *he* had actually touched in some way.

Despite all that had happened since the hunt, the memory of that touch persisted; foul, clinging . . . and growing.

Farnor found he was hunching up his shoulders after the manner of Gryss. With an effort he straightened up and made them relax, but it was not easy.

Somewhere there was an end to this confusion, surely? An end to this hurt. The word came unbidden and surprised him. Hurt? Who was being hurt?

261

We all are, he realized. Both the creature and the gatherers were intrusions from outside, and both brought disruption and anxiety in their wake. And what was anxiety if it wasn't a hurt? It marred the present and clouded the future. Yet it came to him with this revelation that what was truly disturbing him was the thought, hovering like a tiny, distant light at the fringes of his mind, that he could help in some way if he could but see it.

He paused. There was a certainty about this that set it aside from any general, vague wishing everything was all right again. But it was elusive, also, and though it remained with him it refused to make itself further known.

He looked at the retreating figures of Marna and Gryss, and frowned. They seemed different. As if the confusion and the hurt that they, like he, bore were wrapped about them like a cloying mist. Part of him reached out to clear the way for them and allow them to walk unhindered.

Both of them stopped and turned round.

'Sorry?' Marna said.

'Did you say something?' Gryss said at the same time.

Farnor suddenly felt a little dizzy, but he managed to avoid staggering by crouching down and fiddling with his shoe.

'No,' he said. 'My shoelace snagged a bramble.'

Marna reached up to her face as if to brush away a stray hair and Gryss shook his head slightly. Then a gust of wind stirred the trees and threw a light splatter of newly hoarded raindrops on to them and they set off again, briskly.

There was an odd companionship in their common flight from the rain and, to Farnor, it seemed that they had passed some unseen boundary.

'I think they're nothing more than bandits,' Marna said, as prosaically as if she were simply just passing the time of day. 'I think they came here by accident and—'

'Shush,' Gryss said urgently, moving his hand up and down as if to beat down her enthusiasm like a boisterous pup. They had come to the end of the pathway and he glanced along the lane as they joined it. 'Don't say things like that too loudly,' he said.

But Marna was barely listening, she had formed the words and they were too potent to remain unspoken. She did lower her voice a little, however.

'I think they're . . . bandits,' she said again. 'I think they found us by accident and when they realized we thought they were gatherers they decided to make the most of it. I'll wager they're not checking our tithe, they're eating it.'

Gryss grimaced. He did not want to hear this. 'I'm not saying you're right or wrong,' he said. 'I can't pretend to be happy about these people, but, please, *please* don't say such things.'

Marna turned surprised eyes on him. 'Why not?' she demanded.

'Think, Marna,' Gryss said, a touch wearily, and shaking her arm a little. 'Think. If they're really gatherers, then you're defaming the King's servants and who knows what kind of an offence that might be? And if they're not, if they're bandits as you call them, you're telling them we know who they are and what will they do then? Probably drop any pretence at being a legal force, and that might put all of us in danger.'

Marna's brow furrowed. 'I didn't think,' she said, after a long pause.

'You certainly didn't,' Gryss replied, though he added immediately, by way of consolation, 'Not that you're alone in that.' He looked fretful. 'Have you spoken to anyone else about your . . . ideas?'

Marna shook her head.

'Good,' Gryss said, in some relief. 'Don't.' He turned to Farnor. 'We must keep discussion like this between the three of us. If you hear anyone else talking the same, just listen and take note, but say nothing. Do you understand?'

Both Marna and Farnor nodded, then they spoke simultaneously. 'But we've got to do something.'

Concern filled Gryss's face. 'Yes, we have,' he said. 'But not until we know a lot more than at present.'

'I could go downland and over the hill to the next village.' Marna's suggestion came out with a purposefulness that indicated that it was no new thought.

Gryss's eyes widened in horror. He levelled a stern finger at her. 'You just stay where you are, young woman,' he said. 'For one thing, that's a good few days' walk for someone who knows the way, and for another, the last thing we need now is someone like you doing wild-headed tricks like that and creating a great stir in the village.'

'I won't tell anyone,' Marna said earnestly.

'Not even your father, I presume,' Gryss retorted sharply.

Marna looked flustered.

'No, you hadn't thought about that either, had you?' Gryss went on. 'You do nothing, either of you. Nothing at all. Except keep your eyes and ears open and let me know whatever you see and hear.'

The rain suddenly began to fall more heavily, putting an end to the conversation, and the three of them scurried back to Gryss's cottage.

'Hello, old thing,' Marna said, crouching down and stroking Gryss's dog as it emerged to greet them. It wagged its stub of a tail briefly, turned and barked at Farnor, and then retreated back to its current lair.

'It's getting more like you every day, Gryss,' Marna said, smiling as she stood up.

Gryss flicked a brusque hand towards the back room. 'In there,' he said. 'And less of your cheek.'

Gryss placed his two guests opposite one another at the long table, and, unusually, sat himself at the head of it. He laid his hands on theirs.

'I want you two to promise me, now, that you'll keep silent about what we've discussed today,' he said.

'We already have,' Farnor protested lightly.

Gryss shook his head. 'No Farnor, this is not some game, some sunset watch prank. This is serious and I want your solemn word that not only will you not tell anyone about what we've been discussing, but that you won't do anything . . . unusual . . . without talking to me about it first.'

His manner was uncharacteristically severe, and the two young people watched him in silence.

'You're frightening me, Gryss,' Marna said, after a moment.

'Good,' Gryss replied, though not unkindly. 'Because you frightened me with your foolishness. Running off to the next village, indeed.'

Marna shrugged apologetically, but Gryss continued before she could speak.

'And you're more than capable of doing it, so don't protest otherwise,' he said. 'You'd have got yourself in a rare pickle wandering the countryside, lost.' He shook his head, irritated by his own distraction. 'I've a great fondness for you, Marna, you know that. And I admire your independence and . . . your rightheadedness. But you're too impulsive for your own good at times, and while we don't know what's going on, we need thought, not impulsiveness. Now I

265

want your promise, especially, that you'll do nothing foolish.'

'What about him?' Marna said, nodding towards Farnor in an attempt to deflect Gryss's intention.

'Farnor and I . . . understand one another,' Gryss replied.

Marna looked at Farnor, and then back at Gryss. Her eyes narrowed. 'What's going on?' she said suspiciously.

Gryss closed his eyes. When he opened them, he met Farnor's worried gaze. It had occurred to him to make some flippant comment in an attempt to fob Marna off. But Farnor's expression reflected not only his pain, but also a peer's deeper knowledge of Marna's character. And he, the elder and thus outsider, would have to accept that judgement.

'We don't know,' he said quietly, looking straight at her. 'Something . . . strange . . . is happening up at the castle, or in the woods beyond, but . . .' He gave an unhappy smile and he looked around the room as if searching for inspiration.

'It's not just to do with the gatherers, Marna.' Farnor's voice forestalled him. 'It began before they came, and it's to do with me.'

Marna started at his voice. Not so much at the unexpected interruption but at the appeal in it. Her expression was suddenly uncertain. Gryss sat very still and watched them both intently.

Farnor went on, some inner need forcing his tale from him. 'Something's happened . . . perhaps still happening . . . to me. Something to do with whatever . . . creature's . . . been worrying the sheep. And I think it's something to do with Rannick as well.'

Marna threw a quick glance at Gryss for confirmation but his face was impassive.

'What do you mean, happening?' she asked.

Farnor grimaced, then told her hesitantly of his apparent contact with the creature, and of Rannick's strange behaviour.

Marna looked again at Gryss, hoping that his enigmatic expression would suddenly become a mischievous smile and the whole scene end in boisterous laughter. But there was not a vestige of lightness there.

'I've no explanation,' Farnor concluded. 'Neither has Gryss. All I know is that it frightens me.' He looked flustered. His words gave no measure of what he was feeling. They seemed flat and empty; incongruous, almost. But Marna saw the look in his eyes, full of naked pain and distress; more eloquent than any number of words.

She was silent for a moment, then, 'It's all true, isn't it?' she said nervously, looking at Gryss.

The old man nodded. He was quietly reproaching himself for failing to notice the burgeoning maturity of these village 'youngsters'. Marna took a deep breath and when she spoke, her voice, though unsteady, was gentle and full of concern. 'I can't make any sense out of any of this,' she said. 'And I think you must both be misunderstanding something, somewhere. But, whatever it's all about it's hurting Farnor and I'll help if I can.'

Slowly she wrapped her arms about herself, more in a protective gesture than as if she were cold. 'All this, *and* the gatherers,' she said.

'All this *and* the gatherers,' Gryss echoed. He put his hand on hers and looked into her eyes. 'Farnor's trusted you with this tale,' he said. 'You mustn't . . .'

'I know,' she said, before he could finish, her voice edgy. 'I'm like a mole in a trap. I walked in of my own accord and there's no way out.'

'No,' Gryss said anxiously. 'No. You're free to walk away. All I . . . we . . . ask is that you keep this to yourself. Tell no one. At least until . . .' He hesitated.

'Something else happens,' Farnor said bleakly.

Rannick stood up and joined Nilsson at the window as the noise from the courtyard filled the room.

'What have they decided?' he asked.

Nilsson craned forward. 'It looks as if there's about twenty getting ready to ride out,' he said. 'What will you do to them?'

The question had been a deliberate risk, and he sensed Rannick's angry reaction. Nevertheless, he turned away from the window and met his gaze squarely.

Rannick made no denial of the implicit accusation. 'The north of the valley is a bad place,' he said, coldly.

Nilsson knew it would be foolish, not to say, dangerous to press his presumption further, but certain things had to be said.

'Mainly sheep down there,' he said, indicating the courtyard with a nod of his head. 'Followers, not leaders for the most part. But they're *all* good fighters. Fighters with a history of fighting *together*. It'd be serious if we lost too many. It would wreak havoc with morale and substantially reduce our operational strength.'

The hubbub from the courtyard filled the room.

'The north of the valley is a bad place,' Rannick repeated, his face impassive. 'Sheep get worried all the time. If they go there, they must take the risks that lie there.'

Nilsson nodded. 'Let's hope they get sheared rather than slaughtered,' he said still keeping his eyes on Rannick. It was as much of a plea for his men as he dared make, and he became immediately brisk. 'Come on, let's go down and see what the mood is.'

'You go,' Rannick said. 'The men are your affair, not mine. I want nothing to do with them. Just ensure that they understand the realities of their new command. I will tolerate no dissension or opposition, but those who follow me I will lead to power and wealth, to their true destinies.'

'And those who don't follow you?' Nilsson asked.

'Should stand well aside, or look to die,' Rannick said, simply, turning back to the window again.

The courtyard was in noisy disarray when Nilsson reached it. Those who had decided to venture north were reloading the pack animals with reduced amounts of supplies while those who were now remaining at the castle were removing their horses from the column, helping with the reloading or just standing around watching. A few residual arguments were continuing about the rights and wrongs of the decision reached.

'Congress is finished,' Nilsson said as he reached the more heated discussions. 'Each man stands by his decision. No reproaches. Whatever happens, we stand or fall together.'

Spots of rain began to splatter on to the stone floor to form a muddy starscape.

To Nilsson's relief, if hardly to his surprise, he found that both Yeorson and Storran had decided to remain. It was probably their decision that had resulted in the final patrol being as small as it was. Still, he thought fretfully, we can't afford to lose this many.

But there was nothing he could do, he knew. His authority was vested in him through the congress of the men and, while he could manipulate it, to attempt to overrule it would be to undermine his own position, perhaps fatally. This group had decided freely to scout a route to the north and he could not oppose them. All he could do was hope that whatever Rannick intended would not be too disastrous.

At the head of the column he found Haral. That was both fortunate and unfortunate: unfortunate in that

Haral was a good man, fierce, determined, straightforward and definitely not a man to be casually discarded. But, equally, he saw things for what they were and would not needlessly risk either himself or the men under his command. He was brave enough to know when to fight and when to run. It gave Nilsson some assurance.

He waited until the confusion had died down a little, then he put two fingers in his mouth and whistled loudly. The courtyard gradually fell silent, and all attention turned towards him.

The rain became heavier and the muddy stars joined to become a pattern of shining stones.

'You've had your debate and made your decision,' he said. 'You might be right, you might be wrong. So might we who're staying back. But whatever, we still belong together, so I'll be sending out smaller patrols to keep your line of retreat open and, if need arises, to act as rearguard.' He stepped back a few paces so that he could see the full column. He could not speak of his forebodings, but at least he could counsel caution.

'I don't know what there is out there,' he went on. 'But I want no risks taken, nor any stupid heroics. You ride equipped for action at all times. You ride in close order and you camp in close order. And you post sentries in pairs.' There were one or two wry faces pulled at these orders. He singled them out. 'You getting yourself killed is bad enough, but you know what'll happen if you get someone else killed because of your stupidity.' His voice was soft, but more intimidating than any amount of raucous shouting.

Still addressing the whole column, he said. 'Haral, do your best to get everyone back in one piece. If any of them choose to ignore the orders I've just given . . .' He drew his finger across his throat.

Haral gave him a casual salute then the column was

on its way. Nilsson followed them to the gate and stood there for some time watching until they disappeared in the undulating countryside, itself slowly disappearing into grey swathes of wind-blown rain.

He became aware of a presence behind him.

'A horse, Captain.'

He turned. It seemed to him that Rannick was untouched by the rain, and again that he was being buffeted by winds in another place. There was an eerie sensation of movement about him even though he was motionless.

'You startled me, Lord,' he said.

'A horse,' Rannick repeated.

'Certainly, Lord,' Nilsson said. 'But, with respect, they don't seem to take to you.'

'They obey me,' Rannick replied. 'That's sufficient.'

Nilsson signalled to Dessane. 'Escort the Lord to the stables, Arven. Let him pick whichever horse he wishes.' He turned back to Rannick. 'Do you need a pack horse, Lord?'

Rannick did not reply, but motioned Dessane to lead on.

Nilsson watched as the men in the courtyard moved away as Rannick approached, forming a wide pathway for him. Stand well aside, or look to die, he thought.

Chapter 20

Haral's group made good progress. It helped, of course, that several of the men had travelled this way before, and that the trail was well marked. He kept Nilsson's injunction at the forefront of his mind however. He didn't like the smell of this so-called, *Lord* Rannick with his claims to have the power like their old lord. That he'd doubt until he'd seen it for himself, but he had no doubts that the man was treacherous and self-seeking and was up to no good, and that he would undoubtedly have something in mind for the group as it moved further into the forest.

Inherit our master's mantle, he sneered inwardly. You'll need more than fancy words if you're looking to inherit anything other than a shroud, meddling with us. Half a chance and I, for one, will gladly cut your throat for the trouble you've already caused.

And, yet, it couldn't be denied that there was something familiar about his . . . manner . . . his attitude . . . ?

And Nilsson was no man's fool. He wouldn't be taken in lightly by some market trickster. And he'd been closer than many to the Lord. And to Rannick.

Suppose this Rannick could use the power? He was obviously a healer of some skill, judging by what he'd done for Meirach, and the Lord had been a healer when it suited him. It was an intriguing thought, and Haral found it fanning a glow into embers that he had thought long dead. With someone like that in charge you could do well for yourself. He savoured again the near-forgotten feeling of riding forth, tall in the saddle, and looking down at a population that knew that your every word was law and that your arm could punish faults summarily and without appeal.

Good days. It would be truly splendid to have them back again. Provided you didn't get involved with internal army politics and did as you were told, almost anything you wanted was available for the taking. Life had been good indeed.

With a snort he dismissed his daydream. They were days that were gone for ever. Rannick no more had the power than he did. That kind of thing wasn't given to ordinary folk. It was given to those who already had power and wealth. That was the way of things. All that lay ahead of him and the others now was more of what they had been doing for the past years: wandering, stealing, acting as bodyguards for some petty warlord here, fighting as mercenaries for some inconsequential lord there; never knowing where the next night's bed might be, or when they might next eat. And, always, looking over their shoulders for those who were pursuing them. It was a bitter prospect and one that he did not choose to dwell on whenever it came to mind.

To hell with Rannick and the disturbance he'd caused.

He looked around. The rain was falling relentlessly, and cold water which had been seeping around the collar of his leather cape for some time was now beginning to seep through the seams.

It helped him turn his attention back to matters of the moment. Whatever, if anything, was amiss in this forest, it would be foolish to spend too much time in idle musing about either the past or the future.

Though they had made good progress they were still some way from the place in which they had camped previously, and there was little point in forcing the pace in an attempt to reach it. He called a halt in a small clearing and within minutes tents had been pitched and fires coaxed into smoky life.

Despite Nilsson's orders, there was some resistance to the performance of sentry duty. Haral quelled it scornfully with, 'You want this Rannick to cut your throat while you're snoring and then go back and take charge of all that loot, claiming to be the lord returned, and the only possible protection against the curse of the ancient forest?'

The sentries took up their positions as the camp gradually fell silent.

Haral performed a brief circuit of them before he too retreated to his tent.

'I don't know what this Rannick's up to,' he told them. 'But it's for his good, not ours. He's playing for some big prize of his own and I don't think he'll scruple to kill a few of us if it'll help him, especially as we've defied him. He's not stupid and this is his country, so keep out of sight, keep your backs covered and keep your eyes and ears open.'

Now!

It was released again. A wordless command had given it his unfettered will. Find, kill . . .

The thought released old savours into its mouth.

Good . . .

It followed the trail through the damp, lush rain-scented darkness. A trail, faint at first and then glaringly vivid, marked by that old, familiar scent.

There was no taint of the old watchful enemy in it but reflexes, ancient in its breed before it had been fashioned thus, made its every movement silent. Each footstep tested before being taken. Each slight noise a cause for deep stillness and waiting.

It felt lesser creatures sensing its passage and falling fearfully silent, though a few scurried away frantically, luring part of its deeper nature after them. But it could not be deflected. A special prey was to be sought tonight. The old prey. The best prey.

And it was there. Ahead. Mingling with the scent of fire and bruised foliage and trampled earth.

Good . . .

Caution, though. True enemies they might not be, but dangerous and subtle they were. Watch. Listen. Scent the air.

Were there, after all, tangling nets and sharp points silent all about? Was there that hint, acrid in the rich dampness, of fearful, expectant watching . . . waiting?

No. All was as it had been told. All was stillness and forest, save for the silent, sleeping lairs that did not belong. And the fire . . .

And . . .

There, alone. Crouching in the shelter of a tree, head nodding, lulled by the steady drip of rainwater falling from the branches above.

Down, low. Soft and silent through the damp grasses.

Nearer.

Nearer.

Drip, drip.

Then an ancient malevolence wilfully bred into it. The need for prey to be alive.

And screaming.

Drip, drip.

It growled. Soft, but low and frightful.

The prey jerked awake at the ominous rumble, eyes bewildered. They looked around. And then forward. Slowly they focused. And widened. The mouth opened, a black void in the firelit night.

And the scream began. Drawing it forward faster and faster as its intensity grew . . .

Claws extended . . .

Jaws foamed . . .

Farnor jerked bolt upright in his bed, eyes wide and mouth gaping in imitation of the face that had just rushed towards him, growing larger and larger until it had filled his entire vision. His mouth ran with saliva and his skin bristled with unholy desires. He spat out the imagined contents of his mouth with desperate and disgusting urgency, then he plunged forward and buried his face in the blankets, wiping his still sodden mouth to and fro frantically until it was dry and his lips were raw and matted with hairs.

Slowly he swung upright, then crashed back down on to his pillow, his breath coming in laboured gasps. His hand shook violently as he reached out to strike the small lantern by his bed.

After two clattering attempts he succeeded, and it bloomed gently into life.

Its welcome and familiar light filled his bedroom and began to melt away the vivid horror of the last few seconds. Began to melt it away until it had only the intensity of a nightmare.

A nightmare. His breathing began to ease. He hadn't had a nightmare in years.

This was a nightmare, wasn't it?

But it was only a flimsy token of resistance against the grim certainty that stood stark in his mind.

It had not been a nightmare. It had been the creature. He had been with it. He had *been* it. Been it as it stalked the damp forest in search of the prey it had been sent to kill. He had felt its every subtle, muscular movement, its formidable power, its every desire. He shuddered and wrapped his arms about himself at the memory.

He felt sick. He wanted to call out to his parents as he had when he had been a child. Wanted the solidity of their gentle reassurance and smiling understanding to dismiss into nothingness the tortured vapours that had risen to assail him in his defenceless sleep. Wanted them to turn his room and his bed back again into the haven that it really was.

But he could not. Despite the childish clamour rising from within him, he knew it was not possible. Whatever he was now he was no longer that child. Those old reassurances had been a part of his journey to here and they belonged to another time. Now his cry would not be that of their child, it would be that of a man. And alarm and concern would tinge any reassurance.

And questions. Questions which he would not be able to answer, or be able to answer only with more lies.

There must be no more lies. That he knew now. So there must be silence.

He gazed at the beamed ceiling with its well-mapped cracks and stains and shadows. His breathing had eased and, somewhat to his surprise, he found his quaking spirit bolstered by a resolve. An unclear resolve, admittedly, but a resolve nonetheless. One framed through the years, had he known it, by the love that had given him those parental reassurances and made his cracked and twisted ceiling – and, indeed, everything about him – into an impregnable fortress capable of withstanding all ills. Until such time as he should learn that only he could be his own fortress.

He felt suddenly alone. He had his parents and Gryss and, unexpectedly, Marna, who would be a truly staunch ally, he knew. But still he was alone. Yet even as he realized this, so his fear lessened. Somehow, this last . . . contact? . . . vision? . . . by its very intensity had made him understand, and to some extent perhaps even accept, that he was not some inadvertent spectator of a strange and unfolding happening, but a player in it, whether he willed it or no.

It was like going to Gryss with the toothache, he supposed. Thinking about it was worse than being there

278

– usually. The 'usually' made him frown mockingly to himself: toothache was perhaps a bad analogy.

He sat up, needlessly wiped his mouth again and then took a drink from the beaker of water that stood next to the lantern. The pool of saliva glistening on his blanket caught his eye. He grimaced. It was disgusting. He shuddered as he remembered the sensation almost of drowning as he had woken to find his mouth so gorged.

Then more prosaic considerations intervened and, without thinking what he was doing, he threw some water on the viscous mass. It was like a purifying blessing. Then he folded the blanket around it and rubbed it vigorously until it became just a damp patch. It would soon dry. He felt cleaner.

He doused the lantern and lay back. Plans formed in his mind. He would seek out Gryss tomorrow and tell him what had happened. He would suggest that Gryss and he visit the castle on some pretext – perhaps to look at the sick, perhaps to see if they needed supplies – and there they would look and listen.

And Marna? Should she be told?

Yes, he decided. Marna must know. Marna had somehow become a part of this.

As he drifted into sleep, he reviewed the events of his . . . contact? . . . with the creature so he could order his telling for Gryss in the morning. He went over it several times, though each time it became more fragmented as intervals of sleep intervened.

Then, at the end, a faint voice inside him whispered softly to him that one day he would have to face this creature. And that he would have to kill it, or be killed by it.

It was a fearful thought, but it was faint and distant and had no power to disturb the ponderous, rolling momentum of his need for rest.

Farnor slept.

There was uproar in the camp.

'What the devil's going on?' Haral thundered as he emerged from his tent, a torch in one hand and a sword in the other. He kicked a nearby figure. 'Get that fire built up, and fast.' There was no protest at the blow.

Other figures were tumbling from the circled tents.

'Guard the perimeter!' Haral bellowed.

A sentry ran over to him. He was wide-eyed and trembling, and his voice was almost hysterical. 'It grabbed him. Just appeared and grabbed him. I've never seen anything like it . . .'

Haral threw his torch to someone and, seizing the front of the sentry's coat, pulled the man up on to his toes. 'Get a hold of yourself, Bryn. What grabbed who?' he demanded angrily.

'Over there,' the man gasped. 'Mirek. It grabbed Mirek. Dragged him off. Into the trees there. He was screaming.'

Haral's face darkened and he pushed the man urgently in the direction he was pointing. They ran across the small clearing.

'He was here,' Bryn said. 'Leaning against this tree. Then this . . . thing . . . appeared.' His hands reached up as if to cover his ears. 'He started screaming. And this thing picked him up like he was some kid's toy and dragged him off . . . over there.'

There were several men with them now, some with torches, some with swords and axes. They were all talking at once.

'Shut up!' Haral shouted as he moved in the direction that Bryn had indicated. The sentry caught his arm. 'No, Haral,' he said. 'It's no use. He's finished.' He began to stammer. 'He didn't scream long after it'd taken him into the trees.'

Haral looked at him, his face a mixture of anger and alarm.

'And it was big. Very big,' Bryn went on, still gripping his arm. 'You can't go after it. Not at night.'

Haral stared into the darkness and then back at Bryn. The man was frightened, but he was no coward and he would not have stood idly by while a friend was killed. He glanced around at the growing crowd around him. 'I told you to secure the perimeter,' he said menacingly.

'Against what?' someone said.

Haral sent him staggering backwards with a single blow. The bulk of the crowd scattered to do Haral's bidding.

Some of his anger thus released, Haral's thoughts began to quieten. 'What the devil was it, Bryn?' he asked, tugging his arm free. 'And what happened?'

The man gesticulated vaguely. 'I don't know,' he said. 'We'd set up so we could see one another. But I didn't see . . . it . . . coming. It must have come low through that undergrowth there, stalking on its belly . . . until . . .' His voice faded.

'Until?' Haral prompted.

'Until Mirek saw it,' Bryn went on, licking his lips. 'Then he screamed and . . .' His arms shot forward. 'It seemed to rise up for ever out of the ground.' He made a grabbing movement with his clawed hands. 'It was so fast.' His hands twitched towards his ears again as if to cover them. 'And he was screaming. Screaming when it grabbed him. Screaming when it dragged him off into the trees. Then it went quiet.' He looked at Haral, his face drawn, and asked him his own question. 'What in hell's name was it?' he said hoarsely.

Haral put a steadying hand on his shoulder. 'You saw it,' he said, bleakly. 'How big was it? What did it look like? A dog? A bear? A boar, maybe? What?'

Bryn shook his head and held out his hand at waist

height. 'Like a big dog . . . probably,' he said after a moment. He hesitated, frowning. 'But like a cat, too, the way it moved. And it was strong. Very strong. It didn't even falter when it picked Mirek up. Just like he was no weight at all. And he wasn't little, was he?'

'Is that all you saw?'

'It was over too quickly, Haral. I only got a fleeting glimpse. A movement, then the screaming, then . . .' Bryn grimaced. 'I saw its teeth, though. Jaws like a mantrap.'

Haral peered into the darkness again as if still contemplating pursuing the creature. Bryn shook his head.

'No,' he said. 'Believe me. Even if you manage to find it, it'll be long too late for Mirek and it'll kill you before you can raise your sword arm.'

'What the devil kind of a creature could have done that?' Haral muttered, half to himself.

'The same as killed that horse,' Bryn replied. 'If anyone still wants to sleep, I think the rest of us had best double our guard and close in so we're all visible.'

But no one wanted anything but vengeance and the recovery of Mirek when the initial turmoil and alarm had died down.

Haral struggled to beat down the anger that was rapidly gathering momentum. 'No,' he shouted. 'Not in the dark. Whatever this thing is, it's big, it's strong, it hunts at night, it's on its own territory and it's not frightened of people. You want to go against it, you go on your own.'

There was some argument but in the end, by a combination of reason and force of personality, Haral had his way.

'As soon as the light breaks we'll go, but not before,' he said.

The rest of the night was eerie and fretful with the

sound of restless sleepers and muttered debates as a double guard prowled the clearing.

Haral sat by the camp fire, his mood growing darker and more ominous as if in opposition to the approaching light of the dawn. One of the men snatched like a sparrow by a hawk. Battle chance was bad enough: a stray arrow, an unlucky sword stroke, a missed footing; but this was peculiarly unsupportable. His men as prey for some animal!

Something would die for it. Unafraid of people this creature might well be. But that was now. Tomorrow it would be a wiser animal by far before they killed it. And kill it they would, no matter how strong and fast it was.

Chapter 21

Daylight came reluctantly the following day, shouldering its way through a grey, rain-filled sky. The camp, however, needed little rousing and the men emerged into the morning dampness grim-faced and purposeful as if the spirit of Haral's vigil by the fire had passed to all of them.

Haral sent three riders back to the castle with the news of what had happened and of the intended hunt. 'Keep together,' was his sole injunction. He was going to say, 'Tell Nilsson to expect this creature's head for a trophy,' but a frisson of superstition bubbled up to stop him.

The remainder of the group set off along the trail left by the creature. It was wide and conspicuous for some considerable distance, marked by crushed grass and broken branches, and then also by splashes of blood.

Soon the rain began again, steady and vertical at first and then whirling hither and thither as a strong breeze began to blow. Untypically, though, grumbling was minimal and the line of men, quietly leading their horses, moved on in almost complete silence.

The trail led them steadily upwards for quite a way, but it levelled off eventually, keeping well away from the edge of the forest. The wind grew stronger and such conversation as the men wished to have became almost impossible in the din of the waving branches above them.

Bryn moved forward alongside Haral. 'Where do you think this thing could live?' he shouted.

Haral shrugged. 'If it's as big as you say, it probably

lives in a cave somewhere,' he replied off-handedly. Then he frowned and stopped.

'What's the matter?' Bryn asked.

'Something's wrong,' Haral answered after a moment, wiping the rain from his face. 'This trail's like a city road. A blind man could follow it. It hasn't stopped once to—' He hesitated. 'To eat. In fact it doesn't seem to have stopped anywhere, either to adjust its . . . load . . . or even to recover its breath.'

'I told you it was strong,' Bryn said. 'Perhaps it's female. Taking food back to its young.'

Haral's frown deepened. It was not a happy thought. A female with young would be *really* dangerous. Still, however dangerous it was there were enough well-armed men here to deal with it. He let Bryn's suggestion blow away in the noisy wind.

Then the trees began to close in on them, reducing the grey light to an eerie gloaming. With the wind angrily buffeting the canopy overhead but little or nothing blowing along the forest floor, Haral began to feel as if he were moving into some strange underground vault. The steady rain above reached them spasmodically, in large-dropped cascades which chilled and soaked whoever they struck.

The change made Haral uneasy.

He glanced back at his men. They were reflecting his own concern, peering intently into the surrounding gloom and instinctively closing ranks. He said nothing, but kept moving forward. There was very little under-growth here, but the leaf litter was thick and still showed quite clearly the careless passage of the animal.

The trees closed in further and became taller, height-ening Haral's impression that they were walking through the cellar of some great castle which soared high above them. The sound of the wind rattling the tops of the trees echoed down, but around them was only stillness.

Then the wind stopped. It did not quietly fade away, so that like the moment of sleep its passing went unnoticed. It stopped abruptly, as if a great hand had seized it. And with it the rain, too, stopped. The damp silence gradually filled with the sound of innumerable raindrops falling from weary, weighted leaves on to the sodden ground below.

Without command, the column stopped also. The men gazed upwards as if expecting to see some cause for this sudden silence.

Haral did the same, then he looked around at the closely spaced trees fading into the distant gloom. His unease grew. Probably because it was a good place for an ambush by men who knew how to use such terrain, he decided. He tried to reassure himself further. It was no hunting ground for a large animal; too little game, too little cover.

His horse whinnied, making him start slightly. As he reached up to comfort it, a movement caught his eye. His head jerked round. Even as he was turning, he saw that Bryn's description had been accurate. Moving so swiftly that he could make out little of its appearance, a black shadow emerged from the darkness and launched itself at the last man in the column.

Haral had scarcely taken a step forward, and his cry was still forming in his throat, as he saw the man tossed effortlessly into the air and dragged off into the trees. The man's nerve-tearing scream struck him like an axe blow.

Some reflex made him cry out, 'Hold the horses!' as he threw his reins to Bryn and began to run along the column.

But few heard the command. Panic struck the rear of the column immediately with a force greater than that of the attacker. The last horse, now untended and screaming like an echo of its erstwhile rider, galloped off into the gloom while men and horses scattered in all directions in a belated attempt to avoid the long-past attack.

Shouting, 'Hold the horses! Hold the horses!' Haral snatched a spear from the nearest horse and set about his panicking men with the shaft, following the established battlefield principle of ousting one terror by means of a bigger one.

'Form up, you dogs! We've got to get after it,' he roared as he laid about him. 'Form up!'

He had some effect despite the gloom and the close-set tree trunks. One man was knocked down by a horse. He staggered to his feet, dazed, then began to run away from the column. Haral swore and, slithering on the wet leafy ground, set off after him.

He took little catching and Haral's angry hand seizing the scruff of his neck sent his feet flying into the air before he crashed down on to the ground. Haral did not wait for him to recover, but maintaining the grip on his collar prepared to start dragging him back to the column.

Then he saw darkness rushing towards him. He heard a stomach-churning rumble of a growl and heard again Bryn's words, 'Jaws like a mantrap'. He stood frozen with terror. Then, somehow, as blazing red eyes formed in the approaching shadow he dropped down flat, landing violently on top of his charge.

With a winding impact the creature's foot landed between his shoulder blades as it ran over him and he rolled over in panic, flailing his arms wildly. The impetus brought him on to his belly, and as he looked up he saw the shadow strike a man as he was mounting his horse and knock both man and horse to the ground.

Haral groped for his spear then staggered to his feet and lurched forward, almost on all fours in his desperation to reach his men. He heard the scream as the second victim was dragged away; heard the shouts of the men, angry and fearful, and the terrified shrieking of the horses. He saw men slipping on the treacherous ground; spears launched to worse than no avail as one of them plunged into a man's thigh. He saw two men struck by bolting horses.

He saw fear teeter into panic and rout.

He saw death for them all amid those dark, crowded, trees if he did not act.

He did not need to ponder the nature of the creature that had sought out one of their men and now returned to attack the entire group. Whatever it was, its intent, its will and its awful power defined it sufficiently. Haral knew that his only tactic now was to stem the rout and beat a fighting retreat. If he could.

If . . . ?

Farnor yawned and leaned his forehead against the flank of the cow. It had been hard getting up this morning and he had been walking around half asleep ever since.

It had earned him a rebuke from his father, and now the cow showed her resentment at his slothful attention by sidestepping away from him. Jerked into wakefulness he reached out to steady himself, whereupon the cow moved back and nearly knocked him off his stool. He swore at the animal as he struggled to keep his balance and also keep the milking pail upright. The cow turned and gazed at him reproachfully.

He patted it and muttered an insincere, 'Sorry,' then started milking again.

That done, his next duty lay in the workshed which leaned raggedly against the barn. He had neglected quite a few of his usual tasks of late while ostensibly 'doing odds and ends' for Gryss, and this morning his father had detailed a long list of items to be completed, earmarking several for immediate attention. Farnor had considered protesting, citing work still to be done for Gryss, but there was a resolution underlying his father's quiet requests that he knew of old would make any appeal pointless. And probably unwise.

Still, he reflected, it wasn't really urgent that he tell Gryss what had happened last night immediately, despite its terrifying vividness. Whatever was happening was happening, and would presumably continue to do so whether he told Gryss or not. And to continue neglecting his duties about the farm would be merely to aggravate and, in all conscience, burden his parents.

And in burdening them he would burden himself also, thereby adding to the worries he already had. He closed the door of the workshed behind him, kicking it expertly until the wooden latch dropped into position. He smiled as he did so. That was another job on his list, but it was at least something that he could apply himself to, and eventually put right. All the tasks he had to perform about the farm were thus. They were clear and well defined and they had a purpose, a logic, which, if it was not evident straight away, invariably became so as the various emergencies of farm life occurred: winds damaging the ricks; lightning firing them; frantic haymaking as black storm clouds piled high in the sky, dwarfing even the mountains; damp torchlit sojourns in the hills at lambing time; and many others. But all needing other things to be prepared, to be ready.

It came to him that the many small, insignificant things his parents had taught and shown him over the years were part of the great rhythm of tending the land which, in its turn, was the culmination of countless generations of learning through trial and error, success and failure.

He glanced out of the window, noting casually that while it was sunny here, the valley to the north was shrouded in mist.

Some culmination, he thought, gazing at the familiar

disorder of the workshed. He picked up a sickle lying amid the confusion covering the work bench. Its edge was turned and rusty. But then, could he have known how to win the metal to make this, had it not been for his conversations with the smith? And could he have known how to beat and shape and sharpen it thus? Or learned unaided the simple, effortless swing that would enable him to use it for long hours at a time without tiring?

He looked at the other tools and pieces of equipment lying about. No, he could not have hazarded even the nature of such as these, let alone made and used them, had it not been for those who had gone before him.

Not too clever, after all, he said to himself, turning back to the window.

Yet even as this revelation made itself known to him, he had a powerful feeling that he too was a part of this unheard, unseen rhythm, and that it would sustain him in some way through his present trials. Its great and ancient momentum, laden with an accumulated wisdom far beyond that of any one person, would not be so easily deflected.

He must not neglect what was simple and mundane. He must let the performing of his routine everyday tasks be a fist raised in opposition to this unsought intrusion into his life. It was more important, not only for the sake of peace with his parents, but for his own peace, that he diligently attend to the ordinary rather than be for ever scuttling round to Gryss with tales of the extraordinary.

Anyway, what could Gryss do?

Precious little, he decided, though with the thought came guilt. Gryss had done everything that he could do; he had listened, and he had cared. And he thought about things.

Farnor's mood swung from confident determination back towards uncertainty and fear again. While Gryss

291

was there, he knew that he would not be totally alone. Gryss was important to him. The great sweep of the ages offered its continuity, but Gryss offered him more human and immediate sustenance. And he needed the one as much as he needed the other if he was to cope with the darkness that seemed to cloud the edges of his every thought.

He *would* go and see him today, but only after he had attended to his tasks here; attended to them correctly and thoroughly.

He took another look at the mist-shrouded valley to the north, then he hefted the sickle and took it to the grinding bench. A rotating shaft driven by water piped down from one of the higher fields gave a protesting judder as, with a push on the foot pedal, Farnor connected the several grinding stones to it.

He watched the circular stones gather speed. I couldn't have invented that either, he mused, as he brought the blade of the sickle delicately into contact with one of the stones.

Sharpening the various cutting tools that were used on the farm was a source of some enjoyment to him. 'A blunt knife is a dangerous knife,' his father had told him for as long as he could remember, and it always gave him pleasure to know that whenever one of his edges was used it would move effortlessly through string or rope or wood, or whatever it was being turned to. Not only did he enjoy sharpening, but he was good at it. So much so that his father had actually admitted it publicly and his mother had solemnly delegated the task of sharpening her kitchen knives to him: a responsibility more forbidding than any other on the farm.

He frowned a little as he examined the blade. What had his father been doing with it? Cutting down trees?

The fleeting sense of superiority heartened him and he smiled to himself. Let his father cut rocks with it if he wished. He could do what he wanted, and when he had finished his son would make all things well again.

The grindstones rumbled round steadily, the blade hissed in response to Farnor's touch and small showers of sparks cascaded on to the floor, bounced hither and thither in confusion and vanished mysteriously into nothingness.

And then it was finished. Farnor turned the blade this way and that, squinted expertly along its curving edge and pronounced it . . . adequate. He hung it on its correct hook – his tasks included tidying the workshed as well as sharpening everything in sight – and took down a lethal-looking machete.

He smiled as his hand closed about the grip and, crouching, he made a menacing face. Handling this always brought to him the memory of his father frantically snatching it away from him once when, fired by one of Yonas's tales, he had chosen it as his magical sword. A sword which could cut through anything, even the anvil on which it had been forged, and which would slay all who were foolish enough to come against him, no matter how great their skill or rugged their armour.

He chuckled. Lot of problems, children, he said to himself, in imitation of his father's remark at the time.

Now, siding understandingly with his father at this childish peccadillo, he looked at the blade seriously and then offered it to one of the stones.

The sickle, with its curving blade, was quite difficult to sharpen, but the machete was simplicity itself and the long sweeping strokes that he was able to use were particularly satisfying.

He soon became engrossed in the work again and all thoughts that were not concerned with the grinding and honing of the blade faded from his awareness. He watched his hands moving swiftly, steadily and surely; carefully testing, retouching, testing again. And gradually the deed became timeless as his whole world filled with the tuneless song he was creating.

But, it was different today. Fuller, more intense. Words could not begin to describe the feeling.

And, without realizing when it had begun, he became aware that beyond the rumbling and hissing of the stones and the blade he could hear – or, perhaps, more correctly sense – a sound. A sound like a distant chorus of countless voices. Yet so natural did it seem that he felt no surprise. Indeed, he knew that he had heard it before, though where and when eluded him. It was as if he was listening to a huge family debating, discussing, gossiping, and though he could hear no words he felt a sensation of surprise . . . enquiry? . . . pervading it. And directed towards him!

What do you want? he found his thoughts asking.

The debate rippled and shifted, the surprise in it now stronger by far. And he detected, some element of denial; refusal to believe.

As he listened, his eyes watched his hands moving the blade to and fro across the stones and he knew that everything was well.

Then a tiny, swirling knot of confusion came into the chorus, and the attention was no longer focused on him. The knot swelled rapidly to become alarm, then disbelief, and finally, in the merest blink of time, outright horror.

Distantly Farnor became aware of the machete beginning to bounce off the stone as his grip faltered.

Then, rising in pitch to a rending shriek but diminishing in intensity in the same proportion, the chorus was gone, as if into an unknowable distance, and Farnor felt himself overwhelmed by pounding, primitive lusts: the taste of fresh blood in his mouth; human screams rendered inhuman by pain and terror resonating through him; the fear and panic of his prey rich in his nostrils.

Men, horses, confusion. Another victim chosen, burdened and scurrying blindly through the dark trees.

Good . . .

It was good to have found such release after so long. Good to have found such as him again. Good to be free to pursue the old ways again.

In a dream somewhere else, Farnor saw his hand snatching away as the bouncing blade began to move upward, its bright edge glinting in the dust-laden sunlight streaking through the workshed window.

And, clearly, he saw the shadowy, stumbling figure glance over his shoulder and see his fate.

As the blade continued upwards, Farnor felt himself reaching into the horror that was possessing him, and denying it.

And it was gone!

There was only the workshed and the grinding bench. With a jarring thud, the machete struck the ceiling and hung there, swaying gently.

Haral dashed forward roaring, 'Regroup, regroup!'

A charging horse narrowly missed him but he made no attempt to stop it. His prime concern was the men. This creature could take them one at a time if they scattered, and, though he had never known the like before in *any* animal, it seemed as though that could be its precise intention.

Using the butt of his spear freely and filling the forest with his thunderous vituperations, he stemmed the scattering of his men. 'Form up! Form up! And hold those damn horses! It won't attack a group.'

It helped, too, that those at the front of the column had been less panicked by the creature's ferocious attacks and had slowed down their terrified companions.

'Where's Bryn? Where in hell's name is Bryn?' he roared.

The man next to him pointed. A figure was running through the trees towards them with someone slung across his shoulders. It was Bryn. Two of the men started forward to help him, then out of the darkness beyond him the shadow came again, moving directly towards him, fast and purposeful.

'He's not going to make it,' someone said, fearfully.

Haral made no answer, but began running forward, his spear held low before him. 'Run, Bryn!' he shouted desperately as he closed with him. 'Run!'

Bryn looked at him, then glanced hastily over his shoulder. The black shape charging towards him through the trees froze all movement and thought in him and left him only terror.

Faintly he could hear Haral's frantic urging, but he could do nothing to escape the will that was bearing down on him.

Then, abruptly, it stopped.

At the same instant Bryn felt himself released.

He turned and ran as he had never run in his life. He felt a hand seize him and drag him forward, then many hands seized him and brought him to shelter. The burden was lifted from his shoulders and he was in the midst of his companions, gasping for air.

'Keep close! Shoulder to shoulder!' he heard Haral shout breathlessly.

Then an eerie silence fell, punctuated only by heavy breathing from the men and the fretful snorting and padding of the horses. Swords and spears pointed uncertainly in the direction from which Bryn had appeared.

Haral quietly and quickly moved others to guard the sides and rear of the group.

But nothing happened.

'Where's it gone?' Bryn asked after a moment. 'It was just behind me.'

Haral peered into the gloom. 'It's gone,' he said. 'It's given up for some reason.'

His mind filled with questions, but he brushed them aside. Retreat was the only thing that could be considered now. 'Pick up the injured and—'

'Something's coming. Listen!'

The whole group turned, weapons levelled, but before anything could be made out a powerful wind came rushing through the trees, blowing leaves and forest floor detritus before it.

Haral swore and lifted his arm to his face for protection.

'Go quickly,' came a voice through the noise of the wind. It was commanding in tone, though it was laced with urgency. Haral rubbed his eyes and looked blearily into the wind to see the speaker.

It was Rannick. He was gesticulating and pointing south. 'Go quickly!' he shouted again. 'I'll restrain it for as long as I can. But it won't be for long. Go now. Move!'

Neither Haral nor his men needed further bidding. Regardless of their comfort or condition, the injured were quickly thrown across saddles and everyone mounted whichever horse was nearest. Several of them had to ride double because of the horses that had been lost.

Haral took the rear of the column. Struggling to control his horse in the hammering wind, he directed it towards Rannick.

It twisted and circled and flayed out its forelegs in opposition.

'Go while you can!' Rannick's voice carried clearly through the noise of the wind. Haral managed to still his horse momentarily, and stared at his apparent saviour intently. His eyes were still watering, and the figure he saw was blurred and streaked.

'Who are you?' he demanded.

The figure shifted, as if it were both there and somewhere else at the same time. Haral rubbed his eyes again.

'You know who I am,' Rannick said. Then he pointed towards the retreating column. 'Do you wish to go forward or do you wish to die?'

A massive gust of wind struck Haral. Leaves overhead hissed in protest while branches rattled and trunks creaked. Haral's horse turned and galloped after the others. He made no effort to stop it.

As Haral disappeared into the distance, the wind around Rannick died away. He frowned. His plan had worked admirably. Such doubters as there were amongst Nilsson's men had been shown the error of their ways very convincingly, and gaining complete control over the entire group would now be an easy matter. From what he had learned from Meirach and from his own observations, he knew they would form an ideal nucleus to the force that he intended to build. If ever there was to be a confirmation of his destiny, the arrival of Nilsson and his men was it. That, and his long journey into the caves.

It was a time for exhilaration. Indeed he *was* exhilarated.

And yet something had gone amiss. Albeit briefly, something had . . . drained? – no; rather strangled, restrained – the new power that he had discovered.

Perhaps he had not yet the skills he imagined? But no skill had been needed here that he had not had for many years.

He reached out and felt the presence of the creature. It had the stillness of a shadowed and silent lake, deep beyond imagining and wending into the far, unknowable distance. And it had the timeless immovability of a towering mountain whose ancient roots held it fast in the depths below. But above all it had desires. Desires that knew no bounds. And a will that knew no restraint. And it bent to *his* will. It was a richness greater than any he had ever imagined. And there would be more. Much more.

The creature stirred and Rannick basked in its contentment.

Farnor's hand was shaking as he yanked the machete out of the wooden ceiling. Not because of the accident he had narrowly avoided, though he was acutely aware of that, but because of the terrible contact with the creature that he had again been drawn into.

And what had been that other contact immediately before? Vast and whispering. Watching and listening. *Surprised*. Not malevolent, certainly, but every bit as mysterious as the creature.

He had to grit his teeth at the effort he found he needed to stop himself abandoning his tasks and running to Gryss with news of this latest happening. His resolve held and a down-to-earth common sense came to his aid. Whatever had happened it had done him no hurt, save to alarm him. He *must* regain the balance of his life. He must remember that he was Garren Yarrance's son, and heir to the substantial lands at this end of the valley. Paper and documents gravely averred that they belonged to the family Yarrance, but, like all the valley dwellers, he knew that the reality was that *he* belonged to the land. His was a stewardship for the lands that fed and clothed far more than just his family; had done for countless generations in the past, and would do so for countless generations in the future. He had a duty to his parents, to those that had gone before and to those that would come and, indeed, to himself, to continue learning the skills he would need to fulfil that stewardship well.

Other things must yield before this need.

He gazed around the workshed. He would finish what he had been set to do here, and the other tasks he had been given. He would quieten his mind. He looked down at the machete, turning it this way and that. The sun bounced off its glistening edge sending slivers of light skittering about the untidy room.

And in placing these unnerving happenings against the weight of his true life, he would temper and sharpen himself to face whatever the future held for him.

Chapter 22

The wind thrashed the tops of the trees and sent twigs and leaves and sometimes whole branches chasing after Haral's fleeing group. The men were oblivious to such urgings however, as the terror of the last few minutes drove them relentlessly forward.

Galloping up and down the column, Haral managed to prevent the retreat from turning into a complete rout, but it was not easy. Independent of the wills of their riders, the horses had clear intentions of their own and many were soon not only lathered, but bleeding about the mouth as restraints were applied by those same riders, fearful of being recklessly dashed into low branches or crushed against trunks.

As they drew further from the scene of the assault, however, the wind began to ease and the headlong flight gradually calmed, first to a more controlled gallop and then to a steady canter.

Haral, riding at the rear, began to count the cost and the probable consequences. Two men dead, plus Mirek taken earlier. At least four others injured by panicking horses, including the man Bryn had brought back; and one man with a spear still sticking in his leg. All this, plus half a dozen horses lost, and who knew how many other lesser injuries to both men and horses incurred during the melee. He was reminded of these by a sharp pain between his shoulder blades. Carefully, he flexed them and tried to assess the extent of the damage that the creature had done when it had trodden on him. With some relief he diagnosed it as probably only bruising; he had had enough injuries in the past to know when one was merely an inconvenience and one was a problem requiring attention.

He grimaced. What a disaster! He issued up a small prayer of thanks that he had not, after all, sent that frivolous message to Nilsson, 'Expect a trophy.' The humiliation of that would have been altogether too much, on top of the reproaches that would soon be coming his way.

But what else could he have done? he pondered. The damned thing was an animal. He had hunted animals before, as had they all. Fierce animals at that: boars, bears, even wild bulls. And while they would turn and fight, this was usually only at the last extremity when all other avenues of escape had been denied them. Certainly they didn't think like men; didn't know that they were stronger, faster and better armed by far than their flimsy pursuers; didn't know to turn from hunted into hunter by laying ambushes.

But this one had known. Despite himself, Haral found himself thinking of the whole incident as being like some kind of trap, with its bait and its lure and its final assault.

'There's nothing for you there but terrible danger and the Great Forest,' Rannick had said.

And you knew that because, somehow, you were at the heart of it, you piece of horse dung, Haral thought viciously, though he glanced about him as he cursed for fear that, in some way, he might be overheard. Any doubts as he might have had about Rannick's involvement in the attack had been dispelled by his seemingly fortuitous appearance and his promise of help.

Such as he, did nothing unless it served his own end.

Such as he, Haral mused, struck by the turn of his thoughts. He no longer saw Rannick as a petty village trickster, and though it was hard to imagine that the man had the power of Haral's former lord, he nevertheless had a great deal. And he had the will to use it. He was beyond debate, someone to be either obeyed or fled from.

Of course, there was always the alternative of killing him, but Haral had seen the fate of others who had thought similarly in the past, and he had no desire to share any part of it. He shuddered at the memory.

Wholly pragmatic, Haral shifted his stance without any qualms. He had followed and obeyed someone all his life: Nilsson, Rannick, it did not really matter. Let *them* have their grandiose plans; just so *he* knew where he stood. He had only modest ambitions, and so long as he got what he wanted he didn't really give a damn who he followed. And getting what he wanted was generally not too difficult once he had a measure of his leaders.

And the clear measure he had of Rannick now was that he wanted the group to remain at the castle instead of heading north. Wanted it to the extent that he was prepared to kill some of them for it. Further, he had some control over the fearful animal that had attacked them. Haral had *no* measure of that thing except that it was to be avoided at all costs.

Perhaps the reasons for Rannick's wish that they remain at the castle would become apparent in time but, for now, Haral knew enough. 'You go north and you die,' Rannick had said, meaning, 'You go north and I will kill you.' And having had that demonstrated, Haral needed to know nothing further. All he had to do now was give a good account of today's happenings, suitably praising *Lord* Rannick for his timely intervention, then he would do what was expected of him and confirm that the valley was too dangerous to risk any more ventures. After that he would stand back to await events.

A noise from the head of the column interrupted his planning.

For a moment his insides turned to ice. Had Rannick decided to make a real example of them by sending the animal after them to destroy them all? He laid his hand on his sword hilt in readiness for action.

But soon the noise identified itself as other riders, sent by Nilsson to act as rearguard to the group. Haral spurred his horse forward to greet them.

The journey back to the castle was uneventful, though it was dark when they arrived and, gallopers having been sent ahead with the news, the courtyard was crowded with men and ablaze with flickering torches.

Nilsson cursorily examined the seriously injured. 'Send someone for that leech, Gryss,' he said. 'Tell him . . . ask him . . . to come and look at these men.'

He turned to Haral, his face grim and questioning. Haral told his tale as he had determined, laying suitable emphasis on the role played by Rannick and duly declaring that the passage to the north was too dangerous.

The telling was received in silence by the encircling men. Despite the losses, there were fewer reproaches than Haral had anticipated. A congress had been held and each man had made his own decision freely. Those who had stayed, for the most part, considered themselves fortunate rather than wise in their choice, and those of Haral's men who had survived considered themselves both wiser now and fortunate.

Nilsson and others shrewd enough read Haral's true message: 'Do as Rannick says, or he'll kill you. And he can do it.'

It was no great surprise. They had all known the power and, whatever questions they had about how Rannick came to wield it, they knew its force. There was some resentment about being held in thrall by this new leader, but it found little or no voice, and indeed, most were beginning to look to the future for the first time in many years, reflecting into it the lives they had led under their former master.

There were some questions about the creature but they petered out as it became apparent that neither Haral nor any of the others could give any indication as to what it might be.

'What about Mirek and the others?' Dessane asked.

'Dead, beyond a doubt.' Haral's face wrinkled in distaste. 'And probably eaten by now.'

Nilsson looked round to see if there was any enthusiasm for a search and found none. Loyalty was loyalty, but this wasn't worth the risk.

He nodded. 'Now we wait,' he said.

Gryss was in no sweet mood when he arrived. He had been preparing to go to bed when Nilsson's messenger had filled the house with his noisy banging, and the journey had been too fast for his taste.

'I'm too old for this rattling round,' he complained as Nilsson greeted him.

'Why's the boy here?' Nilsson asked brusquely, indicating Farnor, hastily collected by Gryss as he had passed the farm.

'He helps me,' Gryss lied, equally irritably, handing a large leather bag to Farnor.

Nilsson said nothing, though he looked as if he wished to object to Farnor's presence. After a moment, however, he gave a curt nod, then pointed to the building in which the injured were being housed.

'I hope you've managed to find somewhere more wholesome than the last place,' Gryss said in an attempt at conversation as Nilsson led them into a long, arched corridor.

The martial tattoo of the Captain's heels on the stone floor was the only reply.

Eventually they stopped outside a heavy wooden door

which Nilsson threw open. He motioned Gryss inside. As the old man went into the room he grimaced. It was clean enough, but it needed no physician's eye to see the pain racking the men lying there. They made little sound, though the subdued hiss of tightly controlled breathing was more distressing to Gryss than any amount of groaning.

'What happened?' he asked, turning to Nilsson.

'Just tend them,' Nilsson replied coldly.

Gryss began to protest. 'I'll need to know if . . .'

'Just tend them,' Nilsson replied, before he could finish.

The two men held each other's gazes for a moment, then Gryss nodded

'Very well,' he said. 'I'll do what I can.' He took his bag from Farnor. 'There's no point you staying, Captain. This is going to take some time. I'll see you before I leave and tell you what I've done.'

'His tune's changed,' Gryss murmured to Farnor when Nilsson had left.

Farnor had other concerns on his mind. 'I can't help you,' he whispered in some alarm. 'I don't know anything about sick people.'

'Just do as I say, and look confident,' Gryss said, rooting through his bag. 'It's the confidence that does most of the healing anyway.' Despite the grim surroundings, a brief twinkle of amusement shone in his eyes as he looked at Farnor's anxious face. 'This'll be interesting for you.'

'What've you brought me here for, anyway?' Farnor went on.

'I want another pair of eyes and ears about this place,' Gryss answered. 'We need to learn as much as we can about these men, in case . . .' He stopped.

'In case what?'

'Just in case,' Gryss said shortly.

A reluctant groan from one of the injured men ended this subdued conversation, and Gryss turned his attention to their needs.

Farnor did not enjoy what followed, but he obeyed Gryss's instructions scrupulously and tried to appear confident as the old man poked and prodded, moved limbs, issued instructions to breathe in, breathe out, move your toes, move your fingers, look this way, look that.

When it came to manipulating bones however, Farnor gave up all attempt at confidence, and simply concentrated on doing as he was told. This consisted mainly of mopping brows and giving the patients a thick leather thong to bite on as Gryss heaved and tugged at reluctant limbs. Some of the clicks and cracks that ensued made his entire skin crawl, but it was the eye contact that distressed him most; seeing the fear, the young boys within, risen anew, being grimly, angrily, fought back by the men.

'What happened?' Gryss asked each man in turn.

'A horse kicked me,' came the standard, and truthful reply.

Gryss wanted to raise a disbelieving eye, but the nature of the injuries forbade it.

'And I suppose a horse kicked you as well,' he said, pulling back the sheet from the last bed. Farnor caught his breath and turned away. The man's hand, clutching a bloodstained rag, fell away from a deep, raw wound in his thigh.

Visions of the slaughtered sheep returned to Farnor at the sight of the torn flesh, and he felt his gorge rising.

'Slow, deep breaths,' he heard Gryss whispering urgently in his ear, as a surprisingly powerful hand gripped his arm. 'Slow deep breaths. Start throwing up when the wound's in *your* leg. You'll be surprised how much pain in other people a good healer can take.'

307

The sternness and the dark, cynical humour in Gryss's voice jolted Farnor into self-control and he returned to his role as healer's assistant.

The old man pursed his lips as he viewed the damaged leg, then he burrowed in his bag again. He emerged with a small bottle, the contents of which he emptied on to a pad. Farnor's nose twitched uncertainly as a heavy, sweet, smell struck it. Then, unhurriedly, but very quickly, Gryss placed the pad over the man's mouth and nose. The man struggled a little then went limp.

'What's that?' Farnor asked in amazement.

'Just something to put him to sleep for a few minutes,' Gryss replied. 'Here, tie him down.'

A length of stout rope appeared from the bag.

'Tie him down?' Farnor gaped.

'Tie him down,' Gryss confirmed insistently. 'I've got to probe this wound, and if he wakes up before I've finished he's not going to enjoy it. And neither am I when he tries to take my head off.'

Unhappily, Farnor did as he was told, trussing the man to the bed as expertly as if he were tying a cover over a wagon. Even as he was doing so Gryss was delving into the wound.

'Look,' he said, beckoning Farnor down. He had struck a small sunstone lantern and its bright light brought out every stark detail of the wound. Farnor clenched his teeth and somehow managed to bring his face next to Gryss's. Rather to his surprise, his unease began to pass as Gryss, using two thin metal probes, confidently lifted back layers of damaged tissue, explaining to the best of his knowledge what each one was: muscle, sinew, blood vessels and the different layers of skin.

The man stirred and mumbled something unintelligible. Farnor glanced at him anxiously but Gryss shook his head reassuringly.

He nudged Farnor. 'Bone,' he said, tapping a white streak at the bottom of the wound. Farnor rubbed his own thigh feelingly. Then Gryss was peering intently into the wound and, tongue protruding, probing further.

'What's the matter?' Farnor whispered.

Gryss shushed him.

The man stirred again, and then Gryss was busy cleaning and sewing, all the time humming softly to himself. Farnor had seen Gryss stitching wounds before and was able to watch this a little more calmly.

At last Gryss stood up.

'Why haven't you sewn it all up?' Farnor asked.

'Too deep,' Gryss replied. 'It'll have to heal from the inside out.'

Farnor shook his head in some wonder. 'How do you know all this?' he asked.

Gryss turned his head from side to side and wriggled his shoulders to ease the stiffness out of them. He smiled broadly. 'Horses, mainly,' he said. 'And some cows.'

He intercepted Farnor's growing look of horror. 'We're not all that much different,' he said, chuckling darkly. 'Why do you think I don't eat much meat?' Then he became serious. 'But I've done similar for people as well. You can get a nasty wound off a scythe or a sickle.' He paused. 'But I'd like to know what's happened here.'

Farnor started. He had been so preoccupied with watching Gryss that only now did he realize that he knew the answer to this. But it could not be told here. He would have to wait until they had left the castle.

'Horses, they say,' Gryss muttered. 'And it could well be, most of them. But this one . . .' He nodded towards the wounded man, whose eyelids were now beginning to flicker. 'This one's been wounded by a sword thrust, or a spear. The bone was chipped by a sharp point of some kind. I'll ask Nilsson when we see him, although

I doubt he'll tell me anything.' He nodded to himself. 'Untie him, please, Farnor,' he said. 'I'll need to talk to him when he wakes up properly. I'm afraid he's not going to enjoy the next few days.'

Later, as he had promised, Gryss sought out Nilsson and told him what he had done. 'I'll have to examine them again every day for some time,' he concluded.

Nilsson shook his head. 'We'll tend them,' he said bluntly.

Gryss seemed about to debate this decision, then he slumped a little and gave a slight shrug. 'As you wish, Captain,' he said. 'They're your men. But please at least let me tell you how to tend them. The man with the wound in his leg needs particular attention if he's not going to lose it.'

Nilsson seemed unconcerned by the news. 'It's not much,' he said. 'I've seen men recover from worse lying in the field.'

'Yes, and you've seen men dying screaming and burned up with fever as their limbs rotted on them as well, I'll wager,' Gryss said, his voice uncharacteristically savage. 'But, as I said, they're your men.' He turned as if to leave.

There was a brief flash of anger across Nilsson's face at this outburst, but it was followed by an equally brief flicker of doubt. 'Very well,' he said, in a voice that gave no concession to Gryss's argument. 'Come tomorrow. After that, we'll see.'

Gryss nodded. 'I'll get myself back to my bed, then,' he said. 'And Farnor here has to be up early.' Nilsson gave him a cursory nod, but did not seem inclined to offer the thanks that Gryss's comment had been designed to elicit. As Gryss reached the door, he turned back as if he had just remembered something. 'Why've you no healer of your own, Captain?' he asked. 'King's men ranging the country and far from their

310

home base. You should have been given someone, surely?'

Nilsson stared at him, then wrenched his thoughts back from the events of the day. Damn this old fool, he thought. But he needed him still. The present pretence must be maintained unless Rannick reappeared and determined otherwise. 'There were none available at the time we left,' he said. 'One of those things. You know the army.'

'No, I don't, really,' Gryss admitted. 'But I'd have thought that someone somewhere would have been ordering affairs better than that. Still, I don't imagine anyone would be expecting you'd be getting involved in combat, would they?' He shook his head pensively. 'Your man's been lucky. If the point hadn't struck the bone it could've severed a vessel that would have emptied the blood from him in minutes. How did he come by such a wound?'

Nilsson smelt the trap coming. Damn this *crafty* old fool, he reminded himself. 'It was a training accident,' he said blandly. 'These things happen. But that's a soldier's lot. As we used to say in my own country, if you can't stand the cold don't sit in the snow.'

'It was worth a try,' Gryss said to Farnor as they walked across the courtyard to their horses. 'But I suppose he's used to guarding his tongue, whether he's a King's man or one of Marna's bandits.'

Farnor ignored the observation. Away from the urgency of his unexpected night journey and the tension of the sick room, his own concerns returned.

'I've something I need to tell you when we're away from the castle,' he said simply. 'It's about all this.'

Gryss shot him a quick glance, but said nothing.

As he mounted up, he looked round the courtyard. There was a great deal of activity going on for this time of night, he thought. Though much of it consisted of groups of men talking. And there was an air of . . . expectancy. As if they were waiting for something.

Once clear of the castle, Farnor told Gryss what had happened that day. Gryss listened in silence, and remained so for a long time after he had finished. 'So *many* questions,' he said, half to himself. 'And there's no point asking you for more than you've already told me, is there, Farnor?' Farnor shook his head. He had omitted no details. Then Gryss seemed to recollect himself and he reached over and laid his hand on Farnor's arm comfortingly. 'How are you?' he asked in a voice full of concern.

'Better, I think,' Farnor answered. 'A little more prepared to wait things out.' He paused. 'But I don't know how long I can stay like this.'

Gryss patted his arm. 'You'll be all right. Having learned to do that, it'll be with you for as long as you need. That's the nature of things. You'll be burdened with no more than you can bear.'

The next day, his mind full of Farnor's strange tale and the evidence of panic that could be read in the damage that had been wrought to the injured men, Gryss returned alone to the castle. The rain that had been confined to the upper part of the valley the previous day had moved to occupy the whole of it and, coupled with a blustering wind, made it more like winter than spring.

There was an almost eerie silence about the castle as Gryss plied his fist to the wicket door. A solitary guard eventually opened it and beckoned him in with a surly grunt.

Gryss attempted some small talk about the weather as they trudged across the deserted courtyard, but the man merely hitched up his dripping leather cape irritably.

'The sick room's over there,' Gryss said, pointing as the man led him in an entirely different direction.

312

'Captain wants to see you,' came the reply.

Gryss knew that asking, 'What about?' would yield no answer, so he followed in silence.

He was, however, beginning to feel increasingly uneasy as the journey took him into a part of the castle that he had not been in before. But it was the stillness pervading the place that was disturbing rather than the place itself. The guard stopped and knocked discreetly on a door.

There was a reply from within, and the guard pushed the door open and ushered Gryss in.

Though uncarpeted and barely furnished, the room was made almost homely by a large fire burning in an ornately decorated fireplace. Nilsson was seated at a table writing something, while another figure stood with his back to the room gazing out of the window.

Gryss smiled. 'I see you've found yourself some more comfortable quarters,' he said. 'The fire's welcome. It's an unseasonable day today.'

Nilsson said nothing, but gestured to a chair on the opposite side of the table. Gryss sat down and waited. He cast a covert glance at the man by the window. There was something familiar about him, but he was silhouetted against the grey daylight and Gryss could not see him clearly enough to identify him.

'Did any of my patients have any problems in the night?' he asked the still-writing Captain, hoping for a reply that might enable him to discover more of what had happened to the men. He had no doubt that Farnor had told him the truth about what he had . . . felt . . . but . . .

Nilsson laid down his pen after a moment. 'Don't worry about the men, Gryss,' he said. 'We'll attend to them.' His manner was easy and casual, but before Gryss could respond it became serious; grim, even. 'A great many things have changed since last night, and I

. . . we' – He nodded towards the figure by the window – 'are going to need your help in explaining them to the villagers.'

Gryss frowned. Images of invading armies marching down from the north returned to him again, to displace his immediate worry about the injured men and the mystery of Farnor's tale. What had these people done with their prying to the north? He brought his attention back to Nilsson sharply; he was still speaking; and hurriedly, as if to get the matter over.

'It's been decided that the castle here will become a permanent garrison. It's to become a . . . training centre . . . and local headquarters for the army to help strengthen what has become a very weak north-eastern border.'

Gryss's mind reeled. Of the many things he had thought might happen since the arrival of these men, this had not been one.

'I don't understand,' he blurted out. 'Why now, all of a sudden? Who's made this decision? What's it going to mean to the village . . . ?'

Nilsson raised a hand for silence. 'Listen, Gryss,' he said, a sterner note in his voice. 'I'll tell you what I can, but I'm speaking to you now in your capacity as one of the village's senior elders; probably its most influential. So listen, because you'll have to explain it to the others. I've neither the time nor the inclination to do it myself.'

With an effort Gryss held back his questions.

Nilsson continued: 'The why of all this is neither yours nor mine to question,' he said. 'Such decisions are made by the King and his ministers, for whatever reasons they think fit. The who is of no relevance. Suffice it that the order is the King's and that I'm both obliged and empowered to put it into effect.'

Despite the admonition however, Gryss could not

contain himself. 'Why didn't you tell us sooner?' he interjected, without waiting for the answer to his third question.

Nilsson scratched his cheek impatiently, and his lips slipped back to bare his teeth. 'Because we didn't know,' he said. 'The tithe had to be collected and certain other matters determined before the decision was finalized.'

'What other matters?' Gryss demanded.

The figure by the window stirred. Nilsson shot it a nervous glance then glared at Gryss. 'Matters which don't concern you,' he said bluntly.

It brought Gryss back to his third question. 'What's it going to mean to the village?' he asked again.

Nilsson thumbed through some of the papers in front of him. 'Probably very little,' he said. 'Technically you'll be under military law because of your nearness to the castle, but for the most part that'll only affect anyone who wants to enter or leave the valley. You can rest assured that we want nothing to do with your routine daily squabbles. You can continue to deal with those as you do at present, providing they don't interfere with our work here or the security of the valley.'

Gryss frowned. Few either entered or left the valley so, apparently, this new regime would indeed have little effect. But somewhere deep inside, a part of him rebelled against this unasked-for and unwanted constraint. He held it in check; his head was still spinning with this unwelcome news.

'And you'll feed the garrison, of course,' Nilsson added, almost as an afterthought. 'And supply servants – tradesmen and the like – as they're needed.'

Gryss latched on to a practicality to try and calm his confusion. 'Feed you?' he queried. 'How many will there be? We're only a small village.'

Nilsson raised his open palms and shrugged. 'I've no

315

idea,' he admitted. 'But the valley's big and fertile, much of it lying fallow. I'm sure it'll present no problems.'

Gryss put his hand to his head. 'This is all rather a surprise,' he said. 'Not to say a shock. You'll have to allow me a moment to take it in.'

'I understand,' Nilsson said, now almost avuncular. 'But please don't be too concerned. I'm sure there'll be virtually no disruption to your village life if everyone does as they're told. And such few problems as might arise will probably be nothing that can't be sorted out with a little goodwill and common sense on both sides.'

Gryss felt the manipulation behind the words, but he also felt suddenly very old. Momentous events were happening which were utterly beyond his control. Beyond even his comprehension, he began to realize. He had the feeling that he was running faster and faster down a hillside that was becoming steeper and steeper, and that soon he would be hurtling over the edge of some abyss.

The villagers had tended their own affairs for countless generations without aid from anyone beyond the valley, and they could continue thus for as many generations into the future. They lived simple yet rich lives, living off yet sustaining the fertile land that surrounded them. He knew that the intrusion which Nilsson had just outlined to him would destroy this ancient harmony more effectively than if his men had fired the village, and that such destruction would be tantamount to an atrocity.

Why? he cried out to himself, but he left it unspoken, following Nilsson's earlier remark. The why, like the who, was indeed irrelevant. He could do nothing. The villagers could do nothing. They were defenceless. Not merely in the matter of having no weapons to oppose such an imposition should they have so chosen, but in their entire outlook and way of thought. Now the isolation that they cherished and fostered had left them with no one to whom they could turn for help and advice. The word cut through him: defenceless. Totally defenceless, save for their wits and their words.

His mind plummeted into the black depths for a seemingly interminable moment and he saw that, despite their quiet but proud assumption of freedom, the villagers had always been the merest touch away from slavery, and would have always remained so, until . . .

Until . . . ?

Until it was too late. As now.

He rebuked himself. There had been no suggestion of such a fate for the village as slavery. What in the world was he thinking about?

But, suggestion or not, the word would not leave him, and the truth of his revelation about the village's weakness could not be denied. And though perhaps they were not to be slaves, were they not to be held prisoner? There was a profound difference between choosing not to leave the valley and being forbidden.

Then Gryss felt a dark tide of guilt overwhelming him.

He was a senior elder. In many ways the village's chief guide and adviser. But he had never even turned his mind to the possibility that the world from over the hill would so intrude, even though he had travelled in that world and had learned enough to know that by its nature such a world would intrude everywhere, sooner or later.

'Are you all right?'

Nilsson's voice made him start. 'Yes, yes,' he said hurriedly. 'Just a little . . . bewildered . . .'

Nilsson shrugged again. 'It's the way of things,' he said.

'What do you want me to do?' Gryss asked, awkwardly, after a short pause.

317

'Just tell your people what's going to happen,' Nilsson said, gathering together the papers in front of him. 'And reconcile them to it,' he added coldly. 'Everything can carry on as usual providing anyone who wishes to leave notifies me first.' He looked at Gryss almost menacingly. 'That's important. We'll be putting a guard post at the end of the valley. Anyone who tries to leave without permission will be punished. Perhaps even killed. Make sure everyone understands that.'

When Gryss, bowed and fretful, had left, the figure by the window turned to Nilsson.

It was Rannick, and his face was angry.

Chapter 23

Rannick had appeared at the castle in the middle of the night to receive the acclaim of the entire troop following his 'saving' of Haral's group.

Like Haral, Nilsson had no illusions that the ambush had somehow been arranged by Rannick. But, also like Haral, he had no intention of voicing such an accusation. Whatever he or any of his men might think about Rannick and the fate of Haral's group, all sensed that Rannick would have to be followed; and that life would be easier, not to say longer, if he were followed willingly rather than otherwise.

And, chillingly, Nilsson knew now the nature of the strange other presence he had felt at their first encounter: it had been the awesome creature that had hunted and savaged Haral's group. Rannick's dreadful familiar had been waiting in the darkness for the command to kill him.

Struggling to remain composed, he turned to face his angry master as Gryss left the room.

'It irks me to waste such time toying with that old fool,' Rannick said through clenched teeth. 'People are like animals, they only truly understand power. And I have power enough, and you men enough, to make the villagers do whatever we need. Do not let me regret choosing you.'

Nilsson avoided his direct gaze, but watched him carefully. It was essential, he knew, that he obtain a true measure of this man; a complete catalogue of whatever human weaknesses he possessed. But it was proving to be no light ordeal. And this particular conversation had been going on in various forms ever since Rannick had returned.

It had not taken Nilsson long to find the worm that was gnawing at his new master's heart. It was oddly disconcerting. Something in Rannick demanded the humiliation and oppression of this valley and its people.

Bewilderingly to Nilsson, Rannick seemed to have no conception of the consequences of such petty malice against what must necessarily be his home base for some time to come. Nilsson had had to spend a long, difficult and at times terrifying night attempting to persuade him to a more benign subduing of the community.

'It's troublesome and unnecessary,' Rannick had averred. 'I doubt there is a score of weapons in the whole valley, and I know there'll be no will to oppose us. We can do what we want, take what we want, with impunity.'

Cautiously, Nilsson had pointed out that while it was possible that a demonstration of force to bring the villagers to their knees might perhaps be achieved without the loss of any of his men, in his experience, 'Force generally is best avoided, if possible. Chance rides high in such affairs, Lord. Good men get killed. Messengers slip past guards to carry the news abroad. Many things happen other than was intended.'

Then would follow years of slow, sullen opposition from the apparently defeated villagers, draining the morale of the men and drawing them to use more and more brutal means of control. Means that would turn the surly opposition of the many into the active opposition of a few, and lead in turn to yet bloodier repression and an almost inevitable escape of the news from the valley. 'It's a mistake to misjudge both the resolve and the power of execution of the seemingly weak and helpless,' he had insisted. There would be fighting enough in due course, if Rannick's ambitions were to be fulfilled; what was needed now was a secure base from which to operate. And that needed willing workers, or at least keeping workers willing for as long as possible.

Rannick had not appreciated being contradicted, but Nilsson had managed to persist. 'If we can gently constrain the villagers as we build up our strength, then they'll soon become used to us. And by the time they find out we're not who we say we are – *if* they find out – they'll be divided in their opinions about us. That'll give us even greater strength to deal with such of them as wish to object.' He had concluded, 'Arbitrary violence against them now would be to foul your own nest; mar at the outset the future that is your destiny. There'll be little joy in their abasement if your greater intent is spoiled because of it. And does it matter whether they know of your greatness now or later? Isn't there an added relish to be gained in watching them doing your will without them realizing it? In watching them become your grovelling lackeys rather than your cowed slaves?'

In the end he had succeeded, though Rannick's displeasure and dissatisfaction still rumbled dangerously close to the surface. And, though he kept it from his face, Nilsson was as pleased as he was relieved at this outcome. If Rannick accepted his guidance now, it would help entrench him further as his closest aide and thus, in due course, greatly increase his rewards and his own personal power. It was good.

The night, however, had been draining and Nilsson now searched desperately for a reply to this renewed complaint; one that might end this debate once and for all. Then, suddenly, he felt afraid. A warning voice came from within: leave it. Leave it alone. You've been lucky so far. Who knows what drives such a man as this? Who knows what powers he possesses? To be of value to a man like him was one thing, but the slightest hint that they were dependent on you and . . .

'Master, I can say no more than I have,' he said with carefully modulated humility. 'Your will is my command. I am but your servant.'

The anger faded from Rannick's face, though the unreadable, cold impassiveness that replaced it was, if anything, more frightening. He nodded then turned back to the window.

Despite himself, Nilsson fidgeted nervously with the papers on the table in front of him.

There was a long silence.

Then Rannick was behind him.

Nilsson tried to react naturally, but he felt his body stiffening in anticipation of some act of violence. The memory of his first encounter with Rannick and the ease with which he had been hurled from his saddle was still vividly with him. And older memories of the use of the power rose to chill him further.

A hand closed about his shoulder. Nilsson took a slow, deep breath. Then, to his horror, he found he could not breathe out. His fingers curled clawlike, nails squealing along the wooden table. Rannick's hand patted his shoulder affectionately.

'Destroying the village is more the province of you and your men than mine, is it not, Captain?' Rannick said softly. 'Some other time, then.'

Abruptly, Nilsson breathed out, though it was as if the air had been torn from him rather than released by his own need. He slumped forward, gasping as if he had burst through the surface of some deep and drowning lake. His face almost struck the table. Through the sound of his pounding heartbeat and rasping breath, he heard Rannick's voice, now low and resonating as though it came from the echoing bowels of some great pit.

'*Good* . . .' it said.

Gryss rode away from the castle in a daze. His mind was in turmoil. He gazed down the valley. Grey sheets of rain were swirling across it, so that familiar landmarks came and went, their ancient solidity now made ephemeral.

The scene echoed his own tumbling thoughts and feelings: bewilderment, defiance, anger, despair and, ever-present, guilt.

He let the reins hang slack, though his hands were gripping them tightly.

'Grief,' he heard himself say after a long, timeless interval. Rain ran into his mouth.

That's what it was.

'Grief.'

Through his long life he had seen many die including, inevitably, many that he had loved. And he recognized the symptoms he was suffering from. Grief. Grief for the sudden, almost brutal, loss of a precious thing. He guided his horse to a small headland and stopped there. Looking back, he saw the castle. Once no more than part of the landscape, old and affectionately familiar, it seemed now to be new and utterly different, alive with menace and threat. And in the other direction the valley came and went under the shifting curtains of rain.

Like tears, he thought.

He knew only too well that his distress would have to run its course. Grief was an incurable condition. Time alone would ease it.

And yet, that very thought seemed to clear his mind. This was not a death; no one had been lost. This was change, and he could either beat his breast about it or make the best of it. He turned his face towards the grey sky. Despite the rain falling on him, he felt a little easier.

Perhaps after all it was more self-indulgence than true grief he was feeling. He abandoned the debate. It was of no real importance. What was important was this brief time alone. It would at least give him the chance to begin to come to terms with what had happened and to clarify how it could best be presented to the villagers.

A tinge of humour entered the cold grey of his thoughts. The Council meeting that he would have to call would be *very* interesting.

The humour did not survive long, however, as he tried to anticipate what the various responses of his fellow Councillors would be, and then he heard the question that would be asked by someone who was not a Council member: Marna.

'How do we know they're not just bandits?' she would ask.

He patted his horse's neck. Foolishness, he thought. But his denial was not as convincing as he would have wished. Marna's observations about the appearance and conduct of Nilsson's men were accurate, and – something that had not occurred to Marna, yet – Gryss had to concede that he had seen no document identifying them as who they claimed to be.

He grimaced with self-reproach.

And then there was the suddenness of this decision to use the castle as a permanent garrison. Hitherto there had been not the slightest mention of such a development. Now, following what, according to Farnor, had been some fearful confrontation in the woods with . . . that creature . . . and defeat by it, they suddenly decide that they'll stay here.

Unable to leave to the north, unwilling for some reason to leave to the south, they've got to remain, he thought suddenly.

He stared back at the castle, his concerns now doubled. Who were these men?

He could turn his horse about and ask, of course, but the very thought made his stomach tighten with fear. Nilsson might simply produce some document of authorization.

But he might not, and then what?

A knife in his ribs? And, all pretence set aside, the village open and defenceless against whatever Nilsson and his men might then choose to do? Gryss knew the villagers could not stand against such a crew. Yet there was some comfort in this thought. If they were other than the King's gatherers, they wished it to remain unknown. They had reasons of their own for remaining quiet and secret. Gryss felt some relief. Such reasoning would legitimately excuse him from the direct approach he had just contemplated.

Yet what was he to say to the Council?

He wiped the rain from his face. His every instinct was to tell them of his doubts, but what end would be served by that? There would be a rare commotion as it was and, despite any pleas for discretion, the idea would not only be all over the valley within the day, it would be grievously misrepresented; quite stripped of any subtle reservations he might have included in his telling. And who could say what the consequences of that might be? And, too, he could not avoid the feeling that, Marna having voiced her doubts, the same thoughts might be lying unspoken in many hearts, just waiting for the slightest encouragement to bring them noisily to the fore.

But he could not stay silent. Encouraging the people to submit to the will of these men who might be . . .

Might be what?

It was the word 'might' on which his thinking foundered.

Apart from confronting Nilsson personally, the only other way to resolve this was for someone to go over

325

the hill. To go to the capital and the King's palace and seek out some official who could confirm, or otherwise, the credentials of these men.

But who could be sent on such an errand? Who with sufficient wit to find the way, to contend with the difficult journey and to make the necessary enquiries could be sent without their absence also being noticed about the village within the day?

No one.

Gryss clicked his horse forward again. He would compromise. He could do nothing else. He would give the Council a simple statement, without comment, relating what he had been told by Nilsson. But when the meeting was over he would voice his doubts to the few that he could rely on.

Garren, certainly. Yakob too. And Jeorg? He pondered this. Jeorg was not a Councillor and he was pugnacious and outspoken when he chose, but he was reliable and trustworthy if handled correctly. Then there was Harlen, Marna's father. Again this was debatable. Harlen was good-natured and easy-going, a gentle man. Should he be burdened thus? Yet he was shrewd and patient, given to thinking before he spoke – a rare trait. And too, Marna had already been drawn into events more deeply than Gryss would willingly draw any of his other chosen confidants, and it was not inconceivable that she would be drawn in further. Harlen should be at least aware that matters were amiss. And though, like Jeorg, he was not a Councillor he could reasonably be invited to the meeting as an observer. Other names came to mind, equally appropriate. Reliable, sensible men. But too many, he realized. It would be best if his worries were shared by as few as possible. He would confine it to those four.

And Farnor and Marna. It was more imperative than ever now that Marna be told to keep her doubts about

Nilsson's men to herself. He would seek an opportunity to meet both Marna and Farnor soon. In fact today, he decided; before the Council meeting.

Farnor, however, had made a prior decision of his own. Somewhat to his surprise, he had slept well and risen early. He had woken with a clear resolve in his mind and had finished his morning tasks with unwonted speed, though carefully avoiding his father's attention lest more be found.

He had then slipped away and sought out Marna.

Thus it was that the two of them ambushed Gryss as he returned from the castle.

'You're soaked,' were Marna's first words as she and Farnor stepped out of the shelter of a large tree. 'Why on earth didn't you put your hood up?'

Taken aback by her sternly maternal manner, Gryss found himself gaping. Reflexively he began an excuse, 'I . . .' but it faltered before her gaze and other reflexes sent him running to another male for sanctuary.

'What's the matter?' he asked, turning to Farnor. 'Has anything else happened?'

'No,' Farnor replied. 'I wanted to tell Marna about yesterday and last night and she insisted on coming to talk to you about it.'

Awkwardly Gryss dismounted. 'How did you know where I was?' he asked.

'I saw you riding past earlier,' Farnor replied off-handedly. Then, anxiously, he returned Gryss's own question: 'Has anything happened during the night?'

Gryss frowned. He *was* soaked, and cold, and, insofar as he had thought about it at all, this was not how he would have preferred to meet these two to explain the latest developments. However, the chance having arisen, nothing was to be gained by delay. Besides, he could use the two of them to send out notice of the emergency Council meeting for tonight.

'Walk with me to my cottage,' he said. 'I've a lot to tell you.'

As Gryss had surmised, the Council meeting was indeed, 'interesting'. Full Council meetings were rare affairs, and not noted for their strict formality at the best of times. This one, at what was probably the worst of times – certainly within anyone's memory – proved to be almost continuous uproar.

Throughout, however, Gryss gave no indication of his doubts about Nilsson and his men, and was relieved when none was raised by anyone else. The discussion rambled freely and at length over a great many topics, all of which were repeated several times by different individuals and most of which were quite irrelevant. Deliberately, Gryss made no real effort to control the meeting, deeming it better that the effects of the first shock on the leaders of the community be well aired within the tiny Council Hall before being announced publicly. He was also anxious to avoid the development of any serious, coherent thought.

It was thus some considerable time before any semblance of a conclusion appeared, though, inevitably, it was quite simple when it did.

'Well, I suppose there's nothing we can do about it,' they agreed.

Gryss nodded sagely, hoping that he had at last finished repeating his tale. 'Not really,' he said. 'It was announced to me and I've announced it to you.' He sought finally to allay once again the predominant fear that had been expressed. 'The Captain did say he'd no interest in our local affairs and that he expected us to continue as normal. I suppose as matters develop, he'll let us know what he wants in the way of supplies or helpers. I'm sure we'll be able to work together with a little goodwill and common sense.'

Eventually the meeting broke up and the Council members dispersed to their homes, carrying with them the last rumbling echoes of the debate. Discreetly, and separately, during this scattering, Gryss despatched Garren, Yakob, Jeorg and Harlen to his cottage on one pretext or another.

Thus, after being met at the door by his dog wearing the indignant expression of one sorely taxed, he was greeted by a puzzled quartet of friends waiting in his back room.

'I'm sorry for the small deception,' he said. 'But I didn't want to draw attention to the fact that I needed to talk to you away from the others.'

The puzzled expressions turned to concern at this strange admission, and the concern in turn deepened as Gryss added his own doubts to the tale he had told and retold several times to the assembled Councillors.

Unlike the full Council, his listeners were silent when he had finished speaking, with the exception of Jeorg who swore softly under his breath.

'Grim thoughts, Gryss,' Garren said at last. 'What prompted them?'

Gryss shrugged. He had made no mention of Farnor and the creature, nor of Marna's involvement. His friends had enough to contend with as it was. 'They've been brewing for some time, I think,' he lied. 'Treating those injured men last night and the shock of Nilsson's news suddenly seemed to bring them to the fore.' He looked down. 'I feel very responsible for not finding out who they were in the first place.'

Yakob, a tall, dignified man, always smartly dressed and, in many ways the very antithesis of Gryss, laid his hand on Gryss's arm. 'Don't reproach yourself,' he said. 'If there's blame to be allocated, then we're all at fault. We were so surprised to see them at

329

first, then so concerned about our precious tithe, that it never occurred to any of us to ask them for credentials.'

Nodding heads around the small circle confirmed this conclusion.

'It's perhaps as well we didn't ask,' Jeorg said. 'If they're not what they seem they might have turned on us right away.'

'I think Gryss is worrying unnecessarily,' Yakob said. 'They're a rough-looking crowd for sure, but if they're not soldiers, gatherers, then who could they be? Where could such a large armed troop have come from? How could it have come into being?'

Gryss found no reassurance in this. 'It's a big world over the hill,' he said bleakly. 'I saw enough of it when I was younger to know that I hadn't seen a fraction of it. And I saw enough to learn the value of this place here. They could have come from anywhere, believe me. Deserters from some lord or king. Mercenaries. Just plain robbers and bandits. Anything. They *are* foreigners, after all. More to the point, I suspect, is not who are they but what do they want?'

'Is there anything else you haven't told us?' Garren asked.

'I haven't *told* you anything,' Gryss equivocated. 'I just wanted to discuss these concerns with you, quietly and without fuss away from the Council. I might be fretting about nothing, but . . .'

He left the sentence unfinished and the room became silent.

Jeorg blew out a noisy breath. 'Well, we can talk ourselves hoarse here without being any the wiser,' he said. 'It seems to me, like you said, that the only way we'll find out for sure is for one of us to go to the capital and ask someone in authority. And to go quickly, before they put up their . . . guard post or whatever it is.'

Harlen made to speak, but Jeorg, gathering momentum, ploughed on, 'You can tell me the way, Gryss, and I can get the wife to say that I'm sick with . . .' He shrugged. 'Something. I'll leave that to you as well, you're the healer. Then—'

Harlen coughed and waved his hand. Jeorg scowled at the interruption.

'It might be too late,' Harlen said, his round, genial face, uncharacteristically lined. 'I was some way down the valley this morning, early on by the river, and about a dozen or so riders came through. They had pack horses with them.'

Gryss swore.

Jeorg bridled. 'Only a dozen?' he exclaimed. 'I'll sneak past them. They can't watch the whole of the valley.'

Gryss waved him silent. 'No, no,' he said determinedly. 'It's too risky. You'll need a horse, amongst other things, and you're not going to be able to sneak anywhere with that.' He frowned. 'Whatever else he might be, our Captain knows his job. Makes sure we can't leave even before he tells us about it.' He swore again.

The others watched awkwardly. Gryss was not given to such outbursts.

'I could say I hadn't heard about it,' Jeorg said, still clinging to his idea.

'Not if you're caught sneaking through,' Gryss said a little petulantly. 'And if you walk straight into them, they'll just turn you back anyway. And Nilsson did say there'd be punishment for anyone trying to leave without permission.'

Jeorg's mouth worked briefly but no further protest came forth.

'Over the tops?' Gryss said, half to himself.

All four shook their heads and Gryss himself dismissed the notion as soon as he spoke it. That would be far too dangerous; and no chance of taking a horse.

'He's got us,' he said, his jaw set. 'We're trapped.'

The room fell silent again. Gryss's dog made a snuffling noise and rolled over with a thud.

'Then all we can do is watch and wait,' Yakob said. 'I agree with what you said before, Gryss. Whatever they are, Nilsson wants us to think they're King's men and if we behave as though they were then we'll probably find out more about them than if we start doing anything reckless.' He looked significantly at Jeorg who, fortunately, was looking the other way.

'It could be that I'm worrying about nothing,' Gryss said, reverting unconvincingly to Yakob's first remark.

'It could indeed,' Garren said. 'But equally you could be right. There's a lot we've taken for granted. Questions that we should've asked can't be asked now. It's a fair assumption that no one will be allowed to leave and it'll be too risky to try to sneak out, so there's nothing else we *can* do but watch and wait as we decided in the Council meeting.' He leaned forward. 'But we five must keep in touch. Meet regularly to discuss developments. And we must keep our ears open for the feeling in the village.'

Jeorg scowled at this conclusion. 'We should *do* something,' he said heatedly. 'Not just mope around waiting for something to happen. I'd still like to have a go at getting to the capital.'

Gryss looked at him intently. Jeorg was a robustly practical man, and inaction was against his nature. To forbid him to leave the valley would be to store up some future problem almost inevitably.

Cautiously, he said, 'No, Jeorg. Not yet at least. We *must* get more idea of what's actually going on.'

'The longer we leave it, the worse it might get,' Jeorg retorted. 'If they've already set up a guard post it could be a small fort next.' His eyes widened. 'They might even ask us to build it,' he added indignantly.

'No, Jeorg,' Gryss said. 'We none of us here must do anything without telling the others.' He did not wait for any agreement to this idea. 'Think about leaving, Jeorg. I'll tell you the way to the capital, such as I can remember of it, and we can decide what you'll need, and what tale you'll have to tell so that everything will be ready if you get the opportunity to go. But don't do anything without discussing it with us first. Is that agreed?'

Taken aback by this sudden vigour on Gryss's part, Jeorg gaped. 'I – I suppose so,' he stammered.

Gryss looked at the others. They all nodded, Garren smiling a little at Jeorg's discomfiture.

'And we keep this discussion, *all* our discussions and ideas, to ourselves,' Gryss declared with an air of finality.

No one disagreed, and the meeting broke up. Before they parted, Gryss spoke to Harlen and Garren.

'I'd like to take Farnor and Marna partly into our confidence,' he said. 'They're both sensible children . . .' He gave a guilty shrug. 'Young people, I suppose I should say, these days. And they can wander about, run messages and the like, more inconspicuously than we can. And they'll pick up more things than we would – gossip and the like.'

Garren gave him an arch look. 'Well, Farnor's been spending more time here than on the farm of late, so I suppose it'd hardly constitute a change,' he said.

Gryss's hands fluttered apologetically at this bluntness, then he decided to let out at least part of the truth.

'Farnor and I have spent a lot of time talking about Nilsson and his men,' he said. 'He came to me of his own accord with his doubts about them after we'd been up there the first time. He'll work things out for himself when he hears the news, and I think he'd be better off knowing he could turn to you as well as to me.'

Garren looked hurt. 'He can turn to me any time about anything,' he said. 'He didn't have to come running to you.'

'He didn't come running to me,' Gryss said reassuringly. 'It just happened in the course of conversation, as it were. Don't reproach him for it. I've always been a bit of a grandfather to him, and there's things you can tell your grandparents that you can't tell your parents.'

'I suppose so,' Garren conceded, colouring slightly. 'And if he's already bothering about what's happening, then I've no objection to him knowing what we think. To be honest, it'll make things easier at home. He's become rather elusive recently.'

Gryss turned his attention to Harlen. Getting a young man involved was one thing, a girl – a young woman – was another . . .

But Harlen was, if anything, relieved. 'I can't pretend to be happy about it,' he said. 'But Marna's been talking along the same lines as you almost since these people arrived. I think it'd be a good thing if she knew you thought the same. I've been concerned that she might end up doing something foolish.' He hesitated. 'We get on well together, but . . . we don't always talk as well as we should about some things. It's difficult . . . She needs a woman about the house, really. Someone she can talk to properly.'

'I understand,' Gryss said. 'At least I think I do. On the whole I think I understand women less now than I did fifty years ago, but I know she loves you as much as you love her.'

Harlen nodded. 'She's also headstrong and stubborn,' he said. 'If it came into her mind to do so, she wouldn't think twice about marching up to the castle and demanding to see some letter of authority from the King.'

Gryss laughed at Harlen's manner. 'So you don't mind her helping?' he asked.

'Yes, I do,' Harlen replied. 'But, no, tell her what you want and with my blessing. She'll go her own way anyway.'

A little later, Gryss stood at his front door and watched his visitors departing. Idly he fingered the iron ring, feeling the lines of the etched figures sharp beneath his touch. The bell tinkled as he tugged the chain, and a faint, sleepy bark drifted down the hallway. Handling the ring reminded him of Nilsson's almost angry question when he had visited him a few days earlier. No preamble, no subtle introduction to the subject, just, 'Where did you get this ring from, old man?'

Gryss looked at it. 'You know more about these people than we do, don't you?' he said out loud. Then he sighed. He wished he had asked more of the man from whom he had bought it all those years ago. Now he couldn't even remember what he looked like.

Still, that was wind through the trees: long, long, gone. He set the ring down. It rattled slightly against the wall of the cottage.

Gryss took a deep breath. The air was fresh, cool and still now. He looked up. Clouds, rich with blacks and dark blues, ominous with grey and sometimes silver edges, moved to the whim of a wind of their own against a moonlit sky.

He had mixed feelings about what had transpired. He was glad that he had shared at least part of his burden with his friends, but he felt some remorse that he had lied to Garren and Harlen about the involvement of their children. There was nothing else he could have done, of course, and he had promised both Farnor and Marna

335

that he would try to clear the way for them to continue to be involved without bringing parental strictures down on them.

Even so, deceit went against the grain. It had the feeling of a bad omen. He reached up to strike the sunstone as he had done every night for as long as he could remember. Then he hesitated and lowered his hand. Not tonight, he thought. Not tonight.

He turned and went inside, closing the door gently behind him.

Chapter 24

Fortunately, the extensive debate that the Council had held and the final decision to watch and wait, had been well absorbed by the individual Councillors and thus, for the greater part, it pervaded the public breaking of the news about the intended garrison over the next few days.

Inevitably, though, the reaction of the villagers was mixed. Most naturally pondered the reasons for it, but in the absence of any great knowledge about the world over the hill their attempts foundered or became manifest flights of fancy such as Yonas the Teller might have retailed.

One or two, nodding wisely, announced that they had known all the time that something of the kind had been intended. 'Why else would they arrive here, after all these years?' Although it was well noted that these individuals had neglected to share this foreknowledge with their friends and neighbours prior to the public announcement.

No small number shrugged indifferently, regarding the matter as being one beyond their control and thus not worthy of serious concern.

A small minority – a very small minority – by some circuitous reasoning all their own declared that they felt reassured to have an armed force nearby because the fact that an armed force was needed nearby made them feel uneasy.

On the whole, the men expressed varying degrees of indignation – generally in the familiar security of the inn – while the women, wiser by far, fell silent or drew in sharp breaths and lifted their hands to their breasts to still the fluttering fear that rose from their inner depths to greet the news.

Few were really concerned about the positioning of a guard post down the valley. 'Nobody ever goes down there anyway. Besides, it'll keep any undesirable outsiders out.' Though quite when any undesirable outsiders had last visited the valley was a question not pursued.

Gryss and most of the other Councillors found themselves occupied at length in discussing the matter, but this time Gryss was happy to be repeating the same story. The feeling that gradually spread across the village chimed with the villagers' natures.

'Don't rock the haycart.'

'Don't stir the pigswill if you don't want the smell.'

In short, leave them alone and they'll leave us alone. The funeral knell of many a society.

Despite his relief at the reception of the news, however, Gryss's concerns did not lessen. He looked at the complacency he was helping to engender and wondered if he were not once again failing the village as he had failed them when he accepted the arrivals as tithe gatherers without comment.

After a few days, he called another Council meeting and had himself confirmed in the duty that he had already assumed, namely official representative for the village at the castle.

Not that his services seemed to be needed. There was no activity from the castle other than the occasional group of men heading down the valley, or returning. Harlen reported that their guard post was only a few tents, although he remarked also that they were patrolling widely on horseback.

Gryss merely nodded at this intelligence, though he ensured that it was repeated in Jeorg's presence.

Marna and Farnor, now officially seconded to Gryss's command, as it were, found they had nothing to do except pursue their everyday tasks. Gryss would glance enquiringly at Farnor when they met, but the young man had no further strange contacts to report.

Increasingly, though, he kept sensing the distant, unintelligible babbling that he had heard before his last contact with the creature. It tended to come to him when he was at the edge of sleep, yet it was unequivocally from beyond himself, he knew; it was no figment of his imagination.

For no reason that he could have given, he did not mention this to Gryss. Whatever it was, it had none of the malignity that he had felt so sharply in his contacts with the creature.

While the momentum of the villagers' age-old ways began to reassert itself, matters at the castle were less serene.

Rannick came and went to a rhythm of his own, just as he always had, accounting to no one for anything. But each time he returned he was peculiarly elated. The men, however, were less so. They had turned to him partly out of fear, but also because he had given them a vision of the future which they had had once before, and the destruction of which had sent them out from their homeland into their present fruitless and futile wandering.

Now however, apart from manning the guard post down the valley, they found themselves without much to do. When they had stumbled on this castle, they had been exhausted, hungry and almost totally demoralized, their will sapped by the ever-present fear of retribution from the past. Now they were more secure than they had been since they began their travels, and the bonding that a common privation had given them began to weaken.

It needed no great sensitivity on Nilsson's part to detect the growing discontent, but he was at a loss to know what to do. Rannick had bound them to the valley and, to ensure peace, Nilsson himself had effectively bound them to the castle and its immediate environs.

He taxed Rannick. 'The men need to be occupied, Lord,' he said. 'They'll go sour on us left to their own devices for too long. Sour and quarrelsome.'

Rannick, recently returned from one of his absences, was sitting staring into space. He gave no indication that he had heard anything and Nilsson made to speak again, but as he opened his mouth Rannick lifted his hand.

'Every day,' he said softly.

'Lord?'

'Every day,' Rannick said again. He looked at his hands. 'Such things I find.'

Some inner voice told Nilsson not to inquire further.

A long silence elapsed. Then Rannick stood up and turned to face Nilsson. 'Yes, you are right,' he said. 'The men will not only become sour and quarrelsome, they will become soft and useless if they are allowed to continue thus.' His face hardened. 'And they are of no value if they cannot fight, and fight well.'

'Yes, Lord,' Nilsson agreed. 'But what—?'

'We ride,' Rannick said, cutting across his question. 'We ride downland, out of the valley. Begin our journey along the golden road.'

The last remark made no sense to Nilsson, but the import of Rannick's intention did. 'Leave here, Lord?' he exclaimed, unable to keep the surprise out of his voice. 'Why?'

Rannick smiled unpleasantly. 'To get them used to the field again, Captain. The better to appreciate this haven. And to search, to find, to take, to learn, to test our strength. Many things.'

Still little the wiser, Nilsson turned quickly to practicalities.

'As you command, Lord,' he said. 'How many do you wish to go, and for how long?'

'All of us, Captain,' Rannick replied. 'All of us.' He looked round at the plain stone walls and arched ceiling. 'But not for long. There is much to be done here when we return. This place must be made fit for our presence.'

'All of us, Lord?' Nilsson echoed cautiously. 'We must leave a dozen or so to guard the place.'

'Against what, Captain?' Rannick said with a flicker of a malevolent laugh that chilled Nilsson. 'The villagers? They are less likely than ever to come up here now. And what would they do if they did? Nibble at their stolen tithe like mice?'

Nilsson had no answer. 'Old habits, Lord,' he said after a moment.

Rannick turned his attention back to his hands, flexing each of them in turn, then he nodded slowly. 'Besides, *I* will leave a guard here that none will defy.'

Thus it was that, early the following day, the villagers found themselves watching the entire troop trotting noisily through the village. There was some elation at first, but it soon vanished as, in their wake, came the cold-eyed message that Nilsson had left with Gryss: 'We'll be back.'

Nevertheless, their departure opened up opportunities for some, as Nilsson, for some reason, had chosen to tell Gryss that the entire troop was leaving on an exercise, and that nothing would be required at the castle until they returned in a few days.

'Harlen says they've gone all the way downland,' Jeorg said. 'And left no guard posted. We mightn't get another chance. I can leave for the capital right now, and you and the others can go to the castle

341

and see if there are any documents there saying who they are.'

Gryss was unhappy about both ideas, not least because, in an attempt to prevent Jeorg from doing anything impetuous, he had been fulfilling his promise to instruct him in the route to the capital. He had made the instruction quite leisurely, affecting to forget certain parts and spending a great deal of time referring to some very old journals that he had kept during youthful journeyings. Despite Gryss's delaying tactics, though, Jeorg had been attentive, thorough and uncharacteristically patient. And now his reasoning was sound: who could say when the valley would be left unguarded again?

'I suppose so,' Gryss agreed, after some protracted badgering. 'But in the name of pity, Jeorg, take care.'

'I'll keep my eyes open obviously, but I'll tell them I was coming after them to ask permission if I bump into them,' Jeorg said confidently.

His confidence, however, was not contagious, and Gryss could not keep his anxiety from his face as he bade farewell to his friend later that day.

'Don't look so miserable, Gryss,' Jeorg said. 'We've planned it as well as we could. I'm no tracker, but they're a big crowd and I don't think I'm going to run into them by accident.' He looked up at the sky. 'Anyway, it's a fine day for a ride.'

Gryss ignored the false heartiness. 'Are you sure your wife's agreeable to this?' he asked, in a final attempt to deter him.

Jeorg's confidence faltered. 'Yes,' he said, followed immediately by, 'Well, no. Not really. But . . . it's got to be done, hasn't it? She's with me.'

And that was that. Gryss stood motionless, his head forward and his shoulders hunched in tension as he watched Jeorg ride off. The sun was warm on his face and the air was filled with the scents and sounds of burgeoning summer, but inside Gryss roared with anger. Anger at himself for what seemed to be his continuing folly in placating the villagers and allowing Jeorg to undertake this risky journey. Anger at Nilsson for being whatever he was and for bringing such dismay to this quiet and beautiful place. Anger at Jeorg for being so capable, so naive, so . . .

He swore to himself to dash aside such indulgence and began walking back to his cottage. It was time to move on to his next folly.

But he would do this on his own. With the vision of Jeorg's retreating figure etched into his mind, he knew that he did not have it in him to risk any more of his friends, for whatever cause. The searching of the castle had been hastily arranged for the following day, and involved Gryss, Yakob and Garren visiting the castle while Harlen, Farnor and Marna kept look-out along the valley. He squinted up at the sun to judge the time. If he set off now and rode, there would be time enough to be there and back before the light failed.

He would go to the castle *now*, and if he found it empty he would search it on his own.

He had reckoned without Farnor, however. More excited than he chose to admit by the prospect of the venture planned for the morrow, he had spent the afternoon watching the castle closely. He had selected a vantage point on a grassy hillock which gave him a good view and from which he could also see much of the village. Aware of his duties for the next day, he kept glancing back down the valley to the place from where it had been agreed that Marna would signal if Nilsson's troop unexpectedly reappeared. So it happened that he saw Gryss riding along the road when he was only a few minutes out of the village.

Presuming that Gryss was intending to visit Garren, perhaps to make further arrangements for the next day, he paid little heed to him until he saw him pass by the end of the path that led to the farm. Farnor frowned. Where was he going?

Without pondering the question further, and anxious to impart his own new information, Farnor began a cautious descent of the steep knoll. At the bottom the slope eased and he finished the last part at some speed, startling Gryss's horse as he burst out of the bushes in front of it.

Gryss leaned forward and seized its neck anxiously.

'I'm sorry,' Farnor blurted out as the look in Gryss's eyes heralded a particularly fulsome reproach. He took the horse's head and patted it gently.

'I'm sorry,' he said again.

Caught between concern for the fright he had received, the loss of dignity he had suffered and Farnor's swift apology, Gryss was only able to splutter.

'It *is* empty,' Farnor said, capitalizing on this hiatus.

'What?' Gryss managed as the statement cut through his confused indignation.

'It *is* empty,' Farnor repeated. 'The castle. I've been watching it all afternoon and I haven't seen a sign of anyone. Nilsson was telling the truth. They've all gone.'

'Oh,' said Gryss flatly.

'Where are you going?' Farnor asked, abruptly.

Still unsettled by Farnor's sudden appearance, Gryss blurted out the truth. 'To the castle,' he said.

Farnor's eyes widened. 'Why? I thought you were going tomorrow.' He looked around. 'Where are the others?'

Gryss stayed with the truth.

'I decided I didn't want anyone else involved,' he replied.

Farnor frowned. How could anyone *not* be involved in discovering the truth about these people? he thought.

'I'll come with you,' he said.

'No, I don't think so,' Gryss began, but Farnor was already leading the horse forward. Gryss reined it to a halt.

'No, Farnor. This is my responsibility, and I'll carry it by myself. You stay here and keep watch for me.'

Farnor stared at him blankly. 'If that's what you want,' he said after a moment. 'But why—?'

'That's what I want,' Gryss said.

Uncertain, Farnor remained standing in the middle of the road as Gryss rode off. Then he began walking after him.

A little later Gryss approached the castle gate and found Farnor waiting for him.

'It's much quicker over the fields,' Farnor explained before he was asked.

Gryss looked at him pensively, surprised at the mixture of emotions he was experiencing. He was concerned that the boy – young man, he reminded himself yet again – was about to involve himself in something the significance of which he could not begin to appreciate. He was a little angry, too, that his categorical instruction to Farnor had been so blatantly disregarded. And yet he was glad to see him there, young, strong and fit, free of the bodily reluctance and emotional hesitancy with which old age had hemmed in his own true self. It was strange, he thought, how he found Farnor to be such a powerful support, for he had no illusions that he would be of any value against such as Nilsson in any form of combat, mental or physical.

'For your legs, maybe,' he replied, sourly, setting aside his musings. 'But I thought I told you to stay behind,' he said.

'You did,' Farnor admitted. 'But there's no point

me keeping watch if you can't hear me shouting, is there?'

Gryss raised his eyebrows significantly at this attempt to hold what he regarded as an indefensible position.

'Anyway, I'm here now,' Farnor went on. 'Let's go inside.'

'*I'll* go inside, young man,' Gryss said firmly. 'You can do as you're told for once, and wait out here with the horse.' He gave Farnor a look that forbade any defiance then swung down gracelessly from the horse, which skittered slightly as he jostled against it to recover his balance. Farnor took the bridle and murmured softly to the horse.

Gryss gave a terse grunt of thanks and marched over to the wicket door.

The damage that had been done to the lock when Nilsson and his men had first arrived had been crudely repaired. Gryss smiled to himself. Unused to locked doors, it occurred to him only now that all the heart-searching about coming here might well have been pointless. Was it likely, after all, he reflected, that such people as these would have left the place unlocked?

Tentatively he pushed it. To his surprise, it swung open easily.

Farnor, holding the horse and strolling slowly after him, watched his cautious approach. As the door opened and a small part of the courtyard, beyond the dark shade under the archway, came into view it seemed to him that there was something unreal about it; unnatural, even. Without knowing why, he stepped forward urgently.

'Gryss, don't go in!' he shouted.

But it was too late. Gryss, after leaning in and looking round for any signs of life, had, almost incongruously, tiptoed in.

Immediately, the door slammed shut. The sound filled

346

Farnor's head like the tolling of a great bell. He clapped his hands to his ears.

The horse whinnied and reared, tearing itself free from Farnor's loose grip. It galloped away, but Farnor did not notice. He was running towards the wicket door, drawn on desperately by the sounds which were beginning to emanate from behind it.

Then the sound of a roaring wind began to fill the air, rising and falling like some demented creature. And through it came the sound of powerful blows being struck; echoing, booming sounds, as if some giant smith were forging a huge shield. And, threading through the whole, a high-pitched shrieking.

Farnor felt his legs – his whole being – become leaden as he forced himself forward. It seemed as though the gate were at the end of a long tunnel and that it retreated from him as fast as he ran towards it.

'No!' he heard himself shouting distantly, partly in fear, partly in denial.

Faint though it was, the cry shattered the strange, disorientating illusion and he found himself standing before the wicket. He hammered on it frantically. The sound of his blows swelled and rose to mingle with the pounding din coming from within. Farnor felt as though he was trapped in the middle of a grotesque quarrel between two demented drummers. And still the sound of the roaring wind overtopped all with the shrill shrieking weaving in and out of the tumult.

Farnor struck three double-handed blows on the gate shouting, 'Gryss, Gryss!'

Then, a spark of reason shone through his frenzy. He mustn't panic, he must think. He ran his hands over the smooth, planed surface of the wicket. He tried to remember what kind of a lock it had. Surely it couldn't have locked itself? But he could not remember clearly; too many thoughts were cascading through his mind.

What was happening to Gryss? What would his father say about his neglect in allowing the old man to enter the castle alone? What would Nilsson do if he returned to find Gryss locked in there? And many others tumbling wildly over one another. But two emerged above all: what was happening to Gryss? And what was that fearful noise?

He stepped back from the gate with a view to charging it.

As he did so, however, it seemed to him that the wicket was different from the gate which surrounded it. Just as the courtyard had seemed to be in another place when he had briefly glimpsed it before so too, now, did the wicket.

It was itself, here and now, but it was also something else. Or something had been added to it. Some strange influence pouring through from elsewhere.

And it was no benign influence. It was a terrible harm. A terrible rending of reality. A terrible wound.

Farnor's whole body shivered with fear at this unwanted awareness. And, as if the shivering were a birth tremor, he felt something inside him awaken and cry out against this horror: something that he knew nothing of except that it could somehow staunch the wound, stem the flow that was bringing this harm.

No! this inner resolve cried.

No!

Farnor felt as though he had been suddenly jerked wide awake from a twilight doze.

He ran forward and hurled his shoulder against the door.

The wicket door burst open as he struck it and he tumbled headlong out of the sunlight and into the shade of the archway.

He rolled over and clambered frantically to his feet as if expecting to be assailed.

Still he could feel the mysterious resolve inside him setting itself against the harm that was now flowing all around.

He paid it no heed however, for, turning towards the gate, he saw Gryss staggering backwards as if he had been suddenly released from some great pressure. He seized the old man's arm.

At the same time he realized that the noise . . . the harm . . . had weakened . . .

No, not weakened . . .

It had . . . moved away, as if no longer able to reach through . . .

Farnor turned again and looked across the courtyard. There was nothing untoward to be seen, but the sense that he had had of the yard being both there and yet, at the same time, somewhere else, was still with him though now this duality had a quality of hesitancy about it; uncertainty – as if unexpectedly abandoned by a hitherto faithful ally.

Yet it was still there. And it was recovering from whatever had happened to it. Gathering momentum. Whirls of dust were beginning to rise and scurry across the finely jointed stone slabs of the yard.

A breath of wind blew in Farnor's face. He drew back involuntarily. It had had a repellent quality to it, full of enquiry like the touch of a probing hand. Then, as if a signal had been received, the noise began to gather again. Abruptly, the dancing dust devils were scattered into a fine, stinging cloud by a powerful gust. It swirled low and shifted around the courtyard then hurled itself directly at Farnor.

He staggered under the impact. A hastily raised hand protected his eyes, but grit blew into his partly open mouth.

As he turned his face from the impact, he saw that the wicket door was starting to close.

The noise grew louder, triumphant.

Farnor tightened his grip on Gryss and unceremoniously dragged him towards the closing wicket.

He was too slow, however. Gryss staggered, and as Farnor yanked him upright with one hand the wind gusted behind the wicket and slammed it shut, trapping Farnor's upper arm as he lunged forward.

He cried out in pain at the impact, and then in fear as the wind began to pound into him, pressing him cruelly against the gate and pressing the wicket tighter and tighter against his arm.

Tears filled his eyes, so intense was the pain.

He tried to pull himself free, but then something struck him and he heard, 'Push, Farnor!' through the pain. 'Push! Or you'll lose your hand, and it'll have us.'

Vaguely he became aware of Gryss's old hands gripping the edge of the wicket and trying to force it open.

'Push, Farnor!'

His vision cleared momentarily and he thrust his free hand into the gap and hooked it around the edge of the gate. Then, roaring in an attempt to take himself beyond the pain, he pushed.

The noise mounting around him seemed to exult in his cry, picking it up and returning it to him tenfold. But the awful grip on his arm eased slightly, and suddenly his shoulder was in the gap.

And then his whole body.

For an instant it seemed that the wicket would crush him utterly as the pressure behind it was redoubled. But Farnor had both arms firmly against the edge of the gate, his good one pushing with a strength he had never thought he possessed and his injured one pushing, perhaps less powerfully, but with the pain transmuted now into a fury more ancient and terrible than that which was feeding the roaring wind.

The gap widened.

'Get out! Get out! Get out!' he shouted, his voice hoarse with desperation.

From somewhere Gryss appeared to scramble underneath Farnor's straining arms and tumble out through the gap.

No sooner was he through, than Farnor snatched his hands free and jumped. The wicket slammed behind him, giving him a final vicious buffet which sent him flailing wildly out into the sunlight. His legs made a valiant effort to keep him upright, but almost immediately they tangled and he was rolling over and over on the hard-packed ground.

In his ears rang the final, deafening boom of the closing wicket.

As he came to a halt, Farnor became aware of the sound of the roaring wind fading away interminably into a distant nothingness. He became aware, too, that the strange resolve inside him was gone, leaving only a fleeting after-image. He felt oddly empty.

With the dwindling of the terrible noise, sounds of normality began to return.

But they were no solace, for the pain in his arm returned with them and it was fearful. And too, the devil's brew of fear and anger that had given him the strength he needed was not yet fully spent. Clutching his injured arm and wincing at the pain, he twisted himself round and screamed every obscenity he had ever heard at the now silent gate. Eyes wide, mouth gaping, he screamed his defiance and rage, spewing forth not only the horrors of the moment but all the doubts and fears and resentment of the past weeks.

Then he slumped to the ground, hugging his arm miserably.

Only for a moment, though, for no sooner did he begin to become aware of the blue sky overhead than he remembered Gryss. Incongruously he felt himself colouring as he recalled the language he had just been using in front of the village elder. The embarrassment did not last long, however, as an agonizing spasm in his arm made him cry out.

Where the devil was Gryss? Couldn't he see he was injured? Stupid old man!

Propping himself on his good arm he pushed himself up into a kneeling position and looked around. For a moment, his vision still streaky with the tears of pain, he thought that Gryss had abandoned him. Then a nearby blur that he had thought was a rock came into focus. It was the old man, lying on the ground.

He was lying very still.

Chapter 25

Jeorg rode steadily along the winding stone road that led down the valley. Already almost completely overgrown it would soon peter out into little more than a cart track before disappearing completely. Beyond that, all would be strange though Jeorg knew from what Gryss had described to him that, after a while, the mountains would gradually become less steep and turn eventually into rolling, grassy hills.

'Look back at the mountains,' Gryss had said, in passing. 'We live in the middle of a sight of rare splendour.'

But splendid sights were far from Jeorg's mind. He was nervous and at times regretting his impulsive volunteering for this journey.

Still, he reassured himself when his chest began to tighten with alarm, it had to be done. And it might be the only chance they would have to find out who these new arrivals truly were. And too, he had prepared for the journey diligently under Gryss's reluctantly given tuition.

The thought helped.

But not much.

He kept his eyes fast on the far distance for any sign that he might be catching up with Nilsson and his troop. Ironically, he felt that he would feel safer when he was in the completely strange country beyond the valley. At least there he would not be hedged in by the mountains on either side. And it was quite possible that Nilsson would go in a completely different direction to the one that he would be taking.

Thinking about which, he must keep his wits about him lest he miss any of the many landmarks that Gryss had told him about, and which he had so carefully memorized. At least the weather was fine today; he would have been even more nervous had he been attempting this journey on a misty winter's day.

The road ended, and the scenery about him became unfamiliar. He began to feel tense again.

Come on, you're no child, he told himself. You've survived being benighted high in the hills, and being trapped by sudden snows. There's nothing out here that can harm you; even Nilsson and his crowd, providing you can talk fast enough.

His unease passed and he turned his mind to the details of the journey ahead. It was a long way to the capital, and he would have to pass through several villages and towns.

Towns! He had always had difficulty in imagining what such places would be like. Were they wondrous, magical places such as Yonas might describe, or were they just big villages?

The notion taxed him. There was an aura of futility about the idea of so many people living so close together, relying on others to grow and catch their food while they pursued the kinds of tasks that were only necessary because they chose to live so close together. He shook his head as, once again, he failed to break this circle of reasoning.

And Gryss had not been much help. In answer to his questions he had pouted, shrugged and said, 'There's not much to tell, really. They're confusing, noisy and very crowded in places.' Then he had seemed to relent. 'But they're nice sometimes, as well. All manner of interesting things to see. And people? So many strange people, from the wretched to the magnificent.' As for the capital, itself, all that Gryss would say was, 'That *is* worth seeing, without a doubt. But you'll be glad to leave it behind and get back here.'

Ah well, Jeorg mused, philosophically, I'll find out for myself in time, I suppose.

As he went on, he was relieved to see that the way was developing as Gryss had said it would. The old man had affected weakness of memory, 'After all this time,' but, in fact, the route he had taken as a young man was as clear to him now as it had been when he first walked it, so intense had his excitement been, and he had described it to Jeorg with great accuracy.

Jeorg passed by the shore of a long lake, mottled white here and there with flocks of birds and bright blue under the summer sky. It was bigger than any of the lakes further up the valley, and was hauntingly beautiful. Here and there he passed derelict buildings with trees and shrubs growing through roofs and windows, and, for the first time in his life, as he looked at these forlorn remains, he wondered what peoples had gone before in this place.

He allowed his horse to maintain its own steady pace, to ensure that he would not close with Nilsson and his men who were travelling on their larger steeds. But he was still following the route they had taken, there being ample sign of the passage of a large number of horsemen, and he kept himself alert for any indication that he might be drawing too near.

As the afternoon wore on, he remembered Gryss's advice and turned round, for the first time, to look from where he had come. He caught his breath as the vista revealed itself. It was far more than what Gryss had called, simply, a splendid sight. Mountains filled the horizon; massive and majestic. Etched sharp and clear against the blue sky by the low bright sun, they radiated an ancient stillness which held not only Jeorg's gaze for an interval that he could not have begun to measure, but his whole being.

When he came to himself again, another interpretation of Gryss's advice returned to him: 'Look back every now and then especially when you're changing direction.' Gryss had chuckled to himself. 'Believe me, things don't look the same on the way back.'

He understood that now, for the mountains under which the village lay were but a few among many. The thought made him fretful again for a moment. Majestic they might well be, but they were also oblivious to such as he and he could look to no help from them, or anyone, if he lost his way.

As the light faded, he found that he was still following in the footsteps of Nilsson and his men, and he took the precaution of camping in a small copse where the shrubbery would hide him from any casual inspection. And he decided to forego a fire. The evening was warm and he needed no hot meal.

But that he had to behave thus, distressed him, and the restless night he spent was not wholly due to the hardness of the ground and the snufflings and rustlings of the night creatures.

When he woke the following day it took him a little time to remember where he was and what he was doing. He swore when he found that the wife he had just put his arm around was a log in whose lee he had been sleeping.

He swore more than a few times after that, until he had shaken off some of the stiffness that his night's rest had invested him with.

Briefly he pondered lighting a fire and cooking himself a warm breakfast, but he decided against it. It would take time and effort and might perhaps signal his presence to the troop ahead. Besides, though the copse was damp and chilly, the sky overhead was blue

356

and cloudless and promised another warm day. A little walking would soon warm him and dry his dew-soaked bedding and pack.

Indeed, he felt much more his old self by the time he had saddled his horse and soon he was striding out, leading the horse and eating an apple noisily.

His thoughts wandered over a variety of topics as he walked along; up and down, like the terrain he was travelling over. Where he was going, and why. His wife: he struggled to set aside the concern which she tried to hide from him, but which had been all too plain for him to see, in her eyes and the slight set of her mouth. Gryss: had the old man been able to get into the castle, and if so, what had he found? How long was his journey going to take? Would his food last? What kind of people would he meet in the villages . . . and towns! . . . on the way? Would anything untoward happen in the village in his absence?

But, underscoring all, was concern about who lay ahead of him. He was still in the valley, and still following in the hoofprints of Nilsson's men. He wouldn't be truly happy until he saw them turn one way when he turned another, but the country was fairly open and unless he was monumentally careless he should be able to see them before they saw him.

Eventually he came in sight of a conspicuous gap between two hills which Gryss had identified as the point where he should turn west and leave the valley proper. It was at this point that he had hoped he would part company with the troop, but to his dismay, as he turned towards the dip, he found that he was still following the trail of the now familiar tracks.

He mouthed an oath.

Still, the lowest part of the gap was considerably higher than the surrounding countryside. Perhaps when he reached it he would be overlooking the land on the far side and be able to get some indication of how far ahead the riders were.

He mounted his horse and clicked it forward.

It took him longer than he had thought to reach the gap, the scale of the new terrain being deceptive, but as he made his way up the steady slope he began to feel exposed. It occurred to him that if he could see over the countryside from the top, then he in his turn might be seen against the skyline by anyone happening to look back.

He dismounted, feeling quite smug at this insight, and following his own reasoning directed himself to one side of the gap so that he would be even less conspicuous when he reached the top of it.

When, finally, he did reach it, he realized that his precautions had not really been necessary. The ground between the two hills was wide and gently rounded, and the country on the far side came into view only gradually as he walked across it.

Even so, he kept well to one side and proceeded cautiously.

When he was comfortably past the crown of the gap, he paused and looked out over the land that he was about to venture into. It did not have the massive splendour of the mountains, but he found himself held by the sight nonetheless. Hedged all his life by mountains, the vista of rolling countryside fading into the distant morning haze made him feel strangely heady; both excited and uncertain.

Over the hill, he thought to himself, rubbing the palms of his hands together. He could feel the lure that had drawn Gryss onward so many years ago and also, albeit slightly, the comforting pull of the valley at his back.

He turned for a final look at the valley before he set off into this new land, but nothing was to be seen except the sky and the crown of the gap. He smiled to himself and then turned back again to the next part of his journey.

His nervousness returned. Apart from the continuing need to watch for Nilsson and his men, he would have to be careful in this wide, rambling land where, free of the mountains on either side, he would be able to wander in almost any direction. Landmarks would be smaller and less obvious and there would be fewer opportunities to stand high above it and determine his route.

But he had Gryss's descriptions memorized, and he was not exactly stupid, was he?

And, in that connection, his first task now, before descending further, was to check if Nilsson and his men were somewhere in this panorama. He spent some time peering intently over the landscape, but though he could see no line of riders, there were too many folds and dips and extensive areas of woodland for him to move on carelessly. He wrinkled his nose in disappointment. He would have to continue as he had been doing, keeping his eye on the tracks that they had left and as far ahead as the terrain would allow.

He set off down the slope, leading his horse.

By noon he was down from the hills and riding over soft grasses and through light woodlands. All around him spring was hectically preparing for summer, birds singing and nesting, flowers blooming, the occasional small animal pausing briefly to examine this alien passer-by.

But for the fact that he was still following Nilsson's men, Jeorg would have immersed himself in this great awakening. He was old enough to appreciate the joy of the moment while knowing that this same countryside would hold little joy given a good downpour and a strong wind.

At last he reached the point that he had been hoping

to find for most of the journey. The tracks turned suddenly north.

He stood for a little while on the spot, gazing in the direction they had taken. What was up there? Another valley? And what were Nilsson and his men doing, anyway? For a moment he considered going a little way after them to see if he could find an answer to these questions, but the urge soon left him. He had spent much of the journey so far looking to be free of these people and now he was. Now all he had to concern himself about was remembering the way to the capital.

He turned his horse to the west.

As he did so a swirling flock of small birds flew low overhead, the sound of their wings loud and urgent.

Then an unexpected and strong breeze began to blow. His horse shied uneasily.

Nursing his throbbing arm, Farnor struggled to his feet and ran across to where Gryss lay.

'Gryss, Gryss! Are you all right?' he called out as he dropped to his knees beside the old man.

Gryss's eyes were closed and he made no response. For a terrifying moment, Farnor thought that he was not breathing and, without thinking, he took hold of his arm and shook it as if to waken him. Gryss's eyes opened and he drew in a sharp, gasping breath.

'Are you all right?' Farnor asked again, still shaking him.

Gryss yanked his arm free. 'I will be when you stop pulling my arm off,' he said testily. But his face was both pale and covered with perspiration, and belied the vigour of this rebuke. 'Help me up,' he demanded, trying to lever himself on to one elbow. He was breathing heavily.

'In a moment,' Farnor said, putting his left arm

around Gryss's shoulders. 'Just rest a little. You look *awful*.'

Gryss's lip curled. It was almost a sneer, and an expression that Farnor had never seen before on the old man's face.

'Thank you, Farnor,' Gryss said, his tone matching his look. 'You obviously have a natural healer's flare for building confidence in a patient. Now get me up, and let's get away from here before anything else happens.'

But for all his protestations, he lay back on the ground again and made no effort to help himself for some time. When, finally, he did so, it proved no easy task to get him to his feet. He was having difficulty in breathing and Farnor had no feeling in his right arm other than pain, which seemed now to be affecting every part of his body; and both of them were shaking with the shock of the terrifying encounter.

'Where's the horse?' Gryss asked as they began to move hesitantly away from the castle.

'I've no idea,' Farnor replied. 'It ran off when the gate slammed shut.' He shook his head. 'I was half inclined to join it. What happened in there?'

Gryss halted and patted his chest with a clenched fist. Farnor kept his left arm about the old man until, at last, he began to straighten up, and to breathe a little more easily.

'I don't know, Farnor,' he said, without looking at him. 'But I do know that I'm too old for this kind of activity.' He patted his chest again, and coughed painfully.

Gently he shook Farnor's arm from his shoulders and looked around vaguely. 'The horse has probably gone back to the inn.'

'That'll cause a stir,' Farnor said. 'There'll be all sorts of questions. What are we going to say happened?'

361

Gryss frowned. 'We'll have to lie, I'm afraid,' he said. 'I can say I was coming to see your father and something – a fox, maybe – startled the horse, and it bolted and threw me.'

Farnor looked at him unhappily. 'I can't lie to my parents any more,' he said. 'Keeping this business about the creature from them is bad enough. It makes me feel . . . uncomfortable, and my mother knows something's the matter apart from any worries about whether Nilsson's men are gatherers or not.' He grimaced violently and held his right arm tightly. It was growing increasingly painful and he thought he could feel bones moving about under his hand. With an effort he tried to continue talking. 'And staggering in with you half dead . . .'

But the pain was too much and had Gryss not already taken hold of him he would have stumbled.

'I'm sorry, I'm sorry, I'm sorry,' the old man said, the tone of his voice echoing the desperate apology in his words. Quickly he led Farnor to the edge of the road and, sitting him down on a grassy bank, began to take off his jacket.

Now it was the young man who was pale and perspiring.

'I was so busy with my own concerns,' Gryss said as he gingerly worked Farnor's jacket off his arm, 'that I forgot what you did in there.' Self-reproach filled his face as he rolled up Farnor's shirt sleeve to examine the injured arm, but he set his emotions aside and became purposeful. 'Move your fingers,' he said, gently.

After a few minutes of probing and manipulation, during which Farnor simply did as he was told, wincing freely as need arose, Gryss rolled down the sleeve again and draped Farnor's jacket about his shoulders.

'There's nothing broken, fortunately,' he said. 'But it's badly bruised and some of your muscles have been damaged. It'll be very sore for a while. You'll need to rest it. Then it'll be just plain sore for a long time.' His face lightened and he managed a smile. 'And the colours will be something to behold.' He took Farnor's right hand and folded it across his body. 'Just hold it there for now, as relaxed as you can. I'll make a sling out of something when we get to your father's.'

Farnor confined himself to nodding, some reflex from childhood always making him behave thus in the presence of Gryss the healer.

He found that his legs were rather uncertain as Gryss helped him to his feet, but the pain was easier if only for the assurance that no bones had been broken.

They set off down the road at an elderly man's pace.

'You saved my life in there,' Gryss said when they had walked some way. 'I don't know what to say. Thank you seems woefully inadequate. I've never been so frightened in all my life.'

Farnor in his turn did not know what to say by way of reply. 'What happened?' he asked again.

'I can't remember properly,' Gryss said. 'I looked inside and saw no one about, then I went in and . . . something hit me. Threw me into the gate.' His brow furrowed. 'I think I managed to turn round. I recall banging on the gate and shouting, but everything seemed to be sucked up into the noise and thrown back to mock me. It was as if half a dozen winter blizzards were clamouring at my back. And the force . . .' he went on, as if he still could not believe what he had felt. 'So powerful . . .' He turned to Farnor. 'Then it eased. It felt almost as if it had been driven back by something. Like a fierce animal retreating before something even fiercer. And then you came tumbling in through the wicket and dragged me out.'

He looked at Farnor intently. 'What did you hear, on the outside?'

'The same,' Farnor replied. 'A tremendous noise. But there was something else as well. I called out to you before you went in. I had this feeling that something in the courtyard was . . . was both here and somewhere else . . . at the same time. I can't explain. It was as if something . . . some power . . . a dreadful power . . . was coming from that somewhere else. Bringing all the harm.' He shook his head, and nursed his arm once again.

Gryss blew out his cheeks. He felt useless, and it was not a feeling he cared for. Things were happening beyond anything he had ever experienced. Not even in any of Yonas's tales had he heard of anything so strange. He glanced covertly at Farnor. Something in the courtyard from somewhere else? What was the lad talking about? He would have liked to have laughed understandingly and dismissed him as being over-imaginative, or shocked, or deranged even, but the sound and the furious power of the wind that had seized him and pinned him helpless against the castle gate were still with him and all too real. He had no doubts about the threat that he had experienced.

And there was something else too, something he did not want to think about.

Then, as if by their very intensity his wishes could make themselves come to pass, he found his mind filling with an almost desperate longing for everything to be as it was before Nilsson and his troop had arrived. That was a world which he understood completely. Nothing could happen there which he could not turn his mind to and solve eventually. But now . . . ?

He began to feel utterly wretched, and it was only with a great effort that he kept any sign of this inner turmoil from his face. Sternly he reminded himself that, whatever was happening, the young man next to him had been injured in saving his life and that, despite his youth and through no fault of his own, he found himself near to the centre of this mystery. However impotent he, the village elder, felt, Farnor felt no less and needed all the support that could be given.

But what support *could* he offer? There wasn't even anyone he could turn to for advice.

You've sat helpless by enough death beds in your time, just be here for him, came a grim reply from within as he felt the waves of despair about to break over him again. It mightn't be much but it's all you've got.

'What are we going to tell my father?'

Farnor's reversion to his original concerns brought Gryss sharply out of his inner debate.

'I've told you, I can't lie any more. I might fool my father, but not my mother. And it'll upset her if I try.'

The request heartened Gryss. Here, he *could* help. 'We'll have to go halfway,' he said, shrewdly. 'Tell some of the truth. I'll confess to going to search the place on my own, and to dragging you along with me. Then . . .' His head wobbled from side to side as he pondered various alternatives. '. . . We'd better say that the castle was locked, or Yakob and your father will be up there tomorrow.' He fell silent and, brow furrowed, pondered yet more alternatives until: 'We'll have to say that the horse was startled and bolted, after all,' he decided, a little unhappily. 'And . . . that . . . you banged your arm on a rock as you tried to catch me.'

He made an effort to look enthusiastic, but Farnor pulled a sour face.

'Well, you think of something better, then,' Gryss said, a little indignant at this rebuff.

'I suppose we'll have to,' Farnor conceded after a moment. 'We can't tell them what actually happened. It's too . . . complicated. And my father would take

365

Nilsson to task about it in the middle of the village green if he got wind of it. Stealing the tithe is one thing. Hurting people is another.'

Gryss nodded. That was true, and something that he himself had not considered. Garren was a quiet and reasonable man but, as is the way with such men, if roused on a matter he would pursue it, quietly and reasonably, with a dogged relentlessness worthy of any wild-eyed fanatic, until he obtained an explanation that quietly and reasonably satisfied him.

'It was some kind of a trap, you know,' Farnor said.

Gryss frowned, thrown off balance by this strange remark. 'What was?' he asked.

'That . . . wind, or whatever it was. It was a trap,' Farnor expanded. 'It was left there in case anyone tried to get into the castle.'

Gryss stared at Farnor anxiously, afraid that the shock of the young man's injury might be affecting his mind. But even as these thoughts came to him, he realized that their clamour was because he himself did not want to hear what Farnor was saying. Did not want to hear anything that would make him give credence to what he had felt so strongly: that what had happened at the castle was no freak wind. That it was . . .

He twitched away from the thought and turned his attention back to Farnor.

As he knew it would be, Farnor's face, though pale and lined with pain, showed no sign of that detachment which hallmarks a disordered or fevered mind. Farnor was calm and composed, and in full possession of his reason.

'What do you mean, a trap?' Gryss asked hesitantly. 'I don't understand. It was just . . .' His voice tailed off.

Farnor looked at him impatiently. 'It was just what?' he demanded scornfully.

Gryss made no reply. Apart from having no answer to

the question, he knew that he must not hinder Farnor's sudden need to pursue the matter.

'The damn thing was alive,' Farnor went on, urgently, grimacing and hugging his arm as a jolt of pain struck him. His face was angry and fearful, as if he were back in the gloom of the archway again, battling to open the wicket. 'There was a will behind it. It was a guard.'

Gryss wanted to argue. Wanted to say that this was foolishness brought on by his pain. Wanted to say, prosaically, 'If they'd wanted to keep people out all they had to do was lock the gate.' But he couldn't. What he was trying to avoid, he would have to face now or later. Even without Farnor's angry dismissal, he knew that the screaming turmoil that had risen to greet him when he entered the castle had not been any natural happening. There *had* been an intent in the force that had hurled him against the gate and nearly crushed Farnor's arm. A malevolent intent. Even he had felt its burning malice focused on him.

But what did it mean?

He tried to shy away from the only answer that was left, but he could not. Nilsson, or one of his men, had powers beyond the understanding of ordinary people, powers that could control natural forces such as the wind. How such a thing could be he did not pause to consider. He was old enough to know that his ignorance outreached his knowledge by far, and he had seen enough inexplicable events in his life not to be too disturbed by such a possibility. But who it could be? That was different, that seemed to be important. None of the few that he had met had seemed in any way . . . extraordinary – but then what might such a person look like?

He remembered the vaguely familiar figure who had been in Nilsson's room when he had received the news about the intended garrison, but, tantalizingly, face and name eluded him.

367

'And I'm the same,' Farnor said.

The remark, filled as it was with guilt and despair, startled Gryss. 'What are you talking about?' he asked, eyes wide with concern. He stopped and took Farnor's uninjured arm.

'I'm the same,' Farnor said, looking desperately from side to side as if for escape.

'Same as what?' Gryss said, forcefully, shaking him.

Farnor pulled away and moved over to a tree by the roadside. He leaned against its trunk then slid to the ground, his eyes pained.

'I saw it, Gryss. When you opened the gate, I saw it. I knew it was wrong. I knew it drew a power from . . . somewhere else. Something in me recognized it. Something came out from . . . inside . . . and went for it. Like a fox after a rabbit. I couldn't help myself. I attacked it. And it knew it was attacked,' he went on. 'It knew. It retreated. It was hurt. Somehow I'd taken its power from it. Weakened it. I'm the same as the person who set it there in the first place . . .'

He looked down at his hands. Gryss did not speak.

After a long silence, Farnor said softly, 'I'm not going mad, am I, Gryss?'

The question came almost as a relief to Gryss. 'If you are, then so am I,' he said without hesitation. 'And do I look mad?'

Farnor smiled weakly.

'I can't pretend to understand what's happening here,' Gryss went on. 'Or to be other than frightened by it, but it's not in our imaginations, that's for certain.' He took Farnor's face in his hands and gazed at him intently. 'You're not perfect by any means, Farnor, but you've no real evil in you. You may or may not have some strange skill that you knew nothing of, but you'll do no intentional harm with it.'

Farnor's eyes filled with doubt.

Gryss dismissed it utterly. 'Fire is fire, Farnor,' he said. 'Warm yourself by it, cook your food with it, or burn your neighbours' ricks with it. The choice is always yours. And whatever gift you have, you'll always choose rightly. Do you understand me?'

Farnor looked at him uncertainly.

'And remember this,' Gryss went on, 'because I live by it: I might be frightened now – that's part of being alive, part of learning; only fools are never afraid – but really *nothing in life is to be feared. It is only to be understood.* Do you understand that?'

'Yes, I think so,' Farnor said quietly after a moment. Gryss released him gently.

Then, as if following his own advice, Gryss found his mind coldly turning towards what had been happening. 'Maybe it's that creature that's doing it,' he mused. 'It's—'

But Farnor was shaking his head.

'I've touched the creature,' he said. 'And I touched that . . . thing at the castle. They're connected in some way, but they're not the same. It was a man who set that trap, not an animal.'

Suddenly his face went white, and he began to tremble.

Gryss just managed to catch him as he slumped forward.

Chapter 26

There was whirling darkness and chaos, shot through with the cold silver of moonlight and the blood-red of nightmare battlefield sunsets. Tormenting winds blew great storm clouds through it, bringing to him familiar faces that he could not recognize. As they came, so he reached out to them and so they faded.

Somewhere someone laughed at him. The sound wove into that of the storm, rising and falling, taunting him.

He was helpless: the merest autumn leaf, the frailest snowflake. He would be blown where the wind chose.

And in the tumult a dark presence moved. A presence that was both here and . . . beyond . . .

And he must go beyond to still its awful power. It was important that he did it now, before it was too late.

He reached out . . .

A babble of inquisitive voices surrounded him, shattering the dark chaos into a myriad flickering lights. They were full of concern and disbelief. They questioned and argued . . .

And there was fear. An old fear . . .

He spoke to reassure them, but he could not understand his own words.

Surprise shimmered through the disbelief, but still it lingered. And the curiosity and the concern grew stronger.

But the deep and ancient fear grew also.

He strained to speak again.

The laughter returned, though gentler this time. And the lights began to dance and float to its rhythm.

And there was coolness.

371

The voices faded, though he could feel them calling to him. They did not want him to leave. There were so many questions to be asked.

'Don't go . . . We—'

Farnor jerked towards wakefulness, his eyes opening grudgingly. But the coolness on his forehead did not allow him to rise. And there was gentle laughter again.

'Are you feeling better now?' came a familiar voice.

He struggled, but even as he did so his mind began to understand what his eyes were focusing on.

The remains of his sleep washed away from him as if he were emerging into the daylight from the breathless depths of some great lake.

He was in his bedroom staring up at the old, familiar beams that striped its ceiling.

And the coolness on his forehead was his mother's hand.

'Are you feeling better now?' she asked again. 'Muttering away to yourself.'

Farnor tried to sit up, but the pain in his right arm prevented him. His mother put her arms around him and, with an effort, pulled him upright and pushed a pillow behind him.

'The size of you,' she said, with a mixture of pride and reproach. 'You're too big for this kind of treatment these days.'

The pain in his arm, and the buffeting practicality of his mother's sickbed manner brought Farnor fully to his senses. And with his senses came the memory of the events at the castle which, in their turn, brought faint wisps of a need for caution.

'What happened?' he asked. 'How did I get here?'

'How, indeed!' his mother replied. 'Quite the saga, I can tell you.' She did not seemed disposed to relate it, however. Instead she walked over to the door and shouted down the stairs, 'He's awake!'

Farnor glanced round the room. There was something unusual about it. Then he realized it was the light. It had been late afternoon when he and Gryss had gone to the castle. The light coming through the window now was the morning light, and none too early morning at that.

The heavy tread of feet coming up the stairs turned his attention back towards the door. There was some muffled speech then his father entered followed by Gryss.

Garren looked at him with exaggerated sternness. It was an expression Farnor knew well enough. There was humour and relief behind it; he'd been caught red-handed at something, something, however, that wasn't particularly serious. It was a good sign. He gave a guilty smile and shrug in reply. Better play the child until he found out what had happened, and who knew what.

'You're a fine one, aren't you?' Garren said, walking over to the bed and sitting on the edge of it.

But as Garren was speaking, Farnor caught Gryss's eye. Standing behind both Garren and Katrin, Gryss, his hand casually massaging his chin, briefly touched his lips with his forefinger.

Keep quiet.

Farnor nodded as if in reply to his father.

'They're both fine ones,' Katrin said, folding her arms and discarding her caring manner for a matriarchal one. She cast a glance at Gryss that made him wilt as it struck. 'Wandering off to see if they could get inside the castle. Like children sneaking into an orchard. I don't know what—'

Garren lifted a hand gently to silence his wife.

'You've made your point, Katrin,' he said, mouthing softly for Farnor's benefit. 'Two hundred times.'

'It needs making,' she said, directing the errant elder towards her son with a sharp nod. 'See if he's all right,' she demanded. 'He was scowling as if he had the cares of the world on his shoulders, just before.' Then, in high-pitched surprise, she added, 'And he's been talking to someone for the last ten minutes.'

Gryss stepped forward and displaced Garren from the bed rather as if he was seeking cover from a sudden and violent storm. He put on his healer's manner and subjected Farnor to various proddings, pokings and twistings before announcing: 'Fine. I told you he was just stunned. All he needed was a good night's sleep. Let him rest that arm for a day or two and, apart from being every shade from yellow to black that you can imagine, it'll be fine.'

Katrin gave a noncommittal grunt. 'I'll leave you . . . children . . . together,' she said. 'I'll be downstairs, *getting on with the work*.'

'I'll not be long,' Garren said, winking at his son.

When she had gone, however, his manner became more serious. 'I've told you what I think about your little adventure, Gryss,' he said. 'But I'll say it again, in front of Farnor, seeing as he's party to all this, at your request.'

'I know,' Gryss said. 'And I'll apologize again, willingly. And in front of Farnor. He probably saved my life when he tried to catch me . . .'

Gryss had told the tale about the horse bolting then, Farnor registered.

'It was an error of judgement on my part,' Gryss went on. 'I wasn't thinking properly. I was concerned about letting Jeorg go off on his own.'

But, once started, as a rock must reach the foot of a hill, so Garren's conclusion had to be spoken. 'We agreed we were going to work together,' he said, with that special kind of insistence that made those who really knew him nod whether they agreed or not. 'We must stick to that. Who knows what'll happen if we each wander off doing what we fancy without telling each other?' It reminded Gryss that, as Farnor had hinted the previous day, there were times when Garren was not a man to stand in front of.

Then, the reproach out, Garren seemed to become his old patient self. He laid a hand on Gryss's shoulder. Gryss covered it with his own.

'Katrin been giving you a bad time as well?' he said.

Garren raised his eyebrows and blew out a long breath. 'Yes, but I'm not surprised,' he replied. 'You frightened both of us out of five years' growth when you staggered in telling us that Farnor had had an accident.' Garren made a sweeping gesture with his hand. 'Still, no real harm done.'

'Can I get up?' Farnor asked, feeling the need to be a more active participant in this conversation.

Gryss nodded. 'Yes. Just take it easy with that arm for a day or so. Keep it as relaxed as you can, and let me know if it gives you any trouble.'

Despite this permission, however, Farnor showed no particular inclination to leave his bed.

His father prompted him: 'Any time you like,' he said, looking significantly at his son's clothes draped across a nearby chair. 'It's only a couple of hours short of noon.'

This declaration galvanized him more than it did his son, however, reminding him that, with Farnor incapacitated, he had a great many jobs that he should be attending to elsewhere. With a somewhat self-conscious leave-taking, larded with both relief and reproach, he left to get on with them.

As soon as he heard his father's footsteps reach the bottom of the stairs, Farnor pushed back the blankets and swung himself out of bed. He put his hand to his head.

'What's the matter?' Gryss asked.

'Nothing. Just a little muzzy with lying in so long,'

Farnor replied, adding almost immediately, 'Well, every-thing's the matter, I suppose. What happened to me?'

'You fainted, that's all,' Gryss said. 'Shock from the injury to your arm.'

'Or?' Farnor said, picking up the doubt in his voice.

Gryss threw a mask of certainty across his face which had behind it too many long years of experience, as village healer and negotiator, to be penetrated by Farnor.

'Or nothing,' he said, his voice carrying the same certainty. 'It was a nasty and painful injury and you were fretting about everything else that had happened. Both your head and your body needed to get away from it, needed a rest. So they took one when you showed no signs of taking it for them.'

Farnor looked at him suspiciously, but Gryss's mask deflected the gaze as easily as a stout shield would deflect a weakly thrown spear.

Not wholly convinced, but seeing that no further information was to be had from Gryss, Farnor began to get dressed.

'What are we going to do?' he asked, in a low voice, as Gryss helped him thread his right arm into his shirtsleeve.

'Nothing,' Gryss said. 'What *can* we do? I'm not going to the castle again.' He became conspiratorial. 'I've told your father that the gate was locked as we agreed, so at least he and Yakob won't go wandering up there.'

It was important to have the lies consistent, Farnor learned.

'So all we can do is wait,' Gryss went on. 'See what happens when Nilsson gets back, and hope that Jeorg will reach the capital safely.'

Farnor exhaled unhappily.

Gryss became fatherly. 'You take it easy. Get yourself properly well. That was a brave thing you did, but your arm's going to be very sore for a day or two so you'll be in no position to be doing anything strenuous, let alone adventurous.'

Farnor shook his head. 'I've had enough adventures,' he said. 'I think I'm beginning to value a quiet life now.'

Gryss looked at him, his eyes full of compassion but his mouth twitching into a smile. 'That's old man's talk,' he said, his smile rumbling into a chuckle. 'There's plenty of time before you come to that kind of conclusion with any conviction. You just do as I say. Take it easy for a little while. You'll be ready for action again in no time.'

It was an injudicious remark, Gryss realized as soon as he spoke it.

'You think something's going to happen?' Farnor asked, his face alarmed.

Gryss shrugged awkwardly. 'No. I don't think so,' he said uncertainly. 'But . . . ?'

His voice tailed off, and his doubt hung in the silent sunlit air of the homely bedroom. He made no attempt to resolve it, and Farnor, sensing they would be futile, pressed no more questions.

'It's only a month since Dalmas Day,' he said, quietly, after a moment. 'Who could've foreseen all this?'

'Who indeed?' Gryss agreed. And who'd have foreseen *you* changing so much in so short a time, Farnor, he thought. 'It's the way of things,' he said, affecting a worldly ease that he did not feel. 'It's not much fun, but everything'll settle into some kind of order eventually. What we've got to do is keep our wits about us, that's all.' His mouth tightened into a thin line. 'And keep our faith in the basic rightness of things.'

Somewhat to his surprise however, Farnor did not seem disposed to discuss the matter. He was struggling to fasten a loose kerchief about his neck with one and a half hands. Gryss stepped forward to help him, but

377

he shook his head. 'I'll have to get used to it,' he said. A sheepish grin appeared, putting to flight the grimness that seemed to have taken possession of his features. 'My mother's only waiting for half a chance to start looking after me and I'm not too sure I can cope with that.'

Gryss nodded understandingly. Farnor's mood, like a fever, had passed some inner crisis; perhaps one that he himself did not even realize had been reached.

Gryss left the farm shortly afterwards, pausing only to brave Katrin in her kitchen.

'I know you two are up to something,' she declared, waving a long wooden spoon at him like a regal sceptre and jerking her head in the direction of the stairs. 'Though I don't suppose you'll tell *me*, who has to pick up the pieces when you've finished. But I know this, and you know I know it: that inn horse can't lift both front feet off the ground at once, let alone rear and toss someone out of the saddle. And it's seen many a fox before.' Gryss endeavoured to maintain a look of innocent reproach to cover his inner quaking as she closed with him, spoon levelled ominously. 'And that bruise on his arm never came from any rock I ever saw.'

The spoon pinned Gryss to the wall. 'Don't you go getting my son involved in matters he can't handle, Har Grysstson, or you'll have me to answer to. He's only a boy, for all his size.'

'He's near enough a man, Katrin,' Gryss risked ingratiatingly, but with a judicious hint of sternness.

The spoon released him with disdain: he was too unworthy a foe. Retreating to her table Katrin made a disparaging noise. 'Near enough a man!' she echoed scornfully. 'You're all only eight years old. I don't know why we bother about you so.'

When she turned, however, any mockery in her

manner was gone, and the look she gave Gryss was grim and worldly wise. Simple and direct, her words cut to the heart of her need. 'You take care of my son, Gryss,' she said. 'And my husband. And, for that matter, take care of us all in your dealings with that Captain and his men. Whatever else they are, they're all fighting men. Used to brutality, to stabbing and killing and . . .' She paused, struggling to form the words to the measure of her feelings. 'And everything else that goes with such a trade,' she said significantly. 'There's none in the whole valley could stand against any of them and hope to live should need arise.'

'I understand, Katrin,' Gryss said soberly. 'Truly.'

But do you, healer? he thought as he walked across the yard. He gave an acknowledging wave to Farnor, watching him from an upstairs window, then bent to stroke one of the farm dogs that was routinely checking him for interesting smells.

Not like she does, he concluded. Katrin's perception of the reality of events disturbed him. It was no different from his own, but he found himself echoing Farnor's strange phrase: it came from a different place. Beyond a certain point, there was an unknowing between man and woman which could not be bridged by words.

As he opened the gate to the lane he gave the dog a final affectionate pat. Having seen him to the boundaries of its demesne, it wandered away from him, turning its attention to the lure of the richer aromas that were calling to it from all about the yard.

Gryss felt the weariness of his years closing in on him again, despite the warmth of the sunshine and the vigorous optimism of the farm life about him. As he closed the gate, he caught another glimpse of Farnor. He remembered his awkward grin as he had struggled with his kerchief and the shades about him retreated a little.

Resilience, he thought. The dominant hallmark of youth. But the very thought brought back others that he had been holding at bay.

Just stunned, he had confidently declared many times to assuage the alarm of Garren and Katrin as they had raced out to retrieve their unconscious son. But he did not really know. He had peered into Farnor's vacant eyes, searched his pulses, done everything that he knew, but the only insight he had gained was one into his own inadequacy, his own ignorance.

'The body is like a great, well-founded ship. Countless unseen forces work to right it when it is disturbed.'

'The true study of healing lies not in why our bodies become sick, but in why they remain so well against the innumerable ills that constantly assail them.'

Words that he had heard in his youthful wanderings: in his search for knowledge and . . . whatever it is that youth searches for. Words that had seemed wise then, and which time and experience had made seem wiser still. They had returned to sustain him as he had gently lain Farnor on the grass, carefully positioning him so that he would not roll over and choke should he vomit, or swallow his tongue. Indeed, they were all that sustained him in his desperation, for he had no idea what had happened to the young man. Blows to the head, he knew, could produce unforeseeable, alarming effects, but Farnor had received no such injury.

As he had looked down at the motionless figure, Farnor had seemed simply to be asleep. But Gryss had known that he was beyond any normal waking. All he could do was sustain the powerful will to heal that permeated the hearts of Garren and Katrin, and which, perhaps alone, could reach into those unknown regions to where Farnor's spirit might have wandered. By his manner and with his every fibre, Gryss had striven to impart to them his faith in the ancient ability of the young man's body to dispatch its enemies, to right itself, to call back his spirit to its true home.

And it had happened so, though whether or not he had helped in this, Gryss could not guess. It was irrelevant anyway. He could not have done otherwise.

He stopped and looked around the sunlit fields. So full of life and vigour. He shivered. Fear, he diagnosed starkly. How could it be otherwise now? His body was shaking itself loose, telling him to be ready to run.

Or to fight.

He closed his eyes and raised his face to the sun, as if its life-giving warmth would soak into him as it did into the sunstones, bestowing on him an inner light that would dispel the awful chill that had settled over his heart.

And to some extent it did as, for a little while, he revelled in its warm caress and followed the dancing and flickering of the lighted shapes behind his eyelids.

When he opened his eyes again the shapes, though changed in colour, remained, jumping and dancing to their own spasmodic rhythm, and it was some time before he could see clearly. When he could, he found his gaze turning towards the castle. He looked at it pensively. It was no different from what it had been since he was a child. But now it seemed to him to be like a great predatory animal crouching in the lee of the mountains and waiting to spring forward and devour the village.

The analogy brought to him the thought of the creature. And in the wake of this came the village lore about the caves beyond the castle where lay ancient evil creatures from another time, waiting only to be awakened to ravage the world again.

He could not believe such tales, but he could no longer dismiss them as airily as once he would have done.

And Farnor's contact with it had been prior to the arrival of Nilsson and his men . . .

It occurred to him for the first time that perhaps what was happening was the result of some grim coincidence. After all, Nilsson had not ridden into the valley like a man carrying in his train a powerful mover of the elements. He had ridden in at the head of a motley assortment of dispirited, even broken men. Nor had they been any different when he had visited the castle to examine their sick.

Only after they had started to explore the north of the valley had these changes come about.

Could it be the creature using Nilsson in some way?

But Farnor's answer had been unequivocal: 'It was a man who set that trap, not an animal.' And there had been a human quality in the malice that he had felt attacking him yesterday.

There were certain trees that needed an apparently parasitic fungus in their roots in order to be able to survive. Each fed and sustained the other and both prospered, where each alone would wither and die. So perhaps it was now. Perhaps creature and man had encountered one another during Nilsson's foray to the north, and from thence they had grown in strength together.

Gryss nodded to himself. His reasoning had some merit to it, though quite what action he could take as a result of it he did not know.

None, other than watch and wait, he decided yet again. Be aware.

He straightened himself up, taking a deep breath as he did so. For a moment he was twenty years old again. Strong, wilful and determined. It was a good feeling.

He smiled. It *was* good. But not as good as being here now. He would not be that callow youth again for all the life and vigour it put back into his limbs. He had enough life and vigour to get himself around without too much discomfort, and his deeper senses and knowledge were superior beyond measure.

'Take care of us all in your dealings with the Captain and his men,' Katrin had said to him. He would keep her incisive insights into the true needs of the moment at the forefront of his mind, and he would fulfil her demands of him to the fullest extent of his ability.

He felt a faint stirring within him. It was excitement. He crushed it ruthlessly. This was not something to be enjoyed. This was something in which stern discipline and an awareness that others looked to him for their safety must order his deeds.

Nevertheless, as he started back off towards the village there was a spring in his step that had not been there for many a year.

Chapter 27

The only certainty in life is uncertainty, Gryss had decided for himself many years ago, but occasionally one had to conjure out of the confusion a place, a foundation as it were, on which one might stand apparently securely, for a while, just to look around, and make at least some attempt to assess the degrees of probability and improbability of possible events.

In forming his conclusions about what was happening, though knowing that they might well prove incorrect, Gryss had done this. Thus, despite the physical ordeal he had suffered at the castle and the subsequent journey back to the village followed by a night of broken and uneven sleep and a day of heart-searching, he woke the next morning feeling refreshed and with his mind alert and clear, even though his worries about the future were, if anything, greater than before.

He performed his routine stretchings and scratchings as he rose from his bed, and then, yawning noisily, he drew back the curtains.

'Oops,' he said softly to himself as the morning light flooded in. It was a grey, rainy day that greeted him, but he needed no timepiece to tell him that it was much later than he normally rose. Mentally the previous day's earnest reflections may have left him more at ease with himself, but physically he had been sorely tried and obviously his body had insisted on having the rest that it felt it needed regardless of such trivialities as his regular morning activities.

It was of no great consequence. Today he would

further order his thoughts and then decide to what extent he should share them with his confidants.

He opened the window and leaned on the sill. A soft freshness greeted him laden with the moist scents of grasses and flowers. It should be a day for perhaps sitting in the porch and watching the rain, and listening to it, and thinking. Thinking about something . . . anything . . . nothing.

But the prospect of such wholly innocuous self-indulgence did not lure him as once, but a few weeks ago, it would have. Now, despite his determination to watch and wait and to act only as circumstances dictated, there was a dark edge to all his thinking, a constant, nagging wish that all this would be over and forgotten, that all would be as it was. It filled him with a sense of urgency, which told him that he should be doing something even though his mind had told him, beyond dispute, that he could not. And worst of all it left him with a leaden uneasiness in the pit of his stomach.

He breathed in the cool air.

The shades eased a little. Not to savour such moments was some kind of a desecration. But . . .

He shook his head vigorously and closed the window. He would have to learn to live with this new uncertainty. Katrin's words could no more be torn from his thoughts than a barbed arrow from a wound.

'. . . take care of us all in your dealings with that Captain . . .'

She had meant, he knew, 'Do not be reckless as you have been today, you speak for us all.' But he had heard the plea within the command: 'Take care of us all, we depend on you.'

And he would strive to do that, no matter what it cost him in restless nights, burdened with worry and fear. He had done so all his life and he could do no other now.

He turned away from facing what might be the ultimate cost. Matters could not come to that. Somewhere reasoned words would prevail. They always did. Deals could be struck, bargains made, mutual interests agreed and satisfied . . .

Surely . . . ?

He growled irritably and dismissed yet again this variable and shifting mist that was the future. Right now, both he and his uneasy stomach would be satisfied with food.

After a leisurely breakfast he set off for Yakob's with the intention of establishing further the story that the castle was locked and that he had been thrown from his horse when it was startled. He found, however, that Yakob was well acquainted with the tale. Garren, too busy to attend to the matter himself had sent Pieter with a simple outline of events to the inn and to Yakob and Harlen. As a result, Yakob was also in possession of several intriguing details which Gryss had not only not told to Garren, but which had not actually happened.

'It trampled on you, I hear,' was one such.

It took Gryss some time to extract from the message that had reached Yakob the version that he required him to hear. Yakob looked almost disappointed; Gryss's tale was quite prosaic in comparison to that which Garren's too youthful messenger had brought.

'Just a tumble, then?' he summarized finally, through pursed lips. 'I thought that young Pieter was a bit excited.'

Leaving Yakob, Gryss headed towards Harlen's house. Doubtless he would hear the same tale when he arrived there, although, he mused, Harlen's being somewhat farther on it could be even more extravagant by then. He had a fleeting impression of a fabulous bird whose drab plumage grew ever more ornate and colourful as it moved further and further from its humble nest.

'Whimsy, whimsy,' he muttered to himself. A sure sign of aging faculties.

But it transpired that Harlen had brought down the bird in full flight.

'He's gone downland to collect some willow rods,' Marna told him as she took his wet cape. 'He'll probably be gone for some time.' Her face was amused. 'He was going to come up and measure you for a coffin at first,' she went on. 'It took him quite a time to get Garren's proper message out of young Pieter.' She pointed Gryss towards a chair.

'Trampled underfoot and fallen off a cliff, I suppose,' he said, sitting down. The chair creaked, but it was more like a welcome than a protest, and Gryss half closed his eyes in a small ecstasy as Harlen's chair pressed comfort upon him.

'More or less,' Marna agreed, laughing. 'I should imagine that by the time Pieter's finished, there'll be quite a crowd of mourners at your cottage. He's so sweet. And so serious.'

She laughed again. Gryss felt as though the room had suddenly filled with light.

'Perhaps he's going to be a Teller,' he said, chuckling himself.

'What possessed Garren to send *him* with the tale?' Marna asked.

'He's probably got a lot to do, with Farnor hurt,' Gryss replied. 'And I doubt he realized Pieter had such a vivid imagination.'

Marna ran her hands through her hair and shifted it here and there until it looked exactly the same as it had before. 'So, no daring assault on the castle today?' she said mockingly. Though, as Gryss caught her eye, he sensed a sharpness at the heart of the enquiry.

Gryss shook his head and leaned forward and Marna's mockery faded as if it had never been.

'What's the matter?' she asked, uncertainly.

Gryss looked at her. Should he tell her what had happened, or should he not? Would telling her be for her benefit or his own: lightening his own concerns by sharing them? What could she do other than feel the pain and distress of being able to do nothing?

But the choice was not wholly his. As she herself had said, she was like a mole in a trap; she had walked in and could go only forward. And with what she already knew she was likely to give little more credence to the tale that Gryss had had put about than if it were just another of young Pieter's childish ramblings. And she had the strength and the resilience – the word came again – to support the truth where a falsehood from someone she had placed her trust in might well crush her.

He took her hands and, as simply and concisely as he could, he told her what had happened at the castle, together with his own thoughts about what . . . who . . . might be causing it.

She withdrew her left hand to nurse her right upper arm as he told of the gate closing to trap Farnor, but otherwise she remained motionless and silent.

Though patently shocked and bewildered by the tale, she asked no questions about why? and how? when he had finished, but struck to the heart of the matter.

'What are we going to do?' she asked.

He offered her his only conclusion: 'Watch and wait,' he said. 'And hope that Jeorg reaches the capital safely.'

'And Farnor?' she said, with unexpected indignation.

'Oh, his arm'll be sore for some time, but he'll be able to use it well enough in a few days,' Gryss said, reassuringly.

Her face clouded. 'Not his arm,' she protested fiercely, omitting to add, 'You silly man,' though it rang clearly through her intonation. 'All these . . .

things . . . that are happening to him. He probably thinks he's going insane.'

That's why it was right to tell you, Gryss thought almost exultantly. You're his generation. You understand him. That alone would sustain Farnor in his trial. The vision of their youthful strength and courage guided by his knowledge and experience rose before him.

And with it a black thought bubbled up from deep inside him: It's always the old that guide the young to war.

It struck him with an impact like that of a clenched fist. He felt himself gaping.

'What's the matter?' Marna asked. 'You look as if you've seen a tithe gatherer.'

Her inadvertent use of the old village saw, with its now-dark irony, made Gryss smile involuntarily. It released him from the chilling spell of the awful thought.

'Nothing,' he answered. 'Just a bit of reaction, probably, thinking about it all again.'

Marna seemed unhappy with the explanation, but Gryss ploughed on. 'Farnor's well enough,' he said. 'As far as I know, he's told me everything, and he tells me how he feels about things. I think while he's doing that he'll be all right . . . And you knowing as well, Marna, and being his friend will help him also, even though none of us knows what's really happening. Go and see him today if you can. Just a social call, as it were. Following on Pieter's florid tales.'

Marna nodded. Her mouth twisted into a slightly bitter smile. 'And I suppose all Pieter's nonsense will keep people's minds off Jeorg being missing,' she said. Gryss started. He had not expected such a calculated observation.

Then Marna half rose from her chair. 'Someone's coming,' she said. 'Running.'

Scarcely had she spoken than the front door of the cottage was flung open.

'Marna!' a voice called urgently. It was Harlen. His footsteps paused briefly in the hallway, then he burst into the room. His face was anxious and flushed, and in his hand he held Marna's cape which he proffered to her.

'What's the matter?' Marna asked in alarm, as she stepped forward to greet him. Harlen looked at her then at Gryss, surprise and relief mingling with his concern.

'Marna, go to Yakob's now and wait,' he said breathlessly, thrusting the cape into her arms and ushering her to the door. 'Gryss, come with me.'

He had pushed them both from the cottage before either had a chance to speak.

'Father!' Marna protested ferociously, wrenching her arm free from his grasp.

Sensing that a spontaneous and irrelevant family quarrel was about to intrude on what was obviously urgent news, Gryss entered the fray, laying gently restraining hands on the arms of the two potential antagonists.

'Put your cape on, Marna,' he said, as quietly and calmly as he could, then, to her father, 'What's happened, Harlen?'

Harlen looked anxiously at his daughter who glowered at him in reply, still young enough to be indignant at his cavalier handling of her, not least because it had been in front of Gryss.

'Let her hear,' Gryss intervened again. 'She's no child any more. And nothing happens here but what we all hear about it within the day. Spit your news out, for pity's sake.'

Harlen pointed down the valley. 'They're coming back,' he said. His voice dwindled to a whisper. 'They've got Jeorg with them.'

'What?' Marna demanded, craning forward.

391

'Marna, I'd really prefer it if you went into the village,' Harlen said, his tone placating.

But Marna's manner indicated that she had rooted herself to the spot.

'They've got Jeorg?' Gryss said, ignoring Harlen's concern for his daughter, and hoping fervently that he himself had misheard the whispered message.

Harlen reluctantly gave up on Marna. 'Yes,' he replied, his voice pained. 'And it looks as if he's been hurt.'

Gryss's stomach tightened in fear and a cascade of future events poured into his mind, dominant amongst which was the face of Jeorg's wife.

'How badly?' he managed to ask.

Harlen cast another glance at his daughter. 'I couldn't tell,' he said. 'He was draped over a saddle.'

Gryss's eyes widened in horror. Jeorg brought home like a sack of potatoes! Like a dead sheep! The future events faded before the grim present.

'Where are they?' he asked.

'Only a few minutes away,' Harlen replied, pointing again. 'They're not hurrying.'

Without a word, Gryss set off towards the road. Harlen and Marna ran after him. The trio walked on in silence through the thin rain. When they reached the road, Gryss turned downland.

As Harlen had indicated, they did not have long to wait. Very soon the swaying forms of advancing riders appeared ahead. Faced head on, in the misty light, the column could not be discerned as such, but rather appeared to be a single, giant figure of grotesque and unstable proportions. It remained so until it was quite close and the individual riders could be seen.

As they neared, Harlen stopped and took Marna's arm but Gryss continued marching towards the advancing column purposefully, his shoulders hunched and his head craning forward. He heard an order being given and passing down the line, though he could not make it out.

Harlen spoke to Marna and then set off after him, leaving her standing alone.

At the head of the column rode Nilsson, with Saddre and Dessane beside him. They made no effort to stop when Gryss reached them, though Nilsson looked straight at him.

'You have one of our friends, I believe,' Gryss said to him, falling into step by the side of his horse. 'He's been hurt.'

Nilsson gave a flick of his head towards the horse immediately behind him. Gryss stared at it. What he had at first taken to be a pack horse was, in fact, bearing Jeorg, draped across its saddle.

Anxiety lit Gryss's face. 'Stop a moment,' he shouted, stopping. 'Let me have a look at him.'

But Nilsson took no heed, and the column plodded on. Gryss had to catch the horse's bridle to prevent himself from falling.

'Let go of the horse,' came a rough voice from behind. It was accompanied by a none-too-gentle push with a boot that made Gryss stagger again.

He did not look to see who the culprit was, but scurried back to Nilsson's side. 'What's happened?' he asked. Again Nilsson did not reply. Gryss went cold. 'He's not dead, is he?'

'He's not dead. Go to the village.' Nilsson's voice was stark and commanding.

Gryss tried again, more insistently. 'Please stop. If he's hurt he shouldn't be carried like that.'

Still there was no reply. Nothing was to be heard except the sound of clinking harness and the clatter of the horses' hooves on the occasionally metalled roadway.

The healer in Gryss overrode his judgement and he became angry. 'Damn it, will you stop and let me tend him!' he shouted, seizing Nilsson's reins.

Nilsson turned to him sharply, his eyes ablaze. He raised his foot to kick Gryss, but before the blow could be delivered Harlen appeared by Gryss's side and dragged him away hastily.

'Let me go,' Gryss said furiously, but Harlen, easy-going though he might be normally, had no such intention. Without speaking he tightened his grip about Gryss's arm and forcibly marched him ahead of the column, at the same time signalling to his waiting daughter. Without hesitation, Marna turned and ran off into the fields.

'For pity's sake, Gryss, don't antagonize them,' Harlen said urgently as he bundled the elder along. 'They're quiet now, but they were very different when I first saw them. Something's happened while they were away. They're not the same men that arrived here at Dalmas.'

Gryss shook his arm free, but kept up with Harlen's fast pace. 'What do you mean?' he asked, looking back at the column, still maintaining its leisurely pace.

'They were noisy. Singing, shouting, laughing,' Harlen said. 'They've been up to something and something bad, if I'm any judge. And they've got more horses and baggage than when they left.'

Gryss turned to him. 'But Jeorg,' he said. 'We can't just leave him.'

Harlen's face was pained. 'I know, I know,' he said. 'But frankly I wanted Marna out of the way first. I don't want them anywhere near her, the kind of mood they're in. And how are we going to stop them if they don't want to stop? You nearly got kicked in the head for your trouble. Let's do as he said: get back to the village and try again there.'

Gryss could not argue, but Harlen was setting a pace which was barely short of running.

'Slow down, slow down,' Gryss pleaded, breathlessly, after a little while. 'I can't carry on at this speed.'

Harlen cast a glance backwards towards the column and then across the fields. Marna was nowhere to be seen. 'She's gone over the fields to get Yakob,' he said. 'He'll meet us at the green.' Then he slowed. Gryss put a grateful hand on his shoulder and leaned on it freely. Harlen put his own hand over it, at once supportive and apologetic. He did not speak.

When they reached the centre of the village it was raining more heavily, and Marna was standing with Yakob under a tree at the edge of the green.

'What's happening?' Yakob asked anxiously as Gryss and Harlen approached. Harlen explained, while Gryss recovered his breath.

Yakob frowned at the news that Jeorg had been hurt, but Gryss spoke before he could ask any questions.

'We'll try again here,' he said. 'See if we can get them to let me look at Jeorg.' His distress was almost unmanning him. 'This is awful,' he said. 'Poor Jeorg.' He gazed up at the leaden grey sky. 'Well at least the weather'll keep people in their homes,' he went on. 'The fewer who see Jeorg the better.'

It was little consolation to the four as they waited under the dripping tree for the column to arrive, though it was not long before the lead riders came into view. Gryss, Yakob and Harlen stepped forward together.

This time, Nilsson reined his horse to a halt. The column came to an untidy stop behind him. He held up his hand.

'We caught this man trying to sneak out of the valley, after my express instruction that that would not be allowed,' he said. 'You have to understand that you're all under military law now, and that if

395

you choose to disobey orders the consequences will be severe.'

Gryss however, was more concerned for his friend than for an explanation and he moved to his side even while Nilsson was talking. After testing Jeorg's pulse, he gently lifted his head.

His face was badly bruised and bloodstained.

'What the devil have you done to him?' he demanded bluntly. Nilsson looked at him angrily, but before he could speak, Gryss's frustration and rage boiled over, and he began tugging at the ropes that bound Jeorg to the horse. There was a commotion among the riders nearby.

'And you said nothing of the kind,' Gryss burst out furiously. 'You said we'd need your permission, that's all. Jeorg's been planning to go to the capital for months. When he heard what was happening he decided to go now before the garrisoning got under way. Damnit, he was only riding after you to ask your permission. Didn't you even give him time to speak?'

He gave an angry cry as the ropes defeated him, and then reached into his cape. When his hand emerged there was a knife in it.

On the instant, there was the rasping hiss of half a dozen swords being drawn.

Marna let out a scream of alarm, and Yakob and Harlen shouted, 'No!' simultaneously and moved to intervene.

Gryss himself froze, his face suddenly pale and with much of his anger turned to fear as he looked at the ring of points and grim, purposeful eyes that he now centred. Slowly he turned to Nilsson.

'To cut the ropes,' he said weakly.

Nilsson stared at him for a moment and then nodded to one of the riders. Without taking his gaze from Gryss, the man leaned across and, by pulling

396

a single cord, released the ropes that were securing Jeorg.

With difficulty, because his hand was shaking so much, Gryss replaced the knife in his belt.

The swords around him gradually withdrew, and Yakob and Harlen came forward hastily to help him lift down the unconscious Jeorg.

'Gently, gently,' Gryss said, fussily, dithering now and obeying some deep instinct to make himself seem innocuous and innocent while he tried to recover from the shock of the sudden response of Nilsson's men. Their clear intent had terrified him, not least because of its simple casualness. There had been no hesitation. He knew that he would have been given no opportunity to plead a case had he made any reckless movements; no chance to smile and shrug the incident off with the good humour that was his stock in trade with everyone in the valley. These men were stony-eyed strangers, quite indifferent to the fate of some stupid old country bumpkin. Katrin's words rang loud in his head: 'They're fighting men. Used to brutality, to stabbing and killing . . . There's none in the whole valley could stand against any of them and hope to live.'

Jeorg groaned. The sound gave Gryss something to focus on, and his fear began to fade. 'What have you done to him?' he asked again, though more circumspectly.

'Shown him the consequences of disobeying an order,' Nilsson said, starkly summarizing his previous reply. 'He can consider himself more than fortunate that he's not dead. Make sure that everyone understands this, Har Grysstson. We'd prefer to work with your friendship and cooperation, but it's not essential by any means and a few dead by way of example will be of no consequence in the design that's being worked here.'

And without further comment he spurred his horse on.

The three men, supporting the limp form of their friend, stood motionless as the column passed, like a grim parody of royal dignitaries receiving a formal military salute. Indeed, some of the riders did offer mocking salutes as they rode by.

Gryss was chilled not only by Nilsson's callousness but by the aura that seemed to pervade the whole troop. 'They're not the same men that arrived here at Dalmas,' Harlen had said, and Gryss understood now what he meant. Those men had been broken and dispirited, these were alive and vigorous, though there was a quality to their vigour which repelled him; an unnaturalness.

Almost demonic.

The thought startled him, but he realized it was accurate.

'Bandits.'

The whispered word was Marna's. She had come out from the shelter of the tree and was looking after the retreating column. 'Not in a mountain's age could they ever have been King's men,' she added. She wrapped her arms about herself fearfully and shivered.

'Come on. We shouldn't be standing here. Jeorg's in a bad way. Let's get him home and seen to, quickly.' Harlen's words cut through the paralysis that seemed to have gripped the little group.

Gryss started a little. 'No. My cottage is nearer,' he said. 'I can look after him better there.'

'Who's going to tell his wife what's happened?' Yakob asked, awkwardly.

'I will,' Gryss replied reluctantly, after some hesitation. 'But not yet.'

He glanced around the green. Nilsson's men had both entered and left in comparative silence, and no one had ventured into the rain to discover them. Jeorg's return had apparently gone unnoticed.

That, at least, was fortunate, Gryss thought.

That same dark good fortune remained with them as they made their way to Gryss's cottage and they reached it without being observed, softly whispering words of support and encouragement to their injured and occasionally conscious friend.

As they entered the cottage, Gryss's old dog, as if sensing the mood of the group, remained silent, confining its welcome to an encouraging wag of its stump of a tail.

Despite his burdens, Gryss bent down and stroked its head affectionately. Then he motioned Yakob and Harlen to a room at the front. 'Take him in there, get those wet top clothes off him carefully and put him on the bed,' he said. 'I'll get my things.'

That done, Gryss set about his examination of the injured man. The others, having done all that was asked of them, could do no more than sit and wait in the back room.

It was a difficult, restless interlude: Yakob and Harlen silently pondering the implications of what had happened and beginning to assess the extent of their own responsibility for Jeorg's condition; Marna oscillating between the childish urge to flee to safety that the presence of her father invoked, and the adult will which responded to the secret compact she had with Gryss and Farnor. A compact in which she had found a new sense of purpose even as she had watched Nilsson's men standing, menacing and alien, by the village green. Despite her own fears, an awful resolution was beginning to grow within her that sooner or later *she* would have to oppose these men.

And hanging like a grim spectre in all their thoughts

was the sudden and shocking appearance of swords in response to what could only have been an innocent gesture by an old man. Violence in the valley was rare, and when it did occur it was usually due to over-indulgence at the inn and confined to incompetent fisticuffs. Not infrequently it contained no small element of outright farce for the onlookers. The possibility of using knives and swords against people existed only in the distant safety of Yonas the Teller's tales. It was unthinkable in the real world where people tended and slaughtered their own meat; everyone knew only too well what keen, sharpened edges did to flesh and sinew.

Eventually the vigil ended and Gryss came in to them. He struck a sunstone to reveal them all blinking in its sudden light.

'How is he?' Yakob and Harlen asked together.

Gryss motioned Harlen out of his favourite seat and sat down heavily, at the same time waving an apologetic hand for his discourtesy. He looked tired and grim.

'How is he?' Harlen asked again, softly, as if fearing the answer he might receive. 'What did they do to him?'

'He'll be all right . . . I think,' Gryss replied. There was a tremor in his voice, as if he wanted either to weep or to roar with anger. 'There are bruises all over his body,' he went on. 'All shapes and sizes. His arm's broken and two of his ribs. I won't know what happened to his insides for a day or two, but there's no sign of any damage there at the moment.' He put his head in his hands. 'I can't believe it,' he said. 'They must have beaten him with fists and feet and sticks and . . . who knows what? Why, for pity's sake? Why? All they had to do was send him back.'

'They did it to frighten us. To show us they have the power to do whatever they want to us.' It was Marna speaking. 'And they did it because they like doing things like that,' she added.

The three men turned to her. 'Don't be ridiculous, girl,' Yakob said, though his sternness was shot through with uncertainty.

Marna glowered at him. 'There's nothing ridiculous about it,' she burst out. 'If they'd wanted to kill him, they'd have done it and left him out there, over the hill. No one here would ever have found him. They wanted—'

'Can we speak to Jeorg?' Harlen asked Gryss, loudly, at the same time raising his hand to end his daughter's angry tirade before it took full flight. Yakob looked both indignant and relieved.

'You can have a look at him,' Gryss replied, ignoring the tension in the room. 'But we mustn't disturb him too much. He's in a lot of pain and I've given him something to ease it and something that should be sending him to sleep soon. The more time he can put between now and being fully conscious again the better.'

Jeorg was mumbling to himself as the four of them trooped cautiously into his room. Marna gasped in dismay. Jeorg's eyes and mouth were puffed and swollen, while the rest of his face was scarred with bruises and deep, livid cuts.

'Rings,' Gryss said, proffering his clenched fist and answering the question before it was asked. 'Heavy rings.'

Yakob and Harlen shared Marna's dismay and looked from Jeorg to Gryss and to each other. Already powerless to do anything to help their friend, they now suffered the further indignity of not even knowing what to say to one another.

'He's trying to speak,' Yakob whispered, angling his head to catch meaning from the apparently incoherent noises that Jeorg was making. 'Did he tell you anything before? What they did, or why they did it?'

Gryss shook his head. 'He's been mumbling and muttering the whole time,' he said. 'Most of it's been meaningless, although I did get the feeling he was trying to tell me something important. I doubt he'll have anything to say now. A few more minutes and he'll be fast asleep, and likely to remain that way until this time tomorrow.'

Then, as if to give him the lie, Jeorg's swollen eyes opened painfully and searched the room. For an instant they were full of fear then they fell on Gryss and the fear became relief. It was followed by a look of urgency. Jeorg's hand slowly raised itself to reach out to the old man, and his cracked lips began to open.

Gryss pushed Harlen to one side and moved to the bedside. He took the hand gently. 'Lie quiet, Jeorg,' he said softly. 'It's over. It's all over. You're back with your friends. You're safe.'

But the urgency did not leave Jeorg's face and his hand clutched at Gryss's sleeve, trying to pull him downwards. Gryss bent and brought his ear close to Jeorg's mouth.

Then Jeorg's hand went limp, and Gryss straightened up.

'What did he say?' Yakob asked.

Gryss shrugged his shoulders, and began fussily adjusting Jeorg's pillows. 'I couldn't catch it,' he said. 'And he's fast asleep now, so we'll have to wait until he wakes tomorrow. See if he remembers what it was then.' He turned to Yakob. 'He can't tell dream from reality at the moment, anyway,' he said.

But Marna caught his eye and he flashed her a swift and mute appeal. Say nothing. For she had seen his face when he was affecting to adjust Jeorg's pillows; he had been struggling to compose his features.

She had not heard Jeorg's message, though.

'It's Rannick, Gryss. It's Rannick. He's leading them. He's leading Nilsson's men.'

Chapter 28

Later that night, Gryss sat drowsing in a chair by the side of Jeorg's bed. He stirred and muttered something as a subdued knocking drifted into his vague dreams. It was followed by a low, dutiful bark from his dog.

The knocking came again, followed this time by a more querulous bark. Gryss's dreams wavered and began to slip back into the echoing inner darkness from whence they had come. His eyes opened uncertainly.

The knocking was turning into a persistent tattoo, though it was still subdued and discreet. For a timeless moment, the sound mingling confusingly with the fading remnant of his dream, Gryss decided that Jeorg was trying to rise from his bed. The prospect brought him sharply to wakefulness. As both his vision and his mind cleared, however, he saw that Jeorg was still asleep and motionless.

The knocking intruded again. It was coming from the front door and, though soft, it was quite relentless. Frowning, Gryss levered himself up out of the chair and stiffly made his way along the hallway.

Well, he thought, whoever it was, at least they had wit enough not to go clanging the bell with a sick man in the house. His frown deepened at the thought even as he opened the door. Who knew there was a sick man in the house? Apart from . . .

'Marna! What are you doing here at this time of night?'

Marna ignored the welcome and stepped in, easing Gryss to one side. 'What did he say? What did Jeorg

405

say?' she demanded, bluntly, at the same time reaching down to stroke the dog.

Gryss's frown turned to unhappy confusion as it invariably did whenever he had to deal with Marna in one of her 'forthright' moods.

'Come in,' he said, unnecessarily, as he closed the door.

She looked at him impatiently. He motioned her towards the back room. 'Answering your question about how he is, he's still asleep,' he said caustically. 'As was I,' he added darkly, endeavouring to regain a little authority. 'And he's no different now than he was when you left, whereas *I* am markedly more weary.'

Marna coloured at the rebuke, but her demeanour remained unchanged. 'What did he say?' she insisted, though less stridently. 'It upset you, I could tell that. And you lied to my father and Yakob about it.'

A memory returned to Gryss of Farnor once complaining that Marna could and would pester and badger relentlessly to gain information when she was so inclined.

'Sit down, Marna,' he said, with increased firmness. 'And tell me the reason for this urgency.'

Marna did as she was told, folding her hands in her lap demurely. The action was entirely unconscious and the incongruity of it made Gryss smile.

Marna scowled at him in response, and he raised a defensive hand before she spoke. 'You reminded me of your mother for a moment,' he said, then he waved the matter aside. 'Tell me why you've come back to torment me with your curiosity tonight instead of waiting until tomorrow?'

Marna looked uncharacteristically uncomfortable. 'I don't know,' she said. 'I just had to. I've got the feeling that all the time we do nothing, they' – She hesitated, and flicked her hand roughly northwards – 'up there, will get stronger and stronger. They'll be able to do anything they want to us. Turn us out of our houses, destroy our fields, turn us into slaves . . . anything. And we'll be powerless.'

Gryss could not keep the distress from his face. 'That's a stark vision, Marna,' he said. 'And nothing they've done so far indicates they'd want to do that. Don't forget, for all our suspicions, they may still be King's men.'

Marna almost snarled a denunciation of this notion. 'King's men, my behind!' she said, angrily. 'Are all you men completely blind?' She raised her clawed hands in front of her, her arms quivering with tension. It was an oddly male gesture. 'Can't you . . . feel . . . what they're like? Can't you sense what they're up to? Do you have to wait for them to kick in your door and take your goods before you realize something's wrong?'

Despite himself, Gryss found his own temper beginning to flare in response to Marna's rebukes. 'I can feel lots of things I'm not happy about, Marna,' he said heatedly. 'And there's plenty of things been happening of late that I can't begin to understand. But unhappiness and misunderstanding don't tell me what's wrong, or what I should do.'

Caught between Gryss's logic and her own passions, Marna clenched her teeth and banged her heels on the floor. Almost as soon as it appeared, however, this childish outburst faded and Gryss found himself looking into the concerned and determined eyes of an adult.

'I'm sorry,' she said. 'I feel so helpless. It's as if I'm the only one who can see what's happening, and it's all so . . . dangerous, so frightening. Couldn't you see it, feel it, when they were at the green, walking slowly past you, with Jeorg hanging between Yakob and my father?'

Just as her previous angry tone had stirred Gryss's anger, so now her quieter and more compelling manner calmed him.

'Perhaps I was too close to it,' he said.

There was a silence between them for a long moment, then Gryss said, 'They'd have killed me, Marna. Killed me with no more thought than treading on an ant. I looked into their eyes and I could tell that.' He paused. 'And I fear you're right about both them and their intentions, though I don't know how someone so young could have arrived at such a grim conclusion so quickly. They're never King's men, and the longer we do nothing about them the more they'll gain power over us.'

Marna looked at him, unblinking. Questions were bubbling through her head, but central to them was the one she knew she must have answered.

'What did he say to you, Gryss?' she asked again, very quietly.

Gryss answered without hesitation. 'He said that Rannick was in charge of Nilsson's men.'

Marna's eyes widened in disbelief. 'Rannick?' she exclaimed. But she did not cry out, 'Impossible!' as he had half expected. Instead she said, 'How?'

'I don't know. That's all he said. "Rannick's leading Nilsson's men." His voice was weak, but he was quite clear. I didn't mishear him.'

Marna stared at him. 'You've been afraid of this all the time, haven't you?' she said.

It seemed to Gryss that with this simple statement Marna had picked him up and shaken him violently. He felt his breathing become shallow and frequent, and his heart begin to thump.

'Yes,' he heard himself saying breathlessly. He stood up. 'Yes. But how in Murral's name did you know when I didn't even know myself?'

Marna, alarmed at this almost explosive change in her involuntary host, shrugged helplessly. 'Patterns, shapes, bits and pieces . . .' she said, wriggling uncertainly in her chair.

But Gryss was not listening. He found himself teetering between waking nightmare and reality. He sat down again, abruptly, and put his head in his hands as he struggled to bring his rioting thoughts into some semblance of order.

'Rannick's tainted line is at the heart of this,' he said, mainly to himself. 'It wasn't someone that Nilsson brought with him. It was someone here. It makes sense.' Images came and went – Rannick and Farnor meeting by the slaughtered sheep – Rannick disappearing . . . and then reappearing. Still the memory of his meeting with him refused to become clear. And the creature. What part did *it* play in all this? And the terrible fate of the men who had tried to go through the northern part of the valley, the fate that Farnor had indirectly witnessed?

Questions teemed through his efforts to clarify his thoughts. What was the creature? Where had it come from? Were the stories about the caves true? Who and what were Nilsson and his men, and from what distant land did they come? And why? And what was the true nature of the power that ran through Rannick's ancestry like a diseased tap root? And had some part of it branched off to infect Farnor? – if infection was the right word for the lad's strange, seemingly harmless ability.

For an instant he had a vision of uncountable tiny causes and effects stretching back through time, each linked and interlinked, each affecting the other. He shook his head in rejection: it was too complex and, more to the point, it was of no value. Then, like a low rumbling deep beneath the earth, the thought occurred to him that he, and all the others in the valley, were but minor pieces in a game played by some greater, unknowable power. This, too, he rejected because it was of no value, but rejection proved much harder than he would have thought. There were many unknown powers in the world, why not one such? He remembered reproaching Farnor for his ignorance of the simple yellow flowers that grew outside his cottage, but then how much did *he* know about them? Or, by implication, about the power that lay within all living things?

He swore inwardly. These notions were but distractions. Whatever the ultimate cause, if any, of these events, the effect was with him and the rest of the valley *now*, and that was the problem that had to be dealt with.

'It's a coincidence,' he said to the now-bewildered Marna.

'I don't understand,' she said as this single, detached statement appeared in front of her like part of a monologue. 'What's a coincidence? What're you talking about?'

Gryss stared at her. 'Nilsson's being here,' he said, his voice matter of fact. And, as if he had been explaining all the time, he went on, his tone becoming increasingly revelatory, 'Rannick touched the creature, perhaps like Farnor did, but differently.' He curled his lip almost into a sneer. 'Probably because of his naturally curdled instincts. And now he's controlling it in some way. Or it him. Then along comes Nilsson and his men, just by chance, by coincidence, and Rannick sees an opportunity.' His face became thoughtful. 'His powers . . . whatever they are . . . must have grown tremendously if he's now apparently controlling not only the creature but also Nilsson's men.'

Only fleetingly did it occur to Marna that the old man was rambling. What dominated her response was the fact that, whatever the truth of Gryss's conjectures, the sense of evil that pervaded them chimed with her own feelings.

Thus, instead of debating or disputing, when he had

410

finished, she merely asked, 'What would Rannick want? And what can we do about it?'

Gryss had arrived at the same questions, though he too had no answers. 'What did Rannick ever want?' he asked. 'Always something he didn't have. And he compounded his folly by despising whatever he did have. If the family's trait has come, writ large, in a personality like that I shudder to think where it'll end.'

Marna did not seem inclined to disagree. 'What shall we do?' she asked.

'I don't know,' Gryss said.

He pulled a wry face. 'Perhaps I've got it all wrong,' he said, with an airy wave of his arms. 'It's been a bad few days; the business at the castle, Farnor, Jeorg. I'm tired. Perhaps I did mishear him, or misunderstood him. It's all very . . . wild.'

Marna shook her head. 'You heard clearly enough,' she said, starkly. '*And* he repeated himself. I saw that much myself. And however wild your ideas, they're no wilder than what's been happening to Farnor, and what happened to you and him at the castle, are they?'

Gryss's attempted escape into elderly folly collapsed.

'We must do *something*,' Marna insisted.

Gryss remembered again the ring of swords that had suddenly appeared as he tried to release Jeorg, and once again Katrin's words returned to him, though this time they were like a taunt. 'Fighting men . . . stabbing and killing . . . none could stand against them and hope to live.'

'We can't do anything,' he said. 'Not against those swords . . . those men. And not against Rannick if he truly has the power he seems to have.'

'We *must* do something,' Marna repeated, angrily. 'We *know* what's happening. We can't sit idly by and let them slowly take command of the whole valley.'

Gryss felt old again. He wanted to lash out and

411

drive this damned girl away. He wasn't stupid. Whatever happened, he had wit enough to survive. All he needed to do was avoid offending anyone, keep himself inconspicuous, do as he was told. That would be easy enough. And who would want anything from an old man with nothing other than a crooked cottage and a small plot of land? No matter what comings and goings there were through the village, he could live out his life safely and quietly. After all, what more could he ask for? Besides, how much longer did he have?

Then he felt a hand laid softly on his arm. He raised his head.

'Please,' Marna said simply.

Once again, Marna destroyed his escape as, with this light and delicate touch, she shattered the taut and brittle structure of his thinking. The old may send the young to war, he recalled, but this one was girding herself to go on her own. This one not only had a longer life ahead of her, she had a keen measure of the value of what she already had and, seeing the threat to it, she would fight to protect it. This young one was dragging an old one to war. No, that was unfair. This one was asking for the only thing he could give her: his advice and experience. In return she would give him her strength and courage.

Perhaps together they might indeed . . . ?

And yet they were none of them fighters. And fighters would be needed, surely?

'Somehow, we'll have to get help from over the hill,' he said.

Marna showed no surprise. In fact, the manner in which she nodded her agreement indicated that he had merely stated the obvious. 'I'll do that,' she said casually.

The guilt he had felt about Jeorg's fate returned tenfold to Gryss on the instant, and, abruptly, he found himself having to explain to Harlen about the

412

disappearance – or death or worse – of his only daughter.

Before he could protest, however, Marna was continuing. 'We'll have to talk to Farnor,' she was saying. 'He's the one nearest the heart of all this, and what he thinks will be important. Apart from getting the real King's men here, we'll need to convince everyone about what's happening, and I—'

Gryss had recovered from his trip into the future. 'Whoa,' he said firmly, holding up his hand. 'You're going nowhere, miss,' he said, very much elder to younger. 'The journey to the capital would've been hard enough for Jeorg, if he'd been lucky enough to avoid getting captured. It'd be far too hazardous for you.'

Marna's looks darkened. 'You weren't much older than me when you went,' she said. 'And I've coped on my own out in the hills before now.'

Unusually, Gryss held his ground against her. 'No!' he insisted, realizing the danger of becoming involved in a debate with this wilful and shrewd young woman.

Marna faltered a little at this unexpected resistance. Gryss moved in. 'I know you, Marna Harlenkint. I want your old-fashioned promise or die that you'll not do anything foolish like perhaps deciding to go to the capital on your own.' Scarcely were the words out of his mouth however, than he frowned at the levity he had allowed to intrude into his manner. He became serious, pleading almost. 'We'll have enough to worry about if we're right in what we're thinking, Marna, and we must be able to trust one another completely. You understand what I mean? Just think about the pain that's been caused already by Jeorg's venture. And there'll be more when I tell his wife or if he's more badly hurt than I think. And that journey was considered long and carefully.'

Marna's scowl faded. 'I do understand,' she said. 'But—'

'But nothing, Marna,' Gryss said, gently. 'We don't know what we're dealing with in Rannick and those men and we can't afford any act of foolishness antagonizing them . . .'

He stopped speaking and cocked his head on one side as if he had heard an unexpected sound. His movement echoed one Marna had just made. Both of them frowned with concentration. In the silence, a strange mewling sound rose to prominence until it pervaded the whole room. The old dog, which had been lying asleep between them, awoke and let out a quizzical whine.

'What—?'

Gryss did not finish. The mewling suddenly increased in intensity and pitch, and climaxed in an unearthly and unceasing shriek. The dog barked shrilly in alarm and without standing, wriggled backwards until it was under Gryss's chair.

Marna leapt up, her face white and fearful. Gryss rose more slowly but with no less alarm as the awful din echoed around the room until it seemed to come from every possible direction.

Then Gryss identified the sound. 'It's Jeorg,' he said, and was out of the door before Marna had time to realize fully what he had said.

As Gryss entered the dimly lit bedroom where Jeorg lay, it seemed to him for a moment that his images of Rannick's power had been made solid and that the room was alive with battling demons. He hesitated in the doorway, a primitive fear crawling over his skin and robbing him of movement. Then his vision cleared, and he saw a lamp hanging by the bed swinging violently. At its behest, wild shadows were leaping frantically about the room, now skimming from wall to wall, now wall to beamed ceiling, as if performing some

414

mocking dance at the fate of their shaper on the bed. For there Jeorg lay twisting and turning from side to side, his arms alternately flailing in the air and beating the bed. His eyes were wild and desperate, and his mouth was gaping wide.

Gryss stared at the terrible frenzy helplessly for a moment, then moved quickly to the side of the bed. As he reached out to still the swaying lamp, the shadow of his hand grew to fill the room with an ominous darkness then, abruptly, it was light again and the shadows were quiet and ordinary. Marna, pale faced still, moved nervously behind Gryss.

'He's choking,' she said.

Beating his way through the frantic arms, Gryss seized Jeorg's head and peered urgently into his mouth. Marna, unbidden, snatched up the lamp, lifted its dimming cowl and held it high so that it shone brightly on Jeorg's anguished face.

The shadows fled.

Gryss nodded gratefully and, struggling to restrain his thrashing charge, continued his examination. 'No,' he said. 'I can't see anything in his throat, and he couldn't make that amount of noise if his airpipes were blocked.'

Jeorg began to claw at him, and the scream degenerated into a dreadful gasping.

'He's choking,' Marna insisted.

Impulsively, Gryss wrapped his arms about his friend and held him tight. 'You're safe, Jeorg,' he said soothingly. 'It's all over. It's Gryss. You're in my cottage. You're safe. You're safe. Nothing can hurt you here.'

The gasping eased a little, as did the frantic struggling, but did not cease completely. Gryss began to rock him to and fro, as if he were a child who had awakened from a nightmare, all the time whispering gently to him, 'It's over, Jeorg. It's over . . .' On and on.

Gradually, Jeorg's breathing quietened until it became simply that of an exhausted man. Eventually, Gryss released him and laid him back.

'Is he all right?' Marna whispered, but Gryss held up his hand for silence. He was breathing heavily himself, and his face was flushed with effort, but he did not take his eyes from Jeorg.

Then, he nodded slowly. 'I think so,' he said, bending over Jeorg and looking intently at him. 'Jeorg,' he said. 'It's Gryss. Can you hear me?'

Jeorg swallowed several times and, for a moment, it seemed that he was about to begin screaming again. Gryss laid a hand on his chest. 'Gently,' he said. 'Don't distress yourself. You're safe now. There's no hurry.'

The comment seemed to galvanize Jeorg however, as he became immediately agitated. His hand reached out to grab Gryss's arm.

'Yes,' he said hoarsely. 'Hurry. There is a hurry. We mustn't wait. We must—' He gritted his teeth as his physical weakness mastered the intention of his will.

'Gently,' Gryss said again. 'There's nothing any of us can do right now, it's the middle of the night. Please try to relax and talk more slowly.'

Jeorg's eyelids began to close and his face contorted with the effort of keeping them open.

Gryss spoke softly over his shoulder to Marna. 'I don't know why he's awake,' he said. 'I gave him enough sleeping draught to take him through to tomorrow afternoon. He must want to tell us something desperately.'

Jeorg's hand on his arm drew him back.

'Rannick,' he mumbled.

'Rannick beat you?' Gryss suggested.

Jeorg shook his head painfully. 'He stopped them,' he said, with a further agonizing effort. Gryss was pleasantly surprised by this, but only momentarily; there was no hint of gratitude in Jeorg's voice.

416

He started to gasp again, his hands reaching out as if he were trying to hold captive all the air they could encompass.

Gryss managed to quieten him. 'Tell me slowly,' he said. 'What did Rannick do to make you like this if he stopped them beating you?'

Jeorg's hand clawed at his chest, and he drew a long, painful, breath. 'He . . . stopped me breathing,' he managed.

Gryss frowned and lifted a careful hand to examine Jeorg's neck. There was no sign of any bruising. He looked puzzled. 'I don't understand,' he said. 'What do you mean, he stopped you breathing? Did he try to strangle you? Or suffocate you?'

Jeorg shook his head, a grimace of impatience creasing his battered features. 'He stopped me breathing,' he repeated weakly. 'He . . . took my breath . . . the air in my chest . . . and stopped it.' He slumped back on the pillow.

'What did he do?' Gryss persisted, bewildered.

Jeorg managed to raise himself on to his elbows. 'He looked at me,' he said. 'Just looked at me. And I couldn't breathe.' His face became fearful. 'And when I thought my chest was going to burst, he nodded.' Jeorg's eyes widened as the intensity of the event returned to parade its every detail before him. 'Just a slight nod,' he whispered, mimicking the movement with a nervous twitch of his head. 'And I could breathe again. And he did it again . . . and again.' Gryss reached out to him, concerned that he would slip once again into a choking fit, but Jeorg waved him aside. 'I don't know how many times he did it. Then he tore the breath out of me. I could feel him inside me, moving, working.' His face contorted with pain and fear, but there was rage there also, and it was the rage that dominated in his words. 'And they all laughed. They

417

stood around and laughed. They'd already beaten me till I . . .'

His voice faded away as, quite suddenly, his eyes closed. Slowly, he sank back on to his pillow once again.

Marna clutched Gryss's arm in alarm.

'It's all right,' Gryss said. 'He's asleep. It's the sleeping draught catching up with him. I don't think he'll wake again tonight. Not now he's got most of that out of his system.'

He stood up and carefully rearranged Jeorg's pillow and sheets, then he took the lamp from Marna and replaced its dimming cowl. As he hung it back on its hook by the bed he motioned Marna out of the room.

Returning to the room at the back of the cottage, he slumped down heavily into his chair. Marna sat opposite him. Her face was full of questions, but she asked none of them.

'It *is* Rannick then,' Gryss said, after a long silence. 'There was no doubt about it that time, was there? No misheard whispers. No delirious rambling.'

There was a quality in Gryss's voice that made Marna want to turn away. She felt tiny and helpless as the enormity of events became increasingly clear to her. What was she but a pathetic husk of inadequacy? She could not face grown men with their formidable strength, and their swords and their willingness to use them. Nor could she face Rannick with his unbelievable and seemingly diabolical powers; powers that raised a battering wind to protect the castle yet which could be used subtly to torment a helpless, beaten man. What was she against all this?

And even Gryss had been downed and beaten by what was happening. For all her life he had been a man who knew the answers to her questions, a man who saw through her with an eye keener than her father's but whom she could twist to her own ends almost as if he were a mere child. She had not realized before what support she had drawn from him in the past. But now she did, for the support was gone.

Her loneliness was a grim revelation.

She felt as she imagined Jeorg must have felt when Rannick stopped him breathing. She felt the walls and ceiling of the cottage closing in on her, crushing, menacing . . .

She had to get away . . .

A thunderous banging crashed into her waking nightmare, making her start violently. She leapt to her feet, drawing in a raucous, terrified breath, seeing in her mind Rannick and Nilsson and his men circling the cottage, their horses stamping in the darkness and their intent focused on her just as it had been focused on Jeorg.

Her mouth dried and her legs began to shake. She turned to Gryss.

The banging continued.

And someone was shouting . . .

Licking his lips, Gryss half walked and half ran down the hallway.

Reaching the door, he threw it open.

An inarticulate cry greeted him and a figure blundered forward, seizing Gryss in a desperate grip.

Gryss took in the hair, wildly awry, the mud-spattered clothes, the wild, lost eyes and the deathly pale face of the third member of his conspiracy against the invaders of the valley: Farnor Yarrance.

Chapter 29

As they made their way through the village, Nilsson's men remained silent and in close formation. The only sign of interest in their surroundings they had shown had been the ironic salutes that some of them had given to Gryss and the others, as they had stood, bewildered and uncertain, supporting the unconscious Jeorg, while the troop passed by.

Even after they had left the village some way behind, the men maintained their silence and their close formation. Then Nilsson raised his face so that the rain fell directly into it, and let out a low, rumbling laugh.

The sound was a comparative rarity, but it was familiar enough to be recognized and it ran down the column gathering momentum as it went. Soon the troop was a loose, straggling band of men shouting, laughing and jeering.

One rider, the hood of his cape pulled well forward, pushed his horse through the mass to join Nilsson at the front. Nilsson turned to look at him and some of the laughter faded from his face.

'A good trip, Lord?' he asked.

Rannick threw back his hood and ran a hand through his unkempt black hair. There was laughter in his face, too, but there was no humour in it. Not that there was much humour in the laughter that rippled to and fro along the column. It was coarse and raucous and dedicated to the amusement derived from watching the sufferings of others.

'A beginning, Captain,' Rannick replied. 'A beginning. I will confess that it was . . . interesting to watch your men ply their trade. Stimulating, even.'

Nilsson smiled, knowingly. 'The men needed the exercise, Lord,' he said. 'They were becoming restive, and it was only a matter of time before they took it in the village here. Something which would have presented quite a few difficulties for us in the future.'

No sooner had he spoken the words than he cursed himself for a fool. He braced himself for Rannick's response.

It began with a sneer. 'I have told you before, Captain, you concern yourself too much about these people. I know them. A little . . . exercise . . . as you choose to call it would avoid difficulties with them in the future, rather than cause them.'

Nilsson bowed in acknowledgement, but offered no argument. It had been careless of him to touch on the subject of how to treat the local people, and he hoped now that his silence would allow it to fade away. It was sufficient that he had had his own way so far in keeping Rannick from inflicting some horror on them to satisfy whatever malice it was he had towards them.

Fortunately, Rannick chose not to pursue the matter, though Nilsson sensed that it was rankling his new lord and would surface again eventually. He sensed, too, that if it did so then almost certainly he would have to cease his opposition if he wished to survive.

Rannick looked at him directly, and his sneer turned into a malevolent smile. 'I noticed that you too enjoyed the exercise, Captain,' he said.

Nilsson inclined his head. Except for what you did to that villager who followed us, he thought, though this time he managed to remain silent. In that instance he had not had his own way. He would have preferred to let the men have their fun with him and then seen him safely dispatched. It would have been scarcely necessary even to hide the body, so deserted and little-travelled was the region. But Rannick had wanted exercise of his own and, that done, he had ordered that the man be returned to the village by way of an example to others. There had been no debate about it.

It seemed to Nilsson at the time to be a major error, but nothing would have possessed him to even hint at disagreeing with his lord when he saw the look on his face as he worked his fearful way with the choking villager.

He shrugged his concerns aside. If the worst came to the worst as a result, then so be it. He and his men had dealt with worse problems than rebellious villagers in their time. He smiled to himself. It *had* been a good trip. They had not had one such for a long time. And apart from putting heart back into the men, it had also provided them with considerable extra supplies.

Faintly, from the edges of his thoughts like the sound of a distant ocean, came the strains of the grim chorus of the maimed and dying that had risen in the wake of his passing over the years. It was a little louder now, but he paid it no heed. It would fade, and though it was ever there, rumbling to the surface in his quieter moments, he rarely heard it and he *never* listened to it.

Yet that cry for retribution in its harmony was not easily dismissed. Suddenly a chill ran through him. It was not unfamiliar, but there was nothing he could do about it. Somewhere back there they would be following. They would never stop. Never. They would pursue him and his men wherever they went: no boundary, natural or man-made, could offer protection against them, nor the arm of any king or prince. Not even time would give any protection for they would come to his very deathbed to demand an accounting. And there would be no faltering in their resolution; that, he knew; that, they all knew. That much had been known since the first blow had been struck early that misty morning so long ago.

He shivered and, scarcely realizing what he was doing,

glanced over his shoulder. Accidentally catching the eye of Dessane, he forced himself to grin and then passed the act off as a casual inspection of his men.

There had always been the possibility of turning and facing the pursuers and of putting them to the sword, given a chance. But apart from the inherent danger in such a step, to do so would merely be to declare their whereabouts, and there would be others to follow in their wake: always there would be others.

He wiped the rain from his face and turned forward again. Just reaction, he thought. It always happened after a good raid. Perhaps, ironically, it was worse this time because their circumstances were so much improved following the arrival of Rannick. Now, he reminded himself, they were aided by the power. His fear of the past was, in reality, little more than a habit. Rannick may not have the awesome talents of the lord that he had once followed, but Nilsson could see for himself that his skills were growing, and even now no ordinary man could hope to prevail against him.

With an effort, Nilsson set aside his fears and looked again to the future of wealth and power that could be his if he retained Rannick's good will.

The thought brought him back to his original concern. He glanced covertly at Rannick and then allowed himself a discreet moment of satisfaction; his inadvertent rekindling of the dispute about the fate of the villagers had not been fanned into a larger blaze. He had been fortunate this time, but he must remember in whose presence he was. He must weigh his every word just as he had been wont to do in the past.

And, as if in confirmation of this, the rain falling ahead of them began to twist and swirl. Nilsson watched, fascinated, as skeins of water danced hither and thither, merging and dividing, looping and spiralling, now flying high into the air, now slithering along the ground like glistening grey serpents.

His mind filled with questions about how, and why, but he did not speak. Watch and learn were to be his watchwords. Rannick's behaviour had all the hallmarks of childish playfulness, but there was a sinister menace even in these seemingly innocent, dancing shapes whose cause it would be best not to enquire into.

Then the skeins merged into a single solid shape which rose into the air. It stood looming over them for a moment, like a great tree trunk supporting the grey sky above, then it trembled throughout its entire bulk as if something at its heart were trying to escape and, with a strange sigh, burst into a cloud of fine spray.

Nilsson risked a compliment. 'Your skill grows by the day, Lord.'

'No particular skill is needed for such foolishness,' Rannick said, staring at the dispersing mist. 'But you are right. My skill and my power build upon one another. It comes to me that we will be able to pursue my intentions much sooner than I had envisaged.'

Nilsson fought down a frown. One successful raid against a defenceless village did not form a basis for assessing the worth of the men against more prepared adversaries. It was a long time since they had done any serious fighting.

He eased his horse closer to Rannick and lowered his voice. 'The men can't adjust to circumstances as rapidly as you, Lord. And we must build up our strength before we become too . . . adventurous. Sooner or later we'll have to face real opposition as your plans begin to take shape.'

'We must be cautious. Take care not to over extend ourselves?'

Nilsson looked at him, startled by this paraphrasing of the comments he had made so often in their discussions of late. Was it a genuine acknowledgement of their position or did it merely portend an impulsive punishment in response to some fault on his part?

But not to answer could be equally provocative.

'Yes, Lord,' he said, as neutrally as he could manage.

Rannick was silent. Nilsson instinctively held his breath. Then Rannick smiled unpleasantly. 'Holding your breath will avail you nothing, Captain,' he said. 'I can hold it for you for hours, if you wish.' He turned towards him. 'I can do it for the entire troop. Or I can sweep you all into oblivion.'

Nilsson made no effort to keep the fear from his face. 'I'm yours to command, Lord,' he said.

Rannick nodded. 'Yes,' he said simply. The menace in his presence evaporated. 'But have no fear. I shall ask nothing of you that you are not prepared to do willingly. And, as I have agreed with you, those who are loyal and serve me well will be duly rewarded.'

'Lord,' Nilsson said with a bow.

Rannick turned away from him and looked towards the castle which was now occasionally appearing through the rain. Nilsson let his horse fall back a pace so that he could discreetly recover his composure.

Abruptly Rannick leaned forward, as if he were trying to catch a distant sound. Then he frowned. 'Someone's been inside the castle,' he said, his voice an odd mixture of anger and anticipation.

Nilsson swore under his breath. In spite of Rannick's assurances, he knew that he should have left a guard. It was all very well talking about these locals as if they were timid half-wits, but to take such a risk as leaving the castle undefended was folly of a high order. They could have seized back their precious tithe, leaving the troop without supplies other than those that they had just stolen. They could have found such few documents as he had which might reveal the true nature of the troop.

Visions of poisoned food and fouled wells hovered on the fringes of these concerns. And ambush!

'We'll prepare for an attack, Lord,' he said, but Rannick shook his head.

'No,' he said. '*My* guards have done their duty adequately. There's no one there now. Though . . . ?' His voice tailed off with a note in it that Nilsson had not heard before.

Doubt, he realized. What had happened with these mysterious guards he had left behind?

Then Rannick was himself again. 'I am going ahead,' he said icily. 'Follow at the walk. There is no urgency.'

Frightened we might come across some flaw in your schemes, Lord? Patch it up before we arrive? Nilsson thought viciously, though he kept his manner attentive and concerned.

'As you wish, Lord,' he said.

He watched Rannick galloping away, stiff and ungainly, swaying awkwardly from side to side. Whatever else he might be, he was no rider, though he managed well enough on the horse he had eventually chosen. 'Evil-minded, bad-tempered mare, that one. We should've eaten it months ago,' Dessane had said of it. But it seemed to get on with Rannick, prompting Dessane to conclude, very softly, 'Two of a kind.'

'A happy sight, Nils,' a voice said quietly by Nilsson's side. He turned to find Saddre, his restless eyes flicking significantly after Rannick.

'Him riding away?' Nilsson suggested.

Saddre nodded. 'Talk about the old days,' he said, puffing out his cheeks. 'It'd have been kinder to cut that poor sod of a farmer's throat than do what he did.'

Nilsson raised his hand as an injunction to Saddre to avoid the topic.

Saddre missed the movement and continued. 'Do you remember Commander Gro—?'

427

'Yes! Leave it,' Nilsson snapped angrily, favouring Saddre with a look laden unmistakably with danger.

'Sorry,' Saddre said hastily. 'What's the matter with him, anyway?' he went on, gesturing after the now-vanished Rannick.

Nilsson shrugged. 'Doubtless he'll tell us if he wants us to know,' he said. 'But it looks as if something's gone wrong. Keep an eye out for his temper when he gets back.'

It was not mere temper that Rannick was exhibiting when he returned, however. It was a deep, cold fury that he made no attempt to conceal. Even the most oafish of Nilsson's men had wit enough to feel it and stay silent.

Nilsson, increasingly attuned to his new master's moods, sensed it long before any of the others and rode forward to meet him. 'Lord, what's happened?' he asked. 'Has there been an attack? Damage done?'

'We must find the ones responsible immediately,' Rannick said ominously. 'He must be found. If we have to raze every building in the valley he must be found.'

'He, Lord?' Nilsson queried. 'I thought you said—'

'They, they!' Rannick snarled.

Nilsson's horse carried him backwards from Rannick's wrath. 'Have you any idea who it might be, Lord?' he asked when he finally succeeded in bringing his mount under control.

'When I meet him,' Rannick replied, his savagery unabated.

Nilsson let both the vagueness of the reply and the further reference to a single individual pass.

'It's late to organize a full-scale search, Lord, but if the matter's urgent, we can start with the nearest and see how far we get before nightfall.'

'We search until he's found, Captain,' Rannick said, brutally.

'You'll have to come with us, Lord, if you're the only one who can recognize the culprits.'

But Rannick needed no such advice, he was already off, galloping gracelessly towards Garren's farm. Nilsson spurred his horse after him and signalled the troop to follow.

The dogs set up a noisy barking as the troop neared, and rushed out threateningly when they clattered into the yard. Rannick flicked his hand towards them and the two animals abruptly turned tail and fled yelping piteously.

More than the sound of the barking, this brought Garren to the door of the farmhouse. Looking to see what had happened to so frighten his dogs, his gaze lit first on Nilsson.

'What in thunder's name's going on, Captain?' he demanded.

Before Nilsson could reply, however, Rannick had ridden forward to confront Garren. The farmer's anger changed to confusion. 'Rannick? What're you doing here, riding with these men?'

'I'm not riding with them,' Rannick replied. 'They're riding with me. At my command.'

Garren's confusion grew. He gave a bewildered, apologetic smile, as if he had misheard something, though there was some irritation in his voice at Rannick's manner. 'I don't understand. What do you mean?' he asked.

Rannick bent low towards Garren, his face twisted with rage. Nilsson moved his horse forward.

'Who's been into the castle while we were away?' he asked.

His voice was stern and commanding, but free of the rage that was consuming Rannick. It gave Garren the opportunity to turn away from Rannick's strange belligerence. Instinctively, he told as near the truth as he dared. 'No one,' he said, his voice wilfully quiet and courteous. 'Gryss and Farnor set off there to see if there were any sick or injured who needed attention while you were away, but they never got there.'

'What happened?' Rannick intruded.

Garren shrugged. 'Gryss had an accident on the way. A fox startled his horse and it threw him.'

Rannick stretched up in his saddle and stared at the wet rooftops of the farmhouse and its outbuildings.

'Is this the truth?' he asked without looking at Garren.

'To the best of my knowledge,' Garren replied, with some heat. 'I wasn't there personally, but why should either Gryss or my son lie about such a thing? An old man falling off a horse is hardly a matter of any consequence, and Farnor was certainly hurt when he came back. He fell on a rock when he was trying to catch Gryss.' He moved on to the attack. 'What's happened, anyway, to bring you all charging into my yard in the pouring rain?'

A good question, Nilsson thought, realizing that he himself did not know the answer to it, so preoccupied had he been in avoiding Rannick's rage.

'My orders have been disobeyed,' Rannick said. 'You and everyone else will have to learn the consequences of such disobedience.'

Garren's anger overmastered his bewilderment. 'Rannick, I don't know what the devil you're doing here, or what cracked fancy these men have put into your head. I presume it's some private jest of their own, but if you're expecting to get any work from me this summer I'll thank you to moderate your tone.'

A silence descended on the yard. Katrin appeared in

the doorway. Her gaze moved across the watching men, but no reaction showed on her face.

Nilsson felt the storm coming and, almost in spite of himself, moved to forestall it. 'Farmer,' he said, grimly, 'you must understand that many things are changed about here now. You must not address the Lord Rannick thus, on pain of severe punishment. Whatever he may have been, he is now as he says he is: our lord and our leader. It's no jest. As he orders, so we do.'

'*What?*' Garren's single word was filled with both amusement and disbelief. He was about to say more, but Rannick, the force of his anger deflected a little by Nilsson's intervention, spoke first.

'Where's Farnor?' he asked starkly.

'He went for a walk over towards the west-side forest.' It was Katrin who answered, her voice strong but without aggression. 'He hurt his arm when he caught Gryss, and he can't do a lot about the farm. I sent him out because he was pacing up and down like a caged rat.'

This was very nearly the truth, though in fact it was Farnor who had decided to go for a walk. He *was* bored with the enforced inaction, but mainly he felt that he needed time and silence in which to think.

'He's probably sheltering somewhere until the worst of this rain has passed,' Katrin went on. 'We can send him up to the castle when he gets back if you want to speak to him.'

Rannick hesitated. Katrin's manner was direct and open, and spoke of gentler, kinder times. It touched the humanity in him; the humanity that had always sat uneasily with his dark, sour spirit and which was shrivelling further day by day with his increasing use of the power. He teetered on the balance. But in the scales were his old life as a near pariah, a labouring malcontent, and set against them was the glorious, rich

431

and powerful future that lay ahead. There was no true choice for him.

'Speak when I speak to you, woman,' he said contemptuously.

Katrin's eyes blazed momentarily, but her hand went out again to restrain her husband. To no avail however. Garren stepped from the shelter of the doorway and, before anyone could react, his powerful arms had reached up, seized the front of Rannick's cape and dragged him from the saddle. As Rannick thudded on to the wet, hard ground, Garren retained his grip and began to drag him to his feet.

Not by any definition a violent man, Garren's intention was probably to give this lout a good cuffing for his insolence. But he was among men whose knowledge of violence was utterly different and before he could set about his chastisement Nilsson had drawn his knife and, spinning it in his hand, had struck him a powerful blow on the head with its hilt.

Katrin screamed and ran forward as Garren dropped to his knees, both hands clasped over his head.

Rannick staggered to his feet. Nilsson swung down from his horse to catch and support him.

'Lord—' he began, but Rannick was intent on only one thing. He shook off Nilsson's supporting hand and delivered a vicious kick to the kneeling Garren. It was a form of assault that he himself had learned only the other day as he had watched Nilsson's men beating Jeorg. He had never seen, or even truly envisaged, such calculated and personal brutality, and it had exhilarated him. The use of the power was not the only corrupting influence in Rannick's life.

Katrin, who was trying to help her husband, fell backwards as Garren was torn from her hands by the force of the impact.

Stunned by Nilsson's blow and winded by Rannick's

kick, Garren rolled over until he bumped into the wall of the house. Then, gasping, he began to claw himself upright against it.

Nilsson went forward to take hold of him.

'No!'

Rannick's face was so contorted with rage that it was barely recognizable as human. Nilsson abandoned Garren and moved to one side with no pretence at either dignity or courage. He noted, but scarcely registered the fact, that Katrin had disappeared.

Rannick lifted his hand to the stricken Garren. 'You are the second person to defy my will these past two days,' he hissed. 'You have to understand, all of you, what such defiance will mean.'

Garren looked at him, screwing up his eyes in an attempt to bring his tormentor into focus. He staggered forward, his arms nursing his chest. 'You lunatic, Rannick,' he gasped, painfully. 'I think you've broken my ribs. I'm already having to do Farnor's work. How the devil am I supposed—?'

'Your ribs, you pathetic sod-turner!' Rannick shrieked. 'Your ribs!' He turned to Nilsson, who stood very still. 'You see?' he shouted. 'I told you. They don't understand. They have to learn. And there's only one way they can do that.'

'As you will, Lord,' Nilsson said, though he knew that his words did not reach into the whirling maelstrom of ancient bitterness and hatred that had festered and rotted in Rannick's heart, any more than Rannick's declamation to him had been intended for his illumination. It had simply been a step in some obscene, self-imposed ritual that Rannick apparently found necessary before he could bring the encounter to its inevitable conclusion. Nilsson realized that he had not had his own way after all. Rannick was intent upon asserting his will in all matters, and in the treatment of the locals he had not

433

been deferring to experienced counsel, he had merely been waiting for an opportunity.

Talk about the old days. Saddre's words came back to taunt him.

He had no time to ponder them, however, as Rannick had now gathered such resources as he needed.

A violent, gusting wind suddenly sprang up. It blustered angrily around the farmyard, scattering great gouts of rainwater and further unsettling the riders and their mounts. Nilsson staggered under its force and reached for his horse's bridle, both to quieten it and to steady himself.

But it seemed to him that the wind was merely incidental to what was happening. Or a precursor to something.

'Learn! Learn! Learn!' Rannick's scream rose to become one with the increasingly furious wind. Any semblance of discipline left the watchers and the yard became a frenzy of panic-stricken horses and men.

Battered by the wind and by the hatred pouring from his new lord, Nilsson clung to his mount, grimly determined to stand his ground come what may.

He had a fleeting impression of Garren's face, alarm beginning to replace bewilderment, then, although nothing could be seen, a dreadful blow struck him, sending him crashing back into the farmhouse wall. So fierce was the impact that Nilsson heard Garren's breath leave him and his bones breaking even above the din of the wind and the uproar of the struggling men and horses.

Talk about the old days. Yes, this was the way it had been.

Rannick was motionless, though to Nilsson it seemed that he was the swirling focus of the chaos that was filling the farmyard. He was aware of another blow striking Garren. And another. The farmer slammed repeatedly into the wall like a child's doll, his limbs jerking lifelessly.

It was like watching a man being trampled under an invisible cavalry charge.

Nilsson was indifferent to Garren's fate, but there was a demented quality in Rannick's wilful destruction of his body that sickened him.

He's dead, Rannick! he screamed inwardly. You've made your point. You can let him be now.

But he was powerless. This was a time when all he could do was watch. He was bound to this man who was filling his vision with his frenzy.

But another agent intervened to prevent Rannick reaching whatever conclusion he was intending. An image of wild, purposeful eyes, flying hair and a screaming mouth came into Nilsson's distorted focus.

And a knife! Glinting, keen-edged, even in the dull light that pervaded the yard.

Its very sharpness cut through the unreality that was binding him.

The wife!

He swore.

A reflex brought his arm out and his mind watched his hand closing about the sleeve of her dress. He felt its fresh, soft texture.

Without a flicker of hesitation, Katrin yielded her gripped arm to him totally and in so doing remained free to move. Spinning round, she slashed the knife across her would-be captor twice. Again, old reflexes saved him as he released his grip and arched himself backwards away from the blade. He felt it cutting through his cape and jacket and drawing a thin, ice-hot line across his stomach. It was a very sharp knife, he registered.

A survivor of innumerable close-quarter encounters, he knew instantly that, reflexes or no, he was a dead man. He was off-balance and shaken by surprise, while she was so solid in her purpose, so well positioned and *so fast*. He felt his leaden limbs striving to gain control of themselves while at the same time he found himself waiting for the stroke that she would make next and against which he could not begin to defend himself; the one that he had waited for all his life; the one that would spring open his entrails and lay him in this cold, sodden yard. He fancied already that he could feel the wet stones on his cheeks and the cool rain dripping into his gasping mouth. He was strangely calm.

But Katrin was no trained warrior with a catalogue of subtle fighting techniques and skilled slayings at her back. She was simply a woman who had read the signs foretelling the death of her husband and who had responded knowing that he had not her vision. She had little conscious thought about what she was doing. Her whole self knew only that she must strike directly at the source of the danger with all the speed she could rouse. Nothing could be allowed to stand in her way: not her own frailty; not this hulking foreigner.

Thus as Nilsson staggered back he was forgotten, and Katrin returned to the heart of her intent.

'Lord!'

The urgency in Nilsson's distant cry penetrated Rannick's frenzy just as Katrin appeared before him. He glimpsed the upraised knife and her eyes pinioned him. Somehow, a miserable village labourer again, he managed to raise an arm as the knife came down.

Garren's body, freed from its torment, slithered to the ground.

Rannick felt the blow of the knife, but no pain; Farnor's edges were too sharp to allow pain. But he felt a scream of fury and terror at this invasion rising within him.

Katrin did not note what damage she had done. It was irrelevant. He was still there, still conscious, still breathing, still able to hurt her man. She raised the knife again . . .

Rannick mimicked her movement, raising his own arm helpless for all his power against this primordial justice and fury.

Then it was gone.

Nilsson had recovered and launched himself at Katrin.

His powerful grip closed around the hand that held the knife. Katrin made no sound, nor again did she fight him. Instead she slithered and slipped within his grasp, her focus ever on Rannick. Twice Nilsson swung the great fist of his free hand at her, but both times she was gone when the blow should have landed. Briefly they pirouetted in a grotesque dance, then Katrin twisted the wrong way and died with the merest flicker of pain on the blade that her son had so diligently sharpened.

Nilsson felt the life leave her. It was no new sensation to him, but he hesitated for a moment, holding her like a bewildered lover, then he lowered her to the ground with peculiar gentleness at the same time withdrawing the knife. A mysterious twinge of regret rose within him for this warrior who had bested then spared him. But it passed, although in its wake came a spasm of rage that he could not have begun to explain. Furiously, he hurled the knife away from him. It thudded into the stout wooden frame of the farmhouse door. A fine spray of blood left the blade and stained the painted timber.

Nilsson's rage was still alive as he turned to Rannick, who was gripping the arm that Katrin had struck. Blood was oozing lavishly between his fingers, falling drops joining the rain and splattering into the puddles around his feet.

But it was the look on his face that evaporated Nilsson's rage and replaced it with naked fear.

In the woods to the west, Farnor sat fulfilling his mother's prophecy: sheltering under a tree and waiting for the rain to ease before he set off back home.

His arm was sore and he was beginning to feel cold, and his mind was turning with relish to the prospect of the warm, welcoming kitchen, bright with light and bustle and savoury with the odours of his mother's cooking.

He had spent the afternoon wandering idly about the fields and the woods, rejoicing in the soft scents that only the rain can bring forth. Part of the time he had debated recent events yet again, but, despite the violence and strangeness of the assault he and Gryss had experienced at the castle, he had come to no further conclusion than that which he had reached previously: he must watch and wait.

But not here, he decided finally. A glance at the sky told him that the rain was not going to ease and that he should be on his way soon or he would be walking back to the farm in the dark as well as the wet.

Then, suddenly, it was all around him. Stronger and more vivid than he had ever known it before.

The creature.

Its will pervaded everything.

It must be nearby. The thought forced itself into Farnor's mind through the uproar, and froze him with terror.

No, it was everywhere.

And there was blood.

And a demented fury.

He was vaguely aware of the tree at his back. A host of voices whispered to him with a despairing urgency: '*Home. Home.*'

His body took him over and his legs began to carry him on, first staggering, then running. The creature was all around. It was filled with vengeance. And it was hunting. He must reach home. He must reach home.

* * *

Nilsson turned away from Rannick as he looked up. His eyes saw still his new lord, his arm bleeding and his bloodstained hand now reaching forward, clawed in savage reproach. But his inner vision felt the presence of the creature that had slaughtered his men and come near to slaughtering him. And, too, its spirit was everywhere, pervading and drawing strength from the frenzied mass of riders and horses struggling for escape. Somewhere in his consciousness he sensed men falling from their horses, horses bringing down the stone walls of the yard as they scrabbled over them, legs being crushed and twisted in the tight-packed panic at the gate. And, throughout, the rain fell and the wind blew.

But these were fleeting motes caught in the whirlwind that Rannick had now become. And he too, Captain Nilsson, leader and champion of his men, was no more than a mote. To remain where he stood would be to die.

Yet he edged away with a studied caution, for fear that a sudden movement might draw this awful predator down on him.

As he moved he saw Rannick's eyes become alive with an ancient malice. But they were not Rannick's eyes, he knew. They were the eyes of the creature.

The turmoil in the yard grew further in its desperate intensity. Nilsson fended off animals and men alike as he tried to retreat from the farmhouse. Not once, however, did he shift his gaze from Rannick.

Then, just as he had seen the creature in Rannick's eyes, so he heard the creature's voice as Rannick straightened up, threw his head back and roared. It was a fearful sound that wrapped itself around the battering wind and the din of the fleeing men and animals, and drew all together into a terrible focus.

Nilsson's hands began moving to his ears, though the sound was ringing through his entire body, and even as

439

he did so other noises reached him. He turned from Rannick to the farmhouse.

With unbearable slowness, the windows were shattering and blowing inwards, guttering and tiles were being torn from the roof and hurled high into the grey sky, rafters and beams strained after them then quivered and splintered as they fell back.

At the edge of his vision, Nilsson saw Rannick stumbling as if the impact of this destruction had rebounded on him. He caught him.

'Lord,' he said, perhaps in the hope that simple speech might bring back the man from this awful possession.

But it was not yet over. The frenzied presence of the creature seemed not so much to have fled as to have been transformed into something yet more fearful. Rannick was himself again, and, too, not himself.

He leaned heavily on Nilsson and began muttering ecstatically.

'Yes. Yes. I have it now. I have it.'

He pushed himself away from Nilsson and lurched forward, his hands extended towards the shattered farmhouse.

There was a nerve-tearing sound like fingernails drawn down glass and the air in front of Rannick began to shimmer and glow. The sound grew in intensity, until it was finally topped by a great cry of triumph.

Nilsson stepped backwards involuntarily as the shimmering mass crackled into flickering life. A pungent smell assailed his nostrils, then, as if in obedience to Rannick's cry, the light split and divided into great tendrils which surged through the shattered windows of the farmhouse. It seemed to Nilsson that they were like living things, so purposeful was their movement.

Like serpents, he thought.

Almost immediately, the interiors of the rooms were ablaze.

Nilsson watched as flames and smoke poured out of the windows and rose through the gaping roof. It was almost as if they were trying to escape from the horror that had just entered the house. Silhouetted against the scene stood Rannick, his arms held wide, swaying from side to side as if to some unheard music.

Then he sank to his knees and slumped to the ground.

Chapter 30

Farnor ran and ran. The presence of the creature possessed him like a raging fever. He did not see the streams he ran through, the walls he climbed, the fences he slithered under. His mind knew only fear, and his body carried him towards security using reflexes that were older even than the mountains that now stood by, indifferent to the terror that so filled his world.

And yet as he fled he sensed that no matter which way he ran, he could not avoid the creature. It was all around him. And it was more vivid and powerful than it had ever been before.

Then it became worse. Save for a vague, flickering remnant somewhere, he lost even his own sense of being. The world was rasping breath and pounding heartbeat, and . . . the power . . . moving.

Flooding in from . . . ?

Despite his terror, part of him was drawn towards it. Drawn to reach out and stop it. But some deeper instinct pulled him back. He could not stem such a torrent.

And still he fled on, desperately, unhindered by this inner debate; indeed, scarcely even noting it.

Then came . . . light? Lights. Moving, shifting lights.

Flames! He could feel their heat beating on his face, and . . . surging up from within him as if he himself were making them.

A spark of consciousness returned to him. Nightmare. He was dreaming. Soon he would crash out of this terrible flight into the security of his bedroom.

But this revelation affected nothing, for always lurking in the terror of a nightmare is the possibility that one might not indeed awaken. Still he had to flee; flee towards and through these surging flames; flee from the terror at his back; flee until he came to his home.

Then both the flames and the terror faded. As they did so his awareness began to return more fully. It was no nightmare, it was real. And still his body propelled him violently homeward. He must wrap the security of familiarity about him if he was to quench this torment.

A familiar, not unpleasant smell reached him.

A hint of autumn in the air.

Burning.

Something was burning.

It brought him to a halt by a gate. He leaned on it breathlessly. There was nothing to be burned on the farm.

Suddenly, more tangible fears rose within him.

Fire! There'd been a fire in one of the outbuildings. And he hadn't been there! With a cry, he clambered over the gate and began running again.

As he neared the farm, his fears began to be realized. A column of smoke was rising above the small hill that separated him from the farm. Despite his exhaustion, he forced himself on.

What had happened? Visions filled his mind. The barns? The stables? The workshed?

He reached the top of the hill and stopped.

The rain had flattened his hair against his head and ran in streams down his face.

And his world was no more.

A dreadful numbness began to spread through him.

Where had stood the clutter of buildings with the solid block of the farmhouse at its heart – a sight as timeless and immutable as the mountains themselves – stood now a grim mockery of that sight. The buildings were there, though they were different now. Their perspective had been changed. Changed because what had been the farmhouse was now a gaping maw, jagged with shattered walls and blackened rafters. Fires burned here and there, and dense wreaths of smoke swirled in leisurely vortices about the broken carcass like predators at a battlefield before finally twisting upwards and rising into the air to disappear into the grey, rainy sky.

And from somewhere came a noise which, though familiar, Farnor could not identify.

Farnor's mouth worked as he searched for words of denial that would dismiss this sight from his vision.

But none came.

Instead a silent cry of reproach rose up within him.

Move your legs. Get down there. Find out if your mother and father are safe. Find out what's happened.

It seemed to Farnor as he ran towards the smoking ruins that he was in fact motionless and that the house was approaching him, like some injured friend seeking help.

He clambered over the wall and ran round into the yard, calling out.

'Mother! Father!'

But there was no reply, except for the sound of the falling rain splashing on to the waterlogged ground and gurgling along gutters and down pipes into the collection butts. And too there was the noise that he had heard on top of the rise. Though much louder than the rain, it seemed to be coming from a great distance. It was the animals clamouring, panic-stricken, to escape their pens. He hesitated, looking from side to side indecisively, as if debating whether he should attend to these demented creatures or continue to search for his parents.

'Mother! Father!'

He called several times, but there was no response until a single fretful bark pierced the din.

One of the dogs was standing by the blackened,

smoke-streaked gap that had been the front door. It was sniffing at what appeared to be a pile of debris.

Farnor ran over to it.

The dog's tail was dragging along the ground, but it wagged guiltily as he approached, as if it were in some way responsible for the devastation of the farm.

As he reached the dog, the feeling of numbness spread to possess Farnor totally and for a long, timeless interval he stood staring at the shapeless mound that the dog had been sniffing. Then, slowly, he knew it for his father and mother.

As if he were looking at a picture in a book, Farnor noted his father's twisted frame. He was like a broken toy, not a person.

'Mother,' he said.

He knelt down beside her and shook her gently as if she might simply be sleeping out in the rain, not knowing that her house had burned down.

'Mother.'

He put his arm around her shoulder and lifted her into a sitting position.

'Your dress is all wet and crumpled,' he said, quietly, fingering the soiled fabric awkwardly. 'And you've dirtied it too. Look.'

Shaking his head in imitation of his mother's frequent gesture, he ran his hand over the circular stain just beneath the line of his mother's ribcage. Then he looked at his hand. It was covered in blood. He laid his mother down gently, and touched the bloodstained palm curiously with his other hand.

Slowly, he stood up and walked across the yard. Then, quite deliberately and very calmly, he opened the doors of the various stalls to release the distraught animals.

Some brushed him aside in their panic, but others remained where they were. The dog tried to round up some of the escapees dutifully, but after one or two

446

appealing looks at Farnor, who was standing watching them vaguely, it abandoned the attempt.

Farnor went to the gate. It was wide open. Patiently, he pulled it shut and secured it, then he leaned back against the gate post and slid down it until he was sitting on the ground.

The rain continued steadily, and gradually the fires died out and the heavy coils of smoke changed into pale grey wisps. Occasionally some too-charred timber would succumb to the depredations of the fire and the water and tumble apologetically into the rubble.

Farnor sat staring fixedly at the house for a long time without moving. A few pigs and hens wandered aimlessly about the yard, but most of those animals that had not fled had retreated to their opened pens in the face of the rain.

Once or twice his lips moved, but no sound came. The dull afternoon light began to fail. Then, for no apparent reason, he stood up, climbed over the gate as he had done almost every day of his life and walked into the darkening evening.

Gryss staggered as Farnor slumped into his arms.

'Marna!' he shouted, urgently.

She was by his side almost immediately. Taking in the scene at a glance, she pushed the door to with her foot and moved to help Gryss support the collapsing Farnor. They manhandled him along the hallway and into the back room, where he was dropped into a chair.

Gryss took Farnor's chin in his hand and lifted his face up, then he prised open his flickering eyelids and peered into his eyes.

'What's happened to him?' Marna asked, anxiously.

'It's shock, by the look of it,' Gryss said. 'Fetch me some water.'

447

When she returned, Farnor was recovering consciousness. He was talking desperately but incoherently, and he was struggling to rise from the chair while Gryss was trying unsuccessfully to restrain him.

Marna watched for a moment, then shouted angrily, 'Farnor, sit down and be still, will you?' Farnor started, but did as he was told. Gryss gave her a grateful nod.

Marna however did not notice. She was pointing, and her face was full of alarm. 'Look,' she whispered, as if afraid to attract Farnor's attention.

Gryss followed her gaze. It took him to Farnor's hands. He reached down and took hold of them. Farnor offered no resistance.

Gryss frowned. 'Blood,' he said, flatly.

Marna brought her hand to her mouth, and the alarm in her face became fear. She did not speak and for a few minutes the room was silent as Gryss busied himself with cleaning and examining Farnor while he was still compliant.

'It doesn't seem to be his, the blood,' he said eventually. 'He seems sound enough apart from his arm and being wet and cold.' The information did little to ease either his or Marna's anxiety, however. Inevitably, she voiced hers.

'Whose is it, then?' she demanded. 'And why's he in such a state?'

'How the devil do I know, Marna?' Gryss said irritably, then, with a flicker of self-reproach, he laid a hand on her arm in immediate apology.

He pulled forward a chair and sat down in front of Farnor. 'What's happened?' he asked gently.

Farnor's eyes livened a little at the sound of his voice. They drifted to Marna and then back to Gryss, and a pleasant, surprised, smile appeared on his face.

'What's happened, Farnor?' Gryss asked again, his tone anxious now.

He opened his mouth to speak and then realization spread across his face. He stood up with a terrible cry.

'It's all gone,' he said hoarsely. 'All gone! Black rafters and sodden ashes. All gone!' He slumped back into the chair, and looked about agitatedly. 'And the animals are all loose.'

Gryss's eyes widened. There must have been a fire at the farm. 'What's all gone, Farnor?' he asked, trying to keep the alarm from his voice. 'One of the barns? One of the sheds? Burned down?' Despite himself he took hold of Farnor's shoulders and shook him. 'Where are your parents, Farnor? Did they send you for help?'

Farnor screwed up his face in concentration. 'They're gone too,' he said eventually. 'Father's broken. Mother's asleep. She'll catch cold,' he said plaintively. 'She's soaking wet.' He stared at his hand. 'And her dress is all stained,' he muttered. 'She won't want to be seen in that state.'

Gryss had heard enough. Whatever had happened, it was serious, and little more was to be gleaned from Farnor. He turned to Marna. 'Fast as you can. Get to Yakob's, tell him to come straight away and to bring horses. Don't waste any time answering his questions, just get him here. We have to go to Garren's.'

'Shouldn't we raise the Cry if there's a fire?' Marna asked.

Gryss shook his head, and flicked his thumb at Farnor. 'I don't think so,' he said. 'This one's been out in the rain for a long time. Several hours, I'd judge. Go now,' he said, taking her arm and directing her to the door. 'Get Yakob, quickly.'

When she had gone, Gryss looked down at the now motionless Farnor. His every body sign showed deep and profound shock. What the devil had happened to bring the lad to this state?

Concern yourself with matters of the moment, he

reprimanded himself. Farnor had to be made dry and warm and given a sleeping draught before Marna returned if his chilled frame was to be protected from infection and further shock. The truth of what had brought him here would be found soon enough at Garren's.

Even as he busied himself about this task however, possibilities drifted through his mind. Happiest of these, though holding small comfort for all that, was the possibility that something had happened to Farnor that had made his mind succumb to the pressures he had been under of late. Perhaps when he and Yakob went to the Yarrance farm they would find nothing other than the brightly shining sunstone lighting the yard and Garren and Katrin anxiously waiting for the return of their son.

But he tried to give this no more credence than the other, more sinister and ill-formed notions that were plaguing him.

He had scarcely finished installing Farnor into his own bed when the cottage door opened and Yakob strode in with Marna, red-faced and out of breath, at his heels.

The two men looked at one another for a moment. Yakob seemed tired and worried, but he did not look like someone who had hastily dressed.

'Couldn't sleep, either, eh?' Gryss said.

Yakob nodded. 'Too many dark thoughts,' he replied. 'What's happened now?'

'You've brought the horses?' Gryss asked. Yakob made no attempt to press his question.

'We'll talk on the way, then,' Gryss concluded. He drew the sheets up tight against Farnor's chin, and dimmed the lantern by the bed.

'Marna, you keep an eye on him,' he said.

There was a momentary flicker of rebellion in Marna's eyes, but she allowed it no rein. Someone would have to stay with both Farnor and Jeorg lying here in enforced sleep.

The night was cold and damp as the two men rode towards Garren's farm. The rain had stopped and the sky was clearing. A bright moon began to emerge from behind hulking clouds, transforming them for a while into a towering, silver-edged mountain range.

The moonlight lit the road and enabled Gryss and Yakob to make as much speed as their age and unskilled horsemanship would allow. Gryss recounted Farnor's vague tale, but bluntly refused to answer any of Yakob's questions. 'We'll find out the truth soon enough,' was all he was prepared to say. Indeed, it was all he was prepared even to think at the moment.

He sniffed as they entered the lane that led up to the farm, then he grimaced.

'What's the matter?' Yakob asked.

'Smoke,' Gryss said.

The lane, shaded by trees, was quite dark and they were obliged to travel at a slow walk. As he peered ahead, however, Gryss thought he saw brightness in the distance. His heart rose. It was probably Garren's sunstone lighting up the yard in anticipation of Farnor returning home.

But as he reached the gate he realized it was merely the moonlight shining on the remains of the white front wall and contrasting with the darkness of the lane.

'No,' Yakob said in horror as they gazed at the gaping destruction that had once been the Yarrance farmhouse. 'No, no.'

Gryss closed his eyes tightly, as if they would not focus properly.

The smell of charred and sodden timber filled the air, and small tendrils of smoke floated out through the shattered frontage. The moonlight gave them the appearance of some ghastly plant.

Gryss, his stomach turned to lead and his head unnaturally clear, climbed down from his horse and fumbled with the gate latch.

The gate opened silently and easily as he pushed it, mute and poignant testimony to Garren Yarrance's thorough and conscientious life.

'This happened hours ago,' Yakob said softly, almost as if he were in a holy place. 'Why didn't Farnor come sooner?'

Gryss raised his hand. 'We must find out what's happened to Garren and Katrin,' he said, his voice unsteady.

Farnor's words came back to him: 'All gone . . . Father's broken . . . Mother's asleep . . . her dress is all stained . . .'

He started as something nudged his leg. He looked down. It was a pig. It eyed him beadily and then turned away.

'All the stalls are open,' Yakob said, still speaking softly.

'Yes.' The palms of Gryss's hands were sweating with fearful anticipation, and his mouth was dry. He beckoned to Yakob to dismount. 'Stay by me,' he said.

They walked towards the farmhouse. It was dead and haunted in the moonlight. The sight was at once so familiar and so alien that it disorientated Gryss horribly. He knew that, like Farnor, he too was now suffering from shock.

Yakob caught his arm and pointed, but Gryss had already seen the shadowy mound by the front door of the house. As they drew near, the shadow moved and an ominous growl reached them. Both men froze, then Gryss reached into his pocket and took out a small sunstone lantern. It flared into life, banishing the moonlight and turning the world into a small, night-bounded sphere.

The dog, crouching by the bodies of Garren and Katrin, blinked at the light then stood up, its hackles bristling and its upper lip drawn back to reveal its cruel teeth.

'No, no, no,' Yakob whispered to himself in disbelief, his gaze looking past the dog and at the bodies.

Gryss could hardly speak; his tongue felt dry and distended in his mouth. Part of him wanted to dash forward and lay into this stupid dog with feet and fists, but his quieter nature ached for it in its futile vigil over its erstwhile master and mistress.

Handing the lantern to Yakob, he crouched down and began to make soothing noises to the dog, calling its name and holding out his hand gently. Ironically, though the dog's diligence was keeping him from tending his friends, he was glad to have his mind occupied with a simple task. It dispelled the sense of unreality that had descended on him, just as the lantern had dispelled the ghostly moonlight.

It took him a little time, but the dog eventually stopped its growling and moved cautiously towards him, dropping on to its belly as it reached him. He put out his hand and stroked it. 'Good boy,' he said. 'We'll see to them now. Your job's finished.'

Then, keeping his hand comfortingly on the dog's shoulder, he moved over to the two bodies. Yakob followed him.

'Are they . . . ?' he asked needlessly, finishing the question with a trembling gesture.

'Yes,' Gryss said. 'And some time ago, I'd say.' He looked up at Yakob. 'Farnor was deeply shocked when he came to me. I think he'd been wandering round lost for hours.'

Yakob crouched down by him. 'What in pity's name

has happened here?' he said, his voice lower than ever. 'Why are . . . they . . . here? Outside the house? Why are they dead? What . . . ?'

'Hold the lantern still while I look,' Gryss said.

He began to examine the two bodies.

One of the grimmer thoughts that had occurred to him as he had tended Farnor was that indeed the lad's mind had failed under the pressure of recent happenings and that he had committed some terrible atrocity. His whole being rebelled against the idea, but it had its own dark logic and could not lightly be set aside.

His mind was not eased by the rent he found in Katrin's dress and by the broad wound under the arch of her ribs. As he examined the wound, his eye caught sight of the stout kitchen knife embedded in the door frame.

Almost reluctantly, he moved to Garren. Gently he kneaded the crooked limbs, then he placed his hand around Garren's head to raise it.

The softness there made him draw a sharp breath and he had to force himself to examine it further.

'What's the matter?' Yakob said.

Gryss shook his head in an appeal for further patience, and continued his sorry work.

When he stood up his face was puzzled, though there was also a hint of relief in it. Whatever had happened here, Farnor could not have done it. Yakob looked at him expectantly.

'Katrin was stabbed,' Gryss said bluntly. 'Probably with that thing there.' He gestured to the knife. 'As for Garren, he's a mass of broken bones. I've not seen anything like it since we found Menion.'

Yakob grimaced. That incident had been many years ago. Menion had been a young man, who, finding that a long-held and until then secret love was not returned, wandered off into the mountains. Yakob and Gryss had been members of the party that was sent out to search for him two days later. They found him twisted and broken at the foot of a towering cliff. Whether he came there by accident or by intent none could ever determine, but for those on the party the sight of his shattered body remained with them always.

'I don't understand,' Yakob said, his voice unsteady. 'Menion took a terrible fall. How could that have happened to Garren?'

'I've no idea,' Gryss said unhappily. 'If anything, he's in a worse state than Menion . . .'

But Yakob was not listening. He was swaying and rubbing his face with his hands. Quickly, Gryss took his arm and led him away from the two bodies. They had scarcely gone three paces when Yakob doubled over and vomited. Then his knees went and, unable to support his collapsing weight, Gryss eased him down to the ground until he was on all fours.

Yakob lowered his head and his back started to shake with silent sobs.

Gryss extinguished the lantern and turned away from him. There was nothing he could do for the moment except wait.

Eventually Yakob got to his feet. 'I'm so sorry,' he said, shamefacedly, as he took the offered hand for support. 'Such a display. It's the smell of the smoke, and—'

'It's stark, unbelievable horror, and it's too much happening too fast,' Gryss said. 'I can hardly bring myself to think that this is all real and not some frightful dream I'm having.' He looked at his friend, struggling to regain his usual dignified composure. 'There's a butt full of fresh water over there,' he said. 'Give your face a wash. It won't make any of this go away, but it'll make you feel better.' Then, without waiting for Yakob, he walked over to the butt and took his own advice.

'What are we going to do?' Yakob said, after he too had finished a rudimentary ablution.

The question threw Gryss into confusion as a rush of thoughts burst in upon him. What to do about what? About Farnor? Jeorg? About what had happened here? About Nilsson? About telling the villagers? About gathering in these wandering animals and tending Garren's – Farnor's now, he supposed – crops?

'We must put Garren and Katrin somewhere safe,' he said, snatching at the nearest thought to still this rambling. He gazed around the yard. 'We'll have to put them in one of the stalls here. Cover them up, lock the door. We can't do anything else until it's daylight.'

It was an unpleasant task. Katrin was heart-breakingly light and frail and neither man could look at her as they carried her. Garren was much heavier and distressingly bent in the strangest ways due to his massive internal injuries. It lent their struggle with him an element of grotesque farce. Throughout, however, Katrin's words, 'stabbing and killing', kept ringing through Gryss's head to the rhythm of his shuffling feet.

They left the bodies resting on boards carried on trestles and covered with a rough cloth. Gryss pulled the two halves of the stall door shut and bolted them both, then he plunged his hands into the water butt again and rubbed them together desperately. Moonlight glittered brilliantly on the dancing droplets.

The two men did not speak as they walked back to their horses. Yakob mounted his, but before he too mounted Gryss turned and looked fretfully about the moonlit yard.

'What happened here?' he said, half to himself. 'There are gaps in the walls as if something's crashed through them, and everything's scattered all over the place.' He looked up. 'And there are slates missing from some of the roofs. Garren was meticulous about such things. It's almost as if there'd been a great storm here.'

As he spoke the memory of the wind that had arisen in the castle courtyard returned to him, and with it Jeorg's words, 'Rannick's leading them' and his account of how Rannick had tortured him.

A coldness descended on him, stifling his whirling thoughts with an icy grip.

'What's the matter?' Yakob asked, sensing the change in him.

'We're in the hands of a madman,' Gryss said.

'Nilsson?'

'No. Rannick,' Gryss replied.

'Rannick!' Yakob exclaimed. 'What's he got to do with anything? He's probably gone over the hill weeks ago, and good riddance.' Then he looked at Gryss, concerned, fearing, as Gryss had feared for Farnor, that this sudden shock had unhinged him. 'You mean Nilsson, don't you?' he said. 'This could only have been done by him and his men.' His voice shook. 'They must've beaten poor Garren like they beat Jeorg, only this time it went too far and—'

Gryss had been shaking his head throughout. 'Garren wasn't beaten. No beating could do that kind of damage without it showing more. I think this is Rannick's handiwork. I'm beginning to recognize it. He's leading those men now.'

Yakob leaned forward to reiterate his protest at this foolishness, but Gryss turned to him and said, 'Jeorg told me about him, Yakob. It was what he whispered to me before you left. I didn't tell you because I didn't know what to make of it. I wanted to think. Then, later, he was so agitated that he woke up despite my sleeping draught and spoke about him again.'

'You mean it, don't you?' Yakob said, his manner uneasy. 'Are you sure he wasn't delirious?'

Gryss nodded. 'There are other things that've been happening of late that I haven't told you about, Yakob, nor anyone else except Farnor and Marna—'

'Marna! You've been talking about village matters with a slip of a girl and keeping them from the Council?' Yakob was outraged.

'Marna's no more a slip of a girl now than you are,' Gryss said with a quiet resolution that was more compelling that any amount of noisy indignation. 'She's an intelligent and capable young woman, just as Farnor is an intelligent and capable young man. And what's happening in this valley is going to have a greater effect on them than it will on you and me. They're the ones who'll have to do something about matters, and they're the ones who'll have to live with the consequences, good or bad. All we old sparks are going to be able to do is talk.'

Taken aback by this forthrightness, Yakob was composing himself for a further reproach when Gryss swung up into his saddle with unexpected vigour. 'Come on, Yakob,' he said. 'We've had our kin murdered. Whatever doubts and hesitations I've had about all this will have to be resolved tonight, along with such questions as you want to ask.'

Outfaced by this sudden purposefulness, Yakob began to withdraw into his normal cautious dignity. 'Where are we going now, then?' he asked.

'To my cottage,' Gryss replied. 'Then Marna can fetch her father. And for the rest of this night we talk and we cling to one another and we try to look into the darkness that's come amongst us.'

Chapter 31

Footsteps clattered along the stone corridors of the castle, some running, some walking, some firm and determined, others hesitant and fearful. They beat a random, shifting tattoo which threaded its way through the other sounds that filled the castle that night – the sounds that marked a disorder that was teetering perilously near to outright panic. Orders were shouted and disputed, voices were raised in angry quarrels and, too, in laughter, though it was brittle and hard-edged; voices cried out in pain and distress, some pleading, some agonized. Doors creaked and slammed, furniture was overturned, horses whinnied and screamed and pounded their stable walls with violent hooves.

Nilsson sat motionless at the heart of this din, hearing it all, but scarcely heeding. The task of gathering together and calming the men he had curtly delegated to Saddre and Dessane as he had swept the collapsing Rannick on to his horse and dashed with him at full gallop back to the castle.

It had been no easy task for his two lieutenants, not least because they themselves had been badly shaken by the events at the Yarrance farm: not the slaying of Garren and Katrin, which meant little to them, but the unnerving and explosive destruction of the house.

'Do it!' he had thundered at them, bringing to bear the full power of his dark personality in an attempt to replace the terror of the immediate past with terror of the immediate present. 'Do it. Round them up. Crack whatever heads need cracking, but do it or we lose everything. I'll tend to the Lord.'

He had crushed ruthlessly any signs he felt rising to the surface of his own inner quaking at what had happened. He had seen worse, albeit many years ago, and his constant solace when standing near the heart of such events remained with him: it was happening to someone else!

But now this eerie yokel had spent himself in some way. Nilsson cursed to himself inwardly as he stared fixedly at Rannick, lying silent on the bed. His only consolation lay in the steady up and down movement of Rannick's chest. Whatever else he had done, he hadn't killed himself.

Which was good and bad fortune, he found himself thinking. Still a part of him urged him to take his knife and end this monster now, before his overweening ambition took him too high too fast, and invoked some other mysterious power in opposition that might bring them all down like proud oaks blasted by lightning. One stroke could end him now, and he and his men could flee to the north as had been his original intention.

But the greater part of him was well fortified against such urgings. What if this 'illness' were merely feigned as part of a testing on Rannick's part? Or if his flesh were in some way protected and would turn the point of any lunging blade? Both such things he had known. And, too, what of the creature that Rannick seemed to control? Would it flee, howling and lost, back to whatever pit it had emerged from at the death of its master, or would it come crashing amongst them lusting for bloody vengeance?

Nilsson had many and strong defences ever ready to protect him from his wiser self.

He watched Rannick's steady breathing and sought other consolations like a nervous parent. Perhaps in fact Rannick was only in a deep sleep. All of them had been tired after the last few days' activity: the long, hard riding, the rough sleeping, the raid on the village in the adjacent valley, then the business with that oaf of a villager and finally all this.

His hopes waxed and waned. This was no ordinary sleep. He had shaken him as roughly as he dared, and he had called his name. But there had been no response. Hesitantly, he had lifted the eyelids, but that had told him nothing. Nothing except that though his body seemed to be asleep, Rannick's eyes were terrifyingly alert in their fixed gaze.

Out of habit, Nilsson composed his face into an expression of anxious concern to avoid the possibility of his true feelings being visible.

Loud voices in the passage outside roused him from his reverie. Angrily he stood up and went to the door. The source of the noise were two men remonstrating with Dessane. One of them was Bryn, the man who had had such a narrow escape from the creature when he had ridden with Haral's ill-fated group. The other was Avak. That meant trouble.

'We're off,' Avak was saying as Nilsson emerged from Rannick's room. 'This . . . lord's a lunatic. It'll go the same way it went before. Next thing you know there'll be a sodding great army marching along the valley looking for us.' His manner became contemptuous. 'And our precious lord, by the way, won't be able to do anything about them, but he'll save his own neck. Gallop off somewhere, just like—'

'Enough!' Nilsson kept his voice low, as if, paradoxically, he wished to avoid disturbing Rannick, but its power stopped Avak in full flow.

'Nobody's leaving,' Nilsson went on, still quietly. 'We stick together. We make our decisions in congress. That's the way we've survived this far, and that's the way we're going to continue. If you or anyone else wants to leave, then the congress will decide.'

461

His tone was full of a calmness that should have warned the two men, but they were too preoccupied with their own fears to notice.

'To hell with that . . .' Avak began, but his protest was cut short as Nilsson's fist swung up and struck him squarely on the jaw. So swift, direct and unannounced was the blow that Avak had an incongruously surprised expression on his face as he fell to the floor.

Bryn swore, and moved around the fallen body as if to confront Nilsson.

This time it was Nilsson who was surprised. Avak he could always expect problems from – he was too clever by half. But not Bryn. And, normally, the administration of a little summary justice on the leader of any disturbance had a salutary effect on his followers. That this did not appear to be the case here he noted as being potentially very serious.

This consideration, however, did not hinder him as he moved to deal with the continuing opposition. He raised his clenched fist as if to strike Bryn in the face. Automatically, Bryn raised his hands to protect himself, at which point Nilsson's foot shot out and delivered a jarring kick to his shin. Bryn doubled up immediately with a loud cry of pain. As he did so, Nilsson's raised hand came down and seized him by the scruff of the neck. Then, twisting to one side, Nilsson drove Bryn's head into the wall.

'I'm sorry, Nils,' Dessane said, hastily, as Bryn slithered to join Avak on the floor. 'I tried to stop them coming here, but you know Avak. I don't know what . . .'

Nilsson ignored his excuses. 'How many more?' he demanded.

'Not many,' Dessane managed, after a little hesitation. 'And most of them will listen to reason.'

Nilsson held up his hand for silence and inclined his

462

head to catch the sounds drifting along the passage. He frowned, then cast an anxious glance at the door of Rannick's room.

'They're just shouting the odds, Nils, that's all. Getting it out of their systems,' Dessane said. His voice fell. 'That panic in the yard frightened the hell out of me, I'll admit.'

Torn between his vigil by his stricken lord and the need to be amongst his men, keeping this incipient rebellion under control, Nilsson bared his teeth like a trapped animal preparing for a final charge. Dessane discreetly took a short pace backwards ready to flee.

'Frightened,' Nilsson muttered with a snarl. 'I'll frighten them. Too long without proper action, that's the trouble. They've all ridden in battle and most of them have seen the power used worse than that, haven't they?' He kicked the fallen Avak. It eased his mood. 'Get these two old women out of here, Arven. And remind the rest of them who the Lord's anger was directed at. The time to be frightened is when it's directed at *them*. And if any more of them are thinking about leaving, remind them of our rules and the punishment for disobeying them. We stay together until we have a congress that says otherwise.'

Before Dessane could reply, a figure came running along the passage. Nilsson turned, ready for further confrontation. It was Haral and, uncharacteristically, he seemed worried and uncertain.

'Captain,' he said urgently. 'Come quickly. There's something you need to see.'

Nilsson looked at him narrowly, mindful of the two men lying at his feet and half concerned that this appeal might be to lead him into a trap. Then he dismissed the idea. Whatever else he was, Haral was no conspirator. Indeed, he was direct to the point of folly.

'What's the matter?' he asked.

'I think you'd better come and see for yourself, Captain,' Haral said. 'It's . . .' His voice faded away and he gave an awkward shrug.

Nilsson frowned irritably. 'Stay here and guard the Lord's door,' he said to Dessane. 'No one is allowed inside, and if the Lord wants me, I'll be . . .' He looked at Haral enquiringly.

'On the wall by the main gate, Captain,' Haral said.

Despite his basic trust in Haral, Nilsson kept his hands loose and near to his knives as he followed him through the castle. In fact the brief walk reassured him. Such of the men as they passed acknowledged him openly enough, and while he could feel the tension in the air he inclined to Dessane's judgement that it was mainly due to the men shaking off the fear they had experienced at Garren's farm.

Even so, it had been a long time since he had felt anything quite so disturbing and he knew that, independent of Rannick's condition, all under his command was not yet as it should be and he must watch his back more than usual. It came to him as he walked along beside Haral that Rannick's conspicuous use of the power had sent a profound shock deep into the souls of all who had been there, and that many strange impulses could be expected from the resultant resonances. Mud had been stirred that had perhaps been better left undisturbed. He resolved to watch for these consequences, not least perhaps within himself, and to harness them to his own ends where appropriate.

Haral led him across the courtyard. Here it was the sound of the stabled horses that predominated, still badly unsettled by the day's events, though there were small groups of men standing around here and there talking agitatedly in the flickering torchlight.

As they ran up the steps to the top of the wall by

464

the main gate, an anxious looking sentry came down to meet them.

'Is it—?' Haral asked softly.

The sentry nodded, his eyes wide.

'What the . . . ?' Nilsson began, but Haral raised a finger to his lips for silence and motioned him to the parapet. Nilsson moved forward and rested a hand on the wall. Carefully, Haral leaned over and peered into the darkness.

'What is it?'

Nilsson found that he was whispering, still affected by Haral's command to silence.

He was about to repeat the question more loudly when the presence struck him. Instinctively he stepped away from the parapet.

It was the creature. There was no mistaking it. He had not realized how deep and awful an impression it had made on him when he had sensed it at his first meeting with Rannick, but it was quite unmistakable.

'There!' Though Haral's voice hissed quietly through the darkness, it raked jaggedly across Nilsson's suddenly heightened sensibilities. With an effort he forced himself to the parapet again and leaned over, following the direction of Haral's pointing hand.

The rain had stopped and the sky was clearing, but clouds still hid the moon and little could be seen of the ground below. Nevertheless, as his eyes adjusted to the darkness, Nilsson caught the vague impression of a movement.

'I've no idea how long it's been there,' the sentry volunteered. 'I felt something . . . queer, then I thought I heard something . . . sniffing, like . . . then I saw it. Pacing up and down, up and down.' He shivered.

Nilsson raised his hand for silence. Slowly he breathed in deeply in an attempt to quieten his inner turmoil. Fear was the last thing he needed to be showing with his men

465

in the state they were, but this damned thing seemed to be reaching inside him. He felt the knowledge that prey knows when a predator has its scent and when the only escape lies in heart-stopping flight.

He forced his mind to give him reassurance. He was safe where he was, high on the battlements. It was only an animal, after all. Murral alone knew what kind of an animal, but an animal nonetheless.

'It's that thing out of the forest, isn't it, Captain?' the sentry said, his voice trembling. Nilsson looked at him sharply. He was one of the survivors of Yeorson and Storran's patrol. 'I can feel it,' he went on, his fear mounting. 'Like it's come after me.'

The man's fear dispelled some of Nilsson's. He took the man's arm. 'It's just an animal,' he said, forcing his own reassurances into his words. 'It can't get in, can it? And if it did, it's not on its hunting ground here. There's spears and arrows enough to kill a score such creatures, and open space in which to use them.'

The sentry fingered his bow nervously. 'Should I take a shot at it, Captain?' he said.

Nilsson leaned over the wall again and searched for the dim, pacing shadow.

It had gone.

Then he was aware of it streaking towards the wall. He tried to jerk away, but some force held him motionless. The shadow leapt and Nilsson felt a scream forming inside him, but still he could not move. Only when he heard the scrabbling of claws against the stone wall and the heavy thud of the creature landing was he able to step back from the edge. His legs were shaking almost uncontrollably, and he was grateful for the darkness which he knew was hiding a face that was white with terror.

He was safe on top of this high battlement, he told himself again. The creature's leap had been prodigious but it had fallen well short of the top of the wall. Even so, he found little comfort in the knowledge. It seemed that nothing could truly protect him from the malevolent intent and the demented, frustrated rage that had washed over him as the creature had reached the peak of its leap. And the paralysis that had seized him as it had tried to close with him chilled him utterly.

Yes, yes, kill the damn thing, his mind screamed. Get the men up here, shoot every arrow we have into it. But no such order reached his mouth. Instead he merely shook his head. 'No,' he said to the sentry. 'Leave it alone. Dealing with the likes of that is the Lord's province, not ours.'

The sentry stopped fidgeting with his bow with undisguised relief.

Abandoning the battlements, Nilsson made his way back to Rannick's room. He arrived as Dessane was helping Avak and Bryn to their feet. Neither seemed disposed to continue his earlier complaints, but Nilsson still sensed some defiance in their manner. With the creature's blood-lusting intention reverberating through him, he had to fight down an almost overwhelming urge to draw his knife and slay these two where they stood.

In the wake of this urge, however, a subtler device came to mind.

'If you want to leave, leave,' he said, his tone unexpectedly bland and expressionless. 'But you go now, this minute, or you stay and reaffirm your allegiance to our new lord and never seek to leave again except at his express wish. Is that understood?'

The two men looked at one another and then at him, searching for the treachery that they knew must surely lie in his words.

'Now or never,' Nilsson repeated, flatly.

Bryn reached his decision. 'I'll stay, Captain,' he said.

467

'I wasn't thinking straight before. It was just the heat of the moment. I've always been with you and I'm with you now. And if you follow the Lord Rannick, then I do too.'

Avak glowered at him. 'You're a fool, Bryn,' he said, wincing and rubbing his jaw where Nilsson had struck him. 'Take this chance while you've got it. That Rannick's not the man the Lord was by any measure. There's nothing but death here for anyone who follows him.'

'There's nothing but death waiting for us anyway,' Bryn replied. 'At least with Lord Rannick we'll maybe get a chance to die in comfort. I shouldn't have listened to you.'

Nilsson ended any further debate. 'Dessane, take this man to the gate and throw him out,' he said curtly.

Dessane gave him a brief puzzled look. Such a thing had never happened before. Men left the group only one way: dead. He did not linger, however, but motioned Avak forward.

'No supplies, Captain? No chance to talk to my mates?' Avak sneered.

'You've got no mates here now, Avak, and you'll find everything you need outside,' Nilsson said. 'Get out of my sight before I change my mind.'

Avak sneered again and then strode off. Dessane made to follow him, but Nilsson caught his arm and whispered very softly to him: 'Don't linger at the gate. Close it immediately. *Immediately!*'

As the two men left, Bryn remained where he was, his posture unsteady and his hand moving to his head from time to time.

'Not changing your mind again, are you, Bryn?' Nilsson said, grimly. 'Go now, if you are.'

Bryn shook his head carefully. 'No, Captain,' he replied. 'I'm just a little dizzy. I . . .'

He fell silent.

'You what?' Nilsson pressed.

Bryn's face wrinkled. 'It's odd. I feel as if that creature were around somewhere,' he said. 'It's almost as if it were inside me.'

Nilsson waited.

'Funny thing is,' Bryn continued, with an awkward, nervous laugh, 'while I want to run like I ran in that forest, something makes me want to stand still. It's . . .' He shrugged, at a loss for words.

'Go to your quarters and rest,' Nilsson said. 'You're too addled to think straight.'

As he entered Rannick's room, Bryn's remarks hovered in Nilsson's mind. What was this creature that hunted with the murderous determination of a human and seemingly paralysed its prey with fear?

He had no answers, but the arrival of the creature had answered his earlier question. It had not wandered off howling into the darkness, it had been drawn mysteriously to its ailing master. What then would its reaction have been had Nilsson followed the prompting to slay Rannick?

He shuddered. He could not understand how he had stood there unable to move as the creature had leapt at him. Irritably, and with some difficulty, he thrust the concern to one side. A far more serious one lay in the condition of his lord. What could be done to awaken him?

It occurred to him that he might have to send for Gryss, though who knew what reception his messenger might receive in the village when news of the slaughter of Garren and Katrin became known? True, he could ensure Gryss's assistance by taking hostages from among the villagers, but there was no saying what treacherous tricks the old leech might have up his sleeve.

He sat down and gazed at the apparently sleeping form.

Damn you, Lord, he thought. Damn you to hell. You shouldn't have done it. You should've listened to me. Now we've got fifty times the problems we had before.

He let his anger roam freely for a moment, though no sign of it appeared on his face, then he reached out and shook Rannick's arm gently.

'Lord,' he whispered. 'Lord.'

There was no response. Gryss it would have to be, then, though that posed the further problem of how he was to be reached now, with the creature patrolling the castle walls. He let out a weary breath and sagged back into his chair. Perhaps it would have gone by daylight.

He squeezed his eyes with his fingers. As he had accused Bryn, so he accused himself: he was too tired and addled to think straight. He needed to sleep. But how could he with Rannick, his future, lying thus?

Despite himself however, he closed his eyes. In the flickering darkness he found his mind watching the sinuous shadow gliding silently around the castle. He could feel the edge of the creature's bubbling hatred.

He could not open his eyes!

Then on the fringes of his consciousness he felt the slight vibration of the wicket door being hastily slammed shut.

Silence.

And was that a drumming of fists he could hear?

Then a faint, shrill scream cut through his half dream. Suddenly released, he found himself bolt upright and wide awake.

Part of his mind was calculating. One man the less. That was a pity, but Avak had been marked for a long time and it would prove to be a salutary lesson for the rest of the men. Self-satisfaction oozed into his thoughts. He did not imagine there would be many more opportunities when he would be able to use Rannick's creature for his own ends.

But the other part of his mind was listening. Listening to a voice. It spoke one word, very softly, drawing it out and tonguing it with a diabolical relish.

'*Good*,' Rannick said, turning towards him.

Chapter 32

Gryss started awake. About him was the touch of a dark and awful dream, but it vanished on the instant as he became aware of sunlight filling the room. For a moment he was a young child again and the day opened before him, full of warmth and summer scents, soft breezes and everlasting freedom.

He was about to cry out, joyously to his parents when he remembered who he was.

And where.

And when.

Briefly his face creased as if he were about to cry. Then it relaxed into a look of half amused resignation.

He had spent what was left of the night in a chair, and his body was protesting the fact loudly. Carefully, he began to ease his limbs into life and, as he did so, one by one, the events of the previous night reformed themselves in his mind.

He looked across at the bed. Jeorg had scarcely moved.

Time, he thought. Time was what was needed. Time for Jeorg's injuries to heal. Time for Farnor's bewildered mind to calm. Time for himself and the others to reconcile themselves to the cruel deaths of Katrin and Garren.

And time was what they would have, though it was little consolation as it would have to be lived through, second by painful second. He clenched his hands in a combination of self-reproach and anger. The pain of the passing of his time would be as nothing compared with that of Jeorg's and Farnor's and he at least could ease his own pain by seeking to ease theirs.

A noise brought him to the present and dispelled his thoughts. With a final effort he levered himself out of the creaking chair and limped heavily to the door, banging his reluctant leg irritably with his fist.

'Did I disturb you?' Marna said, as he scowled into the kitchen. 'I was making some breakfast for us all.' She stared disconsolately at the pan sizzling merrily in front of her. 'But I don't think I can eat it now. I'm sorry. I took the meat from—'

Gryss waved the apology aside. He looked at her. Her face was drawn and she seemed tired and defeated. She had shed no tears in his presence last night, but her eyes were red with weeping. He turned his face away to hide his distress, then he put his arm around her shoulders and squeezed her comfortingly.

'Thanks,' he said. 'Serve it up, and have some yourself. It'll make you feel better.'

A spasm passed over her face. 'I don't think I want to feel better,' she said. 'It wouldn't seem right, somehow, carrying on with all the ordinary things, when . . .' She could not finish the sentence.

'When Garren and Katrin are lying dead in one of their animal stalls?' he said, finishing it for her starkly but not unkindly.

She nodded and tears filled her eyes.

'It's not something we've any choice in, Marna,' he said. 'You don't need me to tell you that. Weep for Garren and Katrin as much as you want. Rant and rage if that's the way it takes you. And it'll take you many ways, believe me. But in the end, you honour them and everything they were by the way you live your life.'

'Words,' Marna said.

'They're all we've got at the moment, and they're better than nothing. They help to make the time pass, and occasionally they say something that helps someone.'

He looked at her squarely. 'There's no harder thing in life than standing by helpless, and you're never more helpless, more inadequate, more useless, than when someone's died.'

She returned his gaze, then looked down at the pan again, her mouth pouting. 'Do you want some of this?' she asked, dully, turning back to him.

'Not if you're going to burn it like that,' he said, indicating the now smoking pan.

Marna swore, and there was a flurry of activity as meat and eggs were rescued and transferred to Gryss's fine wooden plates and during which Marna burnt the tip of her finger.

Gryss retrieved a loaf from a cupboard and scooped up some cutlery. 'Bring the plates through into the back room,' he said as he left the kitchen. Marna took her finger from her mouth and followed him.

'Eat,' he ordered, as she placed the plates on the long table. Uneasily, Marna did as she was told. It was no celebratory feast, however, and for some time they sat silent, and ate dutifully, rapt in their own thoughts.

Then Gryss recollected himself. 'Where's your father and Yakob?' he asked, guiltily.

'Still asleep. Both of them,' Marna replied. She gave a reluctant smile. 'Like battered bookends, either side of Farnor's bed.'

'My bed, if you please,' Gryss observed, angling like a patient fisherman to keep the smile.

But it slipped away. 'Should I waken them?' she asked.

Gryss shook his head. 'Let them sleep while they can,' he replied. Then he clicked his tongue and frowned. 'I'm not doing too well this morning. I should have looked at Farnor before tending my own needs.'

'He's all right,' Marna said, reassuringly. 'He's fast asleep.'

Gryss looked at her uncertainly. 'I'll have a look anyway,' he decided.

He had to agree with Marna's description as he entered his bedroom. Harlen and Yakob were draped gracelessly in chairs on either side of Farnor's bed. Harlen's head was slumped forward while Yakob's was angled backwards and to one side, and his mouth was hanging open. Farnor, on the contrary, was a picture of repose.

The sight was at once funny and poignant.

Moving delicately past the two sleeping guardians Gryss sat on the edge of the bed and laid his hand on Farnor's forehead. It was cool.

That was a relief. The lad had problems enough without going down with a fever as a result of the soaking and the shock he had had the previous night.

Farnor stirred, but did not wake.

Harlen, however, did. After mumbling a few incoherent words he opened his eyes and blinked vacantly. Then recognition came into his face and he made to move.

'Easy,' Gryss said. 'Your chairs might be comfortable to sit in, but not for sleeping in.'

The soft conversation woke Yakob, who spluttered indignantly for a moment before he too felt the protest of his limbs at having been confined in a chair for so long.

Marna raised a single eyebrow when the three of them entered the back room, bleary-eyed, ill-shaven and unkempt. 'Let them sleep,' she echoed at Gryss. He gave a disclaiming shrug.

At Gryss's urging, the two men made an attempt at the food that Marna had prepared, but it too was little more than an exercise in satisfying bodily needs, and a dark silence soon descended on the room.

Both Harlen and Yakob, like Farnor, were in a state of shock, though Harlen was perhaps the more affected of the two. The previous night he had gone to his home and bed burdened with the knowledge that one of his friends had been brutally beaten for no apparent reason, and that a menace had come silently to the valley, like a tainted autumn mist. Whatever dreams had arisen in the wake of this, though, were as nothing compared to the nightmare to which his daughter had wakened him: a hurried dash through the village to be greeted by Gryss and Yakob with a tale that made Jeorg's beating seem almost trivial. A tale of cruel murder and wanton destruction. The sense of menace had increased tenfold.

And it had become worse as Gryss told of Jeorg's whispered account, concluding with his final torture by Rannick.

The notion that Rannick could be leading such men and possess such powers invoked the same response from Harlen as it had from Yakob. He had looked to Yakob for support, but all Yakob was prepared to offer was an uncertain shrug and a wary, '*He* believes it,' with a nod towards Gryss.

'You know the tales about Rannick's family line, going way back,' Gryss had countered, heatedly. 'It's not just a saga of foul and unpleasant temperaments, is it? There are stories of strange gifts as well. Strange enough for them to be mentioned only in whispers if they're mentioned at all. And you should know this: of our old friends lying murdered up the road, one was smashed as badly as if he'd been hurled down a cliff. No ordinary beating did that.' Tiredness and grief had conspired to make him almost angry with his two friends. 'Do you think I'd be telling you such wild tales at a time like this if I didn't have good reason for thinking they were true? Both of you are old enough to know that there're plenty of things in this world that we haven't the remotest understanding of. Just hear me out.'

Rather abashed following this untypical outburst, Harlen and Yakob had fallen silent and Gryss had given the true account of his visit to the castle and the injury to Farnor's arm. He told, too, of the creature that Rannick apparently controlled, though this he attributed to information given to him by Nilsson's injured men. Some instinct told him not to speak of Farnor's own mysterious contact with the creature. Rannick's powers and Farnor's gift were beyond any logic that he knew of, and opposition to them would thus be visceral rather than reasoned. Who, then, could say where it would stop if once it started? And Farnor had no one to defend him now.

In the end, seeing that Gryss was not noticeably deranged, and in the knowledge that Farnor and Jeorg could be questioned in due course, the two men had reluctantly accepted his tale.

'Though what it all means and what we can do about it I've no idea,' Yakob had concluded in despair.

Gryss, however, had forbidden any debate. 'I can't tell you any more than I have,' he said. 'You have the truth as I know it, grim though it is. Sleep on it as well as you can. We're all too tired and upset to think clearly about anything. And tomorrow we're going to have a lot to do.'

Now tomorrow was on them, and, despite the sunshine streaming in through the window, no light seemed to reach into the hearts of the three men.

Their silence was too much for Marna. 'We can't sit around doing nothing,' she burst out, abruptly, her voice shaking. 'We must do something.'

Yakob cast an awkward glance at Harlen and then, acidly, he said, 'What, you stupid girl? Charge up to the castle on horseback and drag Rannick out to give an account of himself before the council?'

Marna pushed her plate away angrily, contemplated a retort, then swung around to stare out of the window. Her jawline stiffened as she fought back tears. Gryss gave Yakob a reproachful look, but Yakob merely scowled unrepentantly.

Nevertheless, the brief outburst had shattered the leaden torpor that had pervaded the room.

Harlen laid his hands flat on the table as if to push himself up from his seat. 'This is all too much for me,' he said. 'But I do know we must deal with the needs of the moment. We can talk later.' He let out a long breath. He addressed Gryss. 'Yakob and I will go to . . . Garren's and make some arrangement for bringing . . . the bodies . . . back. You and Marna can stay here and look after Farnor and Jeorg.' He stood up. 'Some air, some activity will do none of us any harm.' His easy-going face hardened. 'And, Yakob, I'll thank you not to talk to my daughter like that again, unless she gives you just cause. We're none of us over-endowed with wisdom in the face of all this.'

Yakob coloured and his mouth opened, but he did not reply.

When the two men had gone, Gryss and Marna set about tending to their charges.

'What are we going to do?' Marna asked, as she helped Gryss change some of Jeorg's bandages.

'I don't know,' Gryss replied. 'I don't think I've truly taken everything in yet. I can't even believe that Garren and Katrin are dead.' His voice faltered. 'I don't seem to be able to think properly.'

'I cried a lot last night,' Marna said, flatly, making no attempt to hide her own gnawing distress.

'Maybe I should've done the same,' Gryss said,

pausing reflectively for a moment. 'I probably will eventually.'

Marna moved close to him. 'We'll have to send for help,' she said. 'We can't just do nothing. What's happened is awful. The King should be told, the army should be sent to put things to rights. The proper army.'

Gryss looked concerned. 'One thing at a time, Marna,' he said. 'We need to talk, to clear our thoughts further before we decide about anything. Everything's different now.' He felt a sudden need to explain. 'When I agreed to help Jeorg try to reach the capital, I thought I'd be able to talk him out of any trouble if he got caught, or the worst that could happen was that he might be locked up for a while. Or made to pay a fine of some kind. I didn't think they'd do anything like this, or—'

Unable to continue for a moment, he fiddled nervously with the bandages.

'We can't risk that happening again,' he went on at last. 'They'll kill anyone else they find trying to leave, I'm sure.'

'If they catch them,' Marna said.

'They caught Jeorg easily enough,' Gryss said, missing the tone of her voice.

'He was following behind the entire troop,' Marna pointed out. 'Now they're all back at the castle. They've probably not even left any guards downland. Someone could be through and away before they even realized what was happening.'

This time Gryss did catch the tone. He looked at her. 'And suppose they're not all at the castle. Suppose they have left guards downland. What then, miss?'

'I could move around them,' Marna exclaimed, waving her arms. 'I know everywhere round there. All the streams, the trees, the secret ways . . .'

'Marna, for mercy's sake, stop it!' Gryss burst out.

480

'This isn't some schoolyard game. We've had this conversation before and I told you then the journey to the capital is long and difficult. Almost impossible on foot unless you really know how to live off the land.' Marna made to speak again, but he held up a hand to stop her. His voice became quiet. 'As far as I can see, they'd have beaten Jeorg to death if Rannick hadn't stopped them to play his own game. They'd do far worse to you. Far worse, Marna. Do you understand?' He sighed. 'I don't want to hear any more talk like this. We need to stick together, to rely on one another. You're near enough an adult now, but you've a lot to learn. At times like this, just watch and listen.'

'There's never been a time like this before,' Marna retorted, retreating but defiant. 'And when you've all debated and discussed it'll come to the same in the end. Someone will have to go for help. If Rannick's got anything to do with those men, they'll get worse and worse if no one opposes them. And there's no one here who can stand against men like that.'

This echo of Katrin's words struck Gryss like a blow and he turned away sharply and began removing a bandage from Jeorg that he had only just put on. He swore when he saw what he was doing.

'Damn you, Marna, shut up!' he said. 'You may well be right, I wouldn't pretend to know at the moment. But I know this . . .' He pointed at Jeorg. 'This is the consequence of trying to find help. I shudder to think what they'd do against outright opposition. Jeorg and Farnor need our help right now, and that's all we need to think about at the moment. The needs of the living must be met before those of the dead, no matter how we feel.'

Marna's face darkened ominously, and for the first time in many years Gryss felt real black anger well up inside him.

481

It produced no great ranting, however. Instead he fixed her with a penetrating gaze and spoke very softly. 'Your father's already lost one person that he loved dearly, Marna. He carries the pain of that still. You can't see it because you didn't know him before. But I can. It's in his eyes whenever he looks at you and sees a distant shimmer of your mother there. Just you remember that when you get the urge even to talk about committing some mindless folly such as trying to reach the capital on your own.'

Marna wilted under this quiet onslaught.

Gryss tapped his head. 'We mightn't be able to match these men sword for sword, and certainly we can't match whatever it is that Rannick has, but we can use our heads, can't we? Watch and wait. Be patient. Survive. Now help me with Jeorg.'

'That's what I thought: watch and wait.'

Both Marna and Gryss started at the voice. They turned to find Farnor standing in the doorway. He was pale and weary-looking and there was a deadness in his eyes.

Gryss looked at him anxiously. Some deep agitation within the young man must have made him overcome the effects of the sleeping draught, but his outward appearance gave no indication of anything other than a great calm. It was not a good sign.

'You should be resting, Farnor,' he said. 'You've had a . . . bad shock.'

'Watch and wait,' Farnor repeated, ignoring Gryss's remark. 'I'd decided that that was the sensible thing to do. Make my decisions whenever something happened. *If* anything happened. Wait until it all made some kind of sense. Otherwise I'd go mad, fretting about the next insane thing that might occur. It was quite clear in my mind what I should do.'

Marna moved across to him, but he raised his hand to prevent her coming too close.

'And while I was up in the woods, watching, waiting . . . being sensible . . .' Marna flinched at the anger and bitterness in his voice. 'They came and murdered my parents.'

'We don't know what happened,' Gryss said, fearful at the young man's tone. 'We don't know who—'

'Does it matter what and who?' Farnor blasted, banging the edge of his clenched fist against the door frame. 'They did it! Nilsson's men. Those so-called gatherers. Them, and whoever they have who can control that murderous creature out there and turn the winds themselves to his own will.'

Gryss made to intervene, but Farnor caught sight of the figure on the bed, and stepped forward, his expression irritable, as if this silent intruder had interrupted him.

'Who's this?' he demanded, bending over and peering closely into Jeorg's swollen face.

'It's Jeorg,' Gryss told him.

'Nilsson's men caught him,' Marna added. 'They brought him back yesterday.'

Recognition was dawning in Farnor's eyes and for a moment he was a bewildered young man again. His fingers twitched nervously at the sheets covering Jeorg then, like storm clouds closing around the sun, darkness returned again to his face. 'Yesterday,' he muttered to himself, shaking his head as if confused. Then he straightened up and said, 'At least he's alive.'

Marna bridled at this seeming callousness, but Gryss caught her eye and shook his head.

Farnor returned to the doorway. Reaching it, he leaned heavily against the jamb and yawned noisily. As he finished, he gritted his teeth almost into a snarl as he willed back the slothfulness that Gryss's sleeping draught was attempting to impose on his body.

'Where are my parents?' he asked abruptly.

'Yakob and I put them in one of the stalls at the farm last night,' Gryss said. 'Yakob and Harlen have gone up there now to . . . to see if they're all right.'

Farnor left the room. Gryss threw the bandage he was holding on to the bed and, pushing past Marna, ran after him. He was opening the front door when Gryss reached him. The old man laid a restraining hand on his arm.

'Where are you going?' he asked.

Farnor turned to him. Gryss could barely meet the coldness in his eyes. 'I'm going home,' he said. 'To bury my parents.'

He pulled the door open and stepped outside, obliging Gryss to move aside. As the bright sunlight washed over him he paused momentarily, blinking.

His hand took hold of the iron ring, almost as if for support, and he ran his fingers absently along the sharp-etched carving. When he spoke, his voice was expressionless.

'Then I'm going to the castle to find out who's responsible, and kill him.'

Chapter 33

Yakob and Harlen had had an uneasy journey to the Yarrance farm. Harlen had hoped that they might talk about what had been happening, but then had found himself oddly reluctant to speak. They could not reasonably dispute Gryss's account of recent events, but there was so little in it that they could take hold of and worry into a more familiar, understandable form. And the implications were too alarming for sensible conjecture. They moved like men riding under a thunder-laden cloud, their minds filled only with the possible ills that might befall them.

It came, therefore, almost as a relief when they saw Farnor galloping towards them as they were about to turn up the lane that led to the farm. The relief faded however, as they saw the look on his face.

'This may be a wretched job, Farnor,' Harlen ventured sympathetically. 'It's usual for friends and neighbours to attend to such matters rather than close family. You'd be better off at Gryss's, resting.'

'I'll attend to my parents, thank you, Harlen,' Farnor said coldly. 'And I'll rest when I've killed the man, or the men, who killed them.'

Harlen and Yakob reacted as Gryss had only a little while earlier: with dumbfounded silence. Farnor's manner was a bewildering combination of childish petulance and grim adult resolution.

He was riding up the lane before either of them had recovered sufficiently to move after him.

'What do you mean?' Harlen asked when they caught up with him.

'What I said,' Farnor replied. 'I shall attend to my parents, then I shall go to the castle, find out who did this and kill him.'

'Don't be ridiculous, boy,' Yakob snapped. 'How in the world do you expect—?'

He got no further, his voice failing as Farnor reined to a halt and turned to him. 'Don't call me boy, old man,' he said.

Yakob looked at him, at first angrily and then uncertainly as fear started to stir within him. Whatever else Farnor might be, he was young, fit and strong through his years of working about the farm and his mood now added a menacing perspective to these attributes.

Harlen reached across and took his arm. 'Farnor, Yakob meant no harm,' he said. 'We're none of us ourselves after what's happened. Don't misjudge a hasty word. We are your friends and all we want to do is help.'

Some of the grimness left Farnor and after a moment he eased his horse forward again. The two men moved either side of him, Yakob keeping station a little to the rear.

'You weren't serious about going to the castle, were you?' Harlen asked tentatively.

'Yes,' Farnor replied, starkly.

Harlen and Yakob exchanged glances. 'What do you hope you'll be able to do there?' Yakob asked.

They were at the farm gate. Farnor leaned down and opened it.

'What do you expect to do there?' Yakob pressed.

Farnor, however, was gazing about the yard. Harlen took in a sharp breath and Yakob's face wrinkled in distress. In the daylight the devastation of the farmhouse and the tumbled disorder of the yard seemed even worse than they had at night. Already the house was gaining the air of a long-derelict building.

Farnor showed no emotion as he dismounted. From somewhere the two dogs appeared. One of them barked as they ran towards Farnor and began fawning about him. He bent down and stroked them.

'Where are my parents?' he asked. Yakob looked around for a moment, at a loss to remember in the daylight. Then he pointed. Leaving his horse to wander, Farnor strode towards the stall. Reaching it, he drew the bolts, pushed the two halves of the door open and stepped inside.

Yakob and Harlen dismounted and followed him into the musty gloom, both anxious about his state of mind and searching for an opportunity to know his intentions more clearly. There was an unpleasant warmth in the stall and a few flies rose noisily into the air as they entered.

Farnor looked down at the rough blanket that Gryss and Yakob had covered the two bodies with. After a brief hesitation, he pulled it back and looked down at his parents.

For a moment it seemed as if he were going to weep.

Please, Harlen thought, silently urging the young man's tears on. Let it go.

But the moment passed, and Farnor found no release. Very gently he replaced the blanket. 'We must bury them immediately,' he said.

'Of course,' Yakob said. 'We'll take them down to the village, right away. Old Nath will look after them properly. See that they're in a fit state to be buried.'

'No,' Farnor said. 'We'll bury them here, now.'

Both Yakob and Harlen stared at him in disbelief, but it was another voice that spoke the denial.

'No!' Gryss said powerfully, stepping into the stall. 'Enough's enough, Farnor. I understand your anger and your hurt, but you're still half drugged with my sleeping draught, and you're on the verge of doing things that you'll regret bitterly.'

'This is my family's land, this is where they'd want to be buried,' Farnor said, defiantly.

'Your father's wish was to be buried with the rest of your family in the Resting Field,' Gryss said. 'As was your mother's. That I know for a fact – as, I would think, do you.'

Farnor made to speak, but Gryss, hot and flustered following his chase after him, was in no mood for debate. 'It was their choice to make, Farnor, not yours, nor mine, nor anyone else's. And it's the duty of the Council to ensure that their wish is followed. Do you understand?' He did not wait for an answer, though his manner softened. 'Besides, your parents had many friends, not least those here. They'll need to pay their respects, say what they have to at the graveside. That can't be denied them, Farnor.'

Farnor seemed set to argue the point, but Gryss's demeanour allowed him nothing. Briefly, it seemed again that he was going to weep, but again he did not. His mouth curled unpleasantly.

'Do as you wish,' he said, pushing past the three men and going out into the yard.

'Find a cart and harness it up,' Gryss said to Harlen and Yakob. 'Get them to Nath's. I'll see if I can settle Farnor down a bit.'

Farnor was standing in the doorway of the farmhouse when Gryss emerged into the yard. He had withdrawn the knife that Nilsson had hurled away and that had stuck in the door frame. He was looking at it idly.

'It's one of my mother's favourite kitchen knives,' he said as Gryss approached him. He appeared to be his normal self again, but there was still a distant note in his voice as if his mind were elsewhere. 'Strong blade, good steel, kept its edge for a long time. I wonder who stuck it in the door.'

Gryss briefly considered a shrug of ignorance, then he told the truth. 'It was probably used to kill your mother,' he said, as gently as such a statement would allow. 'She died very quickly. As did your father.'

Farnor hefted the knife. 'I sharpened it only a week or two ago,' he said.

Kicking some charred debris to one side, he went into the remains of the house. Gryss followed him, picking his way carefully. Inside he looked round at the smoke-stained walls of the familiar rooms. Equally familiar furniture lay crushed and broken under the blackened remains of the collapsed roof and floors. Gryss grimaced. It was the very familiarity that heightened his appalling sense of desolation. He wanted to say something, but no great words of solace came to him.

'The walls are sound,' he said weakly after a while. 'It can be rebuilt, Farnor.'

'The cows will need milking,' Farnor said absently.

'We'll get someone along to round up the stock and tend it,' Gryss said, suddenly glad to be practical. 'There'll be no shortage of willing hands, you know that.'

And no shortage of wild speculation and rage and anger, came the thought at the same time. He dismissed it. That would break about his head all too soon. His immediate task was to take care of Farnor. The rest of the village could remain safe and secure in its ignorance for a little while yet.

Farnor put the knife into his belt, then bent down and picked up something. It was a small model cart, neatly carved, and still intact. 'My father made this for me when I was a child,' he said. 'A solstice gift. I played with it for hours on end.' He looked around as if momentarily lost. 'It ended up as an ornament on that shelf there.'

489

He pointed to a clean line on the wall running between two split and charred brackets.

Gryss watched him carefully.

'How did my father die?' he asked, in the same absent tone.

Once again Gryss considered an easy lie, but again such of the truth as he could divine came out almost unbidden.

'A great blow, Farnor,' he said. 'As far as I can tell. Probably several. The only time I've seen anything like it was years ago when someone fell off the crags up east.'

For an instant he had the impression that he was at the centre of a powerful force as he seemed to feel Farnor's scattered attention suddenly draw together into a single hard-knotted whole.

'I don't understand,' Farnor said. 'Do you mean he was beaten, like Jeorg?'

'No,' Gryss replied. 'I'm certain he wasn't beaten like that. The external damage would have been worse and the internal damage less.' He gave a helpless shrug. 'The only way I can describe it is as I have done. He seemed to have been killed by a massive impact, as if he'd fallen from a great height.'

Farnor's brow knitted as he struggled with Gryss's explanation. An image came into his mind from his early childhood. An image of Rannick teasing a cat with increasing roughness until finally it lashed out and scratched him. Rannick had sworn, then with one sweeping action he had snatched up the cat and hurled it into a nearby wall, killing it instantly.

The sound of the impact lingered in Farnor's mind yet, though he had not thought about the incident in many years.

'Or as though he'd been thrown against a wall?' he said, partly to himself.

Gryss stuttered, caught unawares by the attention given to his answer. 'I . . . I suppose so,' he said. 'Yes. But I can't think of how a thing like that could've been done.'

Farnor looked at him coldly. 'Well, he couldn't have fallen off a cliff around here, could he?' he said.

Before Gryss could answer, Farnor had turned around and walked out of the house. Gryss hurried after him, thoughts of Farnor's parting words at the cottage rising to the surface.

But Farnor was standing just outside the door, gazing round the yard. Harlen and Yakob were backing a horse awkwardly between the shafts of a high-sided cart. They stopped when they saw Farnor emerge from the house, but Gryss motioned them to continue.

'What's the matter?' he asked Farnor.

'Hurled against a wall,' Farnor said quietly, as if turning the words over for inspection. Then he pointed and said, 'There's been a great wind here. Look at the damage to those roofs over there. Lines of slates torn off.' He swung his arm round to encompass the yard. 'And look at the mess. Walls damaged, everything scattered everywhere.' He turned to Gryss, his eyes unnaturally bright. 'That wind at the castle snatched you off your feet and pinned you to the gate like a dried leaf, didn't it?' he said. His hand went to his injured arm. 'Whoever set that . . . trap . . . for us there killed my father.' He shivered. 'And that creature had something to do with it as well. I felt it, out there in the woods. I thought it was on top of me, it felt so close. But it was after something else, and it was in full cry.' He bent towards Gryss, confidentially. 'Wherever it is, it draws a power from somewhere else. I could feel that too,' he said. 'Some place that's both here and beyond here. There was a great flood of energy pouring through.

491

Like something alive.' He paused. 'And the creature is a channel for it.'

Gryss gazed at him wildly, understanding nothing, but caught up by the force in his words.

'Now what I have to do is find out who it is who uses this power and controls this creature,' Farnor went on.

Gryss pulled himself together. 'And?' he said.

'And kill him,' Farnor answered, without hesitation.

When Farnor had made this threat at his cottage, Gryss had taken it for no more than an angry, frightened outburst. But here there was such resolve in it that he went cold with fear. He wished he could have laughed and cried out, 'You couldn't hurt anyone, Farnor, it's not in your nature.' But the words would not come, because they were only half true. True in that Farnor would not willingly hurt anything, but not true that he would not kill. He had slaughtered animals in the past as a matter of routine. Slaughtered them quickly and efficiently under the tutelage of his father. The skills were in his hands. All that was needed to bring them to bear on people was the will.

'Is it Nilsson, do you think?'

The question burst in upon Gryss, catching him completely unawares in the middle of his dark reverie. 'No,' he said, shaking his head. 'It's Rannick.'

Even as he spoke the words, his mind sped after them as though it could seize them before they reached their destination.

Farnor spun round and his gaze fixed Gryss just as surely as would one of his long-bladed knives. 'Rannick?' he said, his voice filled with changing shades and nuances: disbelief, doubt, realization.

Every encounter that he had ever had with Rannick seemed to pass through Farnor's mind, culminating in that irritated flick of the hand and the angry buzzing of

492

a cloud of flies restrained by some power beyond their knowing. And with those memories came memories too of subtle familiarities in the contacts he had had with the creature. Familiarities that now fell into place around the name of Rannick, as crystals would form about a single seeding grain. It was sufficient. He needed no further interrogation of his informant to confirm this knowledge.

And, as if Farnor's sudden realization were contagious, Gryss found himself back in that dim castle room with Nilsson telling him about the intention to turn the castle into a permanent garrison. The vaguely familiar figure silhouetted against the window . . . it had been Rannick! Of course. How could he have failed to recognize him at the time? Too tired? Too shocked by Nilsson's news?

But it didn't matter now. It was as if a cold wind had blasted away a cloying mist that had been clinging about his thoughts.

Then welling up into this new-found clarity came a terrible, murderous urge.

Though with that same clarity he knew that they were not his thoughts. They were Farnor's. Gryss could feel the young man's swirling, complex pain and anger. Somehow, through his torment, Farnor's strange gift had reached out to him. He felt no wonder at this revelation, however, only fearful concern for the terrible, purposeful intensity of Farnor's emotions.

He put his hand on Farnor's shoulder.

'No,' he said. 'No. You mustn't do it. Rannick will kill you. Whatever's happened to him, it's given the evil side of his nature full rein.'

Farnor jumped as if he had been struck. He looked at Gryss, his face full of questions. 'You heard me?' he asked, lifting his hands to his head.

Gryss attempted no explanations. 'Come away from

here,' he said. 'Give yourself time to rest and think. Your mind is too full of horrors and your body's half drugged by my sleeping draught. You're not fully yourself. Let's attend to the burying of your parents properly, then—'

Without speaking, Farnor pushed his hand aside and began walking across the yard towards the gate.

'Farnor!' Gryss cried.

Harlen and Yakob turned as the call echoed emptily around the walls of the battered buildings, but made no move to intercept Farnor's departure.

Then Farnor had swung up on to his horse and was gone.

'What happened?' Yakob shouted as Gryss, his face anguished, hurried over to his own horse.

'He's going to the castle to confront Rannick,' Gryss shouted back. 'I'll have to go after him. You take Garren and Katrin down to Nath's, then see how Jeorg's getting on.'

'You told him about Rannick?' Yakob said disbelievingly.

Gryss turned on him angrily. 'It just . . . slipped out,' he said. 'Please. This isn't the time for arguing. Rannick'll kill him. Help me mount then do as I asked.'

They did, but as he galloped away Yakob said, 'This is madness. I can't believe this Rannick business. I think this has all been too much for Gryss. But they're both riding into serious trouble if they go up to the castle, that's for sure.'

Harlen nodded unhappily. He was looking at the cart bearing the bodies of Katrin and Garren. Then he made up his mind.

'You're right,' he said. 'And I'm going after them.' He pointed at the cart. 'They'd expect us to look after their son.'

With an effort he clambered on to his horse. 'Are you coming?' he said to Yakob, urging the horse forward.

Yakob frowned and looked about indecisively for a moment, then he nodded.

The two rode off together.

'Sit with Jeorg,' Gryss had yelled as he had scuttered out of the cottage in pursuit of Farnor. 'He shouldn't wake up for a while yet, but if he does try to keep him quiet. Let him have a little to drink, but don't let him eat anything yet.'

As she closed the cottage door, for the first time in her life Marna had an urge to bolt it.

She left it unlocked, though, and returned to Jeorg's room. As she sat down, Gryss's old dog padded in grumpily and flopped at her feet. She bent down and patted it. 'You've no idea what's going on, have you, old thing?' she said. 'All this coming and going.' The dog gave a heartfelt sigh and rested its chin on her foot.

Now, in contrast to wanting to lock the door, she felt trapped by the room. She hunched her shoulders unhappily. Inevitably, her thoughts returned to the fate of Garren and Katrin, and she began to shake. She had slept only fitfully through what had been left of the night and, as she had told Gryss, she had wept for most of the time that she was awake. Wept for the memory of Garren and Katrin, wept for Farnor and his loss, wept for herself and for fear of what was happening to the valley. Wept for things she could put no name to, because weeping was all she could do.

And the fears were still there. 'They'll do much worse to you,' Gryss had said. She knew that, for pity's sake. But it did not seem to have occurred to Gryss that they would probably do that anyway if they took control of the valley. That was why she was shaking. These were bandits, not soldiers with perhaps some semblance of

495

honour or discipline. When they wanted women they would come and take them, and no one would be able to stop them.

And with Rannick leading them there would be no restraint. At the thought of Rannick her trembling became worse. Of all people. There would be no doubt about which way *his* attention would drift when the urge for female company came over him.

She clenched her teeth violently then clasped her hands together in an attempt to still them.

Ironically, Marna was one of the few people in the valley who had had any time for Rannick. She had always felt a sympathy for him, sensing in him something lost and helpless. But that had been before her ready smile and her pleasant enquiries about his well-being and his activities had been misconstrued for a more ardent concern. Rannick, considerably her senior, had taken the consequent rebuff badly and had been caustically formal with her ever since, though his eyes told a different tale. That she still felt some remnant of that earlier sympathy did little but confuse her now.

She remembered powerful hands holding her as she had never been held before. There had been a faint, unexpected flickering of desire at the contact, but the fear had been the greater and had expunged it: the hands had held her helpless.

'There's no harder thing in life than standing by helpless.' Gryss's words came back to her vividly as she recalled the incident. He had not meant them in that context, but they were nonetheless true.

And here, looking to the future, there was an element of choice.

Marna opened her hands. The trembling had stopped, but the spirit that drove it seemed to have suffused through her entire body, its centre resting solid and cold in the pit of her stomach. And it had changed in character. What had been fear was now anger and determination. She would never be helpless like that again. Frozen like a rabbit before a stoat.

Never!

She looked at Jeorg again. His battered features were an object lesson to her. She could not fight that way, trading blow for blow. She would have to use flight and stealth. But the conclusion was unsatisfactory. The memory of Rannick's grip on her arms returned and her hands started to tremble again. This time she willed them to stop. Sooner or later, flight and stealth would not be open to her and she would encounter such power again. She must be prepared to deal with it.

Her eyes narrowed as she pondered, the fear-driven anger in her giving her a strange creativity. She had teeth and nails which could be used to great effect, but she would need more. She would need a weapon, she realized; something that would do greater damage than teeth and nails and futile fists. Much greater damage.

Swords, spears, clubs she dismissed even as they came to her. They would need strength and skill to use and, anyway, she couldn't possibly carry something like that around all day.

A knife! Or, better still, knives. That was it. She drove a blade into Rannick's arm and felt his grip vanish. Excellent.

And there were plenty about her father's house. She began to run through an inventory of them, at the same time debating where about her person she could carry them.

Unexpectedly, her fear returned, springing upon her like some childish prankster. What about now? Wasn't she defenceless? As before, she had a sudden vision of horsemen circling the house, of an urgent hammering on the door, of Rannick standing in the doorway come to take what he wanted.

Almost in spite of herself, she stood up and went to the window. Cautiously she drew the curtain a little. The sunlit lane stood reassuringly empty. She felt a little embarrassed, but the sense of urgency remained.

She let the curtain fall back and returned to her chair. A restlessness pervaded her and her eyes wandered about the room, though she could not have said what she was looking for.

Then she lit on Jeorg's pack, dropped casually in a corner of the room in the flurry of attending to him.

She went over and picked it up. It was heavy. Quite unscrupulously she took it back to her chair, undid the clasps and began to rifle through it. Jeorg would have a spare knife in here, surely? The contents, however, were uninspiring: clothes, some fruit and dried meat, a few small sunstones, a tin of bandages and salves. Her nose wrinkled unhappily at the sight of these and she glanced again at the massive damage that had been done to her unconscious charge.

Even as she did so, her hand encountered a package. She felt around it carefully, testing its shape and size. Thoughts of a knife vanished in a surge of curiosity and, tongue protruding between her teeth, she gently withdrew the package. Rough string bound a waxed paper parcel.

Untying the string, she opened the paper to reveal a soft leather wallet. She examined it for a moment and then began to open it. It was a cunningly designed and well-made article, with tightly sewn seams and folds and flaps so arranged that, even without the waxed paper wrapping, it was effectively waterproof.

Inside were papers. She looked at them briefly and then, curiosity well aroused, she took them through into the back room where the light was better.

Although her search had been prompted by a need for a weapon with which she could defend herself, for some time Marna would have been oblivious to a noisy army laying siege to the cottage, as she became increasingly engrossed in the papers.

They were the details of the route to the capital that Gryss had prepared for Jeorg. Some of the notes and maps were obviously very old, having perhaps been prepared by Gryss during his own travelling days. Others were much newer.

For the most part, they were written in a neat, curling script that Marna presumed was Gryss's, though there were some more coarsely lettered notes here and there. And they were presented in a clear, logical manner that could only have been Gryss's.

It was all there before her: the way to the capital, laid out for the following. Her mind raced. Fate had transformed an impetuous idea into a real dilemma for her. She could go now, this minute. She could take a horse from the inn, call at her home to gather clothes and food, and go. Go downland discreetly until she saw whether there were any guards posted or not, and then as fast as she could all the way downland and to the capital. Over the hill!

She felt her breath tighten in her chest at the prospect and her palms began to tingle.

What could restrain her? Fear? Perhaps. Responsibility? Suppose Jeorg were to wake suddenly and need reassurance? And what would be the reaction of Gryss if he returned to find Jeorg abandoned and her missing?

Or her father's reaction?

'Your father's already lost one person that he loved dearly.' Gryss's words returned to reproach her.

Marna's mouth pursed. She knew all about that, she thought, but no one had ever expressed it to her so forthrightly, and it proved a winding blow now, as she contemplated flight.

'Damn,' she said, softly and bitterly. She couldn't do it. Not yet. Not like that; not without any warning.

For some time she sat motionless, her hands resting on the papers and her mind drifting idly now that it had been released from the torrential rush of her wild plans.

Slowly however, new patterns began to emerge. Calmer, more reasoned patterns. The threat still remained. The fear and the anger still remained. She must still arm herself. And, if necessary, she must be prepared to make the journey to the capital on her own. She found that she could not avoid that final conclusion, even though the prospect of such a journey was already becoming more daunting.

But she was not a principal in this affair. She must do nothing that would jeopardize whatever efforts Gryss and the others were putting forth.

She looked at the papers again. Then, carefully, she gathered them together in order and replaced them in the leather wallet. For a few minutes she looked at the package thoughtfully, then, reaching a decision, she set about scouring through Gryss's cottage.

Nilsson had spent much of the remainder of the night consolidating the work that he had initially been obliged to leave to Saddre and Dessane, namely the quietening and assuring of his men following their mostly panic-stricken flight from the Yarrances' farm.

It could have been worse, he mused, sitting down on an embrasure and leaning back against the sloping wall that bounded it. A lighter spirit than Nilsson's would have sung out to the warmth of the stone on his back, and the warmth of the sun on his face, and the sight of the valley, green and lush, winding away below him into the distance. But Nilsson was immune to such paralysing infections. His spirit dwelt in the future that he intended to make for himself in the wake of his new lord; the present was merely a passing irritation.

There had been a few injuries in the crush to escape the power unleashed by Rannick but in reality the greatest damage had been done to the men's pride, and it was this that had given rise to much of the trouble as they had returned to the castle in scattered, bewildered groups. As necessary, Saddre and Dessane had soothed injured prides, provided excuses, cracked heads and done the hard work, and subsequently, having stood by his lord throughout, Nilsson had been able to salve most of the remaining hurts by being avuncular and forgiving:

A friendly hand on the shoulder.

'It's been a long time since you saw the likes of that, hasn't it?'

'You weren't there on the palace steps when the old Lord outfaced the southland demon. *That* was something!'

'Who'd have thought we'd ever have come across the likes of him again? Chances like that don't usually come once to a man, let alone twice.'

And so on.

Of course, the destruction of Avak had helped bring a sense of perspective to the proceedings. Pity that. He was a useful fighter, but he was always apt to be troublesome and, all things considered, he was no great loss.

The recollection, however, brought with it the surging malevolence he had felt focused on him as the creature had hurled out of the darkness and leapt up the wall towards him. Momentarily he closed his eyes against the bright day, and, on the instant, he heard again the scrabbling claws and the thud of its landing.

Now, as then, the fact that he was well above any height that the creature could possibly leap gave him

501

no consolation. He had been powerless to move. The only thing he would have been able to do was scream.

Despite the sunshine, Nilsson shivered. And whether he kept his eyes closed willingly or out of fear he could not have said.

But Avak's demise had done more than focus the attention of the men. It had in some way restored the Lord Rannick.

'*Good*,' he had said, with a long-drawn-out breath that had chilled Nilsson utterly. Then he had turned slowly, looked at Nilsson and smiled a smile that was rich with the fulfilment of nameless desires. Nilsson had been grateful for the subdued lighting in the room.

'I need rest now,' he had said. 'I shall sleep. You may go.'

Nilsson had bowed. 'I shall leave a guard outside your door, Lord.'

'I need no guard,' had been the faintly amused response. 'Go, Captain. Tend your men. They will be needed soon, now.'

Nevertheless, concerned for Rannick's safety with the men in such an uncertain humour, Nilsson had cautiously opened the door to the darkened room later to see that all was well.

A blast of air had struck him in the face, stinging his eyes and taking his breath away. It had seemed to pour into his mouth and down his throat and as he had staggered back, retching, the door had closed with a soft, sighing hiss.

Nilsson cleared his throat as he remembered the incident. Then, the lights dancing behind the lids of his closed eyes darkened and the warmth on his face lessened. He opened his eyes abruptly, his hand moving to his knife.

'Sorry to disturb you, Captain,' said the sentry, who

was standing between him and the sun. 'But there's a rider coming.'

Nilsson grunted and stood up. The sentry pointed.

'I think it's that kid from the farm,' he said.

Nilsson leaned forward and screwed up his eyes.

It was the lad indeed. What was his name? Farnor or something, wasn't it?

And coming at the gallop too.

'Should I wake the Lord, Captain?' the sentry asked.

Nilsson shook his head and then smiled. 'No,' he replied. 'I think we can manage one tearful country brat on our own. If he gets this far without falling off that horse, that is. Throw the gate open for him. Let's give him a real welcome.'

His smile broadened and unfurled into a low, unpleasant laugh.

Chapter 34

'What d'you want, boy?' Nilsson said, catching Farnor as he jumped down from his horse, missed his footing and stumbled. 'Charging in like that. Someone's going to get hurt.'

Farnor, flushed and breathless, did not hear the menace in Nilsson's voice. He yanked his arm free. 'Where's Rannick?' he demanded.

Nilsson's eyes darted to the knife in Farnor's belt. 'Lord Rannick, do you mean?' he said.

Farnor scowled, thrown momentarily off-balance by this unfamiliar appellation. 'I don't know anything about any lord,' he said, holding Nilsson's gaze. 'Just get Rannick out here. Rannick the village labourer.' He began to shout past Nilsson, his voice becoming shrill. 'Rannick the village idiot! Rannick the fly trainer! Rannick the coward! Come out and face me, you murderer, Rannick!'

The circle of men that had begun to form expectantly about the protagonists fell suddenly quiet and widened noticeably. Even Nilsson found himself casting a quick glance over his shoulder for fear that Farnor's petulant abuse might result in a violent reproach being brought down on his own head.

Farnor misunderstood the response, taking it to be due to the strength of the passion and hatred that was so possessing him. He made to step around Nilsson but a powerful hand seized his arm and dragged him back effortlessly.

'Stay where you are, boy,' Nilsson said, his lip curling to bare his teeth.

Farnor took a wild swing at him, but Nilsson blocked it irritably and then dealt him an open-handed blow across the face that sent him reeling.

Garren Yarrance had had occasion in the past to chastise his son forcefully, and through the years Farnor had had an average exposure to physical violence in his noisy games and quarrels with his peers. But he had never felt anything like the blow he had just received. Apart from the pain, the body-jarring impact and the ringing in his ears, two things conspired to reduce him instantly to a tiny frightened shadow of what he had imagined himself to be. One was the truly terrifying sensation of having someone, for the first time ever, not only totally indifferent to his true self but actually intent on physically hurting him. The other was a chilling sense of total inadequacy before the power of this man.

Through his unfocused vision and the pounding in his head he was aware of the circle closing round him again, and of laughter urging on his assailant.

'Go home, boy,' he heard Nilsson saying. 'The Lord Rannick won you your inheritance quite a time before you might have expected it. You should show some gratitude.' There was more laughter. 'Go round up your stock and start tending your farm. We'll be needing plenty of food soon enough.'

Frightened child and angry man vied in Farnor. The one urged him to turn and flee. To break out of the circle, dash through the still-open gate and over the sunlit fields until he was surrounded by familiar and kindly faces: faces that knew and understood him; faces that would hold him secure and look after him in his torment. Profoundly shaken as he was by Nilsson's blow, this voice within him was almost unbearably powerful.

Yet, too, there was a fury bubbling within him. A fury that fed on the laughter growing around him and that needed to strike out, to release the pain that he was suffering, to unleash it on anyone, anything, that stood in his way.

And, dimly, underlying everything, there was Rannick. The scowling, surly labourer who had always been a dark stain in his mind and who was now somehow the obscene focus of all that was happening. He felt again the bloodlust of the creature, burning hot and ancient within him. He wanted to see Rannick hurled against the wall like that pathetic squealing cat so many years ago. Hurled and hurled and hurled until he too became a limp rag doll of a thing like Garren Yarrance.

The memory of his slaughtered parents fired the fury beyond any controlling and it welled up to sweep all restraints aside. It seemed to him that his body was filled with a blood-red roaring and that he was scarcely in control of his actions. Distantly, he felt himself bending low and charging at the scornful figure that stood between him and the object of his hatred.

Then all was confusion, cruel pain and winding impact as, strong though he was, his wild inexperience fell easily before Nilsson's greater strength, long-practised and bloody skills and clear-sighted malice.

Pain exploded in different parts of his body, quickly suffusing and accumulating until all he knew was pain. Vague images of the courtyard, of feet and faces and walls and towers, whirled through his vision. And he could do nothing to stop any of it. No part of him seemed to be his own.

Then there was a lull.

The brightness that was percolating through his half-closed eyes began to darken. But it was not the darkness of a merciful unconsciousness, he knew, for he was desperately, painfully awake; it was the circle of men closing around him to finish the work that their captain had started.

Hands seized him and dragged him to his feet. Loud

advice was being shouted to someone followed by mocking laughter. The hands held him firm and an unclear silhouette positioned itself in front of him.

'Leave him!'

The silhouette faltered, and the hands holding Farnor eased their grip.

The words entered Farnor's mind and spiralled through his pain and terror until they evoked recognition.

Gryss!

Nilsson turned to face the source of this interference. Gryss moved forward out of the shade of the gate arch. He was leaning heavily on his horse for support, but his demeanour was angry and determined.

'Leave him,' he said again, 'for pity's sake. Isn't it enough that you've slaughtered his family and destroyed his home? Do you have to break him too?'

'Old man, go back to your salves and potions,' Nilsson said menacingly. 'Before you receive the same. He charged in here and attacked me. He's lucky I didn't kill him out of hand. All he's getting now is a little instruction on how to behave in the presence of his betters.'

Gryss's mouth twisted with rage as he looked from Nilsson's sneering face to Farnor's bruised and bloody one. He caught the twitch in Nilsson's eyes that responded to this and knew that, however justified his anger, he would merely prolong Farnor's beating and receive one himself if he gave vent to it injudiciously. From somewhere he dragged out a reluctant diplomacy.

'I'm sure he understands now,' he said, forcing the anger from his voice. 'He was always a quick learner. Let him go, Captain. He's had enough.'

Nilsson met his gaze. He could feel Gryss struggling to master his fear. It would be no effort to kill the old man right away and then finish Farnor but, just as Gryss had fought down his immediate response, so did Nilsson. Rannick had seized the initiative in the matter of how the villagers were to be treated: perhaps to impose his will on his chosen lieutenant, perhaps for some darker motive that he himself did not fully understand. But it did not matter. The damage had been done, and it would fall to Nilsson now to control a hostile community that would be needed to service what would be a growing number of men at the castle.

And his relationship with Gryss would probably be crucial in this. Despite Rannick's assertion that the villagers would be easily cowed, Nilsson knew from experience that even partly willing servants were far superior to slaves.

Two other figures appeared, hesitantly, in the archway.

Nilsson nodded to the men who were holding Farnor to release him. As they did so, he staggered forward, his arms flailing as if to fend off further blows. Nilsson seized his tunic and dragged him upright and then pushed him savagely towards Gryss. He went sprawling along the ground with a cry of pain.

'That's four people we've had trouble with, old man,' Nilsson said as Gryss bent down to help Farnor to his feet. 'I said you'd be left alone if you behaved, and I meant it. We've more important things to do than deal with noisy yokels. And anyone who causes problems will be dealt with summarily.'

Emotions ran riot through Gryss as he struggled to support Farnor. Starkly he noted that Nilsson had casually admitted responsibility for the deaths of Garren and Katrin. He wanted to scream at him, 'Why, you murderous lout? Why? What could they possibly have done to warrant that?', but he remained silent – though whether through concern for the safety of Farnor or out of simple fear he did not know.

'I understand,' he said. 'And I'll do my best to see that everyone else does.'

'See you do,' Nilsson said grimly.

Gryss took refuge in the immediate needs of his charge. 'Come on, Farnor, let's get you away,' he said gently.

Hesitantly, Harlen and Yakob came forward to help him. Though he was almost sobbing with pain, Farnor somehow managed to stand, supporting himself with a single hand resting on Harlen's shoulder.

There was some raucous abuse from the watching men as the quartet began to move away.

'What's going on?'

Nilsson quailed inwardly at the sound of the voice. It was Rannick's. Go, run while you can, he willed the four villagers, but they stopped and turned as they heard the voice. He swore to himself, and turned to face his lord.

Rannick was wearing a dark brown leather tunic over a linen shirt decorated with a bewildering design of swirling lines. Stoutly woven trousers disappeared into calf-length boots, and were secured by a finely carved leather belt, secured in its turn by a round brass buckle which glinted in the sunlight. Nilsson recognized the clothes as part of the booty they had taken on the raid.

So you've been rooting through the goods, have you, Lord? he thought. Picking and choosing like some old dame at a market.

But there was a quality of both practicality and dramatic presentation in Rannick's choice that for some reason unsettled Nilsson. It betokened both confidence and intent where previously Nilsson had judged there to be mainly bewilderment and spleen.

'Nothing important, Lord,' he said jovially. 'I apologize if we disturbed your rest.'

Rannick saw Gryss and the others.

510

'Ah,' he said, smiling. 'Coming to protest at the treatment of Jeorg and the Yarrances, I presume, eh, Gryss?'

'We've come to take Farnor away,' Gryss said, quickly, before anyone else could intervene.

Rannick nodded understandingly and moved forward. There was a strangeness about him, his clothes and his hair moving as though he were walking through a wind that was blowing in some other place.

As he approached the group, a deep silence fell in the courtyard.

He stopped a little way in front of Gryss. Yakob and Harlen stared at him in open disbelief. Both made to speak at the same time, but Rannick gave them no opportunity.

'What's the matter?' he asked mockingly. 'Can't believe your eyes? Allow me to explain.' He bowed his head.

A small whirlwind of dust formed at his feet. Rapidly it gathered a vicious, whining power and then, like a hunting bird, it flew directly into the faces of the two men. Both of them staggered back, closing their eyes and lifting their arms to protect themselves from the stinging impact.

Rannick laughed humourlessly. 'A little dust in the eyes will help you to see things much more clearly, I think,' he said. 'Give you a picture of the way things are now. Am I not right?'

Gryss raised his hand to prevent Harlen and Yakob from replying. 'We just want to leave, now . . .' He hesitated, then with an effort he managed to say, 'Lord Rannick. We have to tell the rest of the village—'

'Tell them what, Gryss?' Rannick interrupted.

Gryss gesticulated vaguely around the courtyard. 'About the . . . new garrison that's to be posted here. About the need . . .'

511

Rannick shook his head. 'That was Captain Nilsson's jest, Gryss,' he said, smiling again. 'All that nonsense about the army. He and his men are no more King's men than I am. They are fighting men, to be sure, but they are what you might call . . . independent. They fight for themselves rather than for some distant king.'

His manner became suddenly friendly and explanatory. 'They have a fascinating history.' He looked significantly at Nilsson, whose face became expressionless. 'If you knew it, you would never close your eyes in sleep again. Certainly not venture out at the sound of hooves in the street in the early morning. But now they have decided to pledge their swords to me. It is an arrangement for our mutual benefit.' He drew closer to Gryss and his voice became a hissing whisper. 'Just tell the villagers about me, Gryss,' he said. 'Tell them that I am their leader now, and that I require their absolute obedience in all things. Tell them that the penalty for disobedience will depend on my fancy at the time, but is unlikely to be pleasant. And tell them that I have instructed the Captain here to kill out of hand anyone who tries to leave the valley.'

Despite himself, Gryss asked, 'Why did you kill Garren and Katrin?'

Nilsson's eyes narrowed nervously, but there was no outburst from Rannick. Instead his face became thoughtful.

'Garren was insolent,' he said, quite casually, after a moment. He jerked his head towards Nilsson. 'And it was my able new ally who killed Katrin.' He held out an acknowledging hand to Nilsson. 'Or, rather, she killed herself as I remember.' He gave Gryss a look of injured explanation. 'But she *was* trying to kill me, so he could do no other. Had he not done so then I would have had to when I had finished with Garren.'

Gryss shot an anxious glance at Farnor as Rannick

gave this brief and callous account, but the young man, leaning on Harlen, seemed to be barely conscious.

Then Gryss felt Rannick's hand close about his arm and give it a confidential squeeze. He started violently. 'But there was another reason, I see now. A much deeper reason.' Rannick's voice was almost wheedling in its self-justification. 'Why should *I* waste my time brushing an insect like Garren Yarrance from my path?' He looked at Gryss as if he truly expected an answer. Gryss found that he was holding his breath, so awful was Rannick's presence. His arm was released.

'But strange powers are moving here.' Rannick peered at Gryss intently, as if his gaze would give his words greater meaning. 'Powers that are focused on me. Powers that have perhaps been focused on me all my life. Powers that bring my destiny to fruition.' Again the hand closed intimately about Gryss's arm. 'Why else should I have been born with the gift?' A buffeting wind suddenly filled the courtyard, blowing up clouds of dust again and making both men and horses look about them uneasily. And, as suddenly as it had begun, it stopped. Gryss trembled as memories of the wind that had almost trapped him and Farnor, returned.

'Why else should I be drawn to . . . ?' He fell silent and his eyes drifted northwards filled with a strange, smiling secretiveness.

Then he straightened up and continued with the air of an academic carefully following a line of reasoning to a satisfactory conclusion. 'And why else should Nilsson and his lost band of men turn into this of all valleys but to serve my ends?'

Gryss remained silent.

Rannick looked down at his hands. 'And why should have Garren provoked me so needlessly?' His eyes fixed Gryss's again. 'Why should he have elected to provoke me and thus die by my hand?' He curled his fingers so that they looked like talons, then he stretched them out fully and Gryss could feel the tension radiating from his whole body.

'So many questions, Gryss. So many questions.' Rannick bent forward and his voice became intense. 'But only one answer. All this was so that as I made Garren learn what it meant to oppose me, so Katrin would make her sacrilegious assault on me and so, thus, I too would come to a great learning. I would see beyond the totality of my learning thus far. See that it was merely a key to a greater knowledge, a greater strength, a greater power.' His voice fell to a whisper. 'I would be transfigured.'

Sickened and frightened, Gryss could not move away from Rannick even though his arm was no longer held.

'Watch,' Rannick commanded softly.

Gryss felt the air about him come alive with a tingling, unpleasant energy, as though a thunderstorm were about to break. He braced himself for yet another assault by the wind that seemed to guard this place, but instead he found himself trying to focus on a vague, luminous shape that had appeared in front of Rannick. Involuntarily, he made to step back, but Rannick caught his arm and restrained him.

'Watch,' Rannick said again.

Gryss could do no other, so hypnotic was the eerie, dancing light growing in intensity before him. Then there came the fearful screeching that had filled the Yarrance farmyard, and the vague, shifting light became bright, flickering flames. They wove and twisted around one another, merging and separating like sensuous dancers, until they formed a tall column that rose high above the castle walls. The men in the courtyard retreated, as did Harlen and Yakob. Only Nilsson held his ground.

Gryss could feel a heat beating on his face that was

514

worse than any he had ever known. It seemed to him that even the village blacksmith's forge would be as a cool stream after this.

He looked at his captor. Rannick's eyes were glistening in the light, the two tiny columns of flames reflected there seemed to be burning in the heart of the man.

'This is the merest token,' Rannick said. 'Such knowledge I now have. So much more shall I gain. Now I am truly on the golden road to my destiny.'

Every part of Gryss's body was now shaking. Whatever he had thought about Rannick since Jeorg's whispered message, his worst visions had been nothing compared to the reality of the power and the will that was being shown to him here. He knew that he should fall on the man and destroy him somehow before Nilsson or his men could interfere. He could do it; he was near enough. A swift lunge with his knife and he could sever the monster's windpipe. But he knew too that he could not. He knew that with such terror possessing him his hand would not obey any command it received, nor his feet, nor any part of him.

And yet something must be done!

Then he felt Rannick start.

The flames were faltering.

A flicker of anger passed over Rannick's face to be replaced almost immediately by an expression betokening enormous effort.

Yet still the flames waned: slowly, but quite perceptibly.

Sweat formed on Rannick's brow.

Gryss willed himself to absolute silence and turned away from Rannick in an attempt to make himself wholly insignificant. If Rannick was about to fail at the heart of this monstrous boast, then his wrath would be appalling and could fall on anyone at the least provocation.

Rannick began to breathe heavily.

515

Gryss forced words into his mouth. Words that might perhaps enable Rannick to end this display without loss of face. 'Your power is magnificent, Lord,' he gasped. 'Truly awesome. I'd never have thought to . . .'

But above his words and above the noise of the flames a faint, distant sound drifted into the courtyard. It was a terrible, nerve-shredding sound: a howling. It might have been a wolf or some wild feline, but it was both and neither. It was agonized and unnatural; an animal noise, but full of all-too-human malevolence.

It was the creature, Gryss's reason told him; no animal he had ever known would have made such a sound. But he needed no logic; the ancient knowledge in every fibre of his body cried out in response to the sound.

He found his gaze turning back to the flames. They burned less powerfully than before, and a bloody tinge tainted them. Further, there was an aura of struggling effort about them. He was aware of Rannick at the edge of his vision. His face reflected the struggle, grim-shadowed in the light of the flames and glistening with sweat.

It gave Gryss no reassurance to realize that Rannick was not simply struggling to maintain an impressive illusion, but that he was locked in combat with some other power.

Some other will . . . ?

Rescued by Gryss's intervention, Farnor leaned heavily on Harlen's shoulder. Some remnant of childish pride suppressed any outward expression of the inner turmoil that was racking him except for his arm clutched about his stomach and his mouth held tightly shut. Somehow it was enough to keep him from sinking to his knees and crying out at the pain and the fear; crying out for his father to come and take him away from this awful place, and the determined cruelty that had been let loose upon

516

him; crying out for his father to make all well with the looming figure of Captain Nilsson . . . He was sure that he and the big man could become friends and end this misunderstanding. Reproachful inner voices reminding him that it was Nilsson who had killed his parents were, for the nonce, lost beneath the pain.

Indeed, the pain and the effort that he was making to restrain this howling inner plea rendered him almost oblivious to everything that was happening around him.

He could hear familiar voices: disputing, perhaps? But they were distant and unclear and there was nothing in them to draw him from his cocoon of pain.

Until a peculiar unease disturbed him. An unease that was beyond himself. And, like the voices, it was familiar. How long had it been there?

Then it was all about him.

Now here, now gone; elusive. Flickering and intangible, it seemed to dance through and about him. Its touch was foul. A faint memory returned to him.

A memory of the creature, ferocious and cruel. A memory of Rannick. A memory of the torrent of unrestrained emotion that had rolled over him as he had fled across the fields to find his parents slain and his home destroyed.

And they were all one. Brought together in a loathsome totality that had somehow ripped its way into this place where it did not belong.

And then the memories were gone. Swept aside by something stirring deep within him, as if from a long sleep; something like a faint, distant light. And then it was reaching out and forbidding this intrusion.

The unease faltered and shifted, and then trembled.

Then a will emerged to sustain it.

Rannick's will! Farnor's mind thought faintly.

Or the creature's!

It did not matter.

The light that had come from within him flared, and like a predator finding its prey it assailed this opposition.

Somewhere, the merest mote, Farnor watched, helpless, floating in a place that was both here and not here; aware of his beaten body, full of pain and fear and leaning still on Harlen, but unburdened by it; aware that the battle that had just been engaged had been at his will, though it was quite beyond his control.

He was . . .

What . . . ?

That, too, did not matter. He knew only that resolution was needed of him. Implacable determination. What had come here did not belong. In this alien clime, its ability to do harm was beyond measure. The terrible rent through which it had been drawn must be sealed.

And the gift of this sealing lay with him.

But the knowledge meant nothing to him.

Yet he would not be defeated.

He would not be defeated.

He would hold.

There was a timeless interval when all was balanced and still. Somewhere, Farnor knew, the battle was being fought, but he could do nothing other than wait and commit his will to denying this intrusion further entrance.

Then the foulness faltered once again. At first slightly, then with increasing desperation like the scrabbling fingers of a climber at the edge of a rounded ledge.

Was it dying? came the question.

No. That could not be. But it was failing. It was being driven back.

And now it was screaming. But to no avail. It must

be returned from whence it came, and everything made well here.

And, with a dwindling, spiralling spasm, it was gone. And there was stillness.

Farnor felt the light, released now, washing back over him, returning him to himself. He felt a myriad sensations as his body closed about him again.

Painful sensations!

Like a dream, both the intrusion and the mysterious opposition to it had passed away. The light had become now the bright sunlight that was filling the courtyard and forcing its way through his partly closed eyes. And the painful sensations focused themselves in his ribs, and his back and his face and . . . everywhere else that Nilsson had struck.

He heard himself gasp with pain.

The sound seemed to be abnormally loud. He became aware of the silence around him, a silence that rang with tension. He forced his eyes to open further.

Everyone in the courtyard was staring at something, though there was nothing there that he could see.

'What happened?' he heard Harlen say, his voice soft and full of awe.

'It vanished.' It was Gryss replying, in an equally awe-stricken whisper. His hands were by his ears as if he had been covering them. 'That terrible noise,' he said in distress.

'That colour,' Harlen said. 'Like blood. I've never seen flames like that before. Let's get away, Gryss, while we can. Something's gone wrong. Look at Rannick's face.'

At the mention of Rannick, the eerie interlude that had possessed Farnor vanished from his mind utterly, to be replaced by the savage anger that had brought him to the castle in the first place.

It returned to urge him forward to destroy this abomination, as if it had never been halted. Harlen seized him as soon as he started to move, however.

'For pity's sake, Farnor,' he hissed. 'What are you doing? Look at him. We're dead men.'

Chapter 35

'We're dead men.'

The terrible, shaking fear in Harlen's words brought a final awakening to Farnor, heightening the racking pains of the beating that Nilsson had given him. He must have fainted, he decided hazily, and something bad had happened while he had been unconscious.

But what?

He looked at Gryss, who in his turn was staring fixedly at something. Following the old man's gaze Farnor turned to see Rannick. His face was a mask of bewildered fury.

'Down,' Gryss muttered frantically, dropping on to his knees and bowing his head. 'Get *down*!'

Compelled by the urgency in his voice, Harlen and Yakob also fell to their knees. Farnor had little choice, he staggered as the support he had been receiving disappeared, then Harlen's hand seized his arm and dragged him down. He managed not to cry out as the pain of his knees striking the hard paving added itself to the others that were vying for attention. He leaned forward to take some of his weight on his arms.

'Lord Rannick, forgive us.'

Despite his preoccupation with his pain, Farnor became aware of Gryss speaking. Cautiously he looked at the old man. Gryss's head was still bowed and, reminding Farnor of a beaten dog, he was conspicuously avoiding looking directly at Rannick.

'We did not understand how great your power had become . . .' Gryss faltered momentarily then hastened on. 'How great a power you had achieved, Lord. How could we have known of such a wonder as you've just deigned to show us?'

Horror and shame filled Farnor. What was happening? He would not bow to this savage. This was Rannick, the murderer of his parents, the master of that creature . . .

But Harlen's hand held him fast and tightened as he tried to move.

'We have seen the measure of your great power.' Gryss was continuing. 'Forgive us, Lord, we beg of you. Let us go now so that we may spread the news of your greatness through the valley that all may know what we now know.'

There was a long silence. Farnor made another attempt to protest, but Harlen's grip became almost vicious and he could feel the man trembling.

'Go, then. Get out! And see that I am not troubled further with your foolishness.' Rannick's voice was strained and angry.

'Lord,' Gryss acknowledged, bowing lower.

Still avoiding Rannick's gaze, he clambered awkwardly to his feet and motioned the others to follow him. Harlen and Yakob exchanged a quick glance then they stood up quickly, yanked Farnor unceremoniously upright and, eyes lowered, dragged him towards the gate.

'What are you doing?' Farnor said, furiously struggling to keep his balance.

'Shut up,' Harlen and Yakob hissed simultaneously, hustling him on. Harlen's voice was shaking. 'Let's get out of here before he changes his mind.'

Before he fully realized what was happening, Farnor had been dragged through the shade of the gate arch and out into the sunlight again.

He clutched at normality in an attempt to reach

through to his two relentless guides. 'Where are the horses?' he asked.

They did not relax their pace. 'Over the hill and halfway to the capital by now, I expect,' Yakob replied acidly. 'Judging by the speed they left the castle.'

More gently, Harlen sought to reassure. 'No, they'll be grazing their way back to the inn.' Farnor, however, was indifferent to the fate of the horses. He finally gathered enough wit and strength to shake himself free. 'What's going on?' he demanded.

A powerful push in the back sent him lurching forward. He cried out as the impact jarred every pain in his body.

'Just keep moving,' came Gryss's grim voice from behind. 'We can slow down when we're out of sight of the castle.'

Farnor turned on him angrily, but there was a look on Gryss's face that he had never seen before: a profound fear coupled with an equally profound determination. He held the old man's gaze for a moment, then faltered before it. Without speaking he turned away from him and began limping along the road. Harlen and Yakob came either side of him but he rejected their support.

Nothing more was said for some time until, well away from the castle, they moved into the shade of some trees. 'Let's get off the road,' Gryss said. 'I want to have a look at Farnor.'

As they entered the trees the pace eased, as did also the discipline that had kept them stone-faced and silent.

'What happened? What was all that?' Yakob asked nobody in particular, a note near to hysteria in his voice. 'Where did those . . . flames . . . come from . . . or whatever they were?'

Gryss had taken Farnor's arm and was directing him to a grassy embankment. 'That was Rannick,' he replied, savagely, sitting Farnor down and crouching to examine him. 'That was our sour faced village lout coming to full flower. His family taint breaking out in him like a great boil.'

'But . . . ?'

'But nothing. You saw him. Somehow, he's in charge there now,' Gryss said, without turning from his examination of Farnor. 'And don't ask me how any of it's come about, or how he made those flames. It was no conjurer's trickery for sure. I can feel the heat of them still.' He shuddered. 'And that terrible colour as they faded . . .'

'And the noise,' Harlen added.

Gryss nodded and continued: 'From what he said, I suspect he only learned to make those flames yesterday at . . .' He hesitated and looked at Farnor unhappily. 'At Farnor's farm.'

Yakob had been pacing up and down, his face dark and frowning, but the reference to Farnor's personal tragedy made him stop and grimace in self-reproach. 'I'm sorry, Farnor,' he said. 'It's just that . . . what happened up there frightened me so much it made me forget you're the only one who's really been hurt.'

Farnor was in no mood for such concerns, however. 'What did happen?' he demanded. 'And why are we running away from that murderous dog? I want him . . .' He cried out and pushed Gryss away roughly. 'Watch what you're doing, you idiot. That hurt.'

Gryss regained his balance, then his hand shot out and slapped Farnor across his already bruised face. 'And you watch your lip, young Farnor. You nearly got yourself killed, barging in there like that. Not to mention the rest of us for following you.'

'I never asked you—' Farnor began.

'Enough!' Gryss thundered.

524

Then he abandoned his examination and sat down by his patient, his head in his hands.

No one spoke.

A small bird fluttered to the ground nearby, studied the motionless quartet with a cold yellow eye for a moment and then flew off again.

The rapid pulse of its beating wings made Gryss look up.

'Come on,' he said, turning back to Farnor and putting a hesitant hand on his shoulder. 'You've been badly knocked about, and we've all been badly frightened. Let me see if there's anything that needs immediate attention and then we'll go back to my cottage.' He looked round at Harlen and Yakob. 'Perhaps before we get there one of us can think of how we're going to break the news to the rest of the village.'

Rannick rode slowly through the woods. Outwardly he was icily calm, but inwardly his mood oscillated between craven fear and blinding fury: fear that forces were arising that could oppose him in the fulfilment of his destiny, and fury that he could not identify the source of this opposition.

The demonstration of his new-found powers had seemingly been successful. Certainly it had impressed the men, and it had brought that old fool Gryss and the others literally to their knees. That at least was some consolation. He had been right, and Nilsson wrong. All the villagers needed was a display of power and they would present no future problems. Diplomacy and goodwill were items he might choose to use later as his domain spread, but for now why squander them?

But this was trivial. He snatched his mind back to his main concern. His demonstration had been, in reality, a disaster. He rubbed his arm where Katrin had stabbed him. It had been a savage gash, long and deep, but if he rolled up his sleeve he would see now only a thin, well-healed scar. Since his contact with the creature and the knowledge he had gained thereby, his healing skills had developed incredibly. But he would willingly have given his entire arm for the truth that had been revealed to him as a result of Katrin's fearsome attack.

Revealed then, and made manifest by the destruction of the Yarrance farmhouse and revealed further in the darkness into which he had entered afterwards. The darkness of the strange and secret journey that the spirit of the creature had carried him on, taking him to the places between and beyond the worlds where the power was to be found.

Such knowledge!

His hands tightened about the reins of his horse as he recaptured the ecstasy of his discovery; of the vistas opening before him.

And now . . .

His rapture became a hollow, ringing mockery.

Now, when the golden road of his destiny was growing ever wider and easier he was opposed.

He opened his mouth and shouted a cry of fury and hatred at the silent will that had come from nowhere and laid its dead hand across the way through which the power came; had unmade that which he had made and taken the great power from him, leaving him only the power of this world.

Birds rose noisily into the air and his horse pranced its forelegs. Rannick reached out and silenced it. The power of this world was sufficient for most things. But . . .

He reined the horse to a halt. The memory of that other presence loomed dark and ominous in his mind, dominating his every thought, an unexpected shadow across his future. And yet, for all its effectiveness in

526

denying him the power, it had been hesitant, unsure; fearful, almost.

In fact fearful, definitely, he decided.

He clenched his fists. He would not be defied thus! Least of all by some craven interferer. Excuses began to pour into his thoughts. The opposition had taken him unawares, he had been unprepared. It would not happen again, he would be ready for it; he would destroy it if it came again.

But the doubt that permeated his inner ranting enraged him further. Could he risk such another confrontation? Who could say what this other power could do, or from whence it came? He needed to know much more about it.

He knew that the creature, too, had felt it, and felt it powerfully. Yet the very howling of its anger and defiance across the valley heightened the wavering uncertainty that, for the first time, he had sensed in his savage companion.

And it had recognized that which had opposed them! It had known such a power before and feared it. The memory of the creature's doubt mingled with his own to bring his thoughts to their inexorable conclusion: the source of this opposition must be found and destroyed.

He slipped down from his horse and released it. It moved away from him, but it needed no tether to prevent it from wandering for it had been schooled in the consequences of any form of disobedience to its new master. Rannick nodded to himself. He knew now why he had ridden out from the castle after Gryss and the others had left. He had to commune with his dark ally. Had to be close to it. Somewhere silent and away from the oppressive presence of Nilsson and his wretched band.

Together he and the creature must travel the ways

between the worlds until the creature scented the source of the power and he, Rannick, identified the will behind it. For it was someone he knew, he was sure. There had been a familiarity about it that kept returning to him, dancing tantalizingly in and out of his awareness.

But who?

He motioned the horse further away. He needed to be free from its swamping animal fears, needed to touch the ground, to be aware of everything about him so that he could be aware of himself and bring a quietness to his thinking.

He began to walk through the trees. His horse followed him reluctantly, keeping a considerable distance behind him.

Was it one of Nilsson's men? It could have been, Rannick supposed. His acceptance by them was not as complete as they pretended. Some were wholeheartedly his, their lustful greed leaking from them like a rich incense. But others paid only a dutiful obeisance, shot through with fear and doubt.

But these were of no import; lesser spirits, dispensable should need arise.

The familiarity that he had sensed in the power that had thwarted him returned briefly, flitting at the edge of his consciousness. But it defied examination, vanishing when he turned to confront it.

Frustration and anger rose to cloud his mind for some time. As it gradually waned, he dismissed Nilsson's men. The familiarity had stirred vague images of times long before the arrival of the troop, and, apart from that, any difficulties with Nilsson's men would have shown themselves by now.

No, it was someone in the village.

But who?

The anger bubbled up again, but he forced it down ruthlessly, forging it into an icy hatred.

Gryss? Yakob? Harlen? Farnor? Surely not. Three old men and a battered, broken youth who could scarcely stand. There could be no opposition there. The merest touch would scatter their pathetic spirits like dried leaves in autumn.

But who?

He snarled as the question pressed in on him. It did not matter who. He could not answer the question here and now, so he would not allow it to be asked again.

He walked on steadily, following the warm lure of the creature's will. As he passed through a small clearing he found himself moving to its shaded edge, instinctively avoiding the sunshine. He permitted himself a bitter smile at this response to the creature's dark nature, which increasingly mingled with his own: it had little love for the daylight, and none at all for such bright sunshine.

Soon, my pet, he thought. Soon I'll be with you. We can rest together in the darkness of your lair and ready ourselves for the hunt tonight.

A lustful anticipation flooded through him.

In the absence of any inspiration on the weary journey back from the castle, Gryss broke the news of the murder of Garren and Katrin and the seizure of the valley simply and bluntly to a hastily gathered meeting of the Council.

There were as many reactions as there were Councillors present, ranging from the fatalistic to the massively belligerent. Unlike the last meeting, Gryss did not let the uproar continue too long. Then it had seemed that time was ahead of them and that they could patiently await events. Now those events had happened and, they being more desperate in character than anything he could have possibly imagined, Gryss saw no benefit to be gained by allowing a gentle proceeding.

'We have no choice but to accept the reality of this,' he shouted above the din, going straight to the conclusion that the previous meeting had reached. He repeated it as the noise fell. 'We have no choice, my friends. We're trapped in our own valley. Trapped by armed and ruthless men who themselves have been subdued by one of our own.'

The mood of the meeting tumbled between stunned shock at the untimely and brutal deaths of Garren and Katrin – some wept openly – and, initially, open disbelief of the news of Rannick's transformation. However, being valley dwellers, the Councillors had that profound pragmatism that comes as a consequence of living close to the mysteries of the land, and none would fly in the face of the combined testimony of Gryss, Harlen and Yakob, however much they would have wished to. Further, Rannick was known by all and, eventually, both shock and disbelief turned into anger. Gryss allowed some time to be spent in the general telling and retelling of old tales about the ill-natured labourer and his forebears, and in declamations of how none of this would have happened, if he had been treated this way, or that way, or forbidden to do this, or allowed to do that; and so on.

But he was stark in his description of the probable fate of anyone who chose to consider Rannick as the man they all imagined they knew.

'You'll die for your pains, and none too pleasantly either. He regarded it as an honour for Garren and Katrin that they died by his hand.'

The very quietness of the utterance of this revelation brought a fearful silence to the meeting.

'Murder's murder,' someone ventured after a while. 'It's the King's business, I suppose. As is the seizing of his castle. We should get word to the capital.'

'I know,' Gryss said. 'But Jeorg was caught trying

to do just that and he only escaped with his life because of some whim on Rannick's part. Now he's said categorically that anyone who tries to leave will be killed.' He shrugged his shoulders unhappily. 'I don't know what to say, let alone what to do.' He looked at the waiting faces of his friends sitting around the Council table. Their fear and anger were almost palpable. It came over him that all he wanted to do was run away, go back to his cottage, close the door behind him and just . . . sit; leave the problem to someone else. For a moment he found himself wishing fervently that this was all some awful dream and that he would wake up to the sun streaming through his window and to the everyday problems of life that had seemed to be such a penance but a few weeks ago.

But none of his inner turmoil reached either his face or his voice. Instead he said, calmly and authoritatively, 'I think what we have to do is to make sure that everyone understands what has happened and to ensure that no one does anything foolish. In my estimation, crossing Rannick would bring dire consequences not only on the person who did it but on anyone else nearby. You all know what a spiteful swine he was.' He closed his eyes for a moment in self-reproach. 'And no language like that, even in private.' There was a stir amongst his listeners. 'I mean it,' he said sharply. 'Those . . . bandits . . . call him *Lord* Rannick, presumably for a damn good reason. You'll do the same if you—'

Several disparaging voices interrupted him.

'*Lord* Rannick, indeed! I'll lord him, the—'

'Yes you will,' Gryss said, before any of the protests could gather momentum. He pointed to Harlen and Yakob. 'You'll do what we did. You'll lord him, and you'll go down on your bended knees and call him wonderful or whatever else he wants, if you've got two

531

grains of sense in your head. Trust me. You want no demonstration of what he can do.'

His anger subdued the outburst, but other voices had been released by it.

'We can't sit around and do nothing,' they said, quietly and reasonably, echoing Marna's plaint.

'I know,' Gryss said, wearily. He stared down at the table helplessly for some time. 'But all I can think of is watch and wait. Whatever dreadful game's being played here, we're small pieces and easily removed from the board. If we avoid trouble, appease them a little, we'll probably be able to find out more about them. Get to know how they think . . .' He managed a rueful smile. 'Perhaps in a week or so, we might be a great deal wiser than we are now, and far better placed to decide what to do.'

It was an unsatisfactory answer, he knew, but he had no other.

'You don't appease a mad dog,' someone muttered.

'And you don't pull its tail either, unless you've got a stick big enough to deal with it,' Gryss retorted, impatiently.

It was virtually the end of the meeting.

Later a large crowd gathered on the village green to hear the same news. The light was fading when Gryss arrived, and as he climbed on to a table that someone had taken from the inn a few stars were beginning to appear in the purpling eastern sky. They were mirrored by a sprinkling of lanterns and small sunstones amongst his audience.

He told them what had happened as he had told the Council, and their response was the same, though it was louder and wilder and the clamour lasted a great deal longer. More than once some of the younger men had to be restrained from dashing off immediately to storm the castle and drag Rannick to justice. Gryss

532

found the experience of his many years as a negotiator of disputes, as a calmer of quarrels and a soother of hurts sorely stretched. He prevailed, however; here a sharp command, a caustic rebuttal; there a friendly word, a laughing dismissal. Words, gestures, expressions all played their part in swaying the crowd away from hasty action and towards quieter, more serious considerations.

He ended, 'I'll run second to no one in my love for Garren and Katrin Yarrance, or in my desire to see justice done. But Katrin herself saw the truth clearly enough: "They're all fighting men. Used to brutality and stabbing and killing. There's none in the whole valley could stand against any of them and hope to live should need arise."' He paused. 'Her words, my friends. Tragically accurate. And now these men are obeying the orders of Rannick.' He paused again to allow the words to sink in. 'To move against them will gain us only the same fate as she suffered. Living is the way to honour the dead, not dying. Her own son was almost killed when he sought in his grief to confront Rannick. We must be circumspect in all things, no matter what our inner feelings. We find ourselves locked in the pen with a wild bull. Watchfulness, silence and stillness will be our best allies.'

His endeavours, though, left him ill at ease as he watched the crowd disperse into the night, pale faces fading into the gloom to become shadows through which flickered the lights of the lanterns and sunstones.

'I feel as much a murderer as Rannick,' he said softly to Harlen as he took his supporting hand and clambered off the table.

'What do you mean?' Harlen asked.

Gryss shook his head. 'I don't know,' he said sadly. 'I just feel . . .' He brought his two fists down on the table. 'I feel like getting my old axe out, marching up to

533

the castle and hacking my way through everything until I get to Rannick, regardless of what happens. And yet I tell them to be calm, to be thoughtful, to do nothing rash. I can't help feeling that I'm betraying them. Continuing to betray them, in fact. Perhaps that's what we should do. Trust the judgement of the youngsters. March up there and fight them.'

Harlen laid a hand on his shoulder, but made no comment.

Chapter 36

Gryss had returned to his cottage with Yakob and Harlen and the battered and silent Farnor.

'We're all right,' Gryss had said, by way of hasty reassurance to an alarmed Marna. 'I'll tell you everything in a moment.'

Then he had given Farnor a more thorough examination than he had been able to do on the road and, finding he was only bruised, ordered him to stay at the cottage and rest.

'I've got to arrange a Council meeting, then a village meeting,' Gryss said to him, finally. 'While you're here, help Marna with Jeorg if you can.' He put his hand to his brow as he spoke. 'I'll have to see Jeorg's wife, too.' He closed his eyes and blew out an unhappy breath at this remembrance, but no one volunteered to ease his burden.

Farnor ignored him except for a slight nod that some residual courtesy made him make, and Gryss's face was taut with controlled impatience when he turned to Marna and gestured towards Jeorg's room. 'How's he been?' he asked.

'He keeps waking up,' Marna said. 'I've been telling him what happened, but I don't know how much he's taken in.'

'Was he distressed, agitated?'

'Not particularly,' Marna replied. 'Not after I told him you'd heard what he said about Rannick.' She smiled weakly. 'He thought he might have been dreaming.' Then she glanced at the room they had just left. 'What's the matter with Farnor?' she asked, softly.

She clasped her hands tightly in front of her to prevent their trembling as Gryss told of Farnor's beating at the hands of Nilsson, but she went pale as she heard about Rannick and his strange powers. Her only question, however, was about Farnor's dark mood.

'The beating he received was no light matter, Marna,' Gryss replied. 'He'll be hurting badly, and feeling humiliated, degraded. But I think he's the way he is because of his grief.'

Marna did not understand. 'Why doesn't he shout and scream, or cry or something?' she said.

'Grief takes everyone differently.' Gryss grimaced anxiously. 'To be honest, he'd be better if he did shout and scream. He's penning too many things up inside himself.' He shook his head. 'It'll do him no good. These things have to come out sooner or later, one way or another.'

He made a hasty gesture to forestall any further questions. 'I haven't much time, Marna. I'll have to get this meeting arranged. Just talk to Farnor if he wants to talk. Failing that, leave him alone. Just be here.'

Thus, while Gryss was contending with the Councillors and the villagers, Marna found herself sitting opposite Farnor by Jeorg's bedside. Uncertain about the gloomy figure alone in the back room making no effort to light a lantern as darkness came on, she had asked him to help her lift Jeorg into a sitting position. Then to detain him she had forced herself to say, 'Please stay with me, Farnor.' She had not quite managed the plaintive tone she had intended, but Farnor was too preoccupied with his own thoughts to be sensitive to such subtleties. Indeed, despite her concern for him, the look on his face as he sat down in response to this request brought an acid comment to her mouth which took her some effort to bite back.

The effects of Gryss's sleeping draught having gradually worn off, Jeorg, though weak and in some pain, was sufficiently awake to note the tension in the room.

'What's the matter?' he asked, looking first at Farnor and then Marna. 'What's happened?'

Farnor did not reply. Marna hesitated, uncertain what to say: she could not lie and she did not want to tell him the truth.

'What's happened?' Jeorg asked again, his manner both insistent and anxious.

Marna took his bandaged hand and said, very softly, 'Rannick and Nilsson have killed Garren and Katrin, and burned down the farm.'

Jeorg's eyes widened in horror, then his face contorted and his free hand came up to cover it. It was some time before he lowered it, and when he did his eyes were shining with tears. He reached out and laid his hand on Farnor's shoulder, but Farnor brushed it aside. Marna squeezed Jeorg's hand and shook her head, mouthing the words, 'Leave him.'

Jeorg nodded. 'This is awful,' he said, quietly. 'Garren and Katrin. Murdered. I can't believe it.' He shook his head. 'And yet I can, after what happened to me. If only I'd been more careful. I'd have been well on my way to the capital by now. Perhaps . . .' His voice tailed off.

'I don't think it would have made any difference,' Marna said. 'We don't even know why it happened. Farnor came back from the fields, and . . .' Her voice fell. 'Just found them. He went to find Rannick, but Nilsson did that to him.' She nodded towards her silent companion.

Jeorg turned carefully to him. 'You're probably lucky to be alive,' he said, simply. 'As am I. I don't know what's happened to Rannick, but he's a mad dog.'

'He'll be a dead one if I catch him alone,' Farnor said, viciously, still staring fixedly ahead.

537

'Don't be stupid, Farnor,' Marna hissed. 'Jeorg's right. You're lucky to be alive after dashing into the castle like that.'

Farnor's lip curled. 'It wasn't your parents he killed,' he said, sourly. Marna bit her lip, and this time it was Jeorg who took her hand.

'How long have I been asleep?' Jeorg asked, to break the painful silence that ensued. Then, more anxiously, 'Does my wife know what's happened?'

'About a day,' Marna replied. 'And no, your wife doesn't know what's happened yet. Gryss was going to see her after the Council meeting.'

Jeorg pulled a wry face, but the effort made him wince. 'She'll be here shortly then, I expect,' he said, ruefully. 'And I'll be out of the fire and on to the anvil.'

In spite of herself, Marna smiled at his manner.

Then Farnor stood up and moved towards the door.

'Where are you going?' Marna asked.

'Out,' Farnor replied, tersely.

'Gryss said you should stay here and rest,' she shouted after the departing figure. There was no reply, and with an oath she ran after him.

She caught him at the door. 'Gryss said you should stay,' she said again, taking his arm.

Farnor screwed up his face as if he had just eaten something unpleasant, and wrenched open the door despite Marna's restraining hand. 'Gryss can go to hell,' he said, brutally. 'And so can you, Marna. Get out of my way. I've got things to do.'

Then he was limping out into the darkness.

Shocked by this outburst, Marna was unable to respond. It was not until she heard the clatter of hooves as he mounted one of the horses retrieved by Gryss and the others on their return that she found her voice.

'Farnor, where are you going?' she called into the night. But it was to no avail. The only reply was the sound of the hooves gathering speed.

She slammed the door shut and, turning, nearly tripped over the dog. 'Shift, damn you,' she snapped, as she staggered past it.

'What's he doing?' Jeorg asked, trying to lever himself out of the bed as she returned to his room.

Marna's face was a mixture of rage and distress, and she was on the verge of tears. 'I don't know, the stupid sod,' she blurted out. 'And you stay where you are.' An angry finger shot out purposefully at Jeorg, and he stopped his attempted escape. 'There'll be enough trouble with that idiot wandering the countryside trying to get himself killed without you getting up too soon. You can wait for your wife to arrive . . . or Gryss.'

Jeorg lay back, not unrelieved to be the butt of Marna's anger. He could feel the terror of his treatment by Nilsson and Rannick receding a little, but his hasty movement had heightened the weakness and pain that pervaded his body.

'He'll be all right,' he said, in an attempt to comfort Marna. 'He's a sensible lad at heart.'

Marna shook her head. 'They killed his parents, Jeorg. For no reason. Just killed them. It's done something to him. You saw how he was. I think it's driven him crazy. I think he's probably riding back up to the castle right now.' Her face twisted in pain. 'They'll kill him for sure this time. I should have stopped him.'

'Don't be silly, Marna,' Jeorg tried again. 'You couldn't have stopped him. And anyway, he won't be crazy enough to go back for another beating off Nilsson, believe me.' He winced as a casual movement brought him another unexpected pain. 'He probably needed to be alone. Perhaps he wanted to cry. Knowing Farnor, that'd be difficult for him in front of you.'

Marna sat down heavily in the chair that she had occupied for much of the day and, leaning forward, put her head in her hands. Her mind was awash with swirling, nameless fears and with images of Farnor alone in the darkness, and of Rannick, crazed and powerful, and, most sinister of all, though she had not thought about it for some time, images of the strange, savage creature that linked both men.

Farnor rode through the darkness. The moon gave some light, but the horse had sufficient sense to ignore the urgings of its rider and proceeded at a steady trot.

Each jolting step racked Farnor's beaten frame, but for a while he was oblivious to it. His whole being was still consumed by a black, driving desire to confront and destroy Rannick. On his immediate return with Gryss and the others, he had been struggling with the fear and humiliation that he had suffered during his beating by Nilsson. The humiliation in particular had risen to dominate him as the immediate pain of the beating had begun to fade. Its roots seemed to go deeper even than the cringing childishness to which he had been reduced, and as Gryss had surmised he felt degraded in a way that he would never have imagined possible.

But, in its turn, this too had faded – or, rather, been overwhelmed as a terrible urging had arisen to seek out the source of this horror and destroy it. It, too, seemed to come from some depths beyond his awareness, if not from somewhere quite beyond him.

Yet, as Jeorg had declared, Farnor was a sensible lad at heart and gradually the complaints of his body began to force their way through his dark passion, bringing with them shadows of the fear and humiliation once more. He allowed the horse to slow to a walk. His hand went to his belt; the knife that had killed his mother was still there. More humiliation: Nilsson had considered him too trifling an opponent even to be disarmed while he was beating him.

Farnor bared his teeth in unconscious imitation of his tormentor, then drew out the knife. He tested its edge. It was as sharp as if he had honed it only today. But he would have expected nothing else from this. It was a fine knife; his mother's favourite.

'And I'll split you open with it, Rannick,' he said to the night. 'And that obscenity you've conjured up.'

But even as he spoke the words he knew their falseness. They were no more than the petulant swearing of a thwarted child. To go to the castle would be to die.

And yet . . .

And yet, though the words were hollow, the intention was not. That was solid and true. Rannick must be destroyed for what he had done. And destroyed by him, if he was ever to know any peace. A memory of his parents leaning on the farmyard gate suddenly surged over him: his father looking out across the fields and his mother, prompted by some wry remark, turning to slap his arm while at the same time smiling so that the young girl inside burst out through the long-married wife and mother.

The vision was almost unbearable. Farnor clenched his teeth and twisted his fist painfully into his thigh to prevent it from overwhelming him. He must not give way, he told himself. That would be no honour to his parents. He must do what he had to do: finish the task that he had set himself.

The horse had stopped, and he kicked it on again. The sudden, vivid memory of his parents seemed to have left him hollow and empty inside. The future had ceased to exist. Plans that he had never really known he had made were gone. Plans for gradually acquiring his father's knowledge and skills and for taking over the work of the farm as his father grew older. Plans perhaps for marrying and having children, to elevate his parents to the status of grandparents and to ensure the ancient continuity of the line. Vague though they might have been, they were gone utterly now. All that the future offered was a menacing blackness beyond which lay only further darkness.

And it was Rannick's fault!

The hatred began to return, filling the emptiness inside him with comforting purposefulness. He *would* destroy Rannick, one way or another. He closed his hand around the knife hilt. He would indeed split him from end to end for what he had done. He would come to his future again, through Rannick's blood.

Trailing in the wake of this turmoil, and slave to its decisions, came his rational mind. If he could not kill Rannick by confronting him at the castle, then he must kill him by some act of stealth. He must come upon him when he was alone.

Without realizing what he was doing, he turned the horse off the road and into the lane that led to the farm. He was about to jerk it back on to the road when he changed his mind and allowed the animal its head.

Rooting through the blackened rubble of the farmhouse and through the horrific, disordered familiarity of the storeshed was grim work, but he steeled himself to it, once again fighting down those thoughts and memories that strove to unman him and divert him from his purpose. For his purpose would carry him through all things now if he so willed it.

Thus, a while later, Farnor returned to the road with his horse carrying saddle bags filled with food and such tools and other items as he would need to survive alone in the woods.

He could not assail the castle, but he could quietly besiege it. Watching the comings and goings of the men, learning their ways, their routines, watching and waiting until that moment when Rannick would venture out alone. For venture out alone he surely would. Sooner or later, Farnor knew, though he could not have said how he knew it, Rannick would wander to the north to commune with the creature. And when he did . . .

Farnor laid his hand on the knife in his belt.

But he was going the wrong way. This road would lead him directly to the castle. He tugged the reins gently and the horse turned obediently off the road.

Slowly, Farnor rode over the rolling fields in a wide arc, well away from the castle. On the few occasions when it was clearly in view, he could see little or no activity: just a few slits of light along the walls and the odd torch glimmering on the battlements.

Had their fun for the day, Farnor mused bitterly. A brief vision of the future of the valley under the heel of Rannick and these outsiders came to him, but he dismissed it. He had his own problem to deal with. And, in any event, once that had been dealt with, the head of the serpent would have been cut off and the body should not be too difficult to destroy.

Then he was among the trees. The trees that only weeks ago had seemed as far distant from his world as the moon overhead. So much change so quickly. The thought made him feel uneasy. But then he had seen great boulders buffeted from their ancient resting places by streams suddenly swollen by a rapid thaw or a summer storm. And wasn't he himself greatly changed from the person he had been but those few weeks ago?

Change was the way of things. Usually slow, imperceptible even, but sometimes shatteringly fast. It could not be disputed.

He debated which way to turn. Apart from being dark, this terrain was quite unfamiliar to him. Still, woods were woods; these could not be vastly different from those further down the valley. Hiding places would abound, as would food and shelter when need arose. He would have to find something tonight and then explore in the morning.

A night bird flew noisily out of a nearby tree, startling him. His horse whinnied. Calming it, he clicked it forward into the darkness.

Gradually his eyes adjusted to the ill-lit gloom amongst the trees, though he could distinguish little more than shadows within shadows. All around him was silence, except for the tread of his horse and the occasional scuffle of some hunting night creature. He dismounted and led the horse.

He had not walked very far however, when he felt suddenly exhausted. He was still stiff and sore from the beating he had received, and the emotional upheavals of the day had drained him utterly. Without further consideration, he tethered the horse, took a blanket from his bag and lay down between the jutting roots of a large tree. He fell asleep in the middle of a vague, muttered instruction to his horse.

Rannick and his companion moved among the shifting realms that lay between the worlds among which could be found the great sources of power. They were searching, though for what or who they did not know. The creature was fretful and angry, its natural malevolence bubbling uncontrollably into Rannick's mind from time to time so that he felt both its fear and its fury at this ancient enemy which had returned to mar their progress.

Rannick, however, kept his mind above this primeval anger, kept it alert for some sign that he could recognize. Tonight would be the hunt, tomorrow would be the kill – if the prey could be identified. His journeying tonight would be along the screaming highways of nightmare but his journeying tomorrow would be simple and prosaic, and with cutting steel in his hand. He could not risk using his power against this offender, with his unknown skills, nor, for the same reason, could he risk sending Nilsson's men to do the deed. It would be a task of smiling surprise and vicious suddenness and one that he alone must do.

So they searched, an unholy duo bound inexorably together by desire and driven now by a fear of the shadow that had threatened their pursuit of that desire.

Farnor slept, too tired to dream. His young body, older in wisdom by far than its occupant, held him still and silent while it worked to repair the ravages of the day. From time to time the tiny rodents and other mammals that owned the night forest would investigate him, twitching noses cautiously, testing his scent and advising hasty departure. An occasional insect clambered painstakingly over him on its own nightly rounds. His horse stood motionless nearby.

The moon moved slowly across the sky.

The castle lay quiet, as did the village, though there were many troubled dreams there.

Then, abruptly, Farnor was awake. Pain echoed through him as he moved, but some instinct kept him from crying out. He looked around into the darkness. He could just make out the dim form of his horse, silent and undisturbed.

What, then, had woken him? Distantly he seemed to hear voices, though perhaps they were no more than the memory of a fading dream mingling with the soft rustle of the leaves about him.

Yet, faint though it was, it was clear.

'Flee, mover, you are hunted.'

Farnor grunted questioningly, his throat dry. The

coarseness of the sound shattered the delicate texture of the dwindling words, if words they were, and they were gone, leaving only the familiar night sounds of the forest.

Farnor considered lying down again, but he was far from comfortable and, besides, he was now wide awake. Cautiously, he levered himself into a sitting position and peered into the darkness again. Nothing was untoward. No sudden silence had fallen; his horse was not restive. He frowned. 'Mover,' he whispered softly, trying to recapture the subtle meanings that he had felt hidden within the sound of the word.

But it meant nothing. His voice was as far from what he had heard as children's pictures in the dust were from the finely etched figures on the ring that hung outside Gryss's door.

He let out an irritated sigh. Whatever had happened, it had left him too awake to return to sleep while it was still too dark for him to search out a better hiding place.

As these thoughts wandered through his head so the memory of why he was here returned, and the darkness of the night seemed to enter his very soul.

Painfully he wrapped the blanket about himself and settled back against the tree trunk to wait for the dawn.

Slowly, he began to relax. Thoughts of his parents and of the wreckage of his home drifted into his mind, but he set them aside. He did this coldly, but as they continued to return he was obliged to resort to crushing them ruthlessly. There would be time enough for such indulgence when he had destroyed Rannick.

This inner turmoil angered him and after a while he stood up. Despite the warmth of the night, and the blanket around him, he shivered.

Yet he wasn't cold. Why then should he feel such a chill?

Then, with an impact that was almost physical, the presence of the creature was all about him. He flattened himself against the trunk of the tree and cast about desperately, looking for the special shadow within the shadows that would mark the presence of the animal. But there was nothing. Nor too, was his horse distressed, and it, surely, would have felt such a presence if it were nearby.

Yet it *was* all around him.

Farnor stood very still, scarcely daring to breathe. He must learn about this creature, for it was Rannick's creature. Or he its. Either way, to learn of one was to learn of the other.

The memory of the incident in the courtyard came back to him. Of something that had reached out from within him and denied the harm that was being brought here. The images meant nothing to him: places that were here and yet not here? Power that was great only because it did not truly belong?

Yet whatever they meant they were vivid and, he knew, accurately remembered.

As, too, was the memory that he had reached out and stopped this . . . unlawful – dangerous? – flow!

Or some part of him had.

He did not dwell on the thoughts, however; the pervasive presence of the creature forbade that. Farnor clung almost desperately to the knowledge that, whatever was happening, the thing itself was not nearby. He could rely on his horse and the forest dwellers to tell him that.

Nonetheless, he drew the knife from his belt and gripped it tightly.

As he did so, the thought formed in his head: I shall

kill you, you abomination. You do not belong. You never belonged.

The presence about him shifted, as if it had heard something. Farnor could feel its power, drawn again from a place which should not be here. He felt something stir faintly within him, but it faded as the creature's presence moved away again. There was something familiar about the way in which the presence came and went.

It was hunting, he realized sharply.

Then, chillingly, he felt another presence mingling with that of the creature, riding it almost, both guiding and following.

Rannick!

Farnor's grip on the knife tightened further.

He felt anger and hatred surging up inside him . . .

'Flee, mover, you have not—'

Farnor started as the voices whispered softly to him. His mind jerked towards them but that very action again dispelled the subtle sound and the message was lost to him.

Who are you? he thought, but there was no reply. Fearfully, he gritted his teeth and pressed himself back against the tree trunk.

Was he going insane? Quivering in the silent woods beyond the castle, clutching his mother's favourite knife and hearing voices, feeling the presence of a creature that he had never seen?

He felt as though his mind were teetering on the edge of a terrible darkness from which he could never return if he tumbled in. He heard the heavy thumping of his heart and the harsh rasping of his breath. All around he sensed forces moving, though to what end he could only begin to hazard.

It seemed to him that he stood on this fearful edge for an eternity of time, waiting.

Waiting . . .

But for what . . . ?

Faint ribbons of thought flitted through the darkness. Gryss, who had listened and believed; Marna, who had listened and believed; Rannick who had looked into the entrails of the slaughtered sheep and found – what . . . ? A wind that had slammed a wicket door on his arm. His hand reached for the bruised arm and squeezed it hard.

The pain cut through the darkness like distant lightning in the night sky, and the twisting ribbons of thought became like the pennants of an approaching army; sharp-etched against the gloom; confident and bold.

No! For all its appalling strangeness, what was happening was happening and it was real. It was no rambling disorder from inside himself.

I'm here, Rannick! Farnor called into the creature's watching silence.

'*No* . . .' came the voices in despair.

And, on the instant, Farnor felt the truth of their concern. For the presence of the creature was about him now as it had been on his flight back to the ruin of his home. Vast and overwhelming. Power pouring through huge rents in reality that must surely be beyond any repairing.

And with it was Rannick's will, malevolent and wild with rage.

'Farnor Yarrance,' Rannick whispered to himself in the darkness of his communion with the creature. 'Farnor Yarrance. It *was* you who defied me. Who stood in my light and marred my power.'

It was beyond belief that such a thing could be. That a beaten and broken farmer's boy should have such a skill. And that he should come now with a defiant challenge.

But in the same instant, he knew that his concerns had been of no account. For all that happened in the courtyard, the farm boy's will was no more than an autumn leaf caught in a winter wind. He could not prevail against the might that he, Rannick, now possessed: a might that grew daily both in its totality and in the refinement of its use.

Tomorrow Farnor Yarrance would pay the penalty for his rash interference. There could be no escape for him. Rannick smiled. There would be the joy of the hunt and then the joy of the slow destroying. That this would also serve to quell further the spirit of the villagers added an exquisite savour to the prospect.

Rannick wallowed in the glow of his triumph. Truly great powers were guiding and protecting him, to lead him so ingeniously to expose the one person in the valley who might have opposed him. His destiny, as ever, ran true.

But something was amiss.

The creature was disturbed. Rannick sensed its unease, and the awakening of its most ancient hunting instincts.

No, he instructed. Not in the village. Not yet. Your time for that will come. There will be enough to sate even you in the future. But not yet.

But though the creature heard and responded, still it stirred restlessly. Rannick felt his restraint tested, though in anxiety rather than defiance.

He had a fleeting image of fleeing prey.

Fleeing!

He jolted into wakefulness. As he had felt Farnor's puny challenge, so Farnor had felt the weight of his awesome response.

And he was running!

Rannick and the creature became as one.

Go! Rannick hissed into the lusting hunter. Go, hunt him down. He is yours. Let the whole valley be awakened to the ringing of his screams echoing from the peaks!

Chapter 37

Blind fear filled Farnor. The power pervading the eerie presence of both Rannick and the creature was formidable. There were strange stirrings in him, but nothing, he knew, could oppose what was now levied against him. He was a sapling in the path of an avalanche that could sweep away an entire forest.

Just as Nilsson's cruel fighting expertise had casually destroyed his shield of anger and hatred to leave him exposed, shivering and helpless against the icy blasts of reality, so now did Rannick's power.

All his intentions of watching the castle and patiently waiting for the time when he would come upon Rannick alone vanished before the weight of the ancient malevolence that was turning towards him.

He was dimly aware of the voices again, urgent this time, and fear-laden.

'Flee, mover, flee!'

But he needed no such urging. Almost without realizing what he was doing, he was mounting his horse and kicking it forward. Instinctively it turned towards the village.

'No!' said the voices inside him.

They coincided with his own raucous shout, 'No!' The valley was Rannick's now; he could not go that way. He yanked the reins violently. Unused to such treatment, the horse reared and nearly unseated him, but desperation kept him in the saddle. Then the horse leapt forward. Farnor grabbed at its mane to keep his balance then, as a low branch skimmed through his hair, he ducked and wrapped his arms about the horse's neck. As the horse gathered speed, he remained in this position.

All around him – indeed, almost part of him – the presence of Rannick and the creature swung to and fro, searching. It seemed to Farnor that there was nothing in the entire world except these two malevolent wills seeking him out: Rannick taunting, vicious and triumphant; the creature primordial and savage, and focused utterly on its ordained prey.

'Run, horse, run!' Farnor whispered, over and over, as if to cry out would be somehow to draw the attention of the searching creature.

And the horse ran, Farnor clinging to it like a terrified child to its mother, his bruised body begging for relief from the merciless pounding but his fear allowing it no voice. Dark-shadowed trunks flitted by, leafy branches reached down and brushed over him mockingly. Occasionally he became aware of the moon peering through the canopy above, as if it were galloping after him, marking his demented progress for the creature to follow.

And still the presence of the creature was about him, hunting, scenting.

Yet fragments of coherent thought broke through the relentless rhythm of Farnor's flight.

The creature could feel his presence, his naked fear, and it knew that he was fleeing. But it did not know where he was. Briefly he found that his vision was not his own. It was steadier, and closer to the ground; and the sky was different. And, too, strange scents pervaded him, feeding a swirling mass of ancient hatreds that some part of him shied away from, so once again he was himself, pain-racked and frantic, hanging on desperately to his galloping horse.

Whatever else the creature might be, he discovered, it was still an animal and, in seeking him out, it was constrained by the limitations of its body.

The creature's frustration and anger washed over him even as the thought came to him.

'Run, horse. Run!'

So much pain!

'Find him. Find him. He is yours,' Rannick encouraged.

Distance. Surely nothing could outrun this charging animal that he was clinging to? The creature had the woods to roam to find his scent before it could begin to pursue him.

Yet Rannick was gloating. *He* had no doubts about the success of this hunt.

Even before Farnor could ponder the reasons for this, a sudden breeze struck him from one side. The horse veered under the impact, but did not slow down appreciably. To Farnor's horror, the breeze was redolent with the presence of Rannick.

He had searchers of his own.

Farnor's stomach tightened agonizingly. He was found!

'Run, horse. Run!'

The breeze gathered strength and began to tear at him. Farnor wanted to scream his terrifying urgency to the horse, but he knew it would be futile. Besides, the sudden tormenting wind had, in itself, put more fear into the horse. All Farnor could do now was hold on, tighter and tighter.

He caught another fleeting glimpse of the sky. A pattern of stars struck him. They pointed to a solitary star.

North. He was heading north. For an instant, fears mingled. The fear of Rannick and creature, and the fear of what lay ahead in the mysterious land to the north. The Great Forest, whose existence had hovered with an uneasy menace in the background of his childhood years. But that fear was distant, and hedged about by as many years of homely security, and it was as nothing compared to the horror gathering behind him.

The buffeting breeze stopped as abruptly as it had started. Farnor felt Rannick's will luring it back; he knew that it would be carrying its precious perfume back to the creature.

'Run, horse. Run!'

And then the hatred about him changed. It changed from being vague and dispersed to being sharp and focused. Farnor could feel the creature pausing to test the scent that it had been given, and then gathering its terrible resources to commit them to the simple, single-minded pursuit of its prey.

The moon still dashed relentlessly overhead, marking his passage.

And the creature was coming!

Even the horse seemed to sense the change in their common danger. Its neck bent low and its pounding speed increased. It occurred to Farnor that the horse was quite likely to run itself to death, but his own terror swamped any compassion. All that mattered was that it outran this dreadful pursuer and gave him a chance to reach some kind of safety.

'Run, horse. Run!'

Farnor was the creature again. Moving faster now by far than when it had been hunting to and fro seeking his scent. Briefly he tried to use this strange possession to redirect it, to make it stumble, to run it into a tree, a bush . . . anything. But to no avail. He was himself again on the instant, brushed aside effortlessly by a greater will.

There was no hope for him except speed.

And he was moving downhill now, he realized. They must have passed the head of the valley and be heading down into the land to the north.

He wondered where he would find himself if he

survived this chase, but the thought was gone almost before he noted it. He could feel the creature closing the distance between them relentlessly, yet as its presence about him grew stronger, he felt Rannick's growing weaker. A faint spark of hope began to glimmer in the darkness.

But it fanned into no great blaze. The creature's presence was as massive as it was baleful. Indeed, as Rannick's influence seemed to wane so the creature's savagery grew.

And then he could hear it. Penetrating even into the thunderous tumult of his flight came an intermittent baying, partly a frantic, frustrated screaming, partly a demented roaring.

And the horse heard it too. It missed its footing as its fear began to turn into outright panic. Belatedly Farnor's concern turned towards his mount. If the horse stumbled at this speed then, if the fall did not kill him, the creature certainly would. With an effort he changed his goading litany to a more soothing one.

'Easy, easy,' he whispered.

It had no effect; the sound of the creature was growing louder. Farnor's instincts overwhelmed his reason.

'Run, horse. Run!'

Then for the briefest of moments, but with appalling horror, he saw himself, with keen night-eyed vision, draped over the neck of the horse scarcely a hundred paces away, galloping through the trees. As he became himself again he felt an acid, lustful taste in his mouth, and a chilling hint of the ancient and awful emotions now dominating the creature.

He managed to turn his head to peer into the darkness behind, to search for his pursuer, but he could see nothing. He had not the vision of this dweller in the darkness.

He closed his eyes and buried his head in the throbbing neck of the horse.

And waited.

Somewhere in the heart of his terror he knew that he was beyond Rannick's will. But it was of no consequence: his terrible envoy was here to do his bidding, and within a count of heartbeats its dreadful crushing jaws would be upon him.

His whole being filled suddenly and totally with the comforting musty scent of the horse and the rich night perfumes of the trees and crushed forest turf.

But the creature's presence penetrated this flimsy shield and reached right into him. From deep in the darkness of his inner self, Farnor felt a scream forming. And a knowledge that it was what was needed, it was what the creature wanted. It would appease its dreadful lust; turn its rage away.

Yet the scream would not come. Some other inner resource demanded resistance against this pursuing torturer. It reached out and denied the scream, then ensnared and strangled it. But Farnor was scarcely aware of this dispute. Verging on unconsciousness, his dominant thought was to hold on to the horse and to will it forward still faster.

'Run, horse. Run,' he mouthed, but no sound came now.

Behind him, the creature drew nearer with each breathless pace.

Rannick waited, alone in the darkness. Waited for the return of the creature and the knowledge that Farnor was no more. It disturbed him a little to have the creature beyond his influence, but he consoled himself with the thought that it needed no guidance from him to hunt down the fleeing youth, especially after he had given it his scent. And of course, it would return to him. It would never leave him. Brought once again to the world of men by who knew what great upheaval in its deep and ancient lair, it had waited for too long for such as he to abandon him now.

He had not realized it at the time, but the creature had been desperately weak when he had first ventured into the darkness to find it. Perhaps, he mused in his increasingly rare reflective moments, had it not been so, then he might have perished for his temerity in striving to master it. But master it he had. Once again his destiny had guided him truly.

He had kept it silent in its lair as the villagers had first searched for it, and then stood guard, waiting for it to blunder into their feeble traps. Then he had nurtured it on sheep he had stolen in the confusion. And, throughout, he had grown with it as its terrible power had burgeoned, their two ambitions feeding one from the other.

But it had only been after the killing of Nilsson's men that he had come nearer to learning of its true nature. For it drew qualities from the killing of men that it could draw from no other prey – not even the horse it had taken. Qualities other than mere sustenance. Qualities that fed its dark soul.

From wherever it had come, it had not simply been trained to kill men, nor had it accidentally acquired a taste for them. To hunt, destroy and kill men was engrained in the distorted spiralling weave of its very nature. It had been bred for that purpose and seemingly no other and nothing, save death, could divert it. Yet a deeper purpose had been written into the making of the creature and all its kind, and those with the gift could reach into its depths and unleash that purpose. Could be drawn into the places beyond, where the power lay. Could bring it here, where its use was unfettered.

And such a gift was Rannick's.

He closed his eyes ecstatically at the prospect of the creature's return.

It seemed to him that with each journey beyond, his enslavement of the creature increased. The vision to see that it enslaved him also was denied him.

Hitherto, since his meeting with the creature, Rannick's knowledge and skill in the use of the power had grown apace, unhindered by anything other than his own ignorance and inexperience. Then there had appeared that strange marring, that sealing of the ways that had thwarted his demonstration to Gryss and the others. Not that they had noticed it, he presumed, but it had struck him like a physical blow, an icy blast of retribution, and his rapturous vision of his future had faltered and trembled.

But now that he had identified the cause, and found it wanting, all would be well. Nothing further could stand in his path. Soon *all* would kneel before his might.

It was good.

So he waited in the darkness. Waited for the faint gossamer touch that would tell him that the creature was coming near again. For when it came near, it would not merely have fed on its most desired fare, it would have destroyed the only person who could have defied him.

'Didn't you talk to him?' Gryss said, his voice a mixture of anger and hopelessness.

Marna answered the question yet again. 'How many times do I have to tell you?' she said, heatedly. 'Of course I talked to him, but me talking and him listening are two different things.' Her mouth tightened into a thin line and tears of frustration shone in her eyes.

Gryss finally gave up and sat down heavily. He rested his head on his hand. 'I'm sorry, Marna,' he said, quietly. 'I shouldn't rant at you. You couldn't have done other than you did.' He looked at Harlen, who had returned with him from the meeting along with Jeorg's wife. 'And there's nothing we can do either except wait and see what news comes down from the castle tomorrow.'

Marna's voice shook as she said, 'Do you think he'll be all right?'

Gryss wanted to say, 'Of course he will. He's a sensible lad, and who'd want to hurt him? Farnor, of all people. He's not got a hurtful bone in his body.' But he knew that he could not. This was not some child late home for his meal on a sunny evening, or smitten with spots and belly ache. And Marna was no fretful parent.

'No,' he said. 'If he goes back to the castle they'll probably kill him out of hand.'

He heard Marna take in a sharp breath, but he did not relent his words. She did not speak for some time, and the voices of Jeorg and his wife drifted into the room; or, more correctly, the voice of the wife and the occasional submissive grunt from Jeorg.

'Go home and rest,' Gryss said more gently. 'Get what sleep you can. You've done more than enough today.' Then, despite himself, 'I'm sure everything will come right in the end.' He could not meet Marna's gaze as he spoke, however, and she laid a compassionate hand on his arm as she stood up.

Gryss did not notice her unconsciously patting her belt bag as she and Harlen set off towards their home.

Chapter 38

There was turmoil. Fears that had hitherto hovered at the edges of awareness like uneasy dreams rolled inexorably forward, proclaiming themselves beyond any denial. The rumbling doubts of years were focusing themselves into an indisputable and immediate certainty.

'It is *the spawn of the Great Evil.*'

'*And it hunts the strange mover.*'

Yet as many doubts swirled about this enigmatic figure as fears about the manifest evil.

'*His power is unknown.*'

'*He carries a darkness of his own that is beyond us.*'

But the speed of the events now unfolding demanded action.

What was to be done?

'*To stay one darkness will be to admit another, and who can say what consequences might flow from that?*'

'*And who can say what consequences will ensue should the mover fall? There has not been such a Hearer in countless generations. If the spawn of the Great Evil is abroad again, we may have need of such a one, tainted or no.*'

Silence.

The pain and the fear were faced.

'If it is possible, stay the known evil and admit the Hearer.'

The conclusion was definitive.

But the prospect was fearful.

'Run, horse, run!'

Farnor's relentless, inaudible litany had become meaningless to him as his plunging journey carried him onward through the darkness, the creature drawing ever nearer.

He did not look behind. More for fear that he would lose his precarious hold on his terrified mount than of what he might see. For he knew how close the creature was. With almost every heartbeat he seemed for an instant to bond with it; to be possessed by its foul desires, to breathe in the heady odours of the terror of its fleeing prey, to feel his mouth slavering warm, his hair raised stark and stiff. But, worst of all, he would touch fleetingly on the ancient and malevolent will that was powering the still green muscles and sinews.

Yet it was, perhaps, the horror of this that kept his mind focused on the reality of what was happening rather than yielding to the urge to accept this crazed flight as some nightmarish figment from which he must soon awaken to safety and security.

For he knew that, although he was fleeing, he was also fighting a battle of some kind. Whatever unholy kinship he had with this creature, he knew that he must resist to the end.

No.

He must resist. There would be no true end while he did. Only if he faltered would there be an ending.

Hatred and anger wove themselves into the twisted strands of his fear.

He would not fall to Rannick or his creature. He would choke it and slash it even as it seized him. And he would utter not a sound whatever happened.

'Run, horse, run!' he willed silently.

Then, the fear that filled him was not his own. He had the feeling of another will steeling itself for a terrible ordeal. But it was gone before he could respond and, once again, the pounding rhythm of the chase carried him, unwilling, but helpless, into the soul of his pursuer.

There was his prey, almost alongside now: high above, and dangerous hooves flailing, but only a few paces from the kill.

Muscles strained for the extra effort that would turn stride into leap . . .

And the prey was gone!

Ahead lay the looming darkness of a broad tree trunk!

Farnor started violently as he was jolted back into his own consciousness, the creature's surging reflexes alive in his limbs.

Through the din of his flight, he heard a crashing and stumbling behind him.

'Run, horse, run!'

The words rang in his head, but the voice was not his. Nor was the word simply 'horse'. It was rich in many meanings, but, too, it was hung about with great fear.

And, he realized, his awful, pulsing bond with the creature was gone. He was wholly himself again. The presence of the creature was fading. For an instant, he hesitated, but even as he did so the voices filled his mind overwhelmingly.

'Flee, mover! It taxes us sorely to touch this thing so and we have no measure of our ability to help you. Your fate is in your own hands still. Flee!'

'It is done.'

'But the pain, the horror . . .'

'Is passed. And it is done. The spawn of the Evil has been deceived. It returns from whence it came. The mover is safe.'

But there was an awful doubt still. Doubt that robbed this achievement of any true solace for the pain and degradation of touching that which had come in pursuit.

'The mover carries a darkness. We may have committed a great folly.'

'We could have done no other.'

It did not lessen the doubt.

There was a silence, deep and profound. The truth could not be denied. They had allowed an alien darkness to come amongst them.

'It will be ever beyond us. We must call on those who Hear. The Valderen must judge where we cannot.'

And into the night, Farnor, clinging to the neck of his exhausted horse, galloped ever northward into the land of the Great Forest. He was lost and alone, but he knew only one thing: he was no longer pursued. The creature was gone. He was free.

Here ends the first part of NIGHTFALL. It is concluded in VALDEREN.

More Fantasy Fiction from Headline:

ROGER TAYLOR

THE CALL OF THE SWORD

The Chronicles of Hawklan

Behind its Great Gate the castle of Anderras Darion has stood abandoned and majestic for as long as anyone can remember. Then from out of the mountains comes the healer, Hawklan – a man with no memory of anything that has gone before – to take possession of the keep with his sole companion, the raven Gavor.

Across the country, the great fortress of Narsindalvak, commanding the inky wastes of Lake Kedrieth, is a constant reminder of the peace won by the hero Ethriss and the Guardians in alliance with the three realms of Orthlund, Riddin and Fyorlund against the Dark Lord, Sumeral. But Rgoric, the ailing king of Fyorlund and protector of the peace, has fallen under the malign influence of the Lord Dan-Tor and from the bleakness of Narsindal come ugly rumours. It is whispered that Mandrocs are abroad again, that the terrible mines of the northern mountains have been re-opened, and that the Dark Lord himself is stirring.

And in the remote fastness of Anderras Darion, Hawklan feels deep within himself the echoes of an ancient power and the unknown, yet strangely familiar, call to arms . . .

FICTION/FANTASY   0 7472 3117 6

More Fantasy Fiction from Headline:

ROGER TAYLOR

THE FALL OF FYORLUND

The Chronicles of Hawklan

The darkness of ancient times is spreading over the land of Fyorlund and tainting even the Great Harmony of Orthlund. The ailing King Rgoric has imprisoned the much-loved and respected Lords Eldric, Arinndier, Darek and Hreldar; he has suspended the ancient ruling council of the Geadrol; he has formed his own High Guard, filling its ranks with violent unruly men; and Mandrocs have been seen even in Orthlund. At the centre of this corruption is the King's advisor, the evil Lord Dan-Tor, who is determined to destroy the peace won by Ethriss and the Guardians eons ago, and surrender the land to his Dark Lord, Sumeral.

The people look to Hawklan to make a stand against Dan-Tor. But he is a healer and not a soldier – though, deep within himself, Hawklan has felt an ancient power, and when threatened has been seen to fight like a warrior out of legend. Hawklan knows he must confront Dan-Tor before the land falls forever to the encroaching, eternal night . . .

Also by Roger Taylor from Headline
THE CALL OF THE SWORD
The Chronicles of Hawklan

FICTION/FANTASY   0 7472 3118 4

More Fantasy Fiction from Headline:

ROGER TAYLOR

DREAM FINDER

The epic new fantasy from the author of
The Chronicles of Hawklan

The City of Serenstad has never been stronger. Its ruler
Duke Ibris is a ruthless man when his office requires it, but
he is also a man of fine discernment; artists, craftsmen and
philosophers have flourished under his care, and
superstitions are waning in the light of reason and
civilization.

For the Guild of Dream Finders this has proved disastrous.
Since their leader Petran died, their craft has fallen into
disrepute, and Petran's son Antyr is unable to fill the
vacuum left by his father. Antyr finds himself growing
bitter, without the stomach to pander to the whims of the
wealthy, or the courage to offer them his skills honestly and
without fear. His nightly appointments at the alehouse have
lost him customers; and his quarrels with his strange
Companion and Earth Holder, Tarrian, have grown
increasingly unpleasant of late.

Then mysteriously one night, Antyr and Tarrian are taken to
Duke Ibris, who has been troubled by unsettling dreams. It
is the beginning of a journey that leads inexorably to a
terrible confrontation with a malevolent blind man,
possessed of a fearful otherworldly sight, and Ivaroth, a
warrior chief determined to conquer the Duke's land and
all beyond at any cost...

Also by Roger Taylor from Headline Feature:
The Chronicles of Hawklan
THE CALL OF THE SWORD
THE FALL OF FYORLUND
THE WAKING OF ORTHLUND
INTO NARSINDAL

FICTION/FANTASY   0 7472 3726 3

A selection of bestsellers
from Headline

BURYING THE SHADOW	Storm Constantine	£4.99 □
SCHEHERAZADE'S NIGHT OUT	Craig Shaw Gardner	£4.99 □
WULF	Steve Harris	£4.99 □
EDGE OF VENGEANCE	Jenny Jones	£5.99 □
THE BAD PLACE	Dean Koontz	£5.99 □
HIDEAWAY	Dean Koontz	£5.99 □
BLOOD GAMES	Richard Laymon	£4.99 □
DARK MOUNTAIN	Richard Laymon	£4.99 □
SUMMER OF NIGHT	Dan Simmons	£4.99 □
FALL OF HYPERION	Dan Simmons	£5.99 □
DREAM FINDER	Roger Taylor	£5.99 □
WOLFKING	Bridget Wood	£4.99 □

All Headline books are available at your local bookshop or newsagent, or can be ordered direct from the publisher. Just tick the titles you want and fill in the form below. Prices and availability subject to change without notice.

Headline Book Publishing PLC, Cash Sales Department, Bookpoint, 39 Milton Park, Abingdon, OXON, OX14 4TD, UK. If you have a credit card you may order by telephone — 0235 831700.

Please enclose a cheque or postal order made payable to Bookpoint Ltd to the value of the cover price and allow the following for postage and packing:
UK & BFPO: £1.00 for the first book, 50p for the second book and 30p for each additional book ordered up to a maximum charge of £3.00.
OVERSEAS & EIRE: £2.00 for the first book, £1.00 for the second book and 50p for each additional book.

Name ....

Address ....

....

....

If you would prefer to pay by credit card, please complete:
Please debit my Visa/Access/Diner's Card/American Express (delete as applicable) card no:

Signature ....Expiry Date ....